BULLETS OVER BOURBON

The Breakfast Murder Club Series

B Wills

Golden Light Publishing House

Book Cover by: Get Covers

Developmental Edits & Formatting: B Wills

ISBN: 978-1-970692-07-5

For the women who learned to sharpen themselves instead of breaking.
And for the men who chose to stand beside
them—not in front.

Playlist

1. Blood on Her Lips – Raven Knight

2. You(Haunt Me) – Raven Knight

3. Black Delight – Raven Knight

4. Scarred Lips – Cody Marrow

5. GhostFace – Drayce Music

6. Yes Daddy – DVRKTHORN

7. You Shouldn't Want Me – Raven Knight

8. Take You Slow – Cody Marrow

Trigger Warnings

This story does not pull its punches.

It includes graphic violence, stalking, abduction, psychological trauma, corruption, and themes of human trafficking. Characters experience loss, coercion, and sustained threat, alongside adult sexual content and explicit language.

If you are sensitive to these subjects, please proceed with caution—or not at all. Your mental health comes first.

CONTENTS

CHAPTER 1

Kat

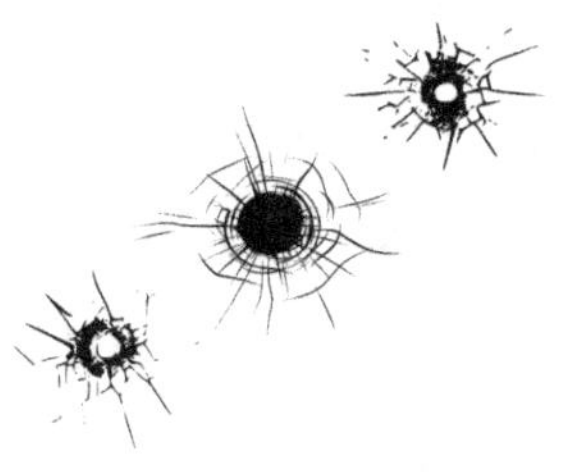

The shop has a pulse when it's empty. Most nights it's gentle—a settling of old wood, the tide breathing against the harbor, the soft rasp of pages shifting as the temperature drops.

Tonight, though, the quiet feels tight. Coiled. Wrong.

I turn the sign to CLOSED, lock the door, and lower the blinds until Driftwood becomes a blur of fog and muted street lamp glow. I should've left twenty minutes ago. Maybe thirty. But the ledger on the counter keeps pulling my eyes back to it like a bruise I can't stop pressing.

Shipping logs. Duplicate invoices. Shell companies stacked like Russian dolls. Every false trail ending at the same point: **Redhaven Foods.**

Jane has no idea I dug this deep. She thinks I'm just doing inventory. Straightening shelves. Living a comfortable, harmless life.

She doesn't know someone has been using her name—using *her*—to launder something far uglier than groceries.

I told her I had something for her to see in the morning. Something important. She laughed, and said I was picking up her bad habits.

Boy, she really has *no* idea.

The overhead light buzzes softly, wavers, then steadies. A draft moves through the aisles despite every door being closed. The air shifts—cooler, sharper, tinged with salt and the faint metallic bite of stormwater. I close the ledger. The paper is warm where my hand was. Then, from the back room—a soft metallic click.

Not settling wood. Not the refrigerator kicking off. Something deliberate, and just enough to spook me.

I slide my hand beneath the counter, fingers curling around the pistol Jane insisted I keep hidden there. The weight fits my palm with an unsettling familiarity.

"Shop's closed," I call, voice even, smooth. The quiet that answers isn't empty. It's listening.

I move toward the storeroom, each step sinking deeper into the thick hush. A faint blue light glows under the door—cold, wrong. The power is never on back there at night. "Jane?" I hear the hope in my own voice and hate it.

I nudge the door open with the gun, only to find shelves, shadows, dust. No one, literally not a single soul is there. But the sense of presence lingers—like stepping into a room where a conversation has just stopped.

I turn to leave, and feel a shift in the air behind me. I pivot, gun rising, but a hand shoots out of the dark, catching my wrist mid-motion. The angle twists my arm, forcing the barrel away from its target. A second hand clamps around my shoulder, pinning me back against the wall with controlled, practiced force.

My breath leaves in a sharp burst, adrenaline flooding my body. He's silent. Efficient. Trained.

I drive an elbow toward his ribs—it connects, but it's like hitting a wall. His grip only tightens, heavy and impersonal. My finger squeezes the trigger anyway—BANG.

The blast tears a display behind us apart, showering the floor with paperback shrapnel. He recoils just enough for me to wrench free. I run, sprinting toward the front door with every bit of strength I can muster. The bell on the door jerks violently as I throw myself out into the wet night air.

Fog swallows the street, thick as wool, muffling everything except the hammering of my pulse. I don't stop moving. I definitely don't look back.

My phone is in my hand before I realize I grabbed it. *Jane.* I hit call, desperately hoping she picks up. The screen lights up.

One ring. Two. Then—*silence.*

Not voicemail. Not static. Just... nothing. The call dies on its own.

Cold slides under my skin. Something tells me my mystery assailant jammed the signal. "Come on," I whisper, hitting redial.

Again—no ring. No tone. Dead on arrival.

I break into a run, boots slapping through puddles as fog curls around my legs like grasping hands. The shop disappears behind me, swallowed by the mist. I try texting her. I NEED TO TALK TO YOU. SOMEONE—message *failed*.

The street goes entirely too quiet. I slow only when I reach the lamppost at the corner, breath ghosting in the cold air. I try one more time to call—and a footstep breaks the silence behind me. The phone dials, Jane's voicemail popping up. "Jane—someone is..."

I whirl—a gloved hand closes over my mouth, cutting off my breath. My phone slips from my fingers, hitting the pavement with a small, final sound.

The grip around my waist is iron-tight, pulling me back into a solid chest. I twist, kick, claw—one good strike lands, a grunt answers it—but he doesn't falter. His other hand presses something soft and chemical-harsh over my nose.

No.

I hold my breath, fight against the arms trapping me, but the world sways sideways, colors running like wet paint. My vision blurs into streaks of blue and orange.

The fog thickens, curling around us as my knees buckle. The streetlight above me pulses once, twice, and then fades to a distant star. The last thing I register is the smell of him—salt and cold metal—and the slow drag of my body being pulled into the dark.

And then—*nothing*.

CHAPTER 2

Jane

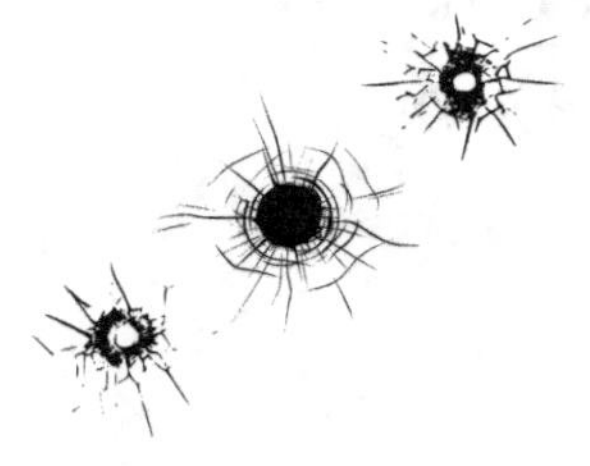

I never thought I'd end up here. No, seriously. Never.

You always hear stories about wrong-place, wrong-time scenarios that spiral into criminal investigations, but you *never*—never in a million years—imagine it will happen to you.

Sure, I've been practically catatonic—gliding through life, drifting through my days like my head's permanently lodged in the clouds.

It wasn't always like this, though. Once—though it feels like a lifetime ago—I was a force to be reckoned with. Somewhere along the way, I lost my will to shine. My spark, if you believe in that sort of thing.

These past few months have been nothing but a weary cycle of ups and downs. One step forward, two steps back. Still... I didn't do this. No, I couldn't have done this. Even if no one believes me.

My day begins like it always does. I walk to Belladonna's for my usual order, then arrive at my bookshop a good thirty minutes before opening. My routine is so predictable I could schedule my bathroom breaks down to the minute—and it still wouldn't be an exaggeration.

The first thing I do when I open the store is check for any notes or paperwork Kat might have left. Nothing seems amiss. Everything is in order: shelves aligned, counters wiped clean, the faint smell of paper and ink lingering in the air like a familiar comfort.

Kat is meticulous, so I don't expect anything less. Polished, professional, punctual—the three P's, as I like to call them. The cornerstone of why I hired her.

So when she not only fails to show up for our meeting... or her afternoon shift... but is found this morning in the upper levels of my bookstore—dead—it feels impossible to reconcile.

I'm the one who finds her. Trussed up, slashed open like a sacrificial lamb awaiting slaughter, the stench of copper and early decay hangs thick in the air, clinging to the back of my throat. Blood pools outward, spreading into a grotesque halo that glistens in the dim light.

And now I'm the one being interrogated, like a common criminal. All because I had the misfortune—the *curse*—of discovering her body.

And the worst part? I *still* don't understand how I ended up here.

Now I sit across from a detective with dark brown hair and slightly graying temples, a scowl fixed on his face like a shield. His storm-gray eyes scrape across my skin, peeling back layers I'd rather keep hidden. The sensation is unsettling, like cold fingers dragging down my spine. His gaze narrows, disdain dripping from every gesture as he flips through the folder. A patronizing smile curves his mouth, his voice a velvet snare meant to coax me into talking. "So, Miss... Jane... Fairhaven, is it?"

I bristle, but he continues, oblivious—or indifferent—to my discomfort.

"When did you last interact with Miss Mathers?"

"As I've told you, *and* your staff, multiple times already... I spoke with Kat yesterday evening. Around five, just before she locked up." My hands pat instinctively at my thighs before I remember they took my phone. "If I had my phone, I could give you an exact time. I'd guess five-thirty, maybe a little earlier. She said she had a few things she wanted to discuss this morning, and I told her I'd arrive thirty minutes early so we could. That was the last of our communication."

He makes a great show of jotting notes, even smiling faintly as if my words amuse him. "I see. And what time did you arrive at your bookstore this morning?"

"Promptly," I snap, patience long since frayed. "Around eight-thirty. That's thirty minutes before opening, as the store opens at nine and closes at six."

"We'll check the camera feed to corroborate your story. Do you always make it a habit of leaving your store in the middle of the afternoon?

Doesn't seem like good business practice to me." His condescending tone grates as he taps his pen against the desk, scattering several papers in front of him.

"Well, seeing as I'm the owner and can make my own schedule..." I let the words hang, narrowing my eyes to catch the name on his badge. "*Detective Rakes*, I figured—why not?"

"Mhhh." He grumbles into his notes, barely registering my response. In his mind, I'm already pegged as the perp. He's biding his time, waiting to keep me here long enough. But... for what? To charge me? The idea is almost laughable.

They have nothing.

I can tell by the way he lingers over the same sheet of paper, the flick of his eyes toward the steel door, the tightening of his jaw every time I speak—like he's biting back some retort stuck behind his teeth.

"Miss Fairhaven, when exactly did you last see your assistant?" His smoldering eyes lock onto mine, a smirk tugging at the corner of his mouth.

I let out a slow breath, keeping my gaze steady, jaw tight with determination. I won't lose my cool. Not here. Not with this asshole. Not like this. "Like I said—yesterday. I left the shop around three in the afternoon. I walked down Main Street, stopped at Belladonna's, and picked up my dinner order."

The scowl on his face deepens. "At three in the afternoon?"

A laugh almost slips out, but the sincerity in his voice stops me cold. "I dine early because I wake early. Or was that not clear from my routine?"

Detective Rakes glares at me, the grind of his teeth sharp enough to make me pause. Interesting. I've rattled him. He's underestimated me—a mistake anyone could make.

His eyes flick to the steel door, then the camera in the corner, then the glass behind me. He's waiting for something. Someone.

I take it all in, cataloging the room the way I would any unfamiliar territory: one door, one camera, one man too focused on posturing to realize how transparent he is. The stale air hums with recycled cold, the overhead light buzzing faintly, the walls too smooth to hide anything useful. It isn't a battlefield I know, but instinct doesn't care about walls or titles. Instinct watches, weighs, waits.

He's sending a message, subtle, just beneath the surface. Maybe for whoever's behind that glass. Maybe for me. Either way, I'll catch it. I always do.

Just as he leans forward to ask another question, a series of harsh knocks rattles the steel door.

"Malcolm, you gotta wrap this up," a disgruntled voice calls from the other side. Rakes grits his teeth again, gnashing them so hard I half expect one to crack.

"Almost finished," he mutters, shooting me a lingering look that curdles the air between us.

Something about this whole encounter gnaws at me. The details don't line up, and the way his attention keeps shifting makes my skin prickle. It feels like there's more in play than he's letting on.

Which, I suppose, is to be expected. My best friend was murdered in my store. Still... something about this doesn't sit right.

Rakes scans the paperwork one more time before exhaling a heavy sigh. "You're free to go," he says, narrowing his gray eyes at me. The words he doesn't speak linger in the space between us. For now. "We'll be in touch. In the meantime, if you think of anything else..." He slides a card across the table. I barely glance at it. "Don't hesitate to call."

I nod, fingers tightening around the card, eyes never leaving him as I rise from the chair and stride toward the door.

"Miss Fairhaven?" he calls after me.

I pause, angling for a clearer look. A small nod tells him I'm listening.

"For what it's worth... I truly am sorry about Kat."

My curiosity stirs. "Did you know her?"

He nods, eyes shining with unshed tears. "Yeah. She's my cousin."

And just like that, pieces fall into place. His hostility. His restless attention. He wasn't signaling some hidden agenda—he was grieving.

I offer him a tight, watery smile. "I'm sorry for your loss."

I leave him with his grief, and he leaves me with mine. Two people bound by the same death, standing on opposite sides of the glass.

The door clicks shut behind me, but the sound doesn't feel like release. It feels like a lock sliding into place.

Chapter 3

Jane

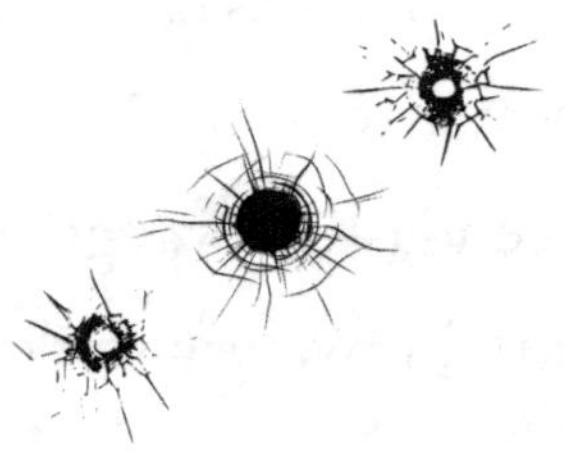

The walk home is arduous, my mind a storm I can't quiet. I keep replaying the morning, every image looping like a film I can't turn off.

Too many details don't make sense. My head feels heavy, my chest weighed down by grief. Kat wasn't just my assistant. Over the last three years, she became *family*.

When I moved to Driftwood—a small coastal town in Maine—I craved quiet. I longed for the sea in the worst kind of way. I met Kat by accident, that first day at Belladonna's.

I'd just finished signing the paperwork for the store, keys to my new house still warm in my hand. A two-story Victorian perched on the best plot of land in town. It overlooks the sea, weathered and practical, yet touched with a kind of magic.

The thought makes me snort. Magic. I toss my long ebony hair over my shoulder, burrow deeper into my jean jacket, and tug the navy scarf tighter around my neck. The salt air stings my nose, sharp and cold, carrying the distant crash of waves against the cliffside.

Kat always had that way about her, though. I didn't know a single thing about her that day in Belladonna's, but she walked right up to me and asked outright if I was the new owner of the Victorian she'd been saving for years to buy.

I stood there, flabbergasted, until she burst out laughing and thrust her hand toward me with all the gusto in the world.

The memory is bittersweet now, sharp enough to sting.

Her goodness is one of the few things that's kept me afloat these last three years. I never told her—I *should've*—but she saved me. In more ways than one.

I swipe at tears, sniffing hard, careful not to invite accusatory stares or pity from the townsfolk.

They don't take kindly to outsiders. Not here. Not *ever*. And even after three years of learning their history, living their rhythms, and donating a fuck-ton of money, nothing changes. None of it softens them toward me.

My footsteps echo against the cobblestone street, my sapphire eyes tracing the same buildings, the same scenes, the same routines. Yet somehow, nothing will ever be the same again.

No more iced chai lattes, extra chai and vanilla. No more of Kat's obsessive tone when she pored over archives and unearthed something new. Never again will I hug her, or call her, just to hear that overbearing voice that somehow managed to comfort me anyway.

It's too cruel an end for someone who radiated nothing but light.

I catch sight of Belladonna—black dress, bat earrings, and her signature black-and-purple curls brushing just above her shoulders. She's every inch herself, A pinch of sarcasm, gothic flair, bold hair. Today, though, she only manages a sad smile and a small wave before beckoning me over.

On any other day, I would've waved back and kept walking, heading home without a second thought. Belladonna knows how much I crave solitude, and she's never once made me feel guilty for it. She always remembers my usual, always slips in a little extra vanilla just for me—one of many reasons why I love her.

But today, I don't even hesitate. I stride toward her, tears spilling freely now, and collapse into her arms. A sob tears from my chest.

"I know, hon," she whispers, voice breaking as she pats my back. "Kat was one of the best and brightest. I'm going to miss her so much."

I pull away, taking in her smudged makeup, the streaks under her crystalline eyes. "I guess everyone knows now?" I murmur, swiping furiously at the mascara running down my own cheeks.

Belladonna avoids my gaze, gnawing at her bottom lip. "You know how it is…"

A harsh laugh threatens to escape, but I swallow it down. "Yeah. Figures."

"It's a small town, hon. News travels fast. Especially when the last murder happened back in the fifties. People are talkin', but only because Kat's death is the most exciting thing that's happened in their pathetic lives so far."

I cringe, pulling back from her touch.

"Hey—I didn't mean it like that," she rushes to add, resting a hand on my shoulder. "Kat was special to me, too."

"I know." I don't add anything else, just keep staring at her while hurt claws at my insides.

She sighs. "Look, I only wanted to check on you. Kat was your best friend—I can't imagine how you're feeling. And to have been the one to find her?" Belladonna shudders, like even the thought is too much, though the image has been seared into my brain since early this morning.

"I just wanted to make sure you're holdin' up okay. I've got your favorite packed for dinner. Figured you could use a pick-me-up. Why don't you wait right here, and I'll run and grab it."

She doesn't give me a second to protest—though, judging by the way my stomach growls, I probably wouldn't have anyway.

When she returns, she's carrying her signature black delivery bag—littered with bats, poisonous flowers, and the Belladonna's Café logo.

The smell hits me instantly, rich and comforting. If I had to guess... "Chicken noodle soup?" I breathe out on a contented sigh. "Tell me you didn't sneak in a whole loaf of your special brioche too?"

She dangles the bag in front of me, mock shock painted across her face. "You know I can't serve chicken noodle soup without that brioche! There'd be a riot in these streets!"

I snort, but don't mention that a riot would be the least of her concerns in a town as small as Driftwood.

"Thanks," I mutter instead, taking the bag from her outstretched hand.

"Don't mention it. If you need anything, you know where to find me." Belladonna presses the bag into my grip, her eyes fixed on the fading sunset. "You better get on home. It's gonna be dark soon."

I frown, unsettled by the sudden shift in her tone. Why does she sound worried about my safety? Does she know something I don't?

For the first time, I'm left with questions I can't shake. Who the hell could be tied to this—and *why* would they mimic *that* kill signature?

"Yeah," I finally call out. "See you tomorrow."

She waves me on, gaze still locked on the last streaks of light, as though she's determined to drink them in. I don't blame her. I would too, if I could.

The streets of Driftwood are nearly empty as I head home. Shops shuttered, lamps flickering, gulls crying overhead as they settle in for the night. The town wears its age proudly—cracked brick facades, rusted signage, cobblestones patched more times than I can count. It should feel comforting by now. Instead, it feels foreign.

I shift Belladonna's bag in my arms, the warmth bleeding through my jacket, grounding me for a moment. Then the sound comes—footsteps. Too light to be coincidence, too measured to be chance.

I stop. The echo stops with me. When I glance over my shoulder, the street is empty, shadows spilling long across the stones.

It's just the wind, or my imagination. That's what I tell myself. But my heart doesn't buy it.

I force my legs to move again, faster this time, the rhythm of my steps too loud in the silence. My throat is dry, my breath ragged, but I keep going until my street finally comes into view.

Relief washes over me at the sight of the old Victorian. She's weathered but proud—two stories, pitched roof, sea air gnawing at her trim but never quite winning. The green-and-yellow wallpaper inside is something out of another decade, curling at the edges, but I never had the heart to strip it. The bannisters groan like tired old men, the antique furniture sagging with history I'll never know.

I climb the steps, fumble the key into the lock, and step inside. The silence swallows me whole, as heavy as the ocean just beyond the windows.

It's a good house. Safe, and solid. The kind of place people think they know me in.

They *don't*. Not even close.

CHAPTER 4

Jane

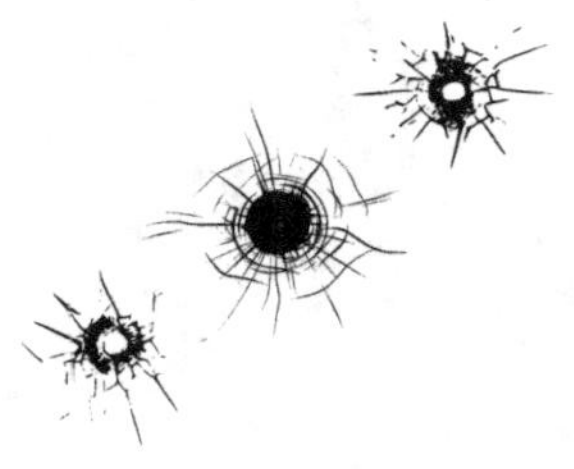

Sunlight trickles through the curtains in my bedroom—too bright. *Wrong.* The gold of it doesn't warm. No, it *sears*, intruding where it isn't wanted.

I force myself out of bed, drag down the rickety staircase I should probably fix one of these days, each step groaning like it resents my weight, and will the gnawing headache to fade. My robe is cinched tight around me, an ineffective shield against the heaviness pressing in on all sides—the weight of what I have to face today.

At the bottom of the stairs, I turn toward the kitchen, deliberately ignoring the open floor plan that leaves Kat's favorite spot in plain view. Fresh tears threaten, but I swallow them back and damn near stomp to the coffee pot.

Lace curtains frame the window over the sink, faintly yellowed with age. The fabric shifts in the draft, carrying the sharp bite of salt air and the faint musk of old wood soaked too long in coastal damp. I move through the motions mechanically—aware, but not.

The coffee begins to brew with a sputter and hiss. I jerk a tumbler down from the cabinet, fumbling with the lid before yanking open the refrigerator for creamer. The cold air curls around me, making the ache in my joints sharpen.

I keep my gaze anywhere but Kat's favorite recliner—the burgundy velvet glares at me like an open wound. I can't stand the sight of it. Not after yesterday.

With a sigh, I stride back to the counter and slam the creamer down harder than necessary. The sharp thud vibrates through the counter, oddly satisfying, cutting through the silence.

Maybe it's all the pent-up aggression bottled inside me after my run-in with Detective Malcolm Thorne Rakes... Thirty-eight. Seven years my senior. Never married. County academy graduate, honors and glowing recommendations. A résumé built for someone who wants the world to think he's unshakable.

None of that matters. It didn't settle my brain last night when I finally gave in to the burning curiosity clawing at the back of my mind.

No. Digging only added fuel to the fire, irritation swirling in my stomach as I scrubbed my hard drives in the dark, the glow of the monitor painting my walls in cold blue. My fingers flew through old keystrokes like muscle memory, too fast, too precise—proof I haven't shed the skin I swore I left behind.

I pour a generous splash of creamer into the tumbler, waiting impatiently as the coffee sputters into the pot. My jaw tightens, teeth pressing until my skull throbs, and I force my gaze out the window. The water stretches deep and blue, sunlight dancing across its surface, gulls dipping low with harsh cries that carry through the glass.

It should be beautiful. Instead, it feels like a betrayal, mocking me with its ease while everything in me fractures.

I need to get the *fuck* out of here.

The alarm on the coffee pot shrieks, jolting me out of my thoughts, steam curling sharp and bitter into the air. I snatch up the tumbler, take a swallow that scalds my tongue, then set it back on the counter before heading for my room. I need to put on something suitable.

What even counts as suitable when you're returning to the scene of a crime you didn't commit?

Taking the stairs two at a time, I tug my ebony waves free from the clip that binds them, working my fingers through the tangles as I rush toward my bedroom like there's a ghost on my heels.

I fling open the armoire and scour the rows of fabric, desperate for something appropriate. Something that screams: *I didn't kill my best friend.*

In the end, I settle on a plain pair of jeans, one of my favorite band T-shirts, and a gray cardigan. The clothes feel thin, flimsy against the weight pressing in on me, but it's the best I can manage.

Dressed, I wander back downstairs and snag my tumbler from the counter, my gaze lingering—just for a moment—on the burgundy recliner. Its velvet sheen catches the light, taunting me with memories I can't bear.

With nothing left to distract me from what has to be done, I grab my purse and keys. Chin lifted, I step out the front door and onto the streets of Driftwood. The hinges groan as the door swings shut behind me, the echo far too final.

***

The walk to Main Street feels longer than it should, every cobblestone carrying the weight of a hundred curious eyes. People don't stop me outright, but I feel them watching, whispering behind cupped hands as I pass.

Outsider. Suspect. Murderer.

The words hang in the air like smoke, even if no one says them aloud.

When I reach the shop, my stomach knots. The yellow tape slashed across the door cuts through the familiar brick facade, jarring and loud against the window displays Kat and I had fussed over just last week. What used to feel warm and inviting now looks like a crime scene.

My crime scene.

For a moment I just stand there, clutching my purse strap so tight the leather creaks. Going inside feels impossible. But avoiding it somehow feels worse.

So I do the only thing I can. Gripping the tape, I yank it down, determined to get inside without so much as a word. I don't have the patience for it. Not today.

My nerves betray me as I fumble with the keys, searching for the right one—the ornate, gothic-looking key I never had the heart to replace. My thumb finds the tiny skull etched into its top, and I wonder, even three years later, if the original owner had a sense of humor or just liked macabre things as much as I do.

I slide it into the lock and turn. The door gives, but something keeps me rooted in the threshold.

My fingers tremble as I wrap them around the knob. Still, I push forward, step inside, and release the breath I didn't realize I'd been holding.

The air inside is colder than I remember, heavy with dust and something sharper that clings to the back of my throat. The faintest trace of blood still lingers—metallic and sour beneath the scent of old paper and ink. A draft sneaks along the floorboards, curling around my ankles, carrying the acrid tang of cleaning chemicals that failed to mask what happened here.

The shop is askew. Books lean at odd angles, stacks half-collapsed, papers scattered across the floor where officers rifled through them. Kat would never have left it like this. Every shelf, every book, every display used to be *meticulous*—her kind of meticulous.

I step further in, my shoes creaking against the warped wood floorboards. The cozy amber glow I've always associated with this place is gone, completely snuffed out. What's left is a hollow shell, a crime scene where my best friend died.

For the first time since moving to Driftwood, the store doesn't feel like mine. It feels like it belongs to someone else now—someone cruel enough to take Kat away and clever enough to make the town think I had a hand in it.

I can't stand looking at it like this.

Before I realize what I'm doing, I'm bending down, gathering scattered papers into a messy stack, sliding stray books back into place. My movements are clumsy, automatic—like if I put the shop back together, I can put myself back together too.

A sigh escapes me when I straighten one of the endcaps Kat had fussed over last week. She'd lectured me for shelving the new releases alphabetically instead of by author popularity. I'd teased her mercilessly for being a control freak, and she'd laughed that laugh of hers—the one that cracked through all the dark corners of this town.

The memory claws at my throat, sharp and insistent, but I shove it down and focus on the work.

Straighten. Stack. Smooth. Repeat.

Order. Kat's order. That's what I need.

It's only when I move behind the counter to align the ledgers that I notice something's... wrong.

One sits crooked, half-hanging from the shelf like it was shoved back in a hurry. The spine juts out at an unnatural angle, pages bent, dust unsettled around it. Kat would never have left it like that.

I pull it free. The leather is older than the rest, worn soft at the edges, the cover darkened from years of handling. Kat's personal ledger. The one thing she guarded like treasure.

The first pages look ordinary—her neat handwriting cataloging sales, dates, the humdrum details she loved. But a few entries in, my breath stutters. A corner is folded, the margin marked with one of her rare asterisks.

Beside it, underlined twice, lies a single word...
Alias?

The name beside it makes my skin prickle. It's a regular. Someone who slips in and out so quietly I barely register him anymore. A face I know, but never thought to question. When I first moved to Driftwood, he struck me as familiar in a way I couldn't place — a tug at the edge of memory, the sense that I'd seen him somewhere that didn't belong to this town. I told myself it was nothing. One of *those* faces. The kind you mistake for everyone and no one. The kind your mind smooths over because it doesn't want to dig.

Now, staring at his name in black and white, that old unease crawls back up my spine. And I can't shake the feeling that I need to listen to it.

Flipping back, I find the same name repeated, but tied to different addresses. Receipts stapled into the margins. Inconsistencies stitched together under one identity. Kat noticed and tracked him.

But *why*? What business did Kat have digging into a customer's lies? She loved records and order, but this wasn't book keeping—this was a whole ass investigation.

And now Kat is dead.

My pulse hammers in my ears as I snap the book shut, hugging it to my chest like someone might reach through the air and snatch it away. The leather smells faintly of old ink, the scent of Kat's hands embedded in its worn cover. She had to have left this behind for a reason.

I force myself to slide the ledger into my bag, hands shaking enough to piss me off. Losing control isn't an option. Not here. Not now.

The shop is silent, but the silence doesn't feel empty anymore. It presses against me, thick and heavy, like someone else is breathing in the room. Watching. Waiting.

I whirl around, scanning the aisles. Shadows stretch across the floorboards, harmless shapes cast by the late sun. Nothing moves, and I feel a little bit silly. It's completely empty. Totally and glaringly obvious—no one's here.

And yet, the hairs on the back of my neck refuse to lie flat.

The air in the room shifts, warping around me until it feels like the place itself is holding its breath. I can't shake the feeling of being watched.

Then a loud thud comes from above—the one place I have *no* desire to go.

Is someone up there?

My jaw tightens. If someone's up there, they picked the wrong damn day.

I move toward the staircase, every board groaning under my weight, the sound too loud in the charged silence. The bannister is smooth beneath my hand, worn down by decades of use, but tonight it feels like a blade's edge.

Halfway up, I pause, straining to listen. Nothing. Just the hiss of the ocean beyond the glass and my own pulse hammering in my ears.

I force myself up the last steps and reach the landing, the narrow hallway yawning ahead of me. The shadows here are deeper, corners thick with dust and silence.

"Hello?" My voice is steady, but it scrapes the air like a warning. No answer. It dies in the hall, swallowed by dust and shadow.

I move slowly, checking each room in turn. The storage closet is empty, shelves lined with old ledgers and cardboard boxes. In the office, the chair has been shoved back and some papers scattered, but nothing else. Finally, I reach the small reading nook at the end of the hall. The armchair sits under the window, its fabric torn at the seams, the cushion indented like someone just rose from it.

My breath hitches, but old habits are hard to break. I immediately begin making notes of everything. The glass is cracked open, sea air curling through the gap, cold and briny against my skin. Leaning out the window, I scan the street below.

Empty. No movement. No sound but the tide gnawing at the rocks.

When I pull back, I can't shake the truth pressing against my ribs.

Someone was here... and they *wanted* me to know.

CHAPTER 5

Jane

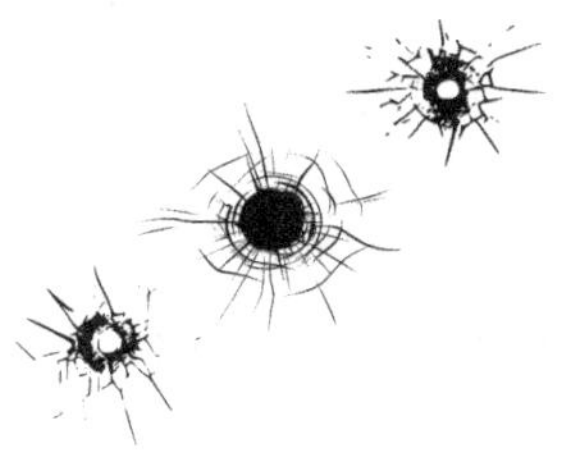

Sleep doesn't come easily—not with the ledger heavy in my bag and the memory of that indented chair upstairs burned into my brain. Even when I finally doze, I jolt awake at every creak of the house, and every groan of the old bannisters. Each sound snaps me back into darkness.

By morning, the weight hasn't lifted. If anything, it's worse. The ledger sits on my kitchen table like a dare, Kat's looping handwriting glaring up at me from the margins.

Alias? Don't trust him.

I trace the letters with my fingertip, wondering why she didn't come to me sooner. Kat noticed something I didn't, and I really wish I could ask her. Now, I'll never get the chance.

I should probably hand this over to Detective Rakes. Let him be the one to comb through the details. That's the normal thing to do, isn't it? The right thing.

But the thought of giving it up feels like cutting out my own tongue. This is the *only* leverage I have, and something in my gut screams that if I let it go, I'll never see it again.

So... in the end, I don't.

I slide the ledger into my bag and snap the clasp shut, the sound louder than it should be in the quiet house—like a gavel, like a vow. That book is mine now—Kat's words, her suspicions, her questions. If I hand it over, it'll vanish into some evidence locker, and with it, the only thread that might lead me to whoever really killed her.

Outside, Driftwood wakes slow. Gulls wheel over the harbor, the scent of salt drifting in with the morning fog, cool tendrils curling through the cracked window. On any other day, I'd stop for coffee, lose myself in routine.

Not today.

Halfway down Main Street, voices carry over the cobblestones. Two dark-haired women linger by the florist's window, paper-wrapped bouquets clutched in their hands. Their words aren't meant for me, but they hit like a dart all the same.

"...such a shame. She was so happy lately, seeing that new fella—"

"Tall one? Comes into the shop? Always polite?"

I don't stay to hear the rest. My pulse spikes, because I know exactly who they mean.

I keep walking, but their words stick, worming into my ears no matter how hard I try to block them out.

Happy? My stomach twists. Kat never mentioned being happy about him. She only mentioned him once—an offhand comment as she restocked the mythology shelf. Something about how his eyes lingered a little too long when she bent to grab a lower title. How his smile felt... just slightly off. But that was... *months* ago.

I see him in my mind now. Cropped blonde hair parted too neatly, like he's trying too hard. Green eyes sharp as cut glass, pale skin like he spends more time under fluorescent bulbs than daylight. Always pressed shirts, polished shoes, paired with manners so smooth they squeak. The kind of man people mistake for trustworthy because he looks like he belongs in a boardroom.

And now... the town wants to paint him as her great romance? No. Not a chance.

I tighten my grip on the strap of my bag, the ledger heavy against my hip.

Thatcher Greeves.

The name coils in my head like poison. To think they're already twisting every piece of this story, and it's only been two fucking days. "Can't even let a dead girl rest," I mutter, curses slipping under my breath as I stomp down the cobblestone street. "Stupid small town, nosey ass bullshit."

I refuse to waste another day wallowing in grief when I should be doing something about Kat's death. I have the means. My past may be full of things best left buried—things only Kat knew—but right now, those shadows are useful.

I'm so tangled in my thoughts, fuming over gossip and lies, that I don't notice the wall of muscle until I collide with it. The impact knocks me back, flat on my ass. My tumbler bounces, lukewarm coffee splattering across the stones, my skirt rucked up around my knees, my bag flung wide open on the ground.

Gunmetal eyes snare me, stopping me in my tracks. An unwelcome wave of heat tumbles down my spine, and I try—*poorly*—to ignore the nervous energy flooding my system. Detective fucking Rakes.

Of course. As if today couldn't get any worse.

"Need a hand?" he asks dryly, scratching at the line of beard shadowing his jaw. He's dressed nice today—hunter-green button-down, worn Wranglers, aviators perched on his head. He leans down, stretching a hand toward me.

I scowl and ignore it, shoving myself upright. With a tug, I arrange my deep burgundy floral skirt so I don't give him a show. "Someone should've been watching where they were going," I snap, crouching to gather my scattered things.

"Well, I sure am happy to see you too, Miss Fairhaven." His tone carries a teasing edge, suspiciously light considering the disdain he dripped on me last time.

"Uh-huh. What can I help you with, Detective Rakes?" I stick to formality—it's safer that way.

"I was looking for you, actually," he says, voice lowering as his eyes track every jerky motion I make while shoving my things back into my bag.

"Oh?" I arch a brow. "Whatever for?"

"For a chat," he says simply, though the way his mouth twists around the word makes it sound like more than that. "Couple of questions I'd rather ask without the badge between us."

I still, my fingers frozen on the buckle of my bag. A chat. Right. That's his word for it—interrogation *without* paperwork. My laugh comes out flat. "Funny, Detective, I don't remember putting myself on your social calendar."

"Humor me." His tone is cool, but those damn eyes are locked on mine like he's trying to peel me open.

"Fine."

"Thank you." A tight smile flickers across his face. "Do you know who Kat was seeing?"

He doesn't waste time. The question blindsides me, though it shouldn't. In a place like Driftwood, word travels fast—whether you want it to or not.

Thatcher's name hits me before Rakes even finishes the question. But handing his name over now? Not a chance. The ledger is all I've got, and I'm not letting him bury it in some evidence box.

I school my features, brushing coffee from my skirt like it matters. "She kept her private life... private," I say evenly. "If she was seeing someone, she didn't tell me."

Rakes studies me in silence, steel-colored gaze narrowing like he's stripping away every layer I've tried to hide.

Then, he finally cracks. "Come on, rumor has it you two were close. Surely she told you about her dates. Girl talk?"

I let out a short, humorless laugh. "Girl talk? What is this, *high school*? Kat and I discussed books, business, and the occasional customer who didn't know how to use indoor voices. That's it."

His mouth twitches, not quite a smile, not quite a sneer. "So you expect me to believe your best friend never mentioned a single man?"

I snap my bag closed with more force than necessary. "Believe whatever helps you sleep at night, Detective. I'm not in the business of rewriting the dead just to fit a narrative."

His jaw clenches, fists tightening at his sides, knuckles bone-white. "Watch it," he snarls.

Good. A nerve struck.

"Just stating the truth." I shrug, flicking my dark waves back over my shoulder.

"I don't fucking buy it," he growls, stepping closer, fury blazing in his smoke-gray stare.

"Everyone knows you two were practically glued at the hip."

I refuse to shrink. Instead, I step in closer, until we're almost nose to nose. "Detective... at the risk of sounding insubordinate—" my smirk cuts sharp at the corner of my mouth, "—she never once mentioned her relation to you. Much less some guy she might've screwed."

"Goddammit!" He huffs, yanking back, his face blanching, then flushing red in quick succession. "You don't have to put it like... like *that*—for fuck's sake."

I school my features, strangling the grin that threatens to slip free. "I only meant—"

"I know what you meant!" His voice spikes, rough with more than anger. Color creeps high on his cheeks, betraying a crack in his composure.

"Like I tried to tell you, sir... Kat wasn't one for idle gossip or chit-chat. That's one of the things I respected about her most." My voice wavers, grief clawing its way up before I can shove it back down. "I honestly don't know what I'm going to do without her."

For a long moment, he just stares at me, jaw tight, chest heaving like he's holding back everything he wants to say. Then, almost too quiet to catch, he exhales.

"Yeah," he mutters, the fight draining from his voice. "She wasn't one for that. Always straight to the point, just like *you*."

The words hang there between us, heavier than the accusations. His eyes shift—no longer cutting, but clouded with something else, something raw.

I swallow hard, hating the way my throat tightens. Sympathy is dangerous. Especially for a man who wants me in cuffs.

He scrubs a hand over his face, the anger gone, leaving him looking older, heavier. The faint scrape of stubble carries in the space between us. "The service is tomorrow morning," he says finally, voice low. "Kat deserves... better than whispers and rumors. Thought you'd want to know."

For once, there's no accusation in his tone. Just exhaustion.

I nod, unable to trust my voice, my fingers curling tight around the strap of my bag until the leather bites my palm. When he steps back, giving me space, it feels like the first olive branch he's ever offered.

"See you there, Miss Fairhaven." His eyes linger for half a heartbeat, pale and inscrutable now—less steel—before he turns and disappears into the crowd.

I let out the breath I didn't realize I'd been holding. The air tastes faintly of salt and exhaust from passing cars, the murmur of town life resuming around me like nothing happened.

Tomorrow, I'll bury my best friend. After that… *all* bets are off.

CHAPTER 6

Rakes

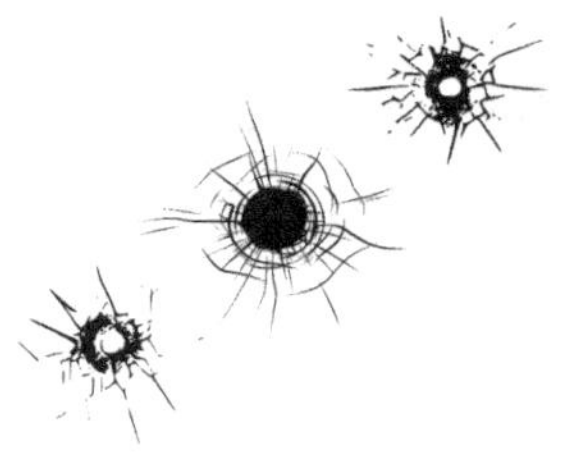

K at always said lilies smelled like death dressed up pretty. Now they choke the chapel, crowding the altar in pale blooms, their cloying sweetness curling in my throat until I can't breathe without tasting them.

And it's not just the fucking lilies. Someone had the gall to send a towering spray of blood-red roses, black-edged calla lilies, and dusky orchids. Too lush, and theatrical. The kind of arrangement you send to make yourself seen, not to honor the dead. Nobody else seems to notice, but I do. The scent hangs heavier than the rest, thick and almost mocking, like beauty tipped just enough to spoil.

I sit rigid in the front pew, fists pressed together so no one sees the tremor in my hands. People file past in black, whispering condolences they don't mean, glancing at me like I'm part of the exhibit.

Cousin. Cop. The man who couldn't save her.

She deserved better than this—better than hushed voices, better than a closed casket, better than being reduced to gossip two days after she bled out on that floor.

My jaw tightens until it aches. The investigation is going *nowhere*. We've got a body, a handful of shaky statements, and Jane Fairhaven sitting square in the middle of it all. Too convenient. Too damn neat.

And yet...

My eyes drift to the back of the chapel, and there she is. Standing apart, like she always does. Chin high, black dress cutting a stark line against her pale skin, ebony hair tumbling loose around her shoulders in rippling waves. Her expression is sour. Grief. Guilt. Both wear the same mask from where I sit.

She found Kat, and she lied to me—I'd swear it. But when her voice cracked yesterday, when she said she didn't know what she'd do without her... for a moment, I almost believed her.

The hymn begins, voices rising thin and off-key. Organ pipes groan under the weight of the song, air thick with pollen and candle smoke. I don't sing. I never could. Instead, I watch everyone around us—especially *her*. And Jane doesn't sing either. She stands unmoving, her hand wrapped too tight around the strap of her bag, knuckles white. Like she's carrying more than a purse. Like she's carrying a secret.

And God help me—whatever that secret is, I need to tear it open.

I can't focus on the hymns or the sermon. My attention keeps snagging on the woman at the back—the one who arrived like she belonged nowhere and somehow everywhere, her record so clean it looks curated. Like she planted herself in Driftwood and never let anyone look too closely.

That's what keeps me keyed on her. It's the single thing that won't let me drop her as the prime suspect, no matter how much grief or office politics tells me to move on. They think I'm forcing patterns where none exist. They tell me it's a coincidence.

But my gut doesn't lie. She's got something I'm not seeing yet. I just don't know what.

I'm so caught in my own thoughts I almost miss the pastor calling my name. Damn it. I forgot I was supposed to speak. As one of Kat's only surviving relatives, the burden falls to me.

I force myself up, each step to the front heavier than the last. The chapel quiets, pews creaking as bodies shift, every eye locking on me. Grief clamps hard on my chest, but I press forward anyway.

My fingers curl around the podium, the wood cool and worn smooth beneath my palms. I scan the crowd—faces I've known all my life, neighbors and family friends, each lined with sympathy I can't bear to meet. The perfume of flowers presses down from the altar, thick and suffocating.

I clear my throat, but my voice still comes out rough. "Kat was... Kat was the kind of person who never let you get away with bullshit. She called things the way she saw them. Always honest. Sometimes too honest."

A ripple of soft laughter moves through the room, hushed but genuine, and for a moment, the pressure on my chest eases.

"She loved this town. Loved her work. Hell, she loved just about everyone she met. If you needed a hand, Kat was there—no questions asked. She... she deserved better than this." My throat tightens, words catching hard. "Better than whispers. Better than suspicion. Better than being taken from us too soon."

I glance up, scanning the crowd. My gaze snags at the back—on her. Jane stands stiff, dark eyes hollow, jaw set against the tide of grief surrounding her. The black fabric of her dress catches in the dim light, severe and striking. I drag my eyes away before anyone notices, gripping the podium until my knuckles ache.

"She was family," I finish quietly. "And she'll be missed more than I can say."

***

Jane

The sound of his voice lingers in the chapel long after he leaves the podium. For a moment, his grief threatens to pull me under with it—but I slam the door shut on that impulse. Sympathy is *dangerous*. It will get me killed if I'm not careful.

My eyes fix on the coffin, smothered in lilies. Kat despised lilies, and said they reeked of false sweetness masking rot. Now their cloying perfume clogs my throat, heavy as syrup, and I fight the urge to gag. Roses and orchids crowd the spray too, gaudy against the pale wood, but it's the lilies that suffocate. It's those damnable lilies that keep drawing my attention, no matter how hard I try to focus on anything else.

The insult astounds me. But, what astounds me even more? That *no one* else notices.

The pastor drones on, words about peace and eternal rest, but none of them touch the jagged wound left behind. Kat's absence is louder than any hymn. I sit stiff in my pew, chin high, while whispers stir around me like gnats.

She found her. Always thought she was strange. Makes sense, doesn't it?

I don't need to hear the full sentences. Their stares finish them for me.

The final hymn rises, a thin chorus straining against grief. I don't sing. My throat is too raw, too tight. When the pastor dismisses us, I move with the crowd, filing toward the doors, the cool draft of salt air brushing my skin before I even step outside.

The sun is too bright out here, too cruel. Clusters of mourners huddle together, trading memories, trading theories. I stand apart, grief heavy on my chest, the weight of their eyes heavier still.

And then, as if pulled by a string, my gaze finds him—Detective Rakes. His eyes pin me across the crowd, pale and relentless, like a storm rolling over the sea.

His stare pins me, sharp enough to raise the hairs along my arms. I break it first, shifting my weight, fingers flexing against the strap of my bag until the leather bites.

Bootsteps crunch over gravel, steady and deliberate. I don't have to look to know he's closing the distance between us.

"Miss Fairhaven." His voice is lower this time, stripped of the sharp edges he used in interrogation—condolence threaded with something heavier.

I square my shoulders before turning to face him. "Detective."

"Kat was…" He stops, jaw flexing before the words scrape out. "She was family. And I know she was family to you too, in your way. I just wanted to say again—I'm sorry."

I study him, searching for the catch, the angle. But there's nothing in his voice except grief, raw and unvarnished. The honesty unsettles me more than his questions ever could. "Thank you," I say carefully, the words stiff on my tongue. I don't know if I mean them, but they're the only ones that fit.

His gaze sharpens. "Still, if there's any-thing—*anything at all*—you remember about the last few weeks with her, now's the time." Then, a brief pause, like he's toying with the words still running through his mind. His voice drops dan-gerously low, "Don't let me hear it secondhand."

Ah, there it is. The hook beneath the olive branch. *Malice* hidden behind kindness.

I let my lips curve in the smallest of smiles, more deflection than warmth. "If I think of something, you'll be the first to know."

Rakes studies me for a long moment, weighing every syllable I've just spoken against some unspo-ken truth. His mouth tightens, like he wants to press harder but knows this isn't the place—not with half the town gathered on the chapel steps, their ears sharp as blades and the cloying perfume of lilies still clinging to the air.

Finally, he gives a single, short nod. "Don't make me chase you for answers, Miss Fairhaven."

The words are quiet, almost civil. But the look in his eyes promises otherwise. I watch him turn away, his broad shoulders cutting through the throng of mourners until he disappears into the blur of black coats and bowed heads. Only then do I let out the breath I've been holding, the ledger heavy at my side like a second heartbeat.

He's not done with me, that much is clear. But... I'm not done with him either.

What's worse? I'm not sure which part of that scares me more.

CHAPTER 7

Jane

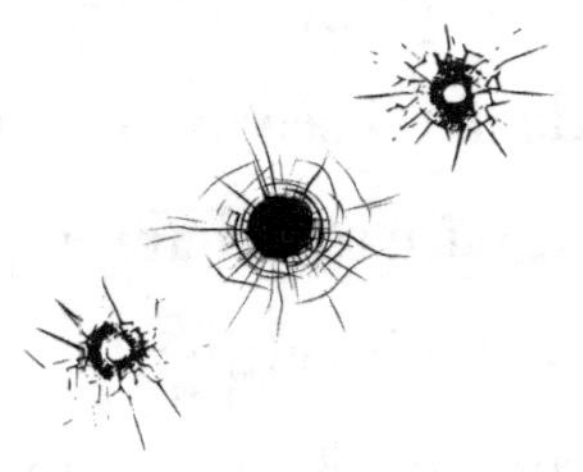

I don't wait around for condolences or the curious stares that follow me down the chapel steps. What's the fucking point?

Let them whisper. Let them clutch their pearls and invent whatever story suits them best. I have no energy left for Driftwood's vultures.

The walk home is quiet except for the scuff of my boots on the cobblestones and the wind rippling across the water. It carries a briny chill that cuts through my dress. Grief gnaws at me in strange ways—some moments too sharp to breathe, others hollow, leaving me numb. It's a vicious cycle that keeps taking me by surprise. By the time my house rises into view, pale and lonely against the gray sky, I feel scraped raw.

Inside, the silence swallows me whole. The old bannister groans as I shut the door, and the wallpaper's faded greens and yellows stare back like a house pretending to be cheerful. Kat used to tease me about it—said the place had "*haunted charm.*" Now the walls feel heavier, every shadow longer, the air tinged faintly with salt and old wood.

The ledger waits where I left it on the kitchen table, leather cover dull in the weak light. I drop my bag beside it and stand there, staring, like if I wait long enough the damn thing might open itself.

My fingers find the edges of the ledger, flipping through pages one by one. Each entry is neat, *precise*—red ink, dates underlined the same way, receipts clipped or referenced. The pattern is obvious, deliberate even. Borderline obsessive? Absolutely. And yet, that's exactly what makes it useful. Kat saw something in Thatcher—something worth watching.

Now... I need to know *what*.

Old instincts stir, the kind you don't forget even when you pretend you have. Orion taught me how to follow trails that didn't want to be seen, how to read absence as loudly as presence. I was never their best tracker, never their sharpest analyst—but I learned enough. Enough to recognize a pattern when it's trying to hide.

I line the receipts up in my mind, scanning what he bought, the days, the times. A rhythm emerges—too clean to be coincidence. Always during Kat's shifts. Always after three. Always when I was gone. How *convenient*.

Now... *Why*?

Ledger tucked under my arm, I head for the staircase and pause. My fingers find the small latch, pressing until the false wall shudders and groans. A moment later, it clicks free, swinging open to reveal what I keep hidden.

My fingers skim the keys, the monitors flaring to life in a chorus of light. God, I've missed this.

But there's no time to indulge. I slide into the chair, logging in, locking every channel down tight with layers of encryption only I can navigate. Each keystroke feels like slipping back into old skin... *Dangerous* skin.

While the systems boot, I pull the black phone from its drawer. The one I swore I'd only touch in an emergency.

And this? This qualifies as an actual fucking emergency. I already know who I'm calling—my *brother*. Beau Maddox.

He picks up on the first ring, tone clipped, and ever wary. "What do you need, Quinn? Make it quick. I'm in the middle of something important."

Feminine cursing filters through the line. I bark out a laugh before I can stop myself. "Beau Sloane Maddox—what the *hell* are you doing? No, scratch that. Don't answer. I don't need the visual."

He groans, a long-suffering sigh. "*Quinn Blaire Maddox*, if you don't get to the fucking point, I'll come through this phone myself."

I snicker, satisfied that I've rattled him at least once. "Fine. Sorry to interrupt your... *extracurriculars*. But I need your help. Someone killed Kat, Beau."

He swears under his breath. "Shit. I'm sorry, sis. What do you need?"

"I need you to run a list of my jobs for the last ten years. I think someone might be framing me, Beau. They used that same fucking kill signature—right down to the halo of blood at their feet. My old one... you know. Before it all went to shit."

Silence. Then a low, and raw, "*Fuck*."

"Yeah." My breath comes out ragged. "It's bad. And to make it worse, some detective's crawling up my ass because I was the one who found her. In my shop."

"Fuckkkkk," he drags it out this time, and I can practically see him rubbing a hand over his face. "Goddamn it, Quinnie, what the hell did you get yourself into?"

"Don't you *dare* use that awful nickname! Not at a time like this."

He snickers. "Still so easy to rattle you. Focus up—we need to cut this call. I'll send an encrypted file tomorrow. Pulling a decade of jobs takes time. You've been a busy little fuck."

"Yeah, I know." I sigh. "Thanks, bub. Talk soon."

"No problem."

The line clicks dead. I set the phone on the desk and lean back, watching the algorithms crawl across the screen, my patience worn thin.

The silence after Beau hangs up presses in harder than the hum of the servers. I drag both hands down my face, exhaling through my teeth. The glow from the monitors paints my fingers in blue light, the smell of warm circuitry faint but familiar.

It's been years since I let myself sit here, and let the old instincts run. Years since I allowed Quinn Blaire Maddox to breathe. Jane Fairhaven doesn't belong in this chair. Jane Fairhaven doesn't even know how to track shadows or build firewalls no one can breach.

But Quinn does.

And no matter how hard I try to bury her, she's the only part of me equipped to survive what's sure to come. Especially if my suspicions are correct.

I stare at the lines of code racing across the monitors, the ledger open beside me like a ghost of Kat's voice. Whoever framed me knew exactly what they were doing. Which means this isn't some random kill. It's *personal*.

The code runs, pulling receipts, names, cross-checks. I lean closer as the screen spits out its results.

Thatcher Greeves. Expected. He's already been circling this mess like a vulture.

Michael Halloway. Another alias. Sloppy, but nothing that makes my pulse spike.

Then the system pings—highlighting the next name in red.

Jonas Kerr.

The name punches a hole in my chest. I've seen it before—years ago, buried in Beau's files, tied to a contract I never touched but equally never forgot. The kind of thing you can't scrub from memory, no matter how hard you try. This can't be random—it feels too... *calculated*. Thatcher's been wearing masks long before he ever set foot in Driftwood.

I sit back in the chair, the servers humming around me, the ledger still open at my elbow. My pulse steadies now, my decision clear. I'll wait for Beau's file tomorrow, but tonight, I'll play my part. Smile for the town. Pretend to be Jane Fairhaven a little longer.

Because Quinn Maddox knows the truth...

This isn't over. Not by a long shot.

CHAPTER 8

Quinn

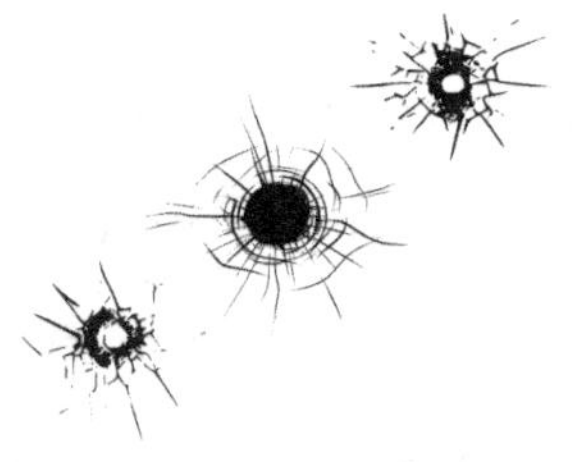

Morning creeps in on a knife-edge of gray light, and I move through the motions like clockwork. Coffee. Shower. Clothes that say respectable shopkeeper instead of woman who spent half the night digging through encrypted files.

By the time I push open the door to the bookstore, the air is sharp with salt and the promise of rain. Inside, the quiet hits me like a familiar weight. I flick on the lights, straighten a stack of returns, check the register. Every detail feels louder now—the scrape of the stool against the floor, the hum of the overhead bulbs, the bell above the door waiting to announce whoever walks through next. Dust motes spin in the shaft of light, and the lemony tang of polish lingers on the counter.

I paste on the same polite smile I've worn for three years. Jane Fairhaven, small-town bookshop owner, connoisseur of baked goods and lattes. No one here needs to know that Quinn Maddox is running the show today.

The bell jingles, and my breath catches in my throat at the sight of him. Thatcher Greeves—pressed shirt, polished shoes, pale skin too smooth to belong in a town like Driftwood.

He looks... vaguely familiar. Not in any concrete way. Not in a way I can place. Just in that unsettling, slippery sense of recognition that could mean everything or absolutely nothing.

The kind of face you see in crowds. In airports. In old reflections. The kind your brain insists you've known before even when you haven't.

Or... maybe I *have* and I just don't fucking remember.

He flashes a practiced smile, the kind that lands a beat too late to be natural. "Morning, Miss Fairhaven," he says smoothly, like nothing at all is wrong with the world.

But in my head, I hear the name that matters more. Jonas Kerr.

The echo of it unsettles me, and I hate that I can't tell if it's memory or imagination, instinct or paranoia. I hate that my pulse reacts before my logic does.

It's odd he's here this early... then again, his routine's been fractured since Kat died. "Anything

I can help you find, Thatcher?" I ask, polite and measured, even though the urge to gouge his eyes out hums under my skin like an electric current.

"Actually, I came to see you," he says, green eyes skimming the shop with a predator's ease—something that doesn't belong in a bookstore.

To anyone else, that glance might pass as nothing more than charm. I don't give him that courtesy.

"Oh?" I murmur, fussing with the stack of papers on the desk, anything to keep my hands busy and mask the tremor in them. Kat was right—he gives me the *creeps*.

"Yes, of course. Kat was special to us all. I felt it improper to approach you at the funeral, but I wanted to offer my deepest condolences and respect."

Right. Of course he does.

"Thank you," I murmur, eyes drifting over the shop as if distracted, sincerity sliding off my words. "It won't be the same without her. I hope they find who did it—and stick it to them *good*."

For the briefest moment, something tightens in his jaw—a quick darkening, like a shadow crossing marble. Then it's gone, replaced by the same polished smile he always wears. "I couldn't agree more," he says smoothly, leaning an elbow against the counter like we're old friends. "Kat deserved better."

I force my lips into a soft curve, even as my stomach churns. "Funny, isn't it? How you always seemed to stop in on her shifts. She mentioned once you were one of her most loyal customers. If I didn't know any better I'd assume you had a small crush on my assistant."

His green eyes sharpen, then shutter, the mask slipping back into place. "*Routine*," he says lightly. "Creature of habit, I suppose."

Before I can press further, the bell above the door jingles again, the sound slicing through the quiet.

Detective Rakes steps inside—all broad shoulders and storm-gray eyes—scanning the shop until they land on us. His gaze flicks between me and Thatcher, sharp as a blade, and the air shifts.

Thatcher straightens immediately, his smile flattening into something more polite. "Detective."

"Greeves," Rakes says evenly, then looks at me. "Miss Fairhaven."

I feel the weight of both their eyes on me, suspicion and interest braided together. Suddenly, the shop feels too thin, the scent of paper and polish cloying in my lungs. I paste on a tight smile, polished enough to pass. "What brings you in today, Detective?"

He hesitates, eyes cutting between us. His gaze narrows ever so slightly at Thatcher before sliding back to me. "A few follow-up questions, if you don't mind. Can I borrow a moment of your time, Miss Fairhaven?"

Thatcher smooths his jacket, a little too quickly. Too practiced. "Ah, I suppose that's my cue to leave. I'll let you two handle your business. Again, my deepest sympathies for your loss. She was a shining star taken far too soon."

His words drip with civility, but the glint in his eyes is anything but.

My fists clench beneath the counter as I watch him walk out of my shop.

The bell jingles again as Thatcher slips out, leaving a silence that feels heavier than before. Rakes doesn't move right away—he watches the door a beat longer, his jaw ticking, before turning those storm-gray eyes on me.

"You always get that kind of company?" His tone is casual, but the edge underneath isn't lost on me.

I shrug, forcing nonchalance. "Bookstore's open to everyone, Detective. Even polished men with bad taste in timing."

One corner of his mouth lifts, though it doesn't reach his eyes. He steps closer, pulling a small notepad from his black leather jacket. "Let's keep it simple. I just need you to clarify a few things about Kat's last week. And, truthfully, I'd rather not do it with an audience."

I lean against the counter, crossing my arms, letting the silence stretch a second too long. I already don't like his tone. "Sure," I say finally, voice even. "Ask away."

"Did Kat often make mistakes at work?" He asks, though it feels like a cheap shot. Especially, coming from him.

My jaw tightens. "Kat was meticulous—you *know* that. If something was off, she would've fixed it before I noticed."

"And you're sure about that? I did some digging, and found some records to suggest otherwise."

"Suggest... *otherwise*," I snap before I can stop myself. "Kat *never* left loose ends. If something truly needed addressed, she brought it to my attention. Immediately."

His pale-steel eyes lift, cutting into me. "Didn't leave loose ends... or made sure you wouldn't see them?"

I lean forward just enough to close the distance, my voice a low slice of glass. "Do you enjoy asking the same question five different ways, Detective, or do you just think I'm too stupid to notice? And, just what exactly are you implying about your... *cousin?*"

A muscle ticks along his jaw. The mask slips—irritation flashes—then he rein's it back, scribbling anyway, the nib biting into paper. "You realize," he says, his voice lower now, "the longer you dance around this, the more it looks like you're protecting yourself."

The words fall like a gauntlet, and I don't miss how he ignores my question. This time, though, I don't bother to hide the slow curl of my smirk.

He watches me for a long beat, pen stilled, weighing something I can't name. He seems to decide it isn't worth pursuing, then the notepad snaps shut, vanishing into his jacket. "That'll be all for now, Miss Fairhaven." His tone is clipped, professional. But as he reaches the door, he pauses. "Tell me," he says over his shoulder, "do you always keep places this tidy—or is Driftwood the only town worth the effort?"

The question cuts clean, deliberate—an insinuation that my neat little life might be a facade. I hold his stare, stretching my shopkeeper's smile until it's paper-thin. "Always a pleasure, Detective."

His mouth twitches—half a smile that never fully forms—before he tips his head and walks out. The bell chimes, a bright sound swallowed instantly by the silence he leaves behind.

My smile collapses. My nails ache where they've dug crescents into my palms. The shop is empty, but the emptiness doesn't mean safe.

Not safe at all.

CHAPTER 9

Quinn

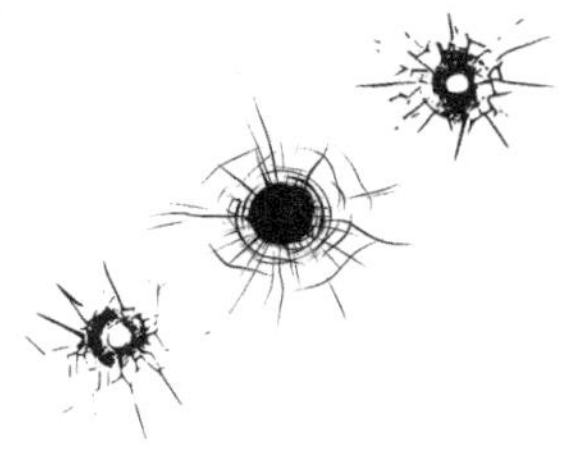

People like to think a bookstore is safe, quiet, harmless. A sanctuary full of words instead of weapons. Those people have never walked into their shop and heard glass crunch under their boots.

The front window gapes like a jagged wound, leaking cold air into the room. My stomach knots as my gaze sweeps the floor—nothing missing, nothing obvious. At least, not to them. But I see it.

The drawer where I kept the ledger has been pulled open, its contents shoved aside, pages bent from lingering fingers. They were searching for Kat's ledger. Too bad for them, it's not here anymore.

I keep my breath steady, tamping down the surge of adrenaline that wants to take over. My body already knows what to do—count the exits, check the shadows, catalog the footprints smudged in glass. Old instincts. Dangerous instincts that will keep me fucking alive.

But Jane Fairhaven doesn't know those things. She's just a shopkeeper with a knack for noticing messes.

So I crouch, straighten a fallen stack of bookmarks, and mutter, "Kids. Probably just some kids looking for cash in the register." My voice sounds steady enough, but my pulse pounds like a war drum. Whoever it was, they weren't after money. They wanted the ledger.

I let my hand drift over the drawer one more time, fingers brushing its warped edge, then push it closed with a snap. Whoever broke in knows more than they should. Which means I don't have time to wallow.

The crunch of boots on glass outside makes me stiffen. Heavy. Measured. Not kids this time.

"Miss Fairhaven?" The voice is low, edged with frustration, and unmistakable.

Detective Rakes. Of fucking course. Can't a girl catch a break?

Trouble clings to me like a shadow, and he's always right behind it. Peace was never on the table—not with *him* involved. I don't know why I assumed otherwise.

He fills the doorway, broad-shouldered in a dark blue button-down rolled to his forearms, jeans worn instead of pressed, scuffed boots grinding glass into the floor. His badge glints at his belt, catching the blue light bleeding through the broken window. His gaze sweeps the wreckage before pinning me in place, sharp as a blade.

I swallow the retort burning at the back of my throat and manage a sad smile instead. "Yes, Detective Rakes?"

"What seems to have happened here?"

And there it is. No pleasantries, no courtesy—straight to the point, like always.

"It appears my store has been broken into," I say dryly, crouching to gather a fallen stack of books, careful not to let him see my hands trembling from anything but irritation.

Rakes steps further inside, boots grinding glass deeper into the floorboards. "You don't say," he mutters dryly, eyes flicking over the broken window, the drawer behind the counter, then back to me. "And nothing's missing?"

I lift my chin. "Not that I can tell, though I'll still need to do a detailed inspection."

His gaze hardens, slate-gray and storming. "Funny. Most break-ins aren't this *neat*. Drawers pulled, things tossed... looks almost like they knew what they were after."

My stomach knots, but I force a careless shrug. "Or maybe they got spooked before they found anything worth taking. We do still live in a small town, Detective. Not every crime is a conspiracy."

He smirks—one of those slow, knowing curves that says he doesn't believe a word I've just said. "No. But some crimes feel... *personal.*"

The words slice between us like a blade. My pulse spikes, but I don't flinch. I meet his stare, my smile razor-thin. "If you're suggesting I staged this to make myself look innocent, you'll need to try harder than broken glass and a messy drawer."

The space between us crackles, tension thrumming, inches from snapping.

"I never said anything of the sort, Miss Fairhaven. What would give you that impression?" His head tilts, eyes glinting, studying me the way a hunter sizes up prey.

He wants me off balance and cornered. No matter how many times I give him the truth, he's convinced I'm tangled in this. It's *insulting*—more than that, it's infuriating.

I arch a brow, folding my arms as if his words roll right off me. "Maybe it's the way you keep circling me like a shark, Detective. Hard not to take it personally."

His smirk flickers—quick, cutting—but he doesn't deny it.

Inside, my pulse is a storm, but on the outside I look bored, almost amused. Let him think I'm just a stubborn shopkeeper clinging to pride. Let him underestimate me. It's safer that way.

"Can't blame me for working the only lead I have."

I swallow the words begging to rip free and turn away, picking my way through the wreckage. He's right about one thing—there's no real devastation. I'm lucky in that regard. Lucky, and better prepared than he'll ever know. Not that I'd ever admit it, but I've got funds tucked offshore, safe in places no one can extradite me from. Beau made damn sure of that.

It would be simple to fix this. Way too simple. But he doesn't need to know that. So I let him stew, play the part, let old instincts prowl at the edges of my skin. My body hums with the thrill of it, dangerous and familiar.

I have to be careful, though. One wrong move and the mask will crack. I can't afford to let go of Jane. Not yet at least. My cover isn't completely blown, and there are worse alternatives...

Out of the corner of my eye, I catch him watching me—still, focused, like a detective searching for any inconsistency. His voice cuts through the silence, low and intentional. "Most people would be rattled. Windows smashed, drawers rifled—yet here you are. Steady as stone."

I force a tight laugh, brushing dust from my cardigan like it's nothing. "Maybe I've had enough grief for one week, Detective. I did just lose someone who was a constant in my life. Did you ever consider... Maybe, I'm just *numb*?"

He doesn't buy it—I can feel it in the weight of his stare pressing against my back. His boots whisper over glass as he steps closer until the space between us hums with tension. "Or maybe," his voice drops, closer now, "you're hiding something."

I keep my eyes on the mess in front of me, refusing to give him the satisfaction of seeing my face. "You always this *charming*, Detective, or is it just me you save the accusations for?"

Behind me, there's the faintest huff of air—half laugh, half growl. He's close enough now that the heat of his presence prickles along my spine.

Silence stretches thin between us, sharp as wire. I don't turn. Not yet.

Finally, I can't stand it—the weight of his stare, the closeness of him at my back. I pivot sharply, my skirt brushing his boots, and suddenly we're face-to-face.

Too close. Way too fucking close. His gaze pins mine, the air between us charged with everything unspoken. My pulse slams in my chest, my breath catching in my throat. For a heartbeat, neither of us moves.

The world narrows to this moment—his suspicion, my mask, and the dangerous spark threading through the space we haven't crossed.

Then—a sudden clatter shatters the silence. Both of us whip toward the sound, nerves drawn tight.

I catch it in him—the flicker when he realizes I'm not totally cowering. I'm steady and braced.

He moves before he fully registers it, hand snapping out, fingers clamping around my wrist. The pull is harder than he intends, and I crash against his chest, unyielding and warm. For the briefest second, something flickers across his face before he smooths it away.

The noise comes again—a broom, sliding where it had been propped against the wall. Nothing more. Just gravity playing tricks.

But neither of us moves. His grip is still locked around my wrist, my pulse drumming against his fingers. I'm pressed too close, close enough to catch the faint scent of cedar and coffee clinging to his shirt.

For one suspended beat, the world is nothing but heartbeats and silence. Then I wrench free, my smile sharp enough to cut. "Looks like your suspect is a broom, Detective."

His mouth twitches—almost a smile, almost not. "Guess even brooms leave traces."

I smooth my cardigan and navy shirt, forcing my pulse into something steadier. "Unless you've got more questions, Detective, I'd like to salvage what's left of my morning."

His eyes linger, searching, weighing. "Questions? Only about a hundred. Answers? Not nearly enough."

I tilt my head, letting the coolest version of my smile slip into place. "Then I guess you'll just have to keep wondering."

The silence stretches again, taut and dangerous, but this time he doesn't close the gap. He just watches me, calculating, before finally stepping back.

"You're a hard woman to read, Miss Fairhaven." His voice is quiet, edged with something I can't name. "But I will."

I hold his stare until he turns and walks toward the door, shards of glass crunching beneath his boots.

Only when the bell chimes in his wake do I let out the breath I've been holding.

I glance at the broken window, at the drawer still slightly ajar, and the hollow quiet of the shop presses in again. Whoever smashed their way inside wasn't finished—they were sending a message. And now, with Rakes circling closer every day, I'll have to decide which mask to wear next...

Jane Fairhaven, harmless shopkeeper... or Quinn Maddox, who knows how to survive when the walls start closing in.

CHAPTER 10

Rakes

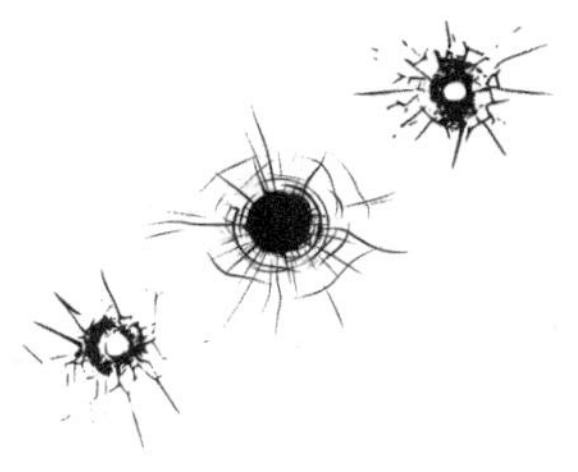

The bell over Fairhaven's door jingles behind me, but she lingers anyway—clinging like smoke I can't seem to shake off.

I drag a hand down my face, boots grinding over glass shards as I step into the salt-stung morning air. She's lying to me. I don't have proof yet—but the truth is there, buried under that polished smile. My gut's never been wrong, and my bones are screaming now. She's involved somehow. I know it.

The problem is, Jane Fairhaven doesn't crack. Most people stammer, fold, get rattled when I press. Not her. She holds steady, hides her tells like she's trained for it. That's not small-town bookshop owner behavior. That's muscle memory. And still, I can't shake the way she stood her ground when the clatter went off in back. Most civilians flinch, shrink, even scream or cry. She didn't. She looked ready, too damn ready.

I tug my notebook from my jacket, flipping it open to the list I've been building since Kat's murder. One name stays pinned to the top—*Thatcher Greeves*. Every time I circle back, his trail stinks worse. Loose alibis. A smile that lands too late. Eyes that linger too long. He feels wrong in ways I can't yet put on paper.

But Fairhaven? She's the one I can't place. I've run her records twice—birth, property, taxes. Everything looks too neat. Like someone scrubbed the edges clean, hoping to distract and deflect.

At the precinct, they already think I'm chasing ghosts. I can hear them now—*Rakes, you're too close. You're letting grief get in the way.* Maybe I am. But maybe grief's the only thing keeping my eyes open.

Jane Fairhaven isn't who she says she is...

And I intend to fucking *prove* it.

***

The precinct hums with its usual chaos—phones ringing, printers spitting, voices bleeding through thin walls. Fluorescents buzz overhead, harsh and cold. But since Kat's murder, even this place feels altered. Conversations drop quicker, footsteps land softer. Like her death rattled something loose in all of us.

I drop my notebook onto the desk. The scrawl of names and half-baked theories stares back—Thatcher Greeves, and Jane Fairhaven. Loose threads I can't ignore.

Mills leans against the corner of my desk, Styrofoam cup in hand, sipping coffee that smells like burned dirt. "You look like *hell*, Rakes."

"Feel worse."

His gaze falls to my notebook. "Tell me you're not still chasing Fairhaven."

I snap it shut, jaw tight. "She's hiding something."

"Or she's *grieving*," Mills shoots back. "Her assistant was murdered in her store. Now the break-in? That's not suspicious, that's tragic. Don't twist it."

But I know what I saw. The broken window. The drawer rifled through—not random, not desperate. Someone was after something specific. And Fairhaven's reaction? Not panic, or fear. She was fucking prepared.

Mills shakes his head, muttering as he pushes off my desk. "You've got ghosts in your head, Rakes. Don't let 'em drag you under."

Maybe he's right. But my gut won't let go.

Jane Fairhaven is hiding—from *someone* or *something*. And sooner or later, I'll find out how deep this runs.

When Mills wanders off to shuffle paperwork, I flip the notebook back open. Her name stares up at me, underlined twice.

I scan the other names on my list, cross-checking details, chasing inconsistencies until my eyes burn. Thatcher's alibis, shaky at best. Loose threads that won't hold. It should be enough to pull focus from her—but it isn't.

No matter how many angles I run, I keep circling back to Jane. Something about her doesn't fit, and if I stop digging now, I feel like I'll miss the one crack that finally breaks her open.

I lean back, staring at the glow of the monitor until my eyes blur. That's when a memory cuts through—Kat, laughing too loud after one too many beers, slouched over the bar stool across from me. Her guard had been down that night, words spilling easier than usual.

She'd mentioned a man. Not serious, she said. Just someone who lingered too long in her orbit. Too polished—eerily *rehearsed*. I hadn't thought much of it then—just Kat being Kat, particular about people. Like she was everything else.

But the name... what was it? Thatcher something.

Thatcher—

The memory locks into place like a round chambering in a gun. It *has* to be a coincidence. Nausea churns in my stomach like a fucking warning bell.

I sit forward, pulse kicking. Maybe this isn't *just* about Fairhaven. Maybe Kat had already been circling the right shark before she died.

My chair scrapes loud against the tile as I push back and stand, the sound cutting through the low hum of the precinct like a challenge. Half the bullpen looks up. Half pretends not to. I don't bother with either. I head straight for Captain Harlan Callahan's office.

His door is cracked, voice pitched low over a phone call. Something about budgets. Or donors. Or both. I knock anyway.

"Yeah," he snaps, not looking up. "Make it quick."

The office smells like aftershave and old paper, the air stale from too many closed doors and not enough truth. Framed commendations line the wall—years of service, community awards, plaques with gold lettering that mean less every time I look at them. Behind his desk, a wide window overlooks the harbor, all gray water and fog, like the town itself is trying to pretend it's clean.

And there—tucked among the official photos, half-shadowed by the window frame—is one that doesn't belong.

Callahan. The mayor. A yacht. All teeth and tan lines and expensive smiles, champagne flutes raised like they're toasting something that isn't legal.

My jaw tightens.

"I need more on Fairhaven," I say. "Full background. Digital forensics. Financials. Anything that doesn't come up on a surface pull."

He finally looks at me then, irritation sharpening his features. "You're still on that?"

"Yes, sir."

He exhales through his nose, pinching the bridge of it like I'm a migraine he can't medicate. "Kat's murder was ugly. I get that. But Jane Fairhaven? No record. No priors. No known associates. You're chasing smoke, Rakes."

"Smoke usually means fire."

His eyes flick to the door, then back to me. "It means you're wasting manpower."

"I'm asking for a cursory—"

"No." The word is flat. Final. He leans back in his chair, folds his hands over his stomach. "You *need* to drop it. We're not dragging a grieving bookstore owner through the mud because you've got a hunch."

That line is way too clean.

I glance again at the photo. The yacht. The mayor's hand on Callahan's shoulder like they're old friends. Like they share something. Something private, or protected.

A slow, cold suspicion coils in my gut. "Sir," I say carefully, "with respect, this feels... premature."

His mouth tightens. "You questioning my judgment, Detective?"

I hold his gaze. "I'm questioning the *timing*."

For a split second, something flickers there—annoyance, yes, but also something else. Wariness. Calculation. Then it's gone. "That's final," he says again. "Drop it."

I nod because I have to. Because pushing here would only put a target on my back. But as I turn for the door, the weight settles in my chest, heavy and certain.

If Callahan's blocking this, it's not because there's nothing there. It's because there *is*. And if the captain's already closing ranks... then the rot doesn't stop at his office.

It runs higher.

Which means whatever Fairhaven's tangled up in... I'm about to be very, *very* alone in it.

Back at my desk, I scrawl a single name at the top of my notebook—**Thatcher Greeves.** The smug bastard hovers at the edges of this whole mess. Kat's voice echoes in my head—her unease, her instinct that he wasn't what he seemed. Thin, yes. But it's a thread I can pull.

If Callahan won't back me, I'll make my own headway.

I shrug into my jacket and grab my keys. Thatcher's hiding something, I'm sure of it. I'll find it, no matter what it takes.

And if Fairhaven is tangled up in this, too?

Well. I'll deal with *that* when the time comes.

Outside, the night air slaps cold against my face, sharp with the smell of rain pushing in from the sea. Thunder rolls low on the horizon, and for the first time all day, the weight of what's coming feels close enough to touch.

CHAPTER 11

Quinn

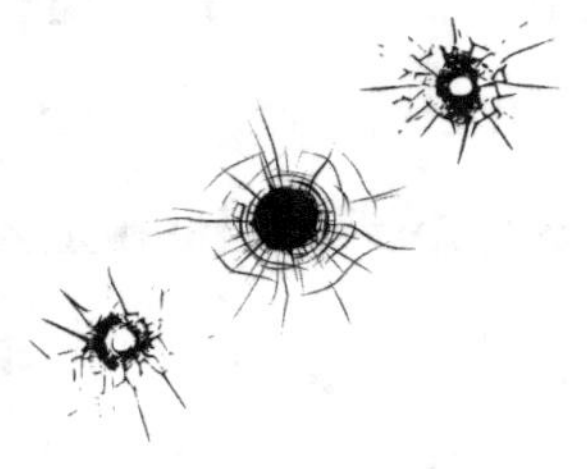

The diner smells like coffee and maple syrup, cloying and familiar. Grease clings to the air, closing around me like a memory I'd rather not keep.

I slide into a corner booth, the teal-blue and crème vinyl sighing under my weight, and pick up the laminated menu I don't need. I could order with my eyes closed at this point.

The bell over the door jingles. I glance up, and my stomach knots when I catch who it is. Of course. Detective Malcolm Rakes—broad shoulders under a navy flannel, gaze sweeping the room until it locks on me.

I duck behind the menu, praying he'll take the counter. He doesn't. His boots echo across the linoleum until he stops at my table.

"Fairhaven," he says, voice rougher today, less detective and more man who hasn't slept. "Mind if I sit?"

I should say no. For whatever delusional reason I would rather not admit... I *don't*.

The waitress appears, pen poised, eyes already tired from the morning rush. "What'll it be, hon?" She asks, nodding to Rakes first.

I nearly roll my eyes.

"Coffee—black, please," he says.

"French toast. Extra cinnamon." The words slip out, automatic. And then—careless, reckless—before I can stop the words and snort from leaving my lips. "My brother would call me a traitor. He thinks pancakes are *sacred*."

The waitress chuckles, scribbles down our orders, and moves on. But across from me, Rakes tilts his head, narrowing his eyes just enough to make my pulse skip.

Silence lingers, broken only by the clink of cutlery and the hiss of the griddle. He leans back, studying me like he's trying to peel layers I don't want touched. "Didn't take you for the French toast type," he says finally, mild on the surface but edged underneath.

I shrug, feigning indifference. "Guess I like what I like."

His gaze sharpens, steel pinning me in place. "Funny, though. You sounded pretty certain about your *brother's* preferences."

My heart stutters. Shit. I should've kept my mouth shut about Beau. I meet his stare head-on, daring him to push. "It was a joke, Detective. Don't tell me you've never made one of those."

For a long moment, he just watches me, jaw ticking, suspicion coiled tight. And then—something eases. His shoulders drop, the hard lines around his mouth softening.

"When Kat was little," he says, almost to himself, "she'd only eat waffles. Wouldn't touch a pancake, wouldn't touch toast. Drove my aunt crazy."

The shift is so abrupt it knocks me off balance.

My breath sticks in my throat, palms sweating against the table. I don't know what to say. It's rare for me to stall—rare to be left without some sharp retort burning on my tongue. But now? I can't string a single sentence together.

It's not even that his admission shocks me. Kat told me that story a thousand times. But I've painted her as guarded and tight-lipped. The truth is she opened up to me a lot this last year—*final-*

ly—after two years of me working to chip past her walls.

She was worth the wait. Our friendship had finally blossomed into something real, something I never thought I'd have again.

No. Not now, Quinn. Jane *has* to stay present. Focus. I can't afford to wander into memories of Kat knowing every dirty secret I buried, or the way she promised to cover the shop next month so I could take care of... *business*.

Not that I wanted to. I like the quiet. I like the life I built after Orion. But when the family calls, ignoring it isn't really an option. And maybe part of me was tempted—one last chance to scratch an itch I'll never scratch again.

I swallow the thought whole, paste on a polite smile, and say lightly, "That sounds like Kat. She was particular."

"She really was," he says, a real smile tugging at the corners of his mouth. "I remember once my aunt drove her all the way to Bangor to find a prom dress. Kat made her stop at every single store until she found the right one."

I smile in spite of myself, the question leaving my lips before I can stop it. "Let me guess—she was fashionable even back then. What did she end up choosing?"

His face brightens, a dimple carving into his left cheek, and my knees threaten to buckle. Thank *fuck* I'm sitting. "She was. She picked an elegant black gown—classic cut, empire waist, made of satin that caught the light just right. The sleeves draped gracefully without being overstated. It *screamed* old Hollywood."

I let the corners of my mouth soften into something dangerously close to real. "Old Hollywood, huh? Let me guess—she probably insisted on pearls, too. Kat always did have a flair for the dramatic."

His chuckle rumbles low, genuine, and for a fleeting second it warms something I'd buried deep. Too deep.

And just like that, I slam the door shut. The smile fades, my spine straightens, and I busy myself with the condensation on my water glass. "She knew what she wanted. Always did. But wanting doesn't change what happened."

A hollow ache lingers in my chest, no matter how tightly I try to lock it away.

Across from me, Rakes tilts his head, the faintest furrow creasing his brow. He's noticed. Of course he has. Suspicion flickers in his eyes, like he's caught a glimpse of something he shouldn't have. "You talk about her like you knew every detail," he says quietly, voice pitched low enough to cut through the clatter of silverware around us. "Funny, considering you've told me more than once she kept things close to the chest."

The air between us sharpens, thin as glass. My pulse kicks up, but I force a smirk, leaning back in my chair like he hasn't just slid a knife between my ribs. "What can I say? Kat had her moods. Some days she shared, most days she didn't. You'd know that if you really paid attention."

Rakes doesn't take the bait. His jaw ticks, his stare unrelenting, like he's peeling back layers I don't want exposed. He leans in, forearms braced on the table, lowering his voice to a rasp that curls right under my skin.

"See, that's the thing, Jane. I did pay attention. I knew Kat better than anyone... or I thought I did. But every time I turn around, you've got another story I've heard before. Makes me wonder—"

The unfinished thought hangs between us like a loaded gun.

The waitress arrives just then, shattering the tension. She slides a steaming plate of French toast in front of me, cinnamon dust spiraling up into the air. Her faded yellow uniform, neat piping worn thin, and brassy ponytail all speak of long hours and practiced cheer. "Here we are, sweetie," she chirps, and bustles off again, leaving sugar and cinnamon where suspicion had been.

I steady my fork but don't move. Across from me, Rakes wraps both hands around his mug, the ceramic creaking faintly under his grip. Around us, the diner hums with low chatter and clinking plates, but between us it's a taut wire waiting to snap.

"Thing is…" He studies me for a long beat. "Every time I think I've got you figured out, Fairhaven, you surprise me. Makes me wonder what else you're keeping tucked away."

The fork finally pierces the crust of French toast. I let the corner of my mouth curl. "Careful, Detective. Curiosity like that? It has a way of getting people burned."

His jaw flexes, the shadow of a smirk tugging at his mouth. "And you strike me as the kind of woman who doesn't mind playing with fire."

I take a slow bite, cinnamon sugar sharp on my tongue, and smile like we're not toeing the edge of something volatile. "Only when I'm sure I won't be the one who gets scorched."

"Funny thing about fire." He rises, dropping a bill onto the table. "It doesn't always care who it takes down with it."

The silence he leaves behind hums hotter than the plate between us. I watch him walk out, the scent of coffee and cologne trailing in his wake, and remind myself—*again*—that he's not the one I should be worried about.

CHAPTER 12

Rakes

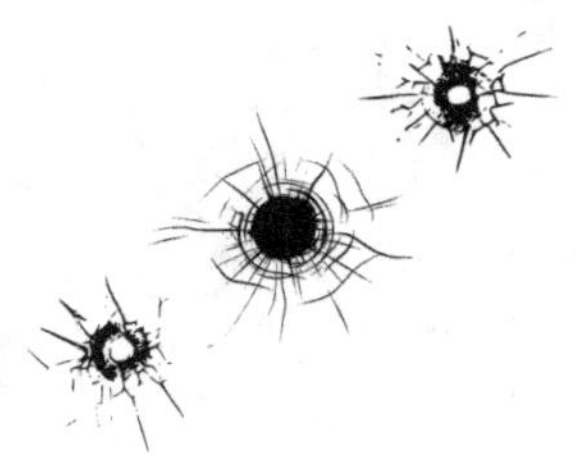

The precinct smells the same as always—stale coffee, copier toner, and a day too long. Different day, same walls, same ghosts.

I walked in this morning with one thought beating like a war drum. Dig deeper into Greeves.

Leave no stone unturned. Then grill him until something cracks.

My patience is fraying. The longer this case drags, the more I have to dredge up. Grief sits on my shoulder like a vulture now, an itch I can't drink away no matter how much bourbon I pour at night.

Today isn't about small talk. I don't want to chat, don't want to smile. I just want to get this done.

I shove my sleeves higher and start hammering the keyboard, fingers drumming like gunfire. Irritation simmers under my skin. I don't even know why it's this bad—other than a certain dark-haired, blue-eyed siren who's managed to crawl under it.

How the hell can I be split like this? Grief gnawing at me, suspicion clawing at my gut, and this raw, *stupid* urge to crush my mouth to hers.

It doesn't make any fucking sense. It's infuriating.

I feel like a goddamn *greenhorn*—distracted, eaten alive by guilt and my own demons—and I *prove* it when Captain Harlan Callahan manages to sneak up on me at my own damn desk.

I jerk, damn near jumping out of my skin. I loathe being snuck up on. He knows it, too—the *bastard*.

"Rakes," Callahan's voice drifts across the bullpen like smoke—lazy, confident, and entirely too pleased with itself. I don't look up right away. I finish lining the edges of my folders, stack my notes with deliberate care. Control what you can. Even when the ground's shifting.

"Captain," I say, finally lifting my eyes.

He's standing in front of my desk, hands hooked in his belt, posture loose. Too loose. Like he owns the room. Like he's already won.

His gaze flicks to the files at my elbow. Lingers. Sharpens.

Fuck.

"I thought I made myself clear about the Fairhaven girl," he says mildly, like we're discussing weather. His mouth curves, but his eyes don't follow. "Or are we having trouble with selective hearing?"

I straighten in my chair, spine going rigid. "You did, sir."

"And yet," he continues, glancing pointedly at the notepad half-hidden under my arm, "I get a call about you playing private eye at the diner this morning."

My pulse kicks—once—hard enough to make my teeth rattle.

I don't bother lying. He wouldn't be fishing if he didn't already have the hook set. "It wasn't an interview. We were in the same place. I spoke to her."

His jaw tightens, just a fraction. Enough to notice. Enough to register as irritation instead of anger—which is worse.

"Off the clock," he says. "In public. In a town where people talk."

I hold his gaze. "I was doing my job."

The bullpen noise seems to dim around us, like the room itself is leaning in. Callahan exhales, slow, through his nose. Drags a hand down his face. When he looks at me again, the irritation is gone. Replaced by something cooler. Heavier.

"Rakes," he says, lower now. "There are lines."

My shoulders tense. "With respect, sir, I don't see any."

That gets me a look. Not anger. Calculation.

He glances past me, quick and subtle, scanning the bullpen. Making sure no one's close. Then he steps in just enough that his shadow crosses my desk.

"You're digging where you shouldn't," he says quietly. "And you're doing it in a way that's going to get noticed."

My jaw locks. "By *who*?"

His eyes flick back to mine. Hold for over ten seconds—I clock it. Doesn't answer.

Recognition strikes my chest like lightning. The room tilts, just a little. "Is that a warning," I ask, keeping my voice even, "or a threat?"

His mouth tightens. Not angry. Tired. Almost... *resigned*.

"It's me telling you to let it go," he says. "Before it costs you something you can't get back."

The weight of it lands hard. Not bluster, or even protocol. This is personal. Controlled. Deliberate.

The last piece clicks into place. That damn yacht photo on Callahan's desk. The *mayor*... all the shut doors. The sudden interest in where I drink my coffee.

He's not protecting the department. He's protecting something else.... or *someone* else.

I lean back in my chair, slow, careful. "And if I don't?"

For a moment, something almost like regret flickers across his face. Then it's gone, and in its place is a stone cold wall. "Then you may not like what you find," he says. "Or who finds you first."

Then he's gone, leaving me anchored to my chair, white-knuckled on the arms. The office hum fades to a dull roar in my ears. Fear coils in my chest like a constrictor, but I smother it under anger.

I knew something about Kat's death stank. Now the smell of a cover-up is everywhere.

Before I even register the choice, I'm moving—keys in hand, jacket yanked on with more force than necessary. The chair skitters back and bumps the desk as I storm out. By the time I hit the parking lot, I've already made the decision that might just cost me my badge.

The cruiser door slams, engine growling to life, and I peel out, tires spitting gravel. The highway opens ahead of me, gray and endless, and I drive it like the bogeyman is breathing down my neck.

The coastline blurs past, trees a smear in the periphery. Callahan's warning still echoes, a weight

I should heed. But I've never been good at letting things go.

By the time I reach Driftwood proper, adrenaline scalds every nerve. My gut narrows to one sharp instinct—*find* Thatcher Greeves.

I cut the siren before I hit Main, coasting quietly through the town. Shops line the street, their windows glowing warm against the gloom. And there—like fuccking clockwork—he's outside the bakery, too polished for this small town, laughing at something the clerk says. Green eyes glinting as he adjusts his cufflinks, every movement calculated.

My pulse spikes, heart pounding in my chest. I kill the engine, step out, and stand long enough to make sure he sees me watching. He does. The smirk that curls across his face says he's been expecting me.

It feels like a trap, bait laid plain in the open, predator waiting in the shadows to strike. My fists clench, but I hold my ground, refusing to give him an inch.

Thatcher takes his time, like he's the one calling the shots. He strolls across the street, shoes clicking on the cobblestones, that grin still plastered on his face. "Detective Rakes," he calls smooth as oil, like my name tastes expensive in his mouth. "What a surprise."

I plant my feet, keeping my tone clipped. "Funny. I was just thinking the same about you. Seems like you're always right where I need you."

He chuckles low, shaking his head. "Coincidences *do* happen, you know."

"Not this many," I shoot back. My eyes scan over his body—every polished detail, every perfect line of his suit. Too curated. Like a man who's rehearsed his role for years.

Thatcher tilts his head, studying me with those too-bright eyes. "Careful, Detective. You look like a man who's chasing ghosts. That sort of obsession? It eats a person alive."

I step in closer, close enough to see the pulse at his throat. "Maybe. But sometimes ghosts leave evidence. And when they do, I'll be there to collect it."

His smile doesn't falter. If anything it widens, glinting under the streetlamp. "*Evidence*, Detective? From ghosts in Driftwood? You'll have to forgive me, but it's hard to imagine what sort of crimes you think lurk in a sleepy little town like this."

"I don't think," I growl. "I know."

Thatcher chuckles softly, brushing a hand along his sleeve as if dust were the thing he feared most. "Well, then. I suppose I'll leave you to your... *ghosts*. But take care—people talk when a man starts seeing shadows everywhere. Might make them wonder if the grief's gotten to you."

He tips his head, polite as a viper, and then he's walking away, each step measured. Like he's the one who just won.

I watch him go, fists clenched at my sides, every instinct in me screaming to drag him back, slam him against the wall, rip that smile right off his face. But I don't. Not here. Not yet.

Because he's right. Push too hard without proof, and I'll look like the detective who lost his grip on reality after burying his cousin. Then he really does win.

The unease stays lodged in my gut. He's hiding something—I can feel it in my bones. One way or another, I'm going to tear his mask off.

CHAPTER 13

Quinn

The house is too quiet.

No lamps lit, no curtains drawn. Just me, the dark, and the groan of old floorboards pacing beneath my restless feet. Kat's ledger waits on the table, its pages bleeding with red ink that glares like a wound I can't cauterize. I've been circling the same entries for hours, hunting a pattern that refuses to surface.

A knock slices through the silence. Not the kind of knock that belongs in Driftwood. It's quiet, hesitant—like it knows it doesn't belong.

I snap the ledger shut, sliding a half-empty tumbler of bourbon across it, amber liquid sloshing against the glass. Thankfully, no spill. My hand ghosts toward the drawer where steel waits—a habit, not a necessity.

Another knock. Louder this time, like they're growing bold and are tired of waiting. My pulse spikes, dancing in a staccato rhythm, but I twist the knob and pull the door open anyway.

Detective Rakes fills the frame, porch light shadowing the lines of his face. His green jacket is rumpled, jaw set, stormy eyes harder than usual—like he hasn't slept, like he's been chasing something that won't sit still. He doesn't bother with permission. He just steps inside, dragging the chill night with him.

"Evening, Miss Fairhaven," he says, voice low and rough. "We need to talk."

I tip my head, spine loose, pulse hammering as if it belongs to someone else. "Detective. To what do I owe the pleasure?"

His gaze flicks across the dim room—shadows swallowing the furniture, the faint glint of glass on the table—before snapping back to me. His jaw works like he's chewing on words before spitting them. "You make it sound like a social call," he mutters. "It's not."

I lean into the doorframe, arms folding, a slow smirk tugging at my mouth. "Well, that's a shame. I don't usually let strange men barge into my house after dark without at least bringing dessert."

His scowl cuts deep, the muscle in his jaw ticking like it might crack. "Jesus Christ, Fairhaven—this isn't a game."

That edge—too loud, too raw—hangs in the stale air between us, heavier than his boots on the floorboards. He's already let more slip than he meant to.

I arch a brow, voice cool as a blade. "Could've fooled me. You storm in here, no warrant, no badge, just a chip on your shoulder and a temper you can't leash. Looks a hell of a lot like a game to me."

The silence between us thrums, taut as a live wire. His nostrils flare, and then he takes a step closer—too close—like he's daring me to keep pressing.

I let my smirk sharpen, chin tilting high. "Careful, Detective. Keep crowding me like that, and people might start thinking you actually enjoy my company."

Something flickers. His breath hitches—just a fraction—but enough. The storm in his gaze shifts, grief bleeding raw through the fury.

"You think this is about *you*?" His voice cracks, rough and jagged, like he's speaking through broken glass. "My *cousin's* in the ground because someone carved her up like an animal. And every damn time I look at you, I can't decide if you're the one holding the knife or the one who's going to bury the truth."

The words hit like a slap, brutal in their honesty. He knows he's gone too far, but it's too late to reel it back. The weight of them hangs thick between us, a silence sharp enough to draw blood.

For a beat, my breath falters. His grief is unvarnished, raw enough to scrape something fragile in me. Kat's smile flares behind my eyes, her laugh reverberating in my chest until the ache threatens to pull me under.

Almost.

I blink, letting my walls slam shut. The smirk returns, cold and clean. "If you're hoping I'll cry on your shoulder, Detective, you've picked the wrong suspect."

His jaw tightens, muscles working like he's grinding words into powder. Then he takes the final step forward, closing the space until the heat of him prickles against my skin. His hand twitches at his side before lifting, hesitant, almost unwilling, until his fingers barely graze the skin of my arm.

Not a grab. Not even a hold, really. Just contact. A tether he shouldn't want, and I shouldn't allow.

The air thickens around us, charged, dangerous. For a heartbeat too long, I stay still, pulse hammering against his touch. Then I move, stepping back, spine stiffening with every movement. The air between us cools instantly, my mask snapping into place like armor. "Don't." My voice is sharp enough to cut. "Don't confuse your grief with attraction."

The words hang like a blade. His hand drops as if burned, his face twisting—grief, anger, maybe shame—it's hard to tell where one ends and the other begins.

"You think I don't know the difference?" he growls, voice low and jagged. "I buried Kat, Fairhaven. I know exactly what grief is… and what it isn't."

For half a heartbeat, the hurricane behind his eyes almost pulls me under again. Then I force myself to breathe, to drag the mask back on tight, because I can't afford to break.

"Then maybe you should spend more time *grieving*," I say coldly, "and less time showing up at my door in the middle of the night."

His lips press into a thin line. No answer. No apology. Just a turn on his heel and the slam of the door. The silence that follows feels louder than the knock that started it.

I sink onto the edge of the couch, dragging Kat's ledger back into my lap. Red ink glares up at me, merciless, every alias and inconsistency screaming at me. Someone wanted us to notice.

A prickle crawls down my spine, and I turn, glancing toward the window. The street outside is dark, quiet—too quiet. For a heartbeat, a pale face flashes between the trees, moonlight glancing off it before dissolving into shadow.

I blink, and it's gone. The trees are empty. Nothing but branches swaying in the breeze.

My chest tightens. Was it *him*—or just my paranoia twisting in the dark?

Either way, one truth gnaws at me. Rakes is pressing in from one side, Thatcher from the other. Both close enough to unravel me.

And I'm running out of places to hide.

CHAPTER 14

Quinn

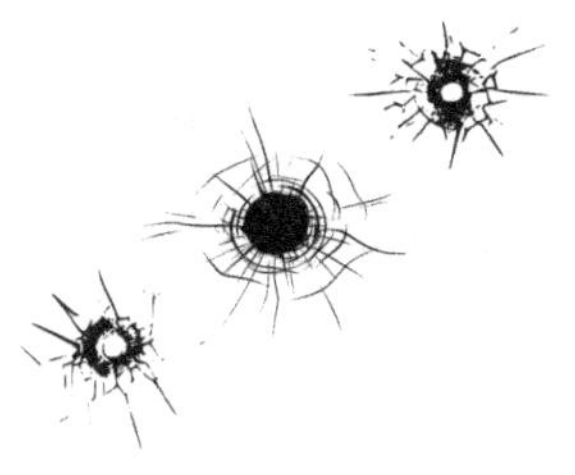

I don't sleep.

Every time I close my eyes, I see it again—that pale flicker of a face in the trees, there and gone in a blink. By dawn, I've convinced myself it was nothing... but my body won't buy the lie. My nerves hum like a struck wire, vibrating with a pitch I can't shake.

I stop pretending. The house is cold and dim, a long exhale of old wood and older ghosts. I pad down the hall, past the framed lithographs I never replaced, past the faint watermarks staining the green-and-yellow wallpaper. At the base of the staircase, I press the hidden latch. The false panel groans, then slides back with the obedient sigh of a secret too used to being kept.

The lair breathes me in.

Blue monitor glow washes the concrete walls. The hum of servers is steady and low, a mechanical heartbeat undercut by the soft whisper of air moving across heat sinks. It usually calms me. Tonight it only reminds me how much there is to lose. I lock the panel behind me and cross to the terminal, palms flat to feel its faint thrum—living, warm, mine.

Beau's email sits at the top of the queue, its subject line a quiet blade: **Maddox Ops Archive — Last Ten Years.**

I sit. I don't open it. My finger hovers over the trackpad. One click and the last decade of who I was—*everything* I did to survive—will be splayed across the screen in neat, damning lines. I could shut it all down instead. Wipe the drives. Salt the earth. Burn Jane Fairhaven and build something new in another sleepy town with a different ocean and different ghosts. I've done it before.

But Kat's ledger sits upstairs like a heartbeat, daring me to keep looking. I can still hear her humming at the shop as she shelved new arrivals, see the way she'd tuck a stray lock behind her ear when a puzzle clicked in her head. She believed in patterns because patterns tell the truth. She believed in me long before she said it.

Running now would be spitting on her grave.

I click. The decryption launches... Cascading glyphs, checksums winking alive and green. I stand and pace while the progress bar crawls, counting the breaths it takes to loop the room—nine, eleven, thirteen—and the faint ticks in the wall where the wiring never quite settled. Paranoia, I tell myself. The good kind. The kind that's kept me upright and breathing. Still, I glance back twice to make sure the hatch's deadbolt is thrown.

The screen pings softly. **Unlocked.**

The first page unfurls like a wound. Dates, locations, wire routes, sums. Names I remember, faces I don't—and the opposite, in equal measure. The archive is surgical. No bravado, no color, just the clean mathematics of consequence. My eyes track down, then down again until I land on a familiar job, the old muscle memory of debriefs waking up in my fingers. Every entry is a door I walked through without looking back.

Seven years ago... *Bangor.* I don't even need to read the rest to feel it hit. The lines on the screen are only proof.

Mark: a financier laundering Orion money through a saint-named shell foundation.

Position: second-floor office, glass wall on a quiet street.

Schedule: seventeen minutes with the door propped open at lunch.

Vulnerabilities: ego, scotch, a fear of dying ordinary.

Outcome: clean. Efficient. My work, and signature.

It's there in tidy font, but I can still smell the citrus of the cleaner, the old paper on his shelves, see the light cutting through blinds. I remember the thrill of a routine so tight it sang. The hush after—the silence that settles once an echo stops bouncing from wall to wall. I used to tell myself the halo meant something—control, precision, a beautiful lie about order. A ring of blood like a crown, a blade-thin promise that nothing was wasted.

Now someone's using it like a fucking spotlight.

My mouth goes dry. Whoever killed Kat wanted me in that room even if I wasn't. They wanted Rakes to suspect me, to uncover a monster who supposedly never retired. They wanted Drift-wood to whisper my name with murderer.

Why?

I scroll deeper. Somerville. Augusta. Two foreign cities I won't name, because saying them is breathing life back into old ghosts. Each entry hits like a cold wave—shock, recoil, breath. The archive is complete—but something nags at me. Beau's thorough, but even he doesn't collate like this unless he's afraid for me. Or unless someone's been pulling his strings too.

A thought I don't like knocks politely...

If Thatcher knows me well enough to copy my signature, then he also knows how I work. And if he knows that, he knows where to dig for the parts of me I tried to bury.

I pull up Kat's scans beside the archive—red ink against black, her handwritten times against my timestamps. Coffee rings on her notes echo the watermarks on Beau's PDFs. To anyone else it's obsession. I see a trail laid by someone who felt hunted and refused to run. A pattern peels away from the noise. A pattern I knew already, but Kat was just as clever.

Thatcher's visits slant toward late afternoons—3:12, 3:28, 3:34—always on the days Kat closed alone. Always fifteen to twenty minutes after the bell rings for the school down the block. An alibi built out of routine. In my world, we called that camouflage.

"He wanted it seen," I murmur, and my voice sounds wrong in here. Too soft, too broken.

The old instincts flare. What Thatcher is doing—*if* it's him—isn't sloppy. It's ritual. Rituals teach the body to move without thinking. It's the same reason I still count steps between shelves and check the corners of rooms I've checked already. The body remembers even when you decide to stop. That makes me wonder where he learned the skill set from.

I lean in, tracing the overlap between a Tuesday Kat circled three times and a Tuesday from my archive with a different city and a different ending. Though, try as I might, I don't see the connection yet.

My shoulders ache. The glow of the monitors sharpens the edges of everything—the keyboard, the mouse, the scrape on the metal rack where I bumped it last spring. The air tastes like dust and copper.

I should feel safer down here. Hidden and cocooned. I don't.

A soft vibration slinks through the floor-boards—January wind pushing along the siding, or... *not*. I freeze and listen, head tilted like an animal scenting. Nothing.

Then—faint—something above, like finger-nails scratching against wood. Too long to be the house settling. Too careful to be the radiator kicking on.

I kill the monitors. The room drops into a humming dusk, and servers go on breathing. I draw the pistol from the shelf under the desk and ghost to the hatch, using the edge of my sleeve to thumb the bolt. It rolls back without a sound.

The panel opens on the underside of my staircase, a wedge of black openings and the older smell of the house—the sea-salt damp threaded through oak. I slip through, count to three, then step up on the outside of each tread to keep the wood quiet. The wallpaper at the landing is a little more scraped than it was. Could be the light. Could be I know where to look.

At the top I pause, listening with my mouth slightly open, catching the subtle push of air along the hall. The Victorian has a way of amplifying small sounds, bouncing them from arch to alcove until you can't tell whether they're coming or going. I move by muscle memory. Right hand low, left hand free. Weight on the balls of my feet. Breathe on the exhale, not the step.

The guest room door stands ajar—no, not ajar, just not latched. A trick of angles. I ease it open with my fingertips and sweep the corners. The quilt Belladonna insisted I keep, the narrow dresser with the stubborn top drawer, the window locked tight and fogged from the cold. Two dust motes spin in a shaft of pale light and settle. Nothing else moves.

Bathroom. *Clear*. Linen closet. *Clear*, except the sheet I folded yesterday isn't as neat as I left it. I tell myself that's petty, that my brain wants something to claim.

The living room waits at the end of the hall like a stage. The burgundy velvet recliner rests in its corner. I hate it for what it holds. The coffee table is centered perfectly in the field of the rug—too perfectly. I hate that too. It makes me feel like a line has been drawn and I'm standing on the wrong side of it.

The ledger sits where I left it after Rakes stormed out—closed now, bourbon ring bleeding light into the cardboard cover. I stop three steps away and take inventory in order.

Front door, deadbolt engaged. Side windows, latched. Fireplace screen undisturbed, the thin curtain to the left breathless in the still air. My eyes skate across the room to convince my brain it isn't missing anything obvious.

I circle the table once, then again, slower the second go around. My pulse thrums in my throat. Nothing leaps out at me, which drives me crazy.

I angle my body to block the street's line of sight and lift the ledger's cover two inches with my fingertips, just enough to peek at the first page.

That's when I see it.

The receipts I stacked on the coffee table last night—edges squared, Kat's handwriting facing the spine—sit at a crooked angle now, one corner bent like a lazy dog ear. A small thing. A nothing, if you don't know me. If you didn't spend three years listening to Kat scold you for leaving ink lines out of alignment. Or, if you weren't trained to spot a half-millimeter shift and know it means someone touched what you love.

My breath goes very quiet. I don't reach for the receipts. I don't touch the ledger. I let the cover fall shut again and stand there in the hush, feeling the weight of that tiny, wrongness settle into my bones.

"Cute," I say to the empty room, because talking makes the silence bearable. "Next time try knocking." No answer. The house goes on, because it's only a house.

I move to the window and part the lace with the edge of my knuckle. The yard is moonwashed and still. Trees at the property line shifting and lean, black against darker black. Nothing moves that isn't wind. I wait for my eyes to trick me, for the pale flicker to cut across my vision again.

When it doesn't, I'm not relieved.

I lock the hatch behind me when I go back downstairs and turn the monitors on one by one, letting the blue spill back into the concrete. The archive is still open where I left it. Bangor bold in the middle of the page, as if the past could reach clean fingers into the present and hold it steady.

Someone touched my life tonight. Not a wrecking ball, like the shop. Just a single, careful press of a fingertip against the glass to say... *I can.*

The receipts stay crooked upstairs, and I let them. I need the reminder. Whoever's doing this wants me to feel them. Wants me to know they know me—how I think, how I stack, how I breathe when I'm counting threats. They want to turn my precision into a map they can follow.

I pull the keyboard closer and start a new file. I title it what it is... **HUNTER.**

Under it, I list what I know, what I can prove, and what I can only feel in my teeth. Then I move to paper. My notes are clean, my columns straighter than Kat's ever were, because now the neatness is a weapon. If he wants patterns, I'll give him patterns he can choke on.

When the first page is done, I sit back, hands folded over the ache in my chest. The ocean breathes against the cliff. The servers keep their low hum. The house waits, listening.

I let the receipts stay crooked. I let the ledger sit where it is. And I keep the pistol on the desk, within reach, while I write the next name in my new file...

Thatcher Greeves — Prime Suspect.

CHAPTER 15

Quinn

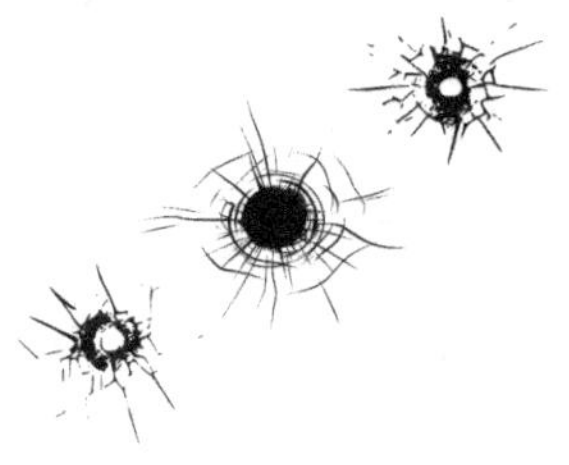

I make my way to the small cemetery at Drift-wood's edge. Rain slicks the cobblestones, a thin drizzle that does nothing to soften the bite of October air. The ocean hisses faintly in the distance, salt sharp on the breeze. Today, it unsettles me further instead of soothing my frayed nerves.

I push through the iron gate, eyes sweeping across headstones — names that meant everything once, now carved into stone for strangers to pass. Kat is where I left her, buried beneath a sprawling oak, surrounded by statues and benches that look almost theatrical in their mourning. Her marker, by comparison, is plain.

Too plain for her. Too muted for the bold woman I came to admire. Another insult, but perhaps all he could afford. I wish he would've asked. I wish for a lot of things... but none of it will bring her back.

Kathleen Leanne Mathers. The name is carved deep, each letter stark against the gray stone. She hated it, always swore being named after her aunt made her sound like an old woman trapped in a young body. But I thought it suited her — strong, rooted, uncommon. Not the kind of name you hear anymore. That's what made it hers.

I sink onto the nearest bench, leather jacket creaking as I fold my arms against the damp chill. Rain beads in my hair, streaks dark down my jeans, but I don't move. I let it soak me through. Maybe the cold will sting sharper than the ache already lodged in my chest.

For a long moment I just stare at her name, willing the edges of grief to blur. Kat should be here — *alive*, perched at the counter in the shop with her ridiculous highlighters and endless commentary. Not silenced.

The quiet presses in, heavy as the clouds overhead. Rain patters against stone, the sea whispers beyond the gates, and my pulse thrums loud in my ears.

When I finally shift, brushing wet strands from my face, my eyes catch on something at the base of her marker. At first, it barely registers — just another bouquet among the many left behind.

But the longer I look, the more wrong it feels. The white blooms are too stark against the dark stone, the fragrance too sweet on the damp air.

Lilies.

Of all the flowers in the world... Unease coils low in my gut. This isn't remembrance. It's a message. One that feels so fucking familiar, tickling the edges of my mind—just out of reach.

I freeze, watching the drizzle turn each petal glassy. Maybe I'm overthinking. Maybe someone grabbed the first bouquet they saw.

But Kat *hated* lilies. Everyone who truly knew her knew that. The perfume curls up into my nose, sharp and sickly sweet, until my stomach lurches. The whole cemetery feels off-kilter now, too still, like the silence is pressing down, waiting for me to react.

My heart pounds in my chest, thumping against my ribcage like a tornado. This wasn't *careless*. Someone chose these with intention.

I glance around—the iron fence, the line of trees, the road beyond blurred by rain. Nothing moves, and no one lingers. Yet, I can't shake the weight crawling across my skin. When I look back, that's when I see it. Not the flowers, but the sliver of paper wedged between the stems. Just enough of an edge to make my throat tighten.

My fingers hover over the stems, then close around the damp slip of paper. The ink has bled slightly from the drizzle, but the words are still legible.

"Burn the past, and the ashes will still know your name."

The breath punches out of me. To anyone else, it's nonsense—a poetic little threat at best. But I know better.

It's *Orion*. One of the mottos whispered in initiation, buried deep enough that outsiders never hear it. I haven't seen it written down in over a decade.

And now? It's sitting on Kat's fucking grave.

The words blur as the drizzle smears the ink, but they've already branded themselves into my brain. My fingers tighten until the paper crumples, disbelief lodging in my chest like a stone. *Orion*. A name I swore I would bury.

My body hums like a live wire, every instinct screaming to move, to disappear, to burn it all down and never look back. But my legs won't obey. I'm rooted here, drenched in rain and my past, staring at the grave of the only person who ever knew the truth about me.

Kat, what the *hell* did you get yourself tangled in?

The air feels too thin, every inhale jagged. I shove the note into my jacket pocket, scanning the cemetery again. The trees, the stones, the mist. All still empty. And yet, I can't shake the feeling I'm being watched.

"Didn't think I'd find you here."

The voice cuts through the silence like a blade. I whip around, heart leaping into my throat—Malcolm Rakes, standing just inside the gate, rain dripping from the brim of his coat, eyes dark as wet slate, fixed on me.

For once, I can't summon a barb. My mask falters, just a fraction, and I know he sees it.

"You look... *surprised*," Malcolm says, his tone softer than usual, though suspicion still threads through it. He steps closer, careful on the slick gravel path.

I drag in a breath, force myself upright, chin tilted in defiance. "Didn't think you were the cemetery type, Detective."

His mouth twitches, not quite a smile. "Didn't think you were either."

I should fire something sharper back, but my mind won't focus. The note in my pocket feels like it weighs a hundred pounds. Kat—sharp-eyed, careful Kat—had to have known something. Maybe even more than I did. That thought gnaws at me, clawing at the neat boxes I've crammed my past into.

"You're distracted," Malcolm says, his gaze heavy, like he's trying to pin me where I stand. "Care to share what's rattling around in there?"

I bark out a laugh, brittle and too loud against the drizzle. "Trust me, Detective, you don't want inside my head."

His jaw flexes, but he doesn't press—*yet*. Rain patters between us, flimsy cover for the storm simmering underneath. "You've got that look," he says finally. "Like you're carrying something you don't want anyone else to see."

I arch a brow, a smirk tugging at my lips though it feels more like armor than expression. "Funny. I could say the same about you."

We stand locked in silence, measuring each other through the mist. My thoughts won't stay put—they slip back to the words on the note, then... to Kat. How much did she uncover? Did she stumble into this, or was she pulled under because of me?

The weight presses harder, but I don't let it bleed through. Not to him. Definitely not here.

Malcolm exhales slowly. "You're *impossible*, you know that?"

"Occupational hazard," I say evenly, though my heart rate hasn't slowed since he appeared.

His eyes linger, searching, like he's waiting for a fracture. But I hold steady. For now.

"Tell me something," he says at last, voice pitched lower, more raw truth in his tone. "Why is it that every time I get close to an answer, you're already three steps ahead of me?"

The words strike sharper than any accusation. He isn't questioning if I'm hiding something. He's telling me he *knows* and is still deciding what to do with that information.

I school my features into something steady, even as the note in my pocket scorches through the fabric. "Maybe I'm just better at paying attention than you give me credit for."

His jaw flexes, but he doesn't look away. "Or maybe you've spent too much time covering tracks, you can't remember what it's like to walk clean."

For a split second, my breath falters. Damn, he struck close. He doesn't know what he's brushing against, but it's enough to twist the knife.

So I lean into the mask, the smirk, the chill in my tone. "You done, Detective? Because right now, you're standing on sacred ground, and I don't think Kat would appreciate your little *theories*."

We hold the silence between us, taut and bitter, until he finally steps back. Not satisfied, not convinced—but contained. For now.

The drizzle thickens, cold needles against my skin, but I don't move. I trace Kat's name with my eyes, trying to unravel how deep she might've been tangled in things I never saw coming. Malcolm shifts closer, boots grinding wet gravel. His patience is thinning—I can feel it radiating off him.

"Enough of the riddles, Jane," he says, voice sharp with a note of desperation. "You know something you're not telling me."

My head jerks up, and the distance between us is gone. He's a shadow at the edge of my grief, looming, shoulders squared, jaw clenched so tight I can almost hear his teeth grind.

"Thatcher," he bites out, spitting the name like poison. "Every time I circle back, *he's* there. *You're* there. Don't you dare tell me that's coincidence."

The name crashes against me like a wave, but I force my face into stillness once again. Inside, though, every instinct screams... *mask, mask, mask.* "Maybe you should spend less time chasing theories," I murmur, "and more time grieving your cousin the right way."

The words sting us both the moment they leave my lips.

His shoulders tense, a muscle ticking in his jaw before he takes an intentional step closer. Rain beads down into the collar of his coat, but he doesn't seem to notice.

"You don't get to tell me *how* to grieve," Malcolm snaps, his voice low but edged sharp enough to cut. "You didn't know her like I did. You didn't *lose* her like I did. So don't you dare stand there and act like you've got the right to lecture me."

The ground between us shrinks to nothing, and I can feel the heat of his fury, close enough to taste it. He wants to shake the truth out of me—I see it in the rigid set of his frame. But there's grief there too, bleeding raw into every syllable.

The bite of his words lingers in the damp October air, cutting deeper than I want to admit.

I hold my breath, forcing my body still, but inside, his fury finds purchase. Because he's right. Maybe I didn't know her—not the way I thought I did. Not if she was tangled up in Orion enough for that clue to be left at her grave.

The rain drums harder against the oak above us, cold rivulets slipping down my neck. I don't answer him. I can't. Silence feels safer than the truth clawing at my throat—truth that would burn me alive if I let it slip.

So I let his anger hang there, thick and unyielding, while mine coils inward. A knot of guilt, paranoia, and the sharpest sting of doubt.

The rain fills the silence for me, spattering against stone and soil, seeping into the fabric of my coat. Every drop feels like a reminder—of how little I knew, of how much I still don't.

He waits, jaw locked, eyes searching me for something I can't give him. When I offer nothing, he exhales briskly, turns on his heel, and storms off. His retreating figure blurs in the gray wash of drizzle, but the weight of his words stays, branding itself into the marrow of my bones.

I stay rooted at Kat's grave, staring at her name until it no longer looks like hers, until the letters blur and run together. Doubt blooms wider, swallowing what little comfort I'd clung to, plunging me into a storm of my own making.

CHAPTER 16

Rakes

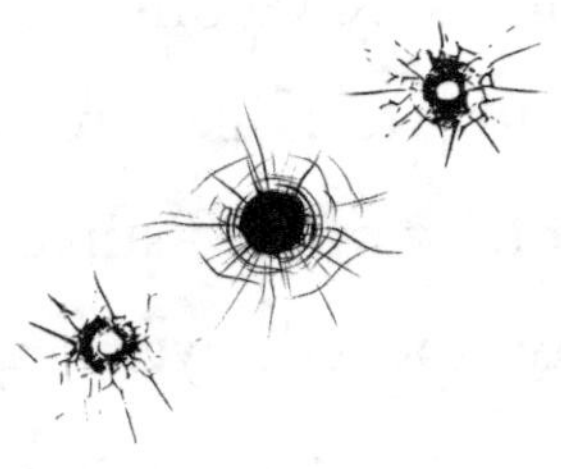

The precinct hums with its usual chaos—phones ringing, typewriters clacking, detectives barking for files across the room. I tune it out. My desk is the only world that matters, buried under coffee-stained reports, printouts, and the stack of documents I've been hammering at since dawn.

I've been circling Thatcher Greeves for days, ignoring the raging thoughts about a certain dark-haired woman, chasing half-formed suspicions and loose alibis. Now the paper trail is finally giving me something real.

A birth certificate that doesn't trace back to a hospital. A social security number that pings in two states. Two addresses—Bangor, Bar Harbor—both tied to utilities, neither lived in long enough to mean a damn thing.

It's not just sloppy bookkeeping. It's a man built from scratch. Completely fabricated.

My heart rate kicks higher as I flip through the files, dragging one folder over another. He's not just *creepy*. He's constructed. Someone polished him until the seams nearly disappeared. But not completely.

I rub a hand over my jaw, stubble rasping against my palm. "Got you, you *son of a bitch*," I mutter, though the words land heavier than I want them to. Because no one scrubs a life this clean alone. Not without resources. Not without protection. Someone powerful *wants* him hidden.

Which means Kat wasn't just unlucky. She was standing too close to something designed to stay buried.

The discovery should feel like a win. Instead it burns cold. Every thread I pull drags me closer to the same wall. And no matter how hard I fight it, her name keeps bleeding through the ink.

Jane Fairhaven.

Or whatever her name really is.

I lean back in my chair, eyes fixed on the chaos littering my desk. Thatcher's mask is flawless—too perfect. But Jane... she's no different.

I've seen it in the way she stays composed when most people would crack. In the tiny slips she tries to bury. In the way grief clings to her like an ill-fitting coat. Two ghosts hiding in plain sight—one pretending to be a man he's not, the other pretending to be a woman she isn't.

The question gnaws at me... Which one breaks first?

I scrub a hand down my face, exhaustion digging its claws in. Bourbon used to dull the edges, but not anymore. Not when the only thing holding me upright is the certainty that if I stop digging, I'll lose the only chance I've got at justice.

And maybe—*just maybe*—I'm terrified of what happens if I find it.

An office door slams loudly, a sound meant to announce itself. Captain Callahan.

He fills the space around my desk, broad shoulders straining against the fabric of his uniform, jaw set tight—the kind of man who doesn't need to raise his voice to make a point, though I've seen him do it when he's pushed far enough.

"Rakes." His voice is flat, warning already woven into the syllables of my name. "You look like hell."

"Appreciate the *concern*, Captain." I lean back in my chair, keeping my tone steady, casual—like my desk isn't littered with evidence I wasn't supposed to touch.

His gaze cuts to the files, the notes, the screen still glowing with Thatcher Greeves scrubbed records. His jaw works once. Twice. "I told you to drop it," he says, each word sharp as a nail. "So explain to me why I walk in the bullpen and find you chasing something I told you to let go of."

My fingers flex against the armrest, the urge to rise and meet him head-on almost too strong. "Because it's sitting in plain sight, sir. And if I don't follow it, we're never going to find out what really happened to Kat."

Callahan steps forward, plants both hands on my desk, leaning down until his eyes bore into mine. "You're not *listening*. I said *let it go*."

My jaw tightens until my teeth ache. "With all due respect, sir, you can keep telling me to let it go, but I won't. Not when everything about Thatcher

Greeves reeks of a setup. Not when Kat's lying in the ground and no one else gives a damn about why."

For a long moment, Callahan just stares at me, the weight of his silence heavier than any words. Then he straightens, slowly, pulling his hands from my desk like he's already washed his own clean of this.

"You're going to dig yourself a hole you can't climb out of, Rakes," he says finally, voice low, almost tired. "And when you do, don't expect me to throw you a rope."

He turns without another word, his footsteps echoing like a lock sliding into place.

I sit there, jaw clenched, blood pounding in my ears, surrounded by files that suddenly feel less like evidence and more like kindling. Because the truth is clear now, sharper than ever. Callahan doesn't just want this case gone. He needs it *buried*.

And if I want answers—for *Kat*, for *myself*—I'll have to dig them out alone.

I shove back from the desk, gather my jacket, and push through the precinct doors. The night air slaps cold against my face, stinging with salt and exhaust, clearing none of the static in my head. I take the steps two at a time, jaw tight, eyes fixed on nothing.

Then I see him.

Thatcher Greeves stands across the street, too polished for Driftwood's grit, his gaze pinned to the bookstore's dark windows. *Jane's* shop. He doesn't move, doesn't blink, just watches like a man casing something he already owns.

My pulse spikes, racing in my chest like a thundering herd.

As if on cue, he shifts his attention to me. A smile slices across his face—thin, calculated. He tips his hat in a gesture slick as oil, then slips into the crowd. One moment there, the next dissolved, leaving nothing but the aftertaste of threat in the air.

The message is clear. He isn't done circling her. And I'm not done digging. Not even close.

CHAPTER 17

Quinn

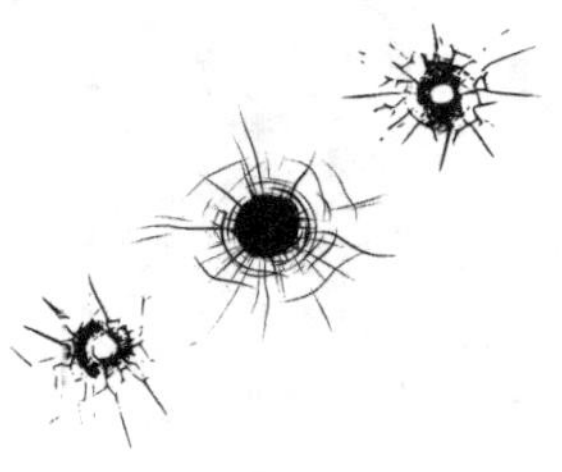

The sky breaks uneven over Driftwood, gray light pressed flat against the rooftops like a hand holding everything down. The kind of morning that promises rain but won't commit, lingering between storm and stillness until the air feels waterlogged. My breath fogs in the chill as I step out, tugging the collar of my jacket higher.

I tell myself I'm only walking into town for coffee, maybe a fresh loaf of bread from Hall's Bakery before the shelves empty. Something simple—ordinary. But the truth is, I *need* to be seen. I need to walk like Jane Fairhaven—local business owner, quietly mourning, keeping her head down. That image has to hold, even when it feels like the floor under me is rotting plank by plank.

The street is quiet at first. A gull flies overhead, its cry sharp against the muted backdrop of tide and wind. My boots scuff the damp cobblestones, the faint smell of salt and brine weaving through the air like a reminder. Driftwood belongs to the ocean, not to the town.

By the time I reach Main, the town has begun to stir. Shops click open their locks. Window displays light up in patchwork color. The bakery releases its usual siren call of yeast and sugar, warm enough to pull almost anyone closer. I fall into the rhythm, queuing behind a pair of women in wool coats, their umbrellas dripping faintly from the mist. Their voices are pitched just low enough to sound like privacy, but the air carries sound differently in Driftwood. A secret whispered here might travel a whole block.

"...*funny*, don't you think?" one of them murmurs, words muffled as she adjusts her scarf.

"What is?" her friend asks, distracted, rifling for coins in her purse.

"That woman. The one with the shop."

The hair at my nape prickles. My gaze fixes on the counter, on the chalkboard scrawled with the daily special, but my ears tilt shamelessly toward them.

"*Jane Fairhaven?*" the friend prompts.

A pause. Then, soft but steady, "Thatcher said she has to be hiding something."

The coins clink together, loud as bells. My pulse snags on the sound, then kicks into a sprint.

The other woman hums, unconvinced. "He talks, that one. Always has. What's he mean?"

Another pause, heavier this time. "Only that trouble seems to follow her. You remember the break-in at her store? And the assistant—*poor girl*—murdered under *her* roof. Thatcher said it was... *odd*. That it's never just chance when so much darkness gathers in one place."

My throat closes around the air.

They move on quickly, conversation slipping back to recipes and errands, their words losing form in the shuffle of the line. But mine stay carved, every syllable branded under my skin.

Thatcher is spreading rumors now? Why? Is he not content with lurking at the edges, with smiling in lamplight and letting implication rot my peace?

Now he's speaking, planting seeds where he knows they'll take root. Driftwood *thrives* on whispers. This town is small enough that gossip doesn't just travel—it *settles*, staining everything it touches.

I keep my face neutral when the baker's daughter hands me a paper bag warm with bread. My hands don't tremble until I'm outside, until the bell above the bakery door clatters behind me and I can let the noise of the street blur the edges of my composure.

The words echo anyway... *She's hiding something.*

It's too clean, too premeditated, the kind of poison you can't scrub once it spreads. By evening half the town will be turning it over like a pebble in the mouth, tasting it, spitting it, passing it along.

By tomorrow it'll be gospel.

I head for Belladonna's shop next, that always smells of roasted beans and cinnamon. The barista greets me with the same practiced cheer, and I murmur my order as though my skin isn't crawling. When I collect the cup, steam fogging the lid, I don't linger. I want the town to see me out and about, but not long enough to invite more whispers.

Outside, the drizzle thickens. Raindrops stipple the street, flattening the scent of sugar and yeast into something sharp, metallic. I tuck the bread tighter under my arm and start back, the paper cup scalding my palm.

All the while, the words gnaw.

Trouble follows her. Not who she claims to be.

By the time I reach the shop, my nerves are so taut they buzz. The store-front looks the same as always—weathered brick, the bell above the door hanging crooked, display window fogged at the edges. Ordinary. Comforting.

That is... Until I reach the door.

The lock slides too easily beneath my key. Too smooth and quick. A small thing, invisible to anyone else, but I know how it should feel. The subtle catch before the tumblers align. This isn't it.

The bag of bread shifts in my grip. I push the door open slowly, the bell jingling a note that feels mocking now.

Inside, the air is still. Too still. The faint scent of old paper and ink lingers, but underneath it is something cloying, something that doesn't belong. My eyes sweep the shelves, the tables, the counter. Nothing looks ransacked. No glass shattered. No drawers pulled.

But there, at the heart of it, sits the message.

On the counter, a single yellow lily lies across the worn wood. Beside it, folded neatly, is a scarf I know too well. *Kat's*—navy with little embroidered stars along the hem, one she'd drape around her neck on colder mornings when she complained about how drafty the shop was. I remember teasing her about its fraying edge, and how she'd stuck her tongue out before tying it tighter.

The scarf is clean. Pressed, even. A relic resurrected. My chest caves inward, breath punched out in silence. The lily's perfume coils thick, sour-sweet, dragging bile up the back of my throat.

Someone was here, close enough to touch what was hers. Someone who knew enough to lay it out like this, not stolen, or destroyed, but *displayed*.

A promise.

My legs carry me forward on instinct, though every nerve screams against it. I stop at the counter, staring down at the flower, the scarf, the quiet mockery of it all. The ledger is safe, hidden where only I can reach it, but that hardly matters. The real wound isn't what was taken—it's the proof that *nothing* here is beyond reach.

I press my palms to the wood, grounding myself in the texture. Grooves cut by three years of Kat leaning on her elbows, tapping her nails, scrawling quick notes. Now those grooves cradle a lily she would've trashed.

My jaw tightens. I want to snarl, to lash, to drag the mask tight and play the role I've perfected. Jane Fairhaven—unbothered, practical, grieving but not broken. That's what the town will see when they pass by the window. That's what Rakes will see if he shows up again, storm-eyed and relentless.

But inside?

Inside I'm quaking. Because the mask isn't enough anymore. Not when someone is dismantling me piece by piece, not when Thatcher's voice is already seeping into Driftwood like smoke through a keyhole.

I gather the scarf in careful hands, the fabric cool and damp from the rain that must've clung to it on its journey here. For a heartbeat I press it to my face, inhaling what's left of her—faint traces of vanilla lotion, old perfume—but even that is tainted now. All I smell is intrusion. Violation. A warning written in threads and petals.

The coffee cup trembles in my grip when I set it down. I lock the door with ease, turning the bolt until the lock bites properly, until the sound clicks sharp against the hush. Then I draw the curtains, blotting out the gray wash of the street.

Alone, I force my breathing even. One beat in. One beat out. Counting until the panic dulls into something I can use.

Kat believed in patterns. If this is the beginning of a pattern, it means something important. It means they want me to feel them circling, to know they can reach me in my sanctuary. They want me off-balance, stripped of the control I've built one cautious brick at a time.

Knowing that doesn't make it any easier to calm the storm raging within. Sadly, it's *working*.

I sink onto the stool behind the counter, the scarf coiled in my lap, the lily still glaring against the wood. My reflection glances back at me faintly from the glass display case—hair damp from drizzle, mouth pressed into a line too sharp to be mistaken for calm.

The mask is cracking—*quickly*—whether I want it to or not.

For a moment I let it. Just here in the silence, with the rain soft against the windows and the scarf heavy across my knees. I let the vulnerability bleed through, raw and aching.

Because the truth is simple, and it terrifies me more than anything else...

Someone is tearing away my cover. And I truly don't know how much longer I can keep Jane Fairhaven standing.

The thought won't leave. It gnaws at me as I cross to the door, twisting the lock, testing it once—*twice*—until my fingers ache from the pressure. The bolt holds, but I don't trust it.

Not anymore. Not after today. Not with lilies and ghosts laid out like offerings in my shop.

The air feels wrong inside these walls, as if the intruder left some of themselves behind. My bookstore, my *sanctuary*, and suddenly I don't belong here. Every shadow stretches too far. Every creak in the floorboards is a step I didn't make.

I try to move like Jane — careful and ordinary. Jane would tidy up, sweep the damp petals into the trash, fold the scarf and place it reverently on a shelf until someone claimed it. Jane would sigh, maybe even laugh nervously at herself for being shaken.

But Quinn counts exit points. Quinn catalogues time of entry, the way the lock sat just slightly off its groove, the exact angle of the scarf on the counter like bait. Quinn knows this wasn't random.

My reflection in the front glass catches me off guard. I look like her — cardigan, hair curling at the ends, polite shopkeeper's smile somehow still etched into place. But my eyes give the truth of me away.

The lily lies where I left it, pale and ugly against the scarred countertop. My stomach twists as another memory forces its way up — another flower, another warning. Years ago...

Different city. Different name. The night I learned just how far Orion went to remind its recruits that the past was inescapable. The flower back then hadn't been a lily. But the message was the same: *we can find you, anywhere, anytime.*

I sink into the stool behind the counter, scarf clutched tight in my hands, and for the first time in years, the tears burn hot and unrelenting. Silent. Stubborn. They carve tracks down my cheeks as I stare at the ledger, still hidden upstairs, and wonder if Kat ever realized just how dangerous her notes had become.

The clock on the wall ticks too loudly. Each second a hammer against glass. I wipe my face with the back of my sleeve, force the tears away, and inhale until my chest steadies. The mask has to come back on. Jane has to come back.

So I sweep the petals into a dustpan. I tuck the scarf into a drawer I never use. I boil water for tea, pretending the mundane ritual is enough to anchor me. Steam fogs the kitchen window, but it doesn't warm me.

Outside, Driftwood is calm, but I feel the town turning, shifting, the way gossip spreads faster than smoke. Thatcher's whispers, the detective's suspicion, the eyes of neighbors that linger too long. It's not just about the ledger anymore, or Kat.

Someone is peeling me apart, layer by layer.

And when I finally kill the lights and let the shop settle into darkness, I realize my hands are still shaking. The mask is still cracked. And Jane Fairhaven feels like she's already halfway gone.

Chapter 18

Rakes

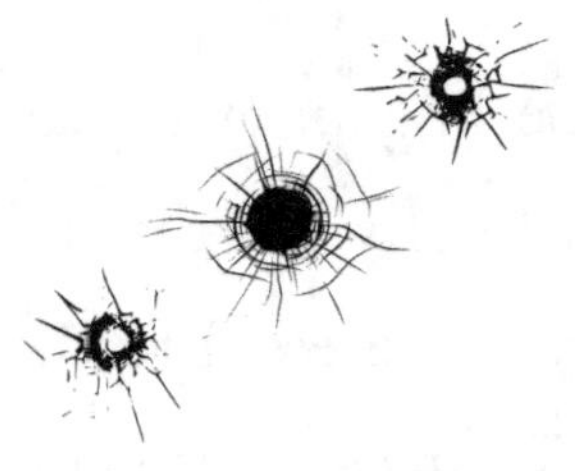

The precinct hums with the same rhythm it always does. Phones ringing, keyboards clacking, detectives barking across desks for coffee and who is getting the next round. The kind of noise that most people would call chaotic. For me, it's white noise, a tide I can let wash over me until I'm not really hearing it anymore. It's easier that way—tune out the chatter, the gossip, the gripes about paperwork—so I can focus on the only thing that matters.

The file is spread across my desk. Jane Fairhaven's file. The one I was *supposed* to let go of.

I've run it a dozen times already. Maybe more. The guys in Records would laugh if they knew how many hours I've burned punching the same search parameters into the system, waiting for something—*anything*—to shake loose. Each time it comes back the same. Neat, ordinary, unimpeachable. A woman with a modest paper trail, small town upbringing, inheritance enough to buy her shop, tax filings in order, no criminal record, not even a parking ticket. *Squeaky* clean.

Still, here I am again, staring at the screen, convinced I've missed something. My fingertips drum against the desk as the system crawls through its databases, spitting out the same tidy lines I already know by heart. Name. Date of birth. Social security. Mortgages. Utilities. Bank accounts.

And then—I stop cold.

It's subtle. Almost nothing. But it's there, waiting for me like it's been laughing at me all along.

2019 to 2022. A gap that should *not* exist. A gap that I'm positive I would've seen...

So, how did it get there?

Not just the missing details. It's a full-on absence. *No* utility bills. *No* tax filings. *No* employer records. *No* credit activity. *No* plane tickets, no hotel receipts, not even a single damn Amazon order. Nothing.

Three years of fabricated nothing.

I lean in closer, narrowing my eyes at the monitor. Run it again. Same result. Try a different search, broader parameters. Same thing. It's like Jane Fairhaven simply blinked out of existence for three years and then reappeared in Driftwood with a bookstore and a spotless record, like noth-ing happened.

Except... things like that don't *just* happen. Not in my world.

I've seen my share of people try to scrub them-selves clean. Old identities, bad debts, dirty his-tories—people think they can bury them under a new name and a fake smile. But it never looks like this. This isn't sloppy. This isn't someone half-assing it on the run. This is surgical. Someone erased those three years so cleanly the file barely remembers they ever existed.

My chest tightens with a mix of dread and vin-dication. Finally. *Proof.*

I sit back, rubbing a hand over my face, stub-ble scraping my palm. My mind is already rac-ing through possibilities. Witness protection? No—the government doesn't build you a new life with this much finesse without leaving their fingerprints somewhere in the margins. A hired cleaner... *maybe.* Private contractors with the kind of skills that cost more money than most small towns will ever see. Or something darker. Something older. Something bigger than anything the system would admit exists on paper.

Who the hell is Jane Fairhaven? Because it's becoming clear someone wanted to shine a light on this. On her *record*.

And now... the big question. Why does someone want her exposed so badly?

I scroll back through the pages, eyes locking on the years that are accounted for. Every box ticked, every bill paid on time, every number lining up exactly the way it should. No mistakes. No human error. That's the part that rattles me most. Real people leave fingerprints—late payments, changed addresses, misfiled tax forms, duplicate charges. Mess, because life is messy. Jane Fairhaven's file isn't messy at all.

And suddenly, all those little moments replay in my head. The way she didn't flinch when the shop got broken into. The way she stood steady when the broom clattered to the ground. The way she parried every one of my questions with just enough truth to make it sting, but never enough to bleed.

For a second, I just sit there, staring at the screen, the glow making my eyes burn. The gap is proof of everything my gut has been screaming since Kat died.

Jane Fairhaven is a lie.

I shove back from the desk hard enough that my chair skids an inch across the floor. The noise draws a glance from Mills, my partner, who's been nursing his third cup of burnt coffee across the room. He arches a brow, but I wave him off before he can ask. Not this time. I don't need another lecture about grief and obsession and chasing shadows. I don't need his pity.

I need answers.

And there's only one man who can green-light me to keep digging.

Captain Harlan fucking Callahan.

***

His office sits at the end of the hall, door always half-shut, blinds tilted just enough to keep you guessing whether he's watching. The man doesn't need volume to command a room—his presence is enough. Heavy, immovable, like granite.

I knock once and push the door open before he can tell me not to.

He looks up from a stack of reports, pen balanced between his fingers, dark brows arching. "Rakes. You look like a man who's either found something or lost everything."

"Maybe both," I mutter, dropping the file onto his desk. The papers fan out, printouts spilling like a hand of bad cards. "Jane Fairhaven. I ran her file again."

His sigh is audible, heavy, the kind of sound that makes you feel like you've already disappointed him before you've said another word. "Christ, Rakes. We've been over this."

"Not like this." I jab a finger at the printouts, at the yawning blank space where three years should be. "Look. 2019 to 2022. Nothing. Not a trace. You ever seen a *citizen* go dark like that? Because I haven't, not without help."

Callahan doesn't look down. Doesn't even blink. He just stares at me, jaw tight, expression unreadable. "So you've got a gap. *Congratulations.* People move. People fall off the grid. You think that's proof of something?"

"It's not just proof," I snap, heat flaring in my chest. "It's a goddamn *beacon*. Someone scrubbed her record clean. You don't just lose three years of a life unless you want it lost. And if you want it lost that badly, there's a reason."

Finally, his gaze flicks down to the papers. He scans them once, twice, and for the first time since

I barged in, something shifts in his face. Not surprise. Not curiosity. Something harder—colder. He sets the pen down, leans back in his chair, and steeples his fingers. "Walk away, Rakes."

The words hit harder than I expect. My stomach knots. "What?"

"You heard me." His voice is even, deliberate, each syllable heavy as lead. "*Drop* it. Now."

"No," I bite out. "Not when Kat's dead, not when Thatcher Greeves stinks of fabrication, not when Jane Fairhaven's file looks like a goddamn tombstone with three years chiseled out of it. You tell me to walk away, I'm going to ask why. You tell me this is nothing, I'm going to say bullshit."

Callahan's eyes narrow, his face hardening into something that feels less like a captain and more like a wall. "This is above your *clearance*, Rakes."

The words land like a punch to the ribs. *Above my clearance.* What the hell does that even mean?

I laugh, sharp and bitter. "Clearance? Since when do murder cases in Driftwood come with clearance levels? What the hell are we talking about here—national security? Witness protection? Organized crime? Which is it?"

"Doesn't matter," Callahan snaps, the first edge of anger slipping into his tone. "What matters is you stop. Now. For your sake."

My pulse spikes. My hands curl into fists on his desk. "For my sake? Or yours?"

Something flashes in his eyes—something I've never seen in him before. Not just frustration. Not just irritation. Something like fear.

It's gone as fast as it came, shuttered behind that granite stare, but it's enough to make my blood run cold.

"I know you chased big fish in Boston, Rakes, but this is Driftwood. Let it fucking go," he says again, voice low, deadly serious. "That's not a request. That's an order."

I push back from his desk, chair legs scraping against the floor, the air between us charged like a storm. "You're protecting someone."

His jaw tightens. He doesn't deny it.

That's all the confirmation I need.

***

By the time I stalk out of his office, the precinct feels different. The noise sharper, the walls closer, every eye on me though no one's looking. I move through it like I'm wading through water, heavy and suffocating, my thoughts a roar in my ears.

Three years erased. A captain telling me to walk away. And the unmistakable weight of someone powerful enough to bury the truth staring me in the face.

I know it's not just a hunch. It's not just my grief twisting shadows into monsters. It's *real*.

I stop at my desk, grab my coat, and ignore Mills's questioning glance. My pulse is still hammering, my chest still tight, but there's clarity in it now. Cold and biting.

If Callahan's willing to threaten me over this, then the truth isn't just dangerous. It's *deadly*. And if Jane's past is tied to Kat's death, then no amount of orders is going to stop me from tearing it open.

Let them come for me. Let them try to bury me under the same silence they've wrapped around her.

I won't stop.

Because for the first time since Kat was murdered, I've got *proof*.

And I'm going to see it through—no matter what it costs me.

CHAPTER 19

Quinn

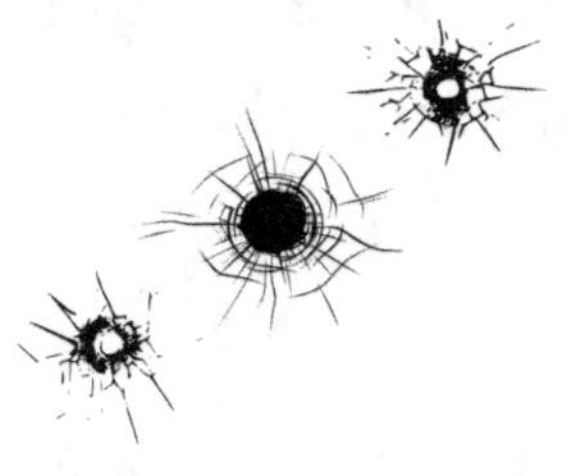

The shop has a different voice after hours. By day, it's paper and chatter and the bell above the door clearing its throat. Tonight it whispers—low and rasping—old floorboards easing, a tired radiator ticking, the far-off hiss of the ocean combing fingers through the rocks. I keep only the lamps glowing. A pool of amber on the counter, a soft halo by the history shelves. Everything beyond those circles is shadow, thick as velvet.

Exactly what I need for what I intend to do.

The ledger lies open like a living thing. Leather warm beneath my palms, spine softened by years, corners blunted, edges darkened. Red ink has bled faintly through a few leaves, ghosting across the next page like a voice after a door closes.

I've read these pages a dozen times. It doesn't matter. Tonight, the teeth of the gears finally catch.

The first alias—*Jonas Kerr*—already hums under my skin, the name that pried the past open. I trace the notation trail with a fingertip. Dates, times, shelves, purchases. Clean, exacting. She marked the days he came after three, slipping in on the wave of noise from the school bell before quiet fell back in. He chooses the slipstream, her hand says. Camouflage.

Camouflage? Like disguises.

I turn the page. More red ink. Receipts stapled to the margins. A corner folded true.

Alias? again—this time underlined harder. Beneath it? *Henry Vale. Black hair, brown eyes with a green iris. Contacts?*

The name chills like a draft under a door. Nothing flashy—just letters that repeat across entries if you're looking. The same handwriting on two return slips a month apart, the same pen pressure on different loyalty cards, the asterisk she saved for certainty. *Same man.*

Henry Vale. Jonas Kerr. Thatcher Greeves.

Three masks, one jawline. The neatness of it makes my teeth ache.

This isn't hobby. It's alarm made orderly. She wasn't just listing him—she was narrowing the circle. Pieces set until a picture formed.

Pride stings against a sharper urge to rip the pages free and lock them where he can't touch them.

I tilt the book toward the lamp and read the rhythm of her notes. Vale buys classics, not new releases. Kerr lingers in local history. Greeves—under the polished skin—asks courteous questions and never purchases what he fingers longest. Obfuscation as habit. He left a trail because men like him can't help it, then doubled back with a cleaner's rag and called the smear coincidence.

She saw through it.

Metal rises on my tongue. The room smells sharper than usual—old paper, lemon from under the sink, sea-damp that sneaks through ancient panes and pearls along the glass. Somewhere in the stacks, a book settles with a soft thup, and my body goes rigid before my mind catches up. Instinct—Quinn's, from long missions and sleepless nights in places better left buried.

I tell myself it's the building stretching. These bones do that when the temperature drops fast. But another sound needles me. Not quite a footfall outside—more like, weight shifting on wet cobbles—then still in a way only a person goes still.

I close the ledger halfway—page held, body unpinned. The pen clicks too loud in the hush. My hand finds the bag strap beneath the counter, measuring—book fits, phone fits, the knife rides light. None of it shows on my face. Jane keeps the mirror calm while Quinn lays out exits.

"*Henry Vale*," I murmur, testing the weight of it. The tone tastes wrong here—old work threaded through new life.

Her notes around Vale sketch a man too pleased with his own cleverness. Twice she wrote, watch when he speaks. I can see it now. Thatcher's practiced smile, the calm of rehearsed manners. I never noticed a tell when he speaks... I will *now*.

My eyes slide past the counter to the streetfront. The glass remembers daylight in a dull sheen, the way skin remembers sun. Beyond it, puddles rippling under lamplight. The bakery sign breathing as wind tests its hinges, and the dark coin of the alley where trash cans build a little city of their own. That's where the shadows thicken, where they make a mouth. Someone could stand there and disappear. Be the idea of a man, a notch deeper than the dark.

I take the kettle to the back sink and let the water run until it goes cold-cold from the pipes. The stream is louder than it needs to be. It covers the faint scrape outside—or the *idea* of one. Steam lifts when I set the kettle on, and the switch's click feels like absurd punctuation as I turn the dial.

I return to the counter because that's the mask—the ordinary rhythm of closing. The second alias tucks neatly under my skin where fear can't chew it.

A reflection catches in the window's corner. The smallest lean at the alley mouth. I don't turn my head. I unfocus the way you do when you're waiting for a deer to lift from brush. A shape edges out, minimal as a shrug. There, then gone—not because it moved, but because whoever owns it knows how to move without being seen.

The kettle begins to mutter. Heat slicks the air. I slide the book into my bag in one practiced sweep and pull the zipper only part way—casual enough, quick enough.

You're not alone, she wrote in a margin six pages back. Tonight the line is a room tone.

I pour water over tea leaves. Bergamot climbs—intrusively lovely. One slow sip, letting the stillness outside wait on me. Petty control is still control. The heat steadies my hands.

If he wants panic, he'll be disappointed. If he wants me to bolt, then he will be bored. If he wants me at the glass, he can keep waiting.

The small brass clock Kat insisted on shudders a minute hand. Ten-fifty-two. Too late for anyone upright on Main who isn't a problem.

I blow across the cup and think of the little stars she penciled beside his names. Big enough to pull her out of her tidy orbit and into mine without either of us knowing. Big enough to make a man wear three faces within half a mile and trust no one would notice.

Except she *did*. And I *do*.

The history-lamp gives a miserable flicker—old wiring wincing as wind fingers the pole—and that's the fissure. I set the cup aside, shoulder the bag, reach for the keys. One to the front, two to the back, a third to the upstairs attic I can't make myself enter.

I douse the lamps one by one, leaving the counter last. The shop folds inward. Shadows reclaim aisles and endcaps and the table she used to stage themes—"haunted towns," "women who saved the world," "ships that vanished." The bell over the door watches like a single bright eye.

I lock the register—Jane would. Then, throw the angle-iron bolt on the back—Quinn would—letting the stillness settle again. The alley doesn't breathe. The wind shifts, and the bakery sign hushes. Attention outside gives a small clinical shrug. Not leaving. Adjusting.

"Coward," I tell the empty store, and I hear the tremor under it and let it stand.

Keys ready, bag secured, I crack the door and step onto the threshold. Night reaches in—damp, cold, tasting of rain that has yet to fall. The street keeps its secrets. A car hisses far off, and a gull cries once and quits.

I lock up without looking away from the glass. My reflection stares back—paler than I remember, darker at the eyes, hair salted with mist. A woman who passes in daylight and survives at night. The weight against my ribs ticks like a second heartbeat.

Something *just* missed me. The air still holds its warmth the way a glass does a hand.

Not paranoia. Perception. The body knows when it was meant to be prey, and I know someone is tailing me. Even if I can't see them.

I don't hurry, or smile for the street. I walk, letting my footsteps announce me. If he wants the music of fear, he'll need another musician.

As I pass the alley mouth, the smell of cold, wet metal rises—trash lid slick, *newly* disturbed—and a hair lifts at my temple like a barometer twitch. I keep my eyes forward and picture Thatcher's immaculate sleeves, Vale's flat signature, Kerr's quiet hands, the faint stars in the margins.

I turn the corner. The shop becomes a dark square behind me. I don't look back, because looking would give them the satisfaction and I choose not to.

I feel it anyway... Watchfulness stretched like wire between us, humming loudly.

***

<u>Rakes</u>

I'm not tailing her.

It's what I tell myself as I sit in the truck across from the shop with the engine off and the heater whining every time the wind shifts. It's not about Jane. Not tonight. The notebook open on my thigh doesn't have her name at the top of the page. It has *his*—Thatcher Greeves. Beneath it, smaller—*Jonas Kerr? Henry Vale?*—and a question mark I hate looking at. I hate how a question mark looks like a hook.

The street is a watercolor of lamp glow and damp brick. Rain's in the air, but it hasn't committed. The kind of night Driftwood wears like a coat—quiet enough to hear your guilt, loud enough to pretend you don't. The bookstore's front room is lit like a stage, warm pools of light inside a box of dark. It's late. She shouldn't be there. And yet if there's one thing I know about Jane Fairhaven, it's that she doesn't live under the word should.

I tell myself I'm watching the shop because Thatcher does. Because he's made a habit of drifting by at odd hours, lingering where sightlines cross, wearing a man's form so politely you forget to notice the edges are wrong. The first time I caught him, he had a fresh coffee in one hand and his other in his pocket—*Ah, Detective, fancy seeing you*—with a sweetness to his voice that felt like someone pressing down on a bruise to make you flinch. I haven't stopped seeing him since.

Tonight, he shows on schedule. A shadow stitching itself to Hall's Bakery awning, then unstitching. He pretends not to look at the shop windows. Pretends to admire the old brick opposite. Pretends the alley's mouth is just an architectural feature. A man who leans without ever touching anything, who always stands a fraction of a step back from where you expect him. It reads as manners if you're generous. Or... it reads as calculation if you've got eyes.

I watch him as he watches her.

Inside, Jane is a figure cut from light and shadow, head bowed over something on the counter. A book, probably. Maybe notes. She moves the way she does when she thinks no one sees—unhurried, distinct, a woman putting objects where they belong and making sure they stay there. People call that meticulous, but I call it control.

The longer I sit here, the harder it is to pretend I don't know why I'm here. The Captain's warning still rings in my ears—*above your clearance*—and I can still feel the heat rising in my throat when he told me to walk away. But there are some people you can't walk away from. Thatcher is one. Kat was another. Fairhaven... I don't have a name for what she is to me yet, and I don't like that I don't. I've had limited interactions with her, but still. Something about her draws me in. It's not love, God no. But *lust*? Maybe. I groan, running a hand across my face, trying to rid myself of the intrusive thoughts.

Then, across the street—*movement.* Thatcher shifts closer to the alley. His head turns a fraction, his lips moving, he's counting. Timing her. Men like him live by pacing and angles, counting windows and seconds the way other people count blessings. He's waiting for something I can't see. Not yet.

My hand finds the door handle without asking me. I check my sidearm out of habit, even though this isn't that kind of night—*yet*—and picture how this goes if I spook him. A polite apology, a thin smile, a promise to donate flowers to the next church fundraiser, a pair of cuffs that feel premature even to me.

I'm not looking for theater. I'm looking for the moment he shows the edge of his mask. I want the slip, so I know where to look next.

A light inside the shop flutters once and steadies. Jane moves in and out of the border of the lamps, a silhouette in motion. I can't hear her through the glass, but my mind supplies the small sounds anyway. The clink of a key ring, the muted click of a kettle, the whisper of leather against wood as something slides into a bag.

She's getting ready to leave. Whatever she came to find, she found it.

Thatcher knows it before I do. He straightens—so subtle a civilian wouldn't clock it—and dampens his presence like turning down a dimmer. If he had feathers, they'd be smoothed. If he had hackles, they'd lie down. It's what predators do when the deer lifts its head. Stillness as camouflage and grace.

I should move now. Get between him and the door, make him choose a direction that isn't toward her. Put myself in the way in a way that doesn't read as territorial even though some feral part of me wants to be exactly that. Instead I hold, because patience is a lever and timing is a key.

The bell above the shop door doesn't ring yet, but the air carries a shift I've learned to trust. You can feel intent if you've lived around it long enough. Inside, she kills the lamps one by one, the shop folding back into itself like an animal curling tighter to keep the night out. Her reflection appears in the window—faint, watery, a double—a woman who looks like she belongs to this town even when the town insists she doesn't.

Thatcher slides a half step deeper into the alley's mouth. The dark catches him like a friend. He isn't leaving. He's picking his vantage point.

"Not tonight," I murmur, opening the truck door.

The hinge gives a soft groan. It's too loud for what my nerves want from the world. The sound carries just enough for him to hear—a small claim, a small threat. Thatcher turns his head, not toward me fully but enough to see me, like I'm an idea he's in no hurry to entertain. His expression doesn't change. The lamplight finds one side of his face and leaves the rest to imagination.

We look at each other across wet brick and old glass. I don't lift a hand—don't call out. I let him know I'm here. Sometimes that's all it takes. Sometimes the knowing is the weapon.

The bell over the door finally speaks—one clean chime—quiet as if it knows not to be dramatic. Jane steps out. Night air lifts her hair, tosses the ends across her cheek, then lays them down again when it doesn't get a reaction. She locks the door without dropping her gaze to the key. Muscle memory and a map in her fingers. Crossbody bag snug against her chest. Shoulders squared. Not a woman leaving late. A woman leaving *right*.

Thatcher doesn't look at her. That's his tell. Not looking as performance. The way a child "hides" by covering his own eyes. It would be funny if the back of my neck didn't feel like a wire about to snap.

I take a step toward the curb, and the fucker moves first.

Not toward her. Back. A small, easy recede that reads like courtesy to anyone not paying attention. He gives the moment a shrug and slides deeper into the alley until the dark takes him. No rustle. No misstep. He leaves the air he was occupying the way a hand leaves water. If I follow now, I lose sightlines on both of them. If I don't follow, he gets what he came for—a look at how we move when we think we've missed him.

Jane passes the alley without turning her head. If she smells the cold-wet-metal that says something shifted in there, she doesn't show it. Her pace is steady. Not careless. Not hurried. The kind of walk that says I see you, but you're not worth my rush. The kind of walk that makes something in my chest lose and gain ground at the same time.

I hover in the space between choices. Confront her and risk driving her deeper into the mask. Dive after him and risk losing the only witness who knows she isn't what her papers claim. It makes me want to laugh and throw a punch at the same time.

The alley gives me nothing but a breath of cooler air and a slick of darker dark. He's gone—either farther back through the service yard or up a metal ladder slick with mist where a man could crouch and watch a town forget he's there. He's practiced, patient, and he's not here for petty thrills.

I let him go.

It isn't mercy. It's triage. Thatcher will circle again. Men like him orbit what they want until gravity does the work. Jane is the body in motion I can't let out of sight without admitting I've chosen a side I keep telling myself I haven't.

She reaches the next corner and doesn't look back. I match her distance without matching her path, cutting across to stand beneath a lamp that hums like a tired bee. She doesn't see me. Or she does and pretends not to. I don't call out. The desire to hear her voice is a small, stupid thing, and I don't reward small, stupid things.

My phone vibrates once, another message from Mills I don't open. The world has shrunk to the breadth of this street and the weight of two people on it, plus a third who's turned himself into a rumor.

I step off the curb, give myself the gift of motion because standing still makes my body feel like a target. Her bag bumps her hip softly, and she disappears around the corner. I follow at a distance that would be ridiculous if anyone else were grading it. I give it another half block before I stop.

The night exhales. The town adjusts the set.

I angle back toward the truck. The shop sits quiet and blind, the bell above the door a small eclipse in the dark. Across from it the alley waits, the kind of black that eats things whole and doesn't worry about indigestion.

I look at it and feel certainty settle bone-deep, clean as a blade.

He isn't circling by accident.

And if I let the orbit hold, it *will* close.

CHAPTER 20

Quinn

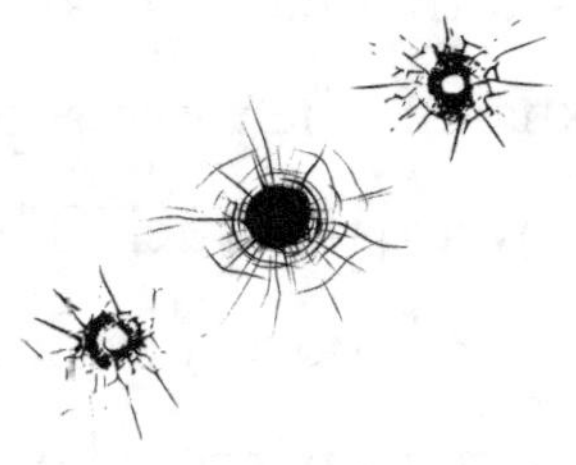

The beach looks different when you stop pretending it's a destination.

Most people come here to be seen—walking dogs, holding hands, taking pictures of the lighthouse like it hasn't been photographed to death. I come because the ocean doesn't ask questions. It takes what you give it and keeps its mouth shut.

Low tide has pulled the water back far enough to leave the sand dark and slick, scattered with stones and kelp and the wreckage of old storms. The air smells sharp and clean, the kind that scrapes your lungs raw if you breathe too deeply. I slip my shoes off at the edge of the path and let the cold shock my feet into the present.

Jane Fairhaven walks this beach the way a local does—head down, hands tucked into sleeves, cardigan pulled close against the wind.

Quinn Maddox walks it differently.

I don't let myself do that tonight. Not fully. But the memories come anyway, surfacing without invitation.

Other shores. Other nights. The weight of a weapon balanced just right in my hand. The sound of water swallowing footsteps. The way the body remembers how to move even when the mind insists it's done with that life.

I stop near the waterline and watch the tide slide in, then retreat again, as if it can't decide whether it wants me.

The wind shifts.

I don't hear footsteps at first—just the subtle change in the air, the way presence announces itself before sound ever does. I turn, already irritated at myself for noticing.

Detective Rakes stands a few yards back, hands in the pockets of his coat, collar turned up against the cold. He looks out of place and perfectly anchored all at once, like the coast carved him out of the same stubborn material as the rocks.

"Oh," I say. "*You.*"

His mouth curves faintly. "Disappointed?"

"Surprised," I correct. "This isn't exactly Main Street."

"No," he agrees. "It's quieter."

"That why you're here?"

"Same reason you are."

I snort softly. "I doubt that."

He steps closer, stopping at a polite distance that still feels intentional. The wind tugs at his coat, threads salt into his hair. For a moment, neither of us speaks. The silence doesn't feel awkward. It feels... assessed.

"You walk a lot," he says finally.

I tilt my head. "Is that an observation or a criticism?"

"Neither." His gaze flicks briefly to the horizon. "Just noticing."

I don't like how carefully he notices things.

"I live here," I say. "That tends to involve walking."

"So does thinking."

I huff a laugh despite myself. "You always this charming, Detective?"

"Only when I'm off the clock."

That earns him a look. "And what brings you out here after hours?"

He shrugs, easy, like the answer costs him nothing. "Couldn't sleep."

Something about that rings closer to the truth than I'm comfortable with.

The ocean roars louder as a wave breaks close to shore, spray catching the fading light. I wrap my arms around myself, more aware of the cold now—and of him.

"You walk this beach like you know it," I say instead. "Like it's mapped into you."

A corner of his mouth lifts, faint and unreadable. "It is. I grew up here."

That shouldn't matter. Somehow, it does.

"But you don't walk it like everyone else," I add, before I can stop myself. "You don't look for anything. You just... stand. Like you're waiting for the tide to tell you something."

His gaze sharpens—not defensive, not amused. Curious. "And you walk it like you're listening."

The words land heavier than they should, slipping under my ribs before I can brace for them.

I look away first, letting my eyes trace the line where the water darkens the sand. "People move how they need to."

"That sounds learned," he says quietly.

"Most survival is."

We fall into silence again, the kind that stretches without snapping. The wind presses against my back, carries salt into my hair. He doesn't move closer, doesn't retreat—but I feel him anyway, the way you feel a shift in pressure before weather turns. It's not threatening. It's not comforting either. It's awareness.

"You always come out here alone?" he asks.

"Yes."

A beat passes. Then, softer: "Because you want to?"

I glance at him, meeting his eyes this time. "Does it matter?"

He considers that longer than necessary, gaze drifting back to the horizon. "Probably not. But I like knowing the difference."

That honesty catches me off guard. I don't respond right away.

A gull cries overhead, sharp and lonely, then wheels back toward the surf. The tide creeps forward, cold water licking my toes until it bites. I step back, grounding myself.

"I should head back," I say—not because I want to, but because staying feels like standing too close to an exposed wire.

"Yeah," he agrees. "You should."

I start toward the path, then pause, glancing back. "And you?"

"I'll stay a while," he says. "Let the noise settle."

I nod, bending to slip my shoes on. "Try not to let the ocean win."

His mouth curves, just barely. "It's been trying my whole life."

As I climb the path toward town, I don't look back.

I don't need to.

I can still feel him there—rooted, watchful, like something that's noticed a fault line and hasn't decided yet whether to test it or leave it alone.

By the time I reach the street, the beach has erased every trace of where we stood. But the sensation lingers. Not danger. Absolutely not safety.

Just the quiet certainty of having been *seen*.

And for reasons I don't yet understand, that unsettles me more than being alone ever has.

Chapter 21

Rakes

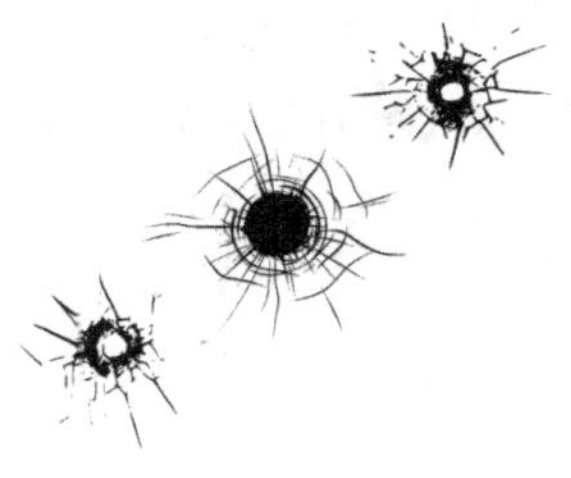

The sky over Driftwood has that late-winter glaze that makes everything look colder than it is—salt-gray light smeared thin, gulls carving slow loops over the harbor like they're looking for something that isn't there. I should've slept.

Instead I paced the length of my house until the floors learned the route, then gave up and came back to the precinct before dawn, trading one hum for another.

I don't boot my work terminal. Not yet. If I touch the department network for what I'm about to do, the audit trail will sing like a choir. I take my phone from my jacket, set it flat on the blotter, and stare at the cracked line across the glass until the name I've been avoiding rises, uninvited.

Elias Ward.

When I first met him, he wore a Bureau badge like it was a dare. Former cyber squad out of Quantico. Before that, two tours with a unit nobody admits exists. Now he's something else—semi-retired, semi-legal, the kind of guy companies hire when they want their skeletons cataloged and their closets reinforced. I helped him on a thing once, and by "*helped*" I mean I kept him from throttling a witness with a power cord.

We aren't best friends, but we aren't strangers either. He's the kind of man you call when the ground under you feels manufactured.

I tap his name. The line clicks after one ring, then a hiss, then his voice—low, unamused, awake like he never went to sleep. "You never call before eight unless something's bleeding." A clink, like a spoon in a mug. "Morning to you, Detective."

"Elias." I glance across the bullpen—empty except for a patrol rookie asleep upright with a report clutched to his chest. "I need a favor."

"That word usually comes with immunity papers." A beat, another clink. "All right. Tell me who you're chasing."

"Thatcher Greeves."

Silence. I can hear him breathing, the soft scrape of a chair leg on wood, a muted radio somewhere in his kitchen playing an AM station that thinks it's still 1997. "Spell it," he says eventually.

I do. "Thirty-seven or thereabouts. Polished. Lives like a man who irons his socks. Spends a lot of time near a bookstore owned by Jane Fairhaven. Everything I can pull is clean in a way that smells like bleach."

"How deep have you gone?"

"State records, credit headers, utility starts, DMV, postal forwards, property filings. Some national plate-read aggregators off the books." I rub the ache between my eyes with a thumb knuckle. "I can make the *shape* of a life. It just doesn't feel like anyone ever lived it."

"Hmm." He draws the sound out until it almost feels like a word. "You want me to run him through the deeper nets."

"I want to know if he's *real.*"

"Everything's real to somebody," he says, which is the kind of thing Elias says when he wants me to understand I won't like his answer. "Text me what you've got. Don't email. Don't send anything that touches government fiber you don't control. And turn off that department phone you pretend is yours."

"It is mine."

"Sure," he says, dry. "And Santa does RICO."

I end the call, switch off the city-issued cell, and use my personal to push a tight packet his way—photo grabs the bakery's camera coughed up, the sanitized data I already regret collecting, the hotel receipt I'm ninety percent sure was paid by somebody else. Then I sit and listen to the building breathe while my stomach ties itself in a sailor's knot.

He doesn't make me wait long. Fifteen minutes from send to reply. That's either a miracle, or he had a cached interest he's not admitting.

Phone vibrates. One line of text first.

ELIAS: Call me. Not at your desk.

I get up, pass the copy room, pass the dead soda machine, push through the back stairwell door where the cinderblock eats sound, and take the steps down until the concrete smells like cold iron and old mop water. Reception bars wobble, then hold.

I call. He answers on the first half-ring.

"You owe me," he says, and he doesn't mean coffee.

"Add it to my tab." I plant a shoulder against the wall, set my heel on the second step, and wait for the floor to tilt.

"Your boy Thatcher," Elias says, "isn't a boy. He's a suit assembled in a clean room."

My grip on the phone tightens. "So the records are fabricated."

"Not the sort you do with a cousin at the DMV and a six-pack." I can hear him moving through his place—cabinet, drawer, the click of a lockbox. "This is layered paper. Layered digital. Synthetic credit files constructed to age out naturally. Employment with a vendor that lives behind four shells and a leased address in Delaware. Healthcare that bills through a concierge practice where the doctor is real, and his patient list is not."

"Who builds that?" My voice comes out lower than I intend.

"People with budgets." Elias sounds almost bored, which is how I know he isn't. "People who don't want a human, they want a front end that passes any ordinary glance and buys you three minutes at the gate when you need it."

"Can you trace it?"

"To a point," he says. "After that point, I like my kneecaps and my retirement fund."

"Meaning?"

"Meaning," he says, and I can hear the smile he isn't wearing, "that the pattern on this reminds me of a contractor I've seen before."

"Name."

He doesn't give me one. He gives me a ghost. "There's an outfit—private, deniable, patriotic in the way that means they invoice. If you said 'Orion' in the wrong conference room, half the people would stand and salute, the other half would stare at the table and hope you stop speaking. They do identities. They do cleanups. They do operations that don't have to make the paper because the paper never learns they existed."

The stairwell feels colder. My breath fogs once, briefly, like the building exhaled through me. I picture lilies—not because Elias said anything about flowers, but because my brain loves symbols and hates me. "You're telling me Thatcher's one of theirs."

"I'm telling you Thatcher is something somebody would make if they wanted a polite man who fits anywhere and nowhere, who could hover at the edges of a small town long enough to become furniture."

"And if I keep pulling?"

"You'll lose skin," he says. No melodrama, no menace. Just honest math. "Listen to me, Rakes. If this is Orion-adjacent, you're in over your head. They don't fight fair because they don't have to. People who chase ghosts like that don't last long."

I close my eyes. An image surfaces uninvited. Jane behind her counter with her jaw clenched like she's holding back a weather system, a single lamp warming the wood, the rest of the shop thrown into suggestion. Her mask is good. I just don't think it was built for this.

"I can't drop it," I say.

"You can," he counters, then lower. "You won't."

"Kat's *dead*." The words fall raw, scrape something on their way out. "And he keeps showing up where he wants to be seen. He was watching that shop last night. He wanted me to notice it."

"Bait," Elias says.

"I know," I say. "I took it anyway."

He lets that sit. "Tell me about Fairhaven," he says, shifting lanes. "Why are you still running her if Greeves is the one with the paper suit?"

I hesitate, not because I don't have an answer, but because the answer shifted while we were talking. "Her file is too neat. There's a three-year void. Not a gap—a *deletion*. Captain told me it's 'above my clearance.'"

"Which is his way of saying he wants to keep you breathing." A pause. "How is she with all this?"

I think about the way she stood at the funeral. Back row, chin up, the town pretending not to stare at her, while she pretended not to stare back. I think about the break-in, the rifled drawer that wasn't really rifled, how steady she stayed when the broom fell, how she didn't cower when every civilian instinct should've begged her to. I think about the diner, the way she revealed and unrevealed facts like she was palming cards, and how my own grief kept mistaking the trick for the hand.

"She's... *complicated*," I manage. "And I can't tell if she's the reason the ghosts showed up or the reason they haven't burned the place down yet."

"That's two different kinds of gravity," he says. "Do you suspect her or want to protect her?"

"Yes." It costs me less than I expected to say. Maybe because saying it out loud makes it real and consequence follows reality. Maybe because the truth was always going to hurt.

"Then here's the part you won't like." He lowers his voice, though nobody's listening on my end. "If Orion is in this, and if Greeves is one of theirs or one their client's, Fairhaven is either part of the machine or *under* it. There *isn't* a third option."

I open my eyes and watch my breath not fog this time. "She's not part of it." It surprises me how quickly I say that. "She's hiding something—*no question*—but the way she hides isn't how those type of people hide. It's not pride, or sport."

"Rakes," he says, almost gentle, "be careful where you set your certainty. It becomes a lever someone else can use."

"Can you give me a dot I can put on a map?" I ask. "Anything I can hold in my hand?"

"I can give you three plate reads within a fifty-mile radius that don't belong to any car he's supposed to own." Keys clink, then a printer whirs faintly on his end. "Two of them cross

Driftwood within the last week. One last night, around 10:40pm, near the bakery. I can also give you a reminder to change your locks and a sermon about opsec."

"I have locks."

"Have better ones," he says. "And stop keeping your heart where people can see it."

"Too late for that," I say before I can stop myself.

He hears it. He doesn't comment. "You want the packet?"

"Send it to the drop we used on the Ponseti thing," I say. "And Elias—"

"I know," he says. "You *owe* me."

He hangs up before I can thank him or argue. I listen to the dial tone long enough to get angry about it, then pocket the phone and climb the stairs back to the bullpen, counting risers to keep from chewing on everything at once. The room looks different with the knowledge in my pocket, like the lights shifted color temperature when I wasn't looking.

I don't sit. If I sit, I'll start building a case with pieces that don't want to touch. Instead I take the long way out. All the way past Records, where the clerk with the purple nails is methodically rubber-banding arrest files. Then past the wall where old commendations gather dust in cheap frames. Finally, past the door to the captain's office, which is firmly closed, blinds drawn tight. If I look, I'll see my reflection in the glass and not recognize the man who looks back.

Outside, the air has warmed half a degree. The ocean smell rides higher, iodine and brine and the wet-metal tang of the pier. Driftwood wakes slowly. Trucks grumble to their first stops. Hall's Bakery throws open its door and lets cinnamon breathe. And a dog drags a man down the block like he's late for something important.

I almost laugh at that... *almost.*

I get in the cruiser, sit a minute with my hands on the wheel, then start the engine and pull away from the curb without a destination I'm willing to admit. The tires hiss on damp asphalt. Wipers thrum. I drive without looking at the clock, which is a lie. I look and pretend I didn't every five minutes.

I take the long curve past the harbor where the boats shoulder each other like sleepers in a too-small bed. I pass Belladonna's café and think about calling in for coffee I won't drink, then don't. I coast by the bookstore and keep my eyes forward because if I look and she's there, I'll stop, and if I look and she isn't, I'll stop anyway.

The phone on the passenger seat chirps once—Elias's packet hitting the agreed-upon place. I don't open it at a stoplight like an idiot. I keep moving. If Greeves is what Elias says he is, he won't show up where anger wants him to. He'll show up where habit does.

A thought I've been holding at arm's length turns and looks at me. It doesn't blink.

Jane is not my suspect.

The admission slides into place with a click I feel in my teeth. It doesn't absolve her. It doesn't make the void in her file make sense, or the mask, or the steadiness that reads like training every time the world lurches sideways. But it rearranges the room. If she isn't the blade, she's the throat the blade is hunting. And if that's true, then every hour I spend proving she's a liar is an hour I didn't spend keeping someone from cutting her open and leaving a ring of blood like a message.

My fingers tighten on the wheel until my knuckles pale. I ease off. The road narrows and lifts out of town—houses thinning, the Victorian bones getting grander as the land pitches toward the cliffs. Her place sits near the end of a street that dead-ends at the sea, a weathered torso of a house braced against wind like it's learned to take a hit. I've been up here more than is healthy for a cop who swears he's not watching a civilian. I tell myself it's the case. I tell myself a lot of things.

I don't turn down her road first. I pass it, loop the block, come in from the cross street that gives me a clean line on the corner without announcing the cruiser's profile to anyone lying in a car with the engine off.

That's when I see it.

Two houses down from the Victorian, half-tucked behind a cypress, a dark sedan sits nose-out at the curb. No plates I can read from this angle. Lights off. Cabin shadowed. A faint bloom of exhaust ghosts the air behind it and dissolves.

My stomach drops, then hardens. I don't hit the brakes. I let the car roll through the intersection like I'm only a man on his way somewhere else, passing through a neighborhood that isn't mine.

In the rearview, the sedan's shape flattens with distance. I take the next right, circle the block, and come back slow from the far side. The road hums under the tires. A different dog barks twice and stops as a porch light clicks on like I triggered it with a thought. Adrenaline threads my fingers, electric and stupid.

I count to five before I turn the corner, then ten when five doesn't feel like enough.

The curb where the sedan sat is empty. No brake drips painting the asphalt. No smear of condenser water. Just a thin curl of vapor lifting in the cold, dispersing as if embarrassed to be seen.

I pull to the far side of the street and park where the cruiser blends with an old pickup that hasn't moved in three days. My mouth tastes like pennies. I let my eyes make a circuit—sidewalk, hedges, porches, the thin column of smoke from a chimney three houses down, the suggestion of movement behind a curtain. I listen. All I hear is wind off the water and the distant, steady breath of the ocean grinding itself to sand.

He was here. Or someone who wants to look like him was. That he left tells me two things. He saw me, and he wanted me to see the absence. Like a fisherman shows you the water after he pulls the net, asking you to imagine what was in it.

I sit another minute, because my body needs to believe I'm deciding and not reacting. Then I ease the car into drive and idle toward her house, slow enough not to spook, fast enough to look like I belong on this street.

Her windows are dark, but that means nothing. A woman who knows she's being talked about ignores the theater. Or she draws the curtains and lets the town write their own play while she rehearses a different one in the back of the house.

I don't knock, and I don't call. I do the thing I've become since I realized the ground under this case is man-made. I mark the information and I carry it like a live wire, careful not to let it touch anything that will ground it before I'm ready for the shock.

On the way back down the hill, I open Elias's packet at a red light because discipline is a story I tell myself and sometimes the ending is weak. Three JPEGs of plate reads with timestamps that bracket the last week, two within a thousand yards of the shop, one with the coordinates I just drove past. One short video—a traffic cam glimpse of a dark sedan slipping through a yellow light without being there at all. The metadata is too clean, which is to say it's been made respectable by someone who knows how integrity checks are supposed to look.

I forward nothing. I save it to nothing. I let the images burn into my head and then lock the phone and set it face down.

At the bottom of the hill, Main Street opens out like a map I've memorized. Hall's Bakery sign winks cheerful. Belladonna's chalkboard reads something acidic and comforting. The bookstore sits steady, a rectangle of glass and wood that shouldn't be able to hold what it's held and yet does, the way a person does because the other option is crumbling.

I pull to the curb across from it and kill the engine. For a moment, the quiet feels like the inside of a seashell—hollow and huge, full of distant noise the body interprets as its own. I picture Thatcher's patient smile. I picture Callahan's face when he said the words *above your clearance*. I picture Jane turning the CLOSED sign with a hand that didn't shake because on some level she knew someone would be watching for the tremor and would write a story around it if they saw one.

I sit there too long. Long enough to watch the reflection of the town bleed into the window and then back out as a cloud parts and returns. Long enough to decide that wanting to protect someone doesn't make you noble—it makes you dangerous to your job.

When I finally turn the key, the engine catches with a cough that sounds older than it is. I pull away slow, eyes on the road, mind four blocks up a hill where a car idled and left because I arrived, where the air still holds a thin thread of exhaust if you go looking for it like a fool.

The message is clear enough to write on the back of my hand. She's *not* safe. And the part of me that wanted to hold onto the suspect label because it kept me clean knows I lost the argument when I called Elias, or maybe earlier, when I realized I was watching the shop not to catch a thief but to ward off a shadow.

I didn't like the man I was this morning—tired, angry, *raw*. I like this one less. He makes promises he can't keep yet.

I'll try to keep them anyway.

CHAPTER 22

Quinn

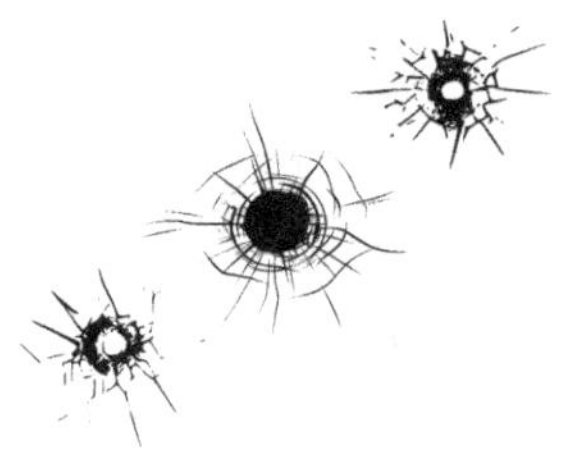

Belladonna's café smells like roasted beans and cardamom buns, comfort ground into air and wood. Normally the place is my haven — an in-between stop where I can sip coffee, tuck into a corner with a book, and pretend that Drift-

wood is the sort of town where masks don't matter. Today, though, the moment I step in, something prickles against my skin. The bell above the
door jingles too sharp. The air feels charged, like
someone's already claimed the stage.

I tell myself it's nothing, that I just need caffeine
and normalcy. I edge toward the counter, coat
damp from the salt wind, boots scuffing against
the old tile.

And then I see him.

Thatcher fucking Greeves.

Polished as ever, suit pressed even in this sleepy
town, shoes shining like he didn't just walk Driftwood's rain-slick streets. He's already holding
court near the window, perched on one of the
café's old iron-backed chairs like he belongs there,
a coffee cup resting in long fingers. Sunlight filters
across his pale face, gilding him with an aura the
townsfolk mistake for charm. His green eyes flick
to me the second I enter, and his smile stretches
slow.

"Miss Fairhaven," he calls, pleasant enough that heads turn. "What a surprise. Out and about so early."

I force my lips into a polite curve. "Morning, Mr. Greeves."

There's no escape. Not without making it obvious. I order my coffee, accept the steaming mug from Belladonna's niece behind the counter, and drift toward an empty table. I keep my posture easy, my movements measured. Jane Fairhaven doesn't flinch when the town's wealthiest patron decides to play at small talk.

Thatcher doesn't let me sit in peace. He rises with calculated grace, crossing the room like it's his drawing room and not a community café. Conversation dips around us, cups clink, chairs scrape. Everyone watches.

He stops at my table, smile gleaming. "Might I join you?"

The question isn't a question. He pulls out the opposite chair and settles in before I can answer.

"Of course," I murmur, folding my hands around the mug so no one sees the way my knuckles tighten.

His voice is velvet, pitched to carry just enough for the nearby tables to overhear. "I must say, Miss Fairhaven, you've kept quite the profile in Driftwood. Bookshop owner, pillar of the community. Admirable, really. Though..." He tilts his head, eyes glinting with something only I can read. "Funny, isn't it, how trouble always seems to follow you?"

A ripple of polite laughter breaks from a table of retirees. They hear banter, not the blade hidden beneath his words.

I sip my coffee, calm and composed. "Small towns do *love* their stories."

His smile widens, showing teeth. "Yes, well. And stories grow so *quickly*, don't they? One day you're a stranger, the next you're the subject of speculation. Fascinating, how fragile reputations can be."

Every word is honey, but the sting is meant for me alone. He's throwing the gauntlet down. Driftwood *thrives* on perception.

I keep my voice even, my tone warm enough to seem genuine. "I suppose you'd know, Mr. Greeves. You've certainly become... *unforgettable* around here."

Another ripple of laughter, this one at his expense, but he absorbs it with a graceful incline of his head. "Touché."

Inside, Quinn snarls. She hears the warning in his phrasing, the claim he's staked — not only on Kat, but on me. Outwardly, Jane smiles, stirs her coffee, and looks like she's politely tolerating the company of a persistent man.

Thatcher leans closer, lowering his voice just enough so only I can hear. "Careful, Miss Fairhaven. Masks slip when pressed too hard."

The smile I give him would fool a saint. "Then it's fortunate mine fits *so* well."

He sits back, satisfied, leaving the line between us taut but invisible. To the room, we look like acquaintances sharing idle talk. To me, it feels like standing in quicksand.

The door opens behind him, the bell chiming again. My eyes flick past Thatcher's shoulder — and catch... Detective Rakes as he enters the door.

He's dressed in his usual mix of rumpled and imposing. Dark jacket, jaw shadowed with stubble, expression carved from stone. His gaze scans the café, and when it lands on us, the air shifts. He doesn't approach us. Not yet. He orders his coffee, and leans against the counter, but I can feel his attention like a hand pressing against my back.

Thatcher notices too, the busybody. His smile sharpens, as though the detective's presence is part of his game. "Ah, and here's our town's finest. Always good to see vigilance at work."

I resist the urge to roll my eyes. "I'm sure the Detective has better things to do than humor us."

Rakes's gaze lingers, suspicion threading through the distance between us. I can't read what he's thinking, but I know what he sees.

Jane Fairhaven, poised across from Driftwood's most polished resident, looking every bit like she belongs in his orbit.

And that — that may be the cruelest cut of all.

Because the truth is, Thatcher's *winning*. Not with threats or violence, but with charm, with carefully placed doubt. To the town, he's respectable, refined, generous. And I? I'm the oddity. The newcomer. The woman who "trouble follows." His needling works because he doesn't need proof. He only needs a stage.

My pulse thunders beneath the porcelain calm of my mask, but Jane Fairhaven doesn't crack. She never does. She sips her coffee, answers in measured tones, and waits for the moment to end.

When it does, Thatcher stands, slipping on his coat with theatrical ease. "Always a pleasure, Miss Fairhaven. Do enjoy your day."

He tips his head, polite as a serpent, then strides out into the drizzle.

The café exhales with him, conversation resuming, cups clinking again. But I feel every eye that lingers too long, every whisper behind bent menus. The damage has been done.

Rakes remains at the counter a beat longer, watching me with that indistinguishable expression, before he finally turns and leaves as well.

I sit in silence, staring into the swirl of coffee gone cold, the mask still fixed to my face while underneath, Quinn claws and seethes.

Because it's not whispers or shadows anymore. Thatcher is dismantling me in daylight. And I don't know how much longer I can keep Jane Fairhaven standing.

I set the cup down. The porcelain still clinks—too loud—and draws a look from a woman by the pastry case. I give her Jane's polite smile, rise, smooth my sleeves, nod to the barista, and leave.

Outside, the air is damp and briny, rain metal-scented in the clouds. Driftwood moves in its coastal rhythm—tailgates thud, gulls heckle over the harbor, two fishermen split a sandwich on the curb. I take the sidewalk. By the time my shop appears—brick warmed by years of wind and salt, the hand-painted sign creaking on its chain—my pulse has settled into that calm adrenaline counterfeits.

The bell greets me. Paper and binding glue, a salt edge, a thread of cinnamon live in the air.

For a breath, safety pretends to be real.

Then the silence changes—not empty, expectant.

I lock the door out of habit. The latch sits flush. No scratches, no drag at the bolt.

Still, something's wrong.

At the counter, the register closed. All the enamel pins fanned just so, and the bookmark bowl half full. Heat kicks on—a faint draft carries dust and last night's rain through the duct. I sweep the room the way Kat taught me, not for chaos, but for what's almost right.

There—midway down literary fiction—a ripple where the spines should be one skyline.

To anyone else, it's nothing. A few books tipped, a couple faced out where they don't belong. But we kept a language here, Kat and I—order with a logic we never explained. You had to love it to speak it.

I walk the aisle as if I'm only straightening. Fingers hover, a breath above the boards. Dust lies unbroken along the tops except at nineteen neat rectangles—spines polished by a stranger's hand.

I read the first letters down the row. Quiet as a prayer. Quiet as a curse.

Q... U... I... N... N...

Next shelf.

B... L... A... I... R... E...

Then... the next.

M... A... D... D... O... X.

My name. My fucking name. Quinn Blaire Maddox, built out of borrowed titles no browser would ever align this way. Whoever did it moved with a librarian's patience and the intimacy of someone who knows exactly how my mind catalogs a room.

My throat goes dry. A clean crack opens under my sternum—too precise to be panic, too neat to be anything but fury.

I don't touch the books. I step back as if the letters burn.

The spines blur for a beat—Quietus, Under Glass, Inland, No Witness, Nocturne—raw material for the only thing that matters. The *message*.

Someone came to speak, not to steal.

I breathe in and cool it out slow, like tempering metal. Jane would fuss, mutter about bored kids, tidy the display and wipe the shelf with a sigh.

Quinn counts exits as a way to calm her racing heart.

Front door. *Locked*. Back hall. *Clear line to stockroom*. Rear exit. *Chain and bolt seated*. Windows. *Latches clean*. Vents. *Dust undisturbed*.

They came the easy way and left the same. They knew how long I'd be at Belladonna's—or watched me go.

A shiver cuts down my spine. I picture Thatcher's pleasant smile. An idling car. A face in glass that isn't mine.

Focus.

I slide my bag onto the counter, pull my phone, and shoot the scene. Wide, then each shelf, then close-ups of the alignment and the scuffs where spines were shifted. Eye-level and low angles. A panorama from the one corner that makes the letters snap into place. My hands tremble once, but I let loose a breath and force them steady. Documentation *before* emotion. It's the only catechism that's ever saved me.

New album: **QBM—PUBLIC.**

I listen to the sounds in the shop. The heater hum, a far window ticking as it adjusts, a gull's brief scream. The street resumes its ordinary noise. The shop does not.

A shadow crosses the display glass—just a passerby. Reflection fractured in imperfect panes. My muscles coil and ease, mind racing as I walk to the front door. I flip the sign to OPEN.

I should close, lock, barricade. But Jane opens, and runs her store. She doesn't show a single crack.

The bell chimes, and a girl in a navy raincoat bounces in, curls damp, tote bag bulging. "Hi! Do you have the new Han?"

"Of course." My voice sounds normal—*good*. One thing going right. "Right over here."

I lead her past the letters. She doesn't see them. Why would she? To her they're just blue and black and cream among a thousand spines. She buys the book, thanks me for a bookmark, and the door jingles her out into rain. The world keeps its pace, oblivious to the stage set for one audience.

I check the drawer—no note tucked inside, no symbol carved under the counter. Whoever wanted me to see this wanted it clean. A whisper only I could hear.

Another customer walks in—older, slicker hood dripping—hesitates near the middle aisle. His gaze skims, catches, slides off. He leaves with a travel guide, promises to return with his grandson.

Enough.

I lock the door, flip the sign to **BACK IN TEN**, and go to the sink. Hot water until steam ghosts off my knuckles, until the tremor in my hands can be named heat, not fear. A glass of water tastes faintly metallic. I set it down with care, then walk back to the aisle. I stand where a stranger would to align the letters and feel something unwilling—*almost* admiration—press against the anger.

The spacing is exact. The verticals align. They took their time, likely counting my minutes.

The urge to tear it all down claws at me. Instead, I take a legal pad and record the titles in order, left to right, top to bottom. A second column for their true homes—Mystery, Essays, Mythology, Travel, a children's classic I've restocked twice. A path through absences I only see now that they've been braided into a name.

A sound scrapes out of me—too thin for a laugh. I wipe it away with the heel of my hand.

If I re-shelve, I erase evidence. If I leave it, I invite questions from the first curious mind who wonders why Quietus is courting M Train. And I can't call Rakes without putting Quinn in his mouth—once he has it, it's *over*. He's already too fucking close as it is.

So I split the difference. Three innocuous face-outs from the new-releases table interrupt the sightline, breaking the clean run of letters. From the center I slide one spine back to its real shelf. It doesn't erase the phrase. It muddies it. To anyone else, *nothing*. To the sender, *I saw you*.

My hands are steady now. Not confidence—*clarity*. The old kind you feel on a rooftop when the guard's smoke break matters more than fear. It has no place in a shop that smells like paper and spice, and it's exactly what I need.

I text Belladonna: ***Running a little off today. Swing by later?***

Her dots appear, disappear, return: ***Of course, babe. You good?***

I hesitate, then type my reply: ***Fine. Just... busy.***

Belladonna: ***I'll bring a lemon tart. Don't argue.***

A smile flickers and dies. I don't want her here if the person who set this comes back to admire their work.

I text her again, telling her I'll swing by instead.

Rain needles the windows, turning the street to watercolor. I flip the sign to **OPEN** again and move through the motions. I dust the front table, tally gift cards, answer two emails about a delayed signed shipment. From the street, it looks normal.

That's the point. Because normalcy is expected of Jane. Jane doesn't have to worry about her past.

Customers trickle in with dripping cuffs. I sell three novels, a true-crime paperback that leaves a copper taste on my tongue, and a pack of postcards a tourist calls *"so vintage."* The message waits, kinked and camouflaged by my edits, visible only to me and the one who wanted it read.

Near closing, the door opens on a gust of wet air. I know the gait before the face. It's Rakes. Rain bright on his shoulders, eyes flat and watchful. He does his sweep—window to back corner, exits and cover—the way professionals and predators read a room.

"Miss Fairhaven." His voice is hoarse from weather or work. "Busy day?"

"Steady." I keep my voice even. "You?"

No answer to that question. He drifts toward the aisle with the letters. My throat tightens. He isn't hunting a message, he's browsing titles like he's killing time. He tests a chair back with two fingers, lets it bounce once. "Greeves bothering you today?"

The question takes me by surprise, but I school my features back into pleasant civility before he notices. "Only the way men with too much time and too little imagination bother all women." Light enough answer to pass for a joke.

His mouth tips, not quite a smile. His gaze sweeps the shop again, slower. He's good at reading more than I say. It's *infuriating*—and, God help me, almost a relief. Since when does he soften toward me? Is it pity, strategy, or something else entirely? Something that unsettles me more than his anger ever did.

"Lock your doors," he says. "Twice."

"I always do."

"Then do it three times."

Something warm scrapes my ribs from the inside, followed by a hint of curiosity. I hate that it feels like comfort. I don't trust the comfort—or the angle behind it. "Duly noted, Detective."

He lingers, then tips his chin and leaves. The bell's echo fades. The shelves hold their breath again.

Night pulls a dark shawl over Driftwood. Lamps turn the shop amber. I take one last photo—the muddied phrase sliced by window-grid shadow—and send it to a secure address with no name. When the confirmation pings back from nowhere, I power the phone down and meet my reflection in the black screen.

"Not today," I tell it. "Not yet."

I close out the register. Back up camera feeds to a drive that doesn't live here. When I flip the sign to **CLOSED**, the street is a slick mirror. Lamplight splinters in puddles, distorting the sky and brick of my store. Something shifts at the mouth of the alley—a trick of rain, or... *not*. I stare until my eyes water and the shape dissolves.

Bolt the door. Then bolt it again, sliding another chain in place. Palm flat to cool glass, as if I can feel through it the hand that touched my name and thought they could pull Quinn out like thread.

I turn and the shop is ordinary again—tables, stacks, a ladder that needs oil. The aisle I blinded to strangers still reads to me like a signature.

Tomorrow I'll re-shelve in a pattern only Kat would recognize, a counter-message under the skin. Jane will smile and sell books, but Quinn will search for someone who might understand the tone.

Tonight, when the ocean mutters against the cliff and the servers hum in the dark below, Quinn will open a new file and write the first line like a vow...

Someone has my true name.

And I will find out who taught them how to spell it.

CHAPTER 23

Rakes

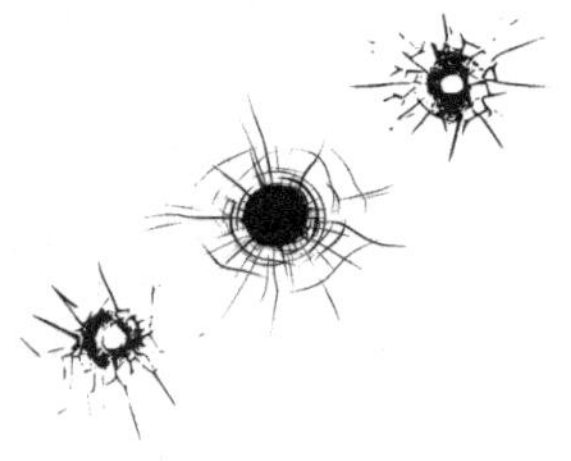

The precinct hums like a machine running too hot—phones shrilling, keyboards clattering, voices cutting too sharp for this early in the morning. I let it wash past me, toning it out as much as possible. My desk is a war zone of crumpled notes, bent paper clips, coffee rings that have bled into reports no one's going to read.

I've been staring at the same stack for an hour, but the words don't shift, don't rearrange, don't give me what I want.

The problem isn't the evidence. It's the *holes*. Nothing but polished surfaces, all shine, no grip. And I've scraped my nails bloody trying to find a hold.

My jaws been clenched so long it aches. I rub at the muscle, but it won't stop twitching. My body's telling on me. Mills knows it too—he glances over the partition like he's waiting for me to blow. "Rakes," he mutters, "you're grinding that poor chair into dust."

I ignore him. What am I supposed to say? That I can't sit still because if I do, I'll have to admit this case is rotting me from the inside out? That every lead I chase circles back to the same brick wall, and I'm half a step from putting my fist through it just to hear something crack?

The truth is, I've already crossed the line. Built my own file. Pulled threads I wasn't cleared to touch. Written things down I shouldn't even be thinking. My desk looks less like a detective's workspace and more like the nest of a man waiting to be stripped of his badge.

Maybe that's what I am.

I close the folder anyway, fingers pressed hard to the cardboard like it's the only thing keeping me tethered. Then I stand, chair scraping loud enough that Mills winces. "You know what he'll do," he says without looking up.

"Yeah," I tell him. "That's why I'm going."

And I head for Callahan's office, pulse loud enough in my ears to drown out the rest of the precinct.

Callahan's office door is half ajar. That's an invitation or a warning depending on who you ask. I don't knock. Knocking is for men who have time to dress their words. Mine are already naked and shivering.

He's standing behind his desk with his jacket off, sleeves rolled. The blinds throw stripes across his tie. He doesn't bother to hide the annoyance that crosses his face when he sees the folder. "What *now*?"

"Thatcher," I say, and lay it down between us like a body. "Not guesses. Not maybes. Holes I can punch my fist through."

He doesn't touch the file. He looks at me instead, and there's something in his eyes I don't like—recognition and the fatigue of a man who knows the ending to a story and hates it anyway. "We've done this before, Rakes."

"No," I say, and feel the cord in my neck pull tight, "we danced around it. I humored your patience while you told me to let it go. I brought you evidence—and it looks like a man with two lives and neither of them breathe."

He taps the folder's corner with one knuckle. A small sound. It still manages to make the office feel smaller. "What do you want me to say?"

"Say you *see* it." I hear how it sounds—how close to pleading a grown man can get and still pretend he's asking a professional courtesy. "Say we pull him off the street for questions that don't have safe answers. Say you'll let me do my *job*."

Callahan leans back, pins me with a gaze I've spent a decade learning to read. It's not anger. It's calculus. "Where'd this come from?"

"Off-grid," I say.

"From whom?"

"A friend," I say. And when he waits I add, "A former fed. Clean as they come."

"Name."

"Not on a phone," I say. "Not in here."

"Then it's not admissible," he says, and the line lands like a tired joke. We both ignore the fact that half the things that save lives in this town don't start admissible. "Anything I can actually use?"

"Yes," I say, and flip the file open. The table of Thatcher's addresses, laid side by side with land registry data that shows utility start and end dates like flatlines. The cross-check against employment records that never lasted more than a fiscal year, always changing when the paper trail got warm. A photo of him outside a bakery laughing at a clerk, duplicated from two different angles because someone wanted to prove he knew he was being watched and liked it.

"He's a mannequin," I say. "And someone spent a lot of money to dress him."

"Or he's a man with a boring life," Callahan says.

"Boring lives have taxes, Captain," I say. "They have neighbors who remember their names and mail carriers who wave because they've been there long enough to be waved at. He's a picture frame. We don't get to pretend that's normal."

Callahan's hand slips off the folder like he touched a live wire. "You're done with this."

"No." The word surprises us both with how fast it comes out. "No, I'm not."

His jaw flexes. There it is. The temper he keeps under lock until a subordinate inspires it. Only this isn't rage. It's something like fear's older brother. "I told you to leave Fairhaven alone. I told you Greeves is *clean*. You don't have clearance to sniff around whatever you *think* you've found."

"Clearance?" I say, and it tastes like bad metal. "We bury my cousin and you're talking to me like I'm the problem because I keep pulling a thread that—"

"—that leads somewhere you *can't* go," he snaps. "That's the point."

"Then why are we here?" My voice isn't loud, but it carries. "Why do I come to this building and put on this badge if the minute I need it to mean something it's a piece of tin and a fucking suggestion?"

The blinds hiss when wind touches them. The light stutters across his desk, dust swirling like glitter in a delicate dance that doesn't match the tension in the room. Callahan picks up the folder and holds it like a contaminant. "You're suspended."

It shouldn't shock me. It still scrapes. "Excuse me?"

"Effective *immediately*," he snaps, holding out his hand. "Badge and weapon."

I laugh, the wrong sound in the wrong room. "For asking you to look at a ghost with footprints?"

"For disobeying a *direct* order," he says. "For jeopardizing an active investigation. For bringing questionable material into my office and asking me to take it on faith. For banging your head against a wall I told you won't move."

"It's moving," I argue. "I can feel it."

He opens a drawer, sets a small felt tray near the blotter. The kind of tray usually used for paperclips and keys. Now it's an altar. "Badge. Gun."

He isn't bluffing. I could make a speech about Kat. I could tell him what Elias told me and start a fire I can't control. I don't. Instead, I take off the leather with the shield stitched in, the one that's worn smooth at the edges where my thumb rests when I think, and lay it down. The Glock follows, and the desk takes their weight like it's been waiting for them all along.

"Rakes," he says, and I hear something in my name I wish I hadn't—regret, pity, a warning he can't file. "Go home."

"What am I supposed to do there?"

He doesn't answer. The question isn't for him anyway.

I turn to leave, and Mills is standing in the doorway with a file he pretends to read, badly. He steps aside without meeting my eyes. I shoulder past him and the bullpen opens like a stage I don't belong to anymore. Phones ring and printers cough and someone tells a story about a dog on a roof and the room pretends it didn't just watch its favorite cautionary tale unfold.

I rush through the precinct, and out the front doors, shoving them open harder than necessary.

Outside, the day hits wet and cold. The sky is the wrong kind of white—the kind that can't decide between rain and snow and settles for a mix that needles exposed skin. I breathe it in and it tastes like coin. My hands are empty in a way I wasn't prepared for. The absence of the badge is louder than the presence ever was.

I cross the lot, gravel spitting under my boots, and stop at the cruiser like I forgot I don't get to drive it today. The passenger window throws my reflection back at me. A man who looks older than he was this morning. I press the heel of my hand to the glass until the cold eats the itch under my skin. Then I drop it and keep walking.

By the time I hit the street a tremor has worked its way up my forearms and set its tent in my shoulders. It's not fear. It's momentum with nowhere to go.

I end up at the river without meaning to, the path I take when my feet outrun my sense. The water runs high and colorless. The reeds on the far bank bending like they learned the word mercy too late. A freight horn floats in from somewhere far enough away to be myth. I lean on the railing, metal slick under my palm, and watch the current worry a branch apart.

Suspended. That's what they call it. Like you're a thing tied up by invisible wire, hung over your own life and asked to admire the angle.

Kat used to send me videos of the sea when I got stuck in my head. Ten seconds of gulls and gray water, her laugh chasing the wind, a text that said... *Breathe, Mal. The world still does it without you.* I delete the thought the second it forms because thinking about her like that—warm and easy—hurts worse than the memory of the casket.

I pull my phone anyway. The screen lights my hand with a sick glow. No badge means no network, no databases, no names I shouldn't know. I scroll past the last text I sent Mills—*cover me*—and the last one I didn't send Callahan—*you're afraid of the wrong thing*—and tap the contact that isn't saved under a name.

Elias answers on the second ring. No hello. "You sound like a man who just got benched."

"You said 'if Thatcher's Orion, she's either apart of it or under it.'"

"I did."

"I just got suspended for asking about his mask."

"Then you're asking the right questions."

The wind lifts and drops my coat like it's trying to shake me out of it. "I'm blind, Eli."

"You were blind *with* a badge," he says, and there's no comfort in it, only accuracy. "Now you're just blind without one. Sometimes that's safer."

"For who."

He lets the silence answer me. "I told you to walk away."

"I don't know how."

"I know," he says softly. "That's why I answered."

The river slaps the retaining wall, cold applause. "You really don't think she's a suspect?"

"She isn't," he says. "Not if your read on him is right."

"You sure 'him' isn't me," I say, and the bitterness surprises even me with how clean it is.

"I'm sure you're making this harder than it needs to be," he says, not unkindly. "But that's your brand."

"She won't tell me anything," I say with an exasperated groan.

"Maybe she can't," he says. "Maybe she doesn't know what you think she does. Or maybe she knows and telling you is the same as handing you a live wire."

"Then what."

"*Stay alive*," he says. "Keep *her* that way if you can."

The line clicks dead. I stare at the river until my eyes ache and then push off the rail. Movement is the only thing that feels like choice.

On the walk back to the lot the town looks at me the way it always does when the uniform comes off—a shade too long, curious without admitting it, weighing me for the story they'll tell at dinner. I climb into the truck that smells like old coffee and last winter's rain and sit with my hands on the wheel until the world narrows down to road and weather and a single sentence that refuses to stop chewing my head. I can't reach her with a badge and I've run out of other tools.

So I do the only stupid thing I have left.

I drive to her.

Rain takes the easy way down the windshield. The wiper blades complain like they haven't forgiven me for ignoring them last year. Driftwood slides past in pieces I know too well—Belladonna's café's purple awning bellied with water, the bait shops bell ringing at a gull, the school's parking lot painted with puddles and chalk ghosts. The closer I get to the coastline, the harsher the wind.

I come around the final bend, and the Victorian clings to the cliff like it was built to withstand more than weather.

Her porch light is off. That's normal for this hour. The streetlamp a house up casts a cone that turns the rain to strings. I park a half-block away and sit long enough to decide whether I'm making the kind of mistake you write apologies for. There's nothing to apologize for that I haven't done already.

I'm halfway to the gate when I see the tire marks in the yard—two arcs in the slick grass where somebody turned a car a little too tight earlier with no weather to excuse it. My stomach climbs two inches higher in my chest. The prints look old enough to be yesterday. They look fresh enough to be today. That's the trouble with heavy rain. It keeps secrets and it tells on you in the same breath.

At the gate the iron is cold enough to sting skin. I push it open and it gives a noise that would be a scream if it were human. The walk is a shred of slate. The windows stare like the house is holding its breath.

I knock, and nothing answers but the sea.

I knock again, knuckles rapping the wood like I'm trying to drum out a heartbeat. Movement crosses the entryway—just a smudge of shadow heading toward the door—and stops. The porch light flares. It turns me into something caught and named. I lift my chin like that makes me taller and less guilty.

The bolt slides. The chain lifts. The door opens four inches and the woman I keep pretending is just a witness looks at me like I'm the thing that might finally make this day worse.

"Detective," she says. Not quite a question. Not a welcome.

The title hits like a punch now that I don't deserve it. I clear my throat and don't bother to hide the edge. "I'm not here for pleasantries."

"Good," she says, and the chain comes off. "Because I'm all out of them."

She opens the door wide enough for me to understand I can cross the threshold if I insist and hate myself for it. The smell that comes out is coffee and old wood and the salt that this house will never stop drinking. Behind her, the brass of a lamp catches and gives a small glow. Behind her house, the ocean works itself raw against the cliff and keeps going.

I step over the line, soaked, raw, suspended in every sense a man can be suspended, and realize I've reached the only place in town where getting answers might actually cost me more than keeping my mouth shut.

She closes the door behind me. The lock turns, and the house breathes, as if relieved to have someone else hold up the ceiling for a minute.

"Say what you came to say," Jane tells me, voice low, steady, dangerous only if you underestimate it.

I look at her and forget how to be careful. "Start with the truth."

CHAPTER 24

Quinn

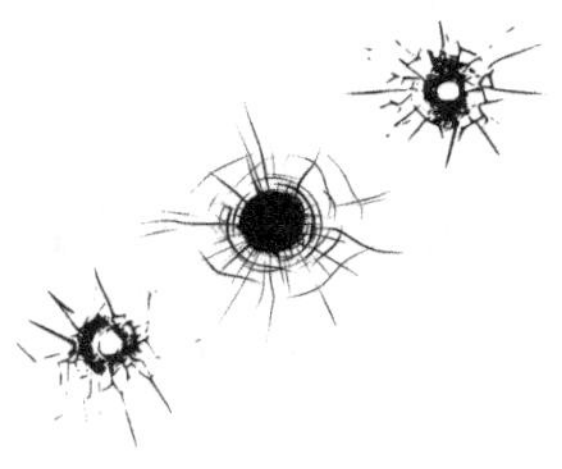

His words hang in the parlor like a match held to paper. The house takes them in, shivers once, and waits to see what burns.

He's dripping onto my floorboards, rain threading off his collar in thin lines, jacket gone the color of wet slate. He looks different without the shield of the precinct on his shoulders—stripped to whatever spine is left. The door clicks shut at his back; the lock slips home. The brass lamp throws a steady circle across the rug, heat gathering under its shade until the metal smells faintly sweet. Sea damp curls in from the sash, climbing the woodwork, making the wallpaper pucker where it's oldest.

"Careful what you ask for," I say. My voice is low, and even. The edges are where the truth lives. I keep mine smooth. "It has a way of taking fingers with it."

He doesn't flinch. "They benched me." The syllables come flat, a card he drops between us, not for pity, but to change the odds. "I'm suspended. They took my badge. They'll take more if I give them a reason."

"That a warning for me, Detective, or for you?"

"A warning for both of us." He steps farther in. The air tightens. "I need something real. Not what you hand me when you want me to leave. Not the store-bought answers."

He's used to people cracking when he asks like that. I can see it in the set of his jaw, the patience that's actually a countdown. He's run out of options, which makes him dangerous. He's lost the uniform, which makes him useful.

"I'm fresh out of confessions," I say.

"Then start smaller." He spreads his hands, rain dripping from his cuffs. "Start with a splinter."

Silence, except for the old clock tonging the seconds and the slow exhale of the heater through the vent. The lamp hums. I stand very still so he can't see how fast my heart is moving.

"Fine." I tip my chin toward the hallway, toward the part of me that hasn't slept since morning. "Someone went into the shop when I wasn't there."

His gaze snaps sharper, like a blade looking for bone. "Took what?"

"Nothing." I let a breath out. "They put things back."

"So... a *prank*."

"Alphabetized, actually." The word tastes wrong coming out of my mouth. "Aisles I don't shelve that way. Titles that don't sit together. Not unless you line them up to make letters."

He takes a slow step. "Letters that spelled what?"

I let him see it then—the smallest fracture at the corner of the mask, a stutter I can't quite tame. "Not...*Jane*."

His eyes darken, narrowing slightly. He doesn't ask the name, though I know he could force it. He studies my face instead, as if the letters are there, ghosted over my skin where only he can read them.

"How long since?" Rakes asks.

"Hours." I hate the tremor I hear. "No windows broken. No pry marks. They came the way everyone comes. And they knew how long I'd be gone."

"Belladonna's," he says, more statement than question.

"Like always."

He scrubs a hand over his mouth, leaving a wet streak along his cheek. The house gathers itself around us, listening. When he moves, it's not toward me. It's toward the corner table.

"What are you doing," I say, not quite a question.

He bends over the lamp. Fingers skim the brass collar, patient and precise, then pause. He tilts the shade and the room slides to one side. The circle of light shaves across the rug, throwing the grain of the wood into relief. He flips open a pocketknife. The click is small and final.

"Don't," I start, because I hate the image of him cutting into my house, into the few things here that still feel uncomplicated.

"Hold," he says softly, which is not an order so much as a promise that this will be quick. He wedges the blade under the collar, worries gently at a seam that isn't supposed to be there. A thread of sweet-scorched odor slips out—split insulation, warmed dust, the coppery tang of something new where only old should live. He wraps his hand in a folded handkerchief, then pinches and coaxes.

A dot the size of a seed rests on the tip of the cloth, black and perfect as an eye.

He doesn't look triumphant. He looks tired. "You've got ears," he says, voice low. "Fresh placement. Probably a week at most. Good range, too."

The world tilts again, this time without the lamp's help. I take one step back, then another. The rug yields and creaks like an old man under my heels.

"So." My throat feels too tight for speech. "It's him."

"*If* it's Greeves," he says, folding the dot into linen with a care that feels like respect for an enemy, "it isn't *just* him. That's not hobbyist hardware. That's someone with a budget."

"You make it sound like comfort."

"It's a boundary." He straightens. Rain ticks from his lashes onto my floor. "It tells me what kind of hunt we're in."

"And what hunt is that, off the record?" I ask, heat blooming under my ribs. "Because this town only knows one. They think you bag me and you get to bring Kat back."

His jaw flexes. Not at the name. At the shape of what I'm *implying*—what everyone is starting to believe even if it's not true.

"If this is who I think it is," he says carefully, "he's not hunting you because you're convenient. He's hunting you because you're the point."

The words land exactly where he meant them to. Right under the ribs, where breath lives.

"So stop treating him like he'll tire out if you keep jogging the same loop." I don't mean to step into him, but I do. The lamp heat licks the side of my neck. The ocean damp has climbed high enough on the walls to make the paint a shade darker near the baseboards. Everything smells faintly like brine and warmed brass and the first bite of a lightning storm, even though there's no lightning. "Stop playing local."

He takes it. The push. The shape of my anger. He doesn't give ground. "I can't keep you alive," he says, very quiet, each word pulled through the fire of his throat, "if you keep me blind."

I almost laugh. It would sound like breaking. "Protection isn't what I need."

"Then what," he asks, not like a cop, not like a man angling for leverage. Like somebody standing barehanded at the edge of a machine he can't switch off and desperate for the one lever that will jam it. "Tell me."

Believe me. Trust me. See me. The answers climb my tongue and line up, but they're all wrong in this room, with this lamp heat and the smell of cut wire.

"Go ahead," I say instead. "Show me what you do with truth when you touch it. Start with that."

He holds my stare long enough that the tips of my fingers go numb. Then he nods once, puts the folded linen in his pocket, and wipes the knife clean with the other side of the handkerchief before snapping it shut. Calm. Competent. As if the space between us hasn't been vibrating like a plucked wire since he walked in.

The old clock sounds the half hour. Rain needles the panes. The house shifts, vibrating with an awareness it shouldn't possess.

My phone pings, the sound startling in the sudden silence.

We both look down. The screen glows on the counter where I left it beside the ledger, an unfamiliar icon pulsing—a red lock overlaid with a thin white line that keeps sweeping from left to right. *Timed relay.* My skin crawls the way it always did when Quinn's tools spoke in codes Jane pretends not to understand. No sender. No subject. Just a countdown unwinding from twenty seconds.

"Don't touch it," he says, already crossing the rug.

"It's already here," I say, because some words you don't cage. "That's the point."

We stand shoulder to shoulder without discussing it. His coat still leaks rain. A cold bead hits my wrist and runs under the cuff of my sweater, sending a shiver down my spine. The lamp hums, the red bar thinning and thinning and then disappearing completely.

The file opens on its own.

Static breathes. Then a voice threads out—familiar in the way a favorite song is familiar, a note you could find in a dark room with your eyes closed. *Kat*. Not the voice I heard in remembrance. Not the recording from last winter pretending to be a voicemail. No, this is new. There's wind moving across the mic, and her breath touches the phone twice, like she's talking fast, walking faster.

"Don't trust—" The last consonant breaks apart. There's a scrape, an exhale like fear yanked short, and then the line snaps. The file ends because the file ends, not because my phone glitches or because the house hiccups. It's a cut. Clean.

For a moment, all I can hear is the tiny tick of heat expanding metal inside the lamp shade, the ocean shouldering itself along the cliff, and the blood in my ears.

He doesn't say he's sorry. He doesn't say she's gone, or someone is playing you, or any of the other stock phrases men reach for when a woman's world has been shoved sideways. He stays exactly where he is and watches me the way you watch a wick to see if it will burn or flood.

"Timestamp," he says at last.

I angle the screen. The file metadata shows in a thin gray strip—encrypted, routed through three relays, origin masked. My phone knows the when because the when was part of the lock. The when is *before* the funeral. While I was at Belladonna's.

"She recorded it that morning," I say. My voice doesn't shake. That scares me more than the message.

He exhales, a sound like a man stepping down into cold water and forcing his muscles not to jump. "Who else gets these."

"*No one.*" The lie tastes like pennies. I let it stand because it's the smallest one in the room.

"You're not safe here," he says.

"Now you sound like a man playing local again," I answer. The old habit is hard to kill. Deflection. Joke. Be the literal thorn in his side. But it comes out softer than I intend.

He scans the room with a hunter's air—corners, drapes, baseboards, the underside of the coffee table. Nothing else. Which feels worse than if he'd filled his pockets.

"Lamp goes in a metal tin tonight," he says. "Out in the shed, if you have one. Phone goes into airplane mode until we can route it through a cleaner. You sleep away from windows. Away from the front rooms. No routine tomorrow. Break it all."

"You issuing orders, or advice?"

"Whatever gets you to listen."

The mask in me wants to slap him for that. The real part—the one locked down in the basement with the servers humming—sets both hands on the counter to keep from shaking.

"What do you need from me," he asks.

"Twenty minutes," I say. "Alone."

He nods once. "I'll be outside."

When the door closes, the house exhales. I take the lamp by its neck, feel the heat of it pulse into my palm, and twist the switch, shoving it unceremoniously in a tin container. Darkness snaps down to the edges.

Tonight, I let the receipts stay crooked. I let the tin sit cold in the shed. I let the ocean talk.

And when I finally lift my eyes to the ledger, Kat's half-sentence still burns in the room.

"*Don't trust—*"

The rest waiting for me in the dark.

CHAPTER 25

Quinn

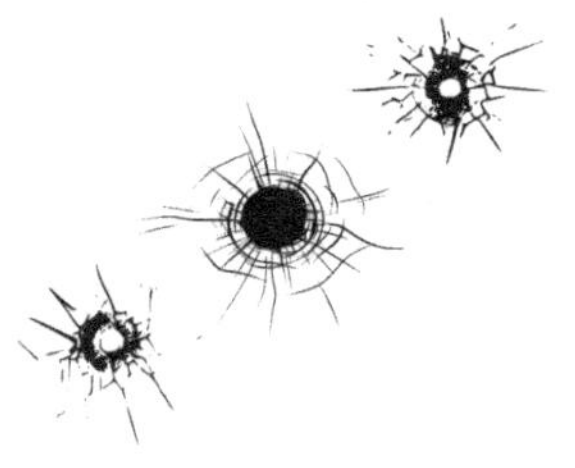

The night hasn't softened by the time I let him off my porch. Rain needles the streetlamps, drumming into the gutters with a persistence that feels personal. Rakes falls in beside me without speaking, his presence broad and deliberate, a man stripped of his badge but not his weight. The lock on my shop door turns cleanly under my key, but my pulse skips anyway, like it expects a different sound — a catch, a drag, some sign of what waits on the other side.

The bell chimes as we step in. It should be comforting. But it isn't.

Paper, glue, cinnamon from a hundred lattes Belladonna carried through this door — the shop smells the way it always does, but the air carries something new beneath it. A weighted pause, like someone is listening.

Rakes moves ahead, slow and measured. He doesn't ask permission. He doesn't need to. His eyes sweep corners, tops of shelves, shadowed angles behind displays. He's reading signs. I force myself to follow, spine straight, mask steady.

I'd left my little signals — Quinn's habits wearing Jane's hands — half-hidden in the daily mess. A paperclip angled across the register. Receipts stacked to a line. A trail of salt at the back door threshold that nobody here would think twice about. They're all disturbed. Only slightly. Paperclip at a different tilt. Receipts bent at one corner. Salt smudged by more than draft.

"You see it?" My voice is tight.

He grunts. Low. Affirmative. But then his hand hovers above the brass latch of the stockroom door. He crouches. Runs his thumb over a faint scrape that wasn't there yesterday. Dust displaced in a line no customer would notice. "They opened this."

My skin prickles. "I would've seen—"

"You were looking at your tells," he cuts in, not unkind but merciless. "They wanted you to. This—" he points at the scrape, the faint shift of dust "—is what they wanted me to see."

I hate that he's right. I hate more that his competence steadies me.

We sweep the rest in silence. Nothing is missing. Nothing obvious, or out of the way. Just the smallest wrongnesses — nudges to prove presence, rearrangements to prove knowledge. Every one of them personal. Every single one meant to crawl under my skin.

When we're done, he leans against the counter, wet hair dripping onto the ledger I'd left closed. He looks at me with that steel-flat gaze of his. "You can't keep routine tomorrow."

I know. I knew it the second I found my name spelled on shelves, the second he pried a bug from my lamp like he was picking glass from a wound. But admitting it aloud is another crack in the mask.

Still — I nod. "Tomorrow. It changes."

"Not tomorrow," he says. "Now."

I bristle. "You going to write me a schedule, Detective?"

"If that's what it takes." His voice is low, even, dangerous because of how calm it sounds. "You keep walking the same streets at the same hours, you might as well hand him a map. Break it. Every step. Every hour."

I half-smile, sharp enough to cut. "Fine. Break it. Six in the morning?"

"Yes." He doesn't blink. "Six. I'll be outside."

The words settle into me like stone. Unwanted. Necessary. A vow I don't want to want.

We close the shop in silence. On the walk back, the rain doesn't let up. He doesn't speak again. Neither do I. But the rhythm between our steps is wrong on purpose — and for once, that feels right.

***

I don't sleep.

The lamp is gone to the shed, sealed in its tin, but the ghost of its heat stays with me, an echo pressed into my palms. Everytime I close my eyes, I hear Kat's unfinished voice in the dark, those two words pulsing like an artery—and then silence. When I open them, the Victorian answers with its own creaks and sighs, as if the house is testing how much weight I can carry before it gives way.

I pace until the floorboards groan their protest. I sit until the clock sounds another useless hour into the air. By the time the sky lightens to a dull, salt-stained gray, my nerves are so raw that the thought of unlocking the shop feels like an invitation to bleed.

I stand at the window, mug cooling in my hands, and watch Driftwood wake. Vans trundle toward the harbor. Fishermen stamp their boots at the corner, laughter carried sharp and thin through the mist. Normally, I'd be moving through these motions too—lights on, kettle whistling, shelves tidied, bell chiming open at nine on the dot. That routine was safety. Predictable. Now it's a map my enemy has already memorized.

Not today.

I set the mug down and turn from the window. The sign stays flipped to **CLOSED**. The lock stays thrown. For the first time since I claimed this name, this town, this mask, Jane Fairhaven doesn't open shop.

When I step outside, the damp air sticks to my skin, briny and cool, pulling me back into my body. And there he is—leaning against the storefront like he's been welded there overnight. Rakes. No badge. Just a man suspended in every sense, waiting on me to begin a day where nothing goes according to plan.

He doesn't speak, and neither do I. Words feel dangerous at this hour, brittle enough to shatter. Instead, he pushes away from the rail, falls into step beside me, and we start walking.

We don't take my path. We don't take his either. Driftwood pulls us forward. The harbor, where gulls wheel and jeer over crates of fish still slick with morning sea. Then to the square, where schoolchildren drag bright backpacks like anchors. Past Belladonna's café, its windows fogged, her silhouette darting between tables with a tray of mugs.

It should feel ordinary. It doesn't.

Every glance catches wrong. A man fixing his rearview mirror for too long. A woman pulling her scarf higher as she passes, head tipped just enough to watch us without turning. A teenager with earbuds who never taps his foot to the beat. Coincidence? Maybe. But once you start reading the world as surveillance, everything speaks.

Rakes doesn't comment. He doesn't need to. His silence is deliberate—like he's waiting for me to name what he already sees.

By the boardwalk, the air thickens with salt spray. The planks groan under our weight, damp rising through the gaps. I keep my chin angled, eyes sliding to the glass fronts of shops we pass, watching reflections instead of pavement.

"You always move this way?" he asks finally.

I cut him a glance. "This way?"

"Head angled. Eyes on glass. Counting people twice."

The mask twitches, but I hold it steady. "Some of us like to know what's behind us."

His mouth tightens—not in disapproval, but recognition. "Then you know we're not alone."

I don't answer. I don't need to. The shadow has been with us since the harbor, loose enough not to spook prey, close enough to smell the hook.

***

At noon, Belladonna spots me through the café window. Her face lights up, hand raised, lemon tart already boxed at her elbow. For a moment, I almost push the door open. Almost let the warmth and sugar and ordinary conversation swallow me whole.

But I don't.

I give her a small wave through the glass, mask pinned in place, and keep walking. Her smile falters before she turns back to the counter. Rakes notices, though he doesn't say a word. He doesn't need to. The distance is its own explanation.

The afternoon pulls long and gray. In the square, vendors close umbrellas against the drizzle. A musician tunes his guitar but never plays. A boy on a bicycle circles twice, too slow, eyes too sharp for his age. Twice I catch Rakes's gaze tracking the same wrongness mine does—reflections bent in window glass, a figure too polished for a town like this.

We don't name him, though. Naming makes things real.

Our silence turns heavier, not hostile but charged. Each footstep feels like a question. What do you believe? How far will you go? What happens when one of us breaks?

By dusk, Driftwood shutters itself against the wind. Shop lights dim. Curtains draw. The town exhales as if settling, but my skin prickles with the opposite... *anticipation.*

We circle back toward my street. The Victorian waits in silhouette, windows dark, roofline hunched like a sentinel. I slow before we reach it, gaze caught on the corner.

The crowd there is thinning, but not gone. For a heartbeat, the air shifts—an outline that doesn't belong, a pause too long before vanishing into the gray. Not a face I can name. Not a gesture I can prove. Just the certainty of eyes.

Rakes' shoulders brace beside me. His hand flexes once, empty, but it's enough. He felt it too.

We don't speak. Not yet.

The night gathers around Driftwood, ordinary on the surface, but I know better. The stage is set. The next act is already written.

And tomorrow, I'll be breaking every pattern I ever built—*again*—because the only way to survive is to become unreadable.

CHAPTER 26

Rakes

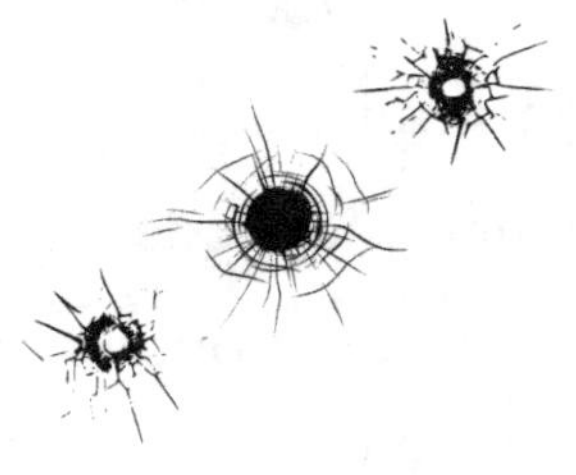

The silence in my house is louder than it should be. My old cottage-style, nineteen-fifties two-bedroom shifts every time the wind pushes in off the harbor, creaking in ways I didn't realize were possible until last night. Every sound rides my nerves raw—pipes groaning, shingles tick-ticking, a draft whispering under the back door.

I didn't sleep. Not really. I shut my eyes, listened to the ocean grind against the cliffs, counted heartbeats until dawn. When the gray light finally bled through the blinds, I gave up. There's a bottle in the cabinet, bourbon I swore I wouldn't touch before noon. All morning, the thought of it has been pacing with me. The smell of char and oak, the warmth, the burn down the back of my throat that would take the edge off for half an hour. My hand itches for the glass, but I don't reach. Not today.

Instead, I dig into the past.

After telling Jane to break her routine, I pulled the old box out of the closet—the files I promised myself I'd never need again. Contacts scrawled in fading ink, numbers that belong to burner phones or disconnected lines. I flip through the Rolodex, a habit that feels half like prayer, half like self-destruction. The cardboard cards rasp beneath my fingertips, grounding me and winding me tighter at the same time.

Most of the names are ghosts—Boston detectives who retired, DAs who wouldn't pick up my calls now if I paid them. I keep thumbing until I stall at one in particular. The edges of the card are bent, thumbworn. I don't have to read the name; I remember the case attached to it.

Jack Lawson, CIA.

Case Reference ID: Bloom 367NW.

Status: Unsolved.

Agent: Retired.

Lawson was the kind of spook who saw patterns where the rest of us only saw static. He'd been on the wrong end of Bloom, a case that bled into my Boston years—the kind that was spoken of in hallways but never in reports, the kind that left more closed coffins than closed files. He retired before I made detective, but his name never left the periphery. Too sharp to be forgotten, too stubborn to vanish.

I dial before I let myself think better of it.

The line clicks alive on the third ring. No greeting. Just silence that stretches long enough to feel calculated.

"Lawson," I say, voice low. "It's Rakes."

A sigh, thin as smoke, curls down the line. "Didn't expect to hear that name again." His voice is rougher than I remember—old gravel over rust. "You digging up Bloom, or did Bloom come to you?"

"Both, I believe," I answer. "Name's Greeves, here in Driftwood. But it doesn't line up. Not clean. Records scrubbed, history fabricated. I've seen empty covers before, but this one feels military-grade."

Another pause, longer. I hear the faint clink of glass—maybe coffee, maybe something stronger. "You should've left it closed."

"I can't." My throat tightens. "Too many bodies. Too many cracks in the wall."

"You think it's Bloom… or Orion?" Lawson asks. His tone sharpens, a note beneath the gravel.

"I know it's one of them. Elias told me before he—" I stop. Don't finish. Lawson doesn't ask. He's the kind of man who fills in blanks without needing confirmation.

"Orion's not the kind of thing you sniff around and walk away from," Lawson says finally. "It's not just organized crime. It's *bigger*. Corporate fronts, shadow budgets, contractors who never existed until they disappear. You tug that thread, you're not just putting yourself in the ground—you're pulling everyone you care about in with you."

His warning cuts cleaner than any blade. For a moment, I picture Jane—her shop, the lamp, the bug no bigger than a seed sitting in my pocket. Her face when the audio file ended mid-sentence.

"You already know too much," Lawson continues. "And if they know you're looking, you're marked. Greeves isn't a ghost, Rakes. He's bait. Orion probably uses him to see who bites. Bloom would do the exact same."

My pulse thrums in my jaw. "Then I've already bitten."

A quiet laugh that isn't humor. "Then you'd better learn how to chew fast, before they reel you in."

I rub at my eyes, the grit of exhaustion burning against my lids. "What do you remember about the LeClair case?"

A sharp inhale. Silence stretches. "That's a name and a file you don't drag into daylight unless you want a visitor before dawn," Lawson says slowly. "LeClair wasn't just a man—he was a network. False shells, charities, food companies, offshore money. We chased him for years and all we found were burned leads and dead assets. The few who got close didn't stay close for long."

"That too late for me?"

Another pause. Then, softer. "If it's LeClair that's tied to Orion, you're not hunting him. He's hunting *you*—" Lawson cuts himself off. When he speaks again, his voice is colder. "Walk away, Rakes. Whatever you think you owe, whatever badge you think you're carrying—it won't cover the cost."

The call ends without goodbye.

I sit with the dead line pressed to my ear, the house creaking around me like it's eavesdropping. The bourbon whispers again, stronger this time. I ignore it.

Instead, I reach for my jacket. Lawson's words sit like stones in my gut, but the warning only sharpens the edge already in me. Jane's shop. The bug. Kat's voice. It all points the same direction, and walking away isn't an option anymore.

Not when the hunt has already begun.

CHAPTER 27

Quinn

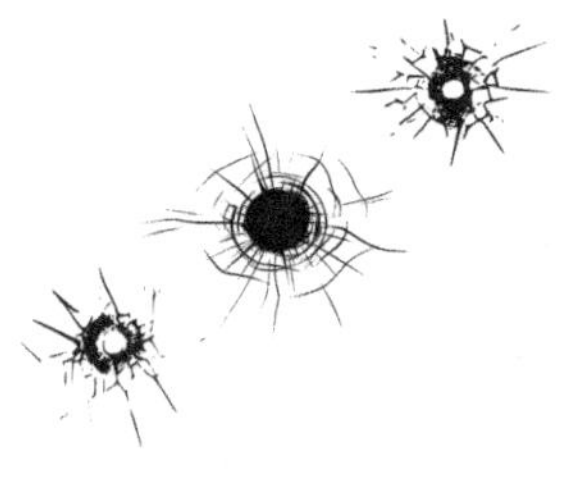

The morning air carries that brittle kind of brightness Driftwood gets after a storm—everything looks clean, but the light feels wrong. Too sharp. The town smells like washed salt and rusted nails.

Belladonna's café is half full by the time I walk in. She's behind the counter, sleeves rolled up, wrist tattoo peeking above her bracelet as she grinds espresso. There's comfort in the sound—the mechanical hiss, the clink of porcelain. I let it anchor me for all of thirty seconds before I feel it—the weight of being seen.

Not hostile. But something new has entered the air—an attention that's been trained.

Belladonna spots me and brightens. "Jane! I was just about to text you." There's a little too much cheer in it, the kind that hides a bruise. She wipes her hands and comes around the counter. "You didn't have to do that, you know."

"Do... *what*?"

Her laugh is easy, unguarded, and that's what chills me. "The sponsorship for the community fund. You'll have half the town singing your praises by next week."

I blink once, twice, too slow. "The what?"

"You didn't see? Oh, honey—Thatcher dropped by last night with the forms. Said you wanted to stay anonymous but he convinced you to let them use your name. The Driftwood Council's already posted about it. Something about a literacy initiative—perfect fit for your shop."

The words hit like stepping into a room where all the furniture's been rearranged.

Belladonna's talking, smiling, grateful, and all I can think is: he's writing me into his story.

"That's... generous," I manage. My voice doesn't sound like mine. "He's persuasive, isn't he?"

She laughs again, not hearing the undertone. "Persuasive is one word for it. You should've seen him—came in with those old-world manners and that goddamn hat. If I weren't taken—"

I let the rest of her sentence fade. My pulse hammers at my throat, steady as a metronome. He isn't just shadowing me anymore. He's curating me. Repainting my edges for everyone else to see.

When Belladonna turns to grab a tray of croissants, I step aside and pull my phone from my pocket. Notifications bloom—two missed calls from the Chamber of Commerce, one from the Driftwood Literacy Fund, a congratulatory message from the councilwoman with a heart emoji and "We're honored to have your support, Ms. Fairhaven!"

I scroll, and there it is... A post tagged to my shop's page.

Jane Fairhaven from Salt & Spine, and Belladonna's Cafe proudly sponsor: The Driftwood Literacy Project.

A smiling photo of Thatcher shaking hands with the mayor, my name printed in elegant script underneath, like a benediction.

I feel my stomach drop. I never signed the form. Never touched a pen.

The café's warmth turns oppressive. My reflection in the glass looks unfamiliar—a woman with perfect posture, polite smile, quiet eyes. Jane Fairhaven, benefactor.

"Hey." Belladonna nudges my arm. "You okay?"

"Fine," I lie. "Just... didn't expect it to go public so soon."

She nods, buying it. "He said you're private, but not shy. That you just need someone to remind you this town's not all water and salt. Sweet, right?"

"Right."

I can't breathe for a moment. *Sweet.* That's what he wants them to think—gentle, charming, civic-minded Thatcher Greeves. The man helping the grieving shopkeeper find her place again.

When I step outside, the sky's gone white with light. The gulls shriek overhead. My hands are steady, but the edges of my vision pulse.

I walk the long way back to the shop, down by the docks where the fishermen are mending nets. Their radios hum static and country. A man in a dark coat stands by the pilings, head turned toward the water. When he glances up, I can't tell if he's looking at me or past me.

Rakes would tell me not to engage. So I don't. I just walk, careful, slowly, until the shop sign creaks into view.

The bell above the door doesn't ring when I open it. I frown. That's... *new*.

I pause, examining the front door. The latch still sits right. The lock's unbroken. But the sound—the small, simple assurance of entry—is *gone*. I bend down, find the bell neatly wrapped in linen and tied with twine. A note pinned through the fabric with an antique brass tack.

The note is blank.

But the paper—I know it. The same stock Kat used for her receipts. The kind only *I* order.

My pulse hits my teeth. He's threading her ghost through my walls again, and I'm getting really fucking sick of it.

I set the bell aside and walk through the aisles, every shelf a mirror of last night's fear. No new rearrangement, no fresh disturbance. Just the silence of a place that's been handled, then left intact.

When I reach the counter, my phone buzzes. I glance down at it, curiosity piqued. It's flashing with... *unknown number*. I answer before I can think. "Hello?"

"Jane Fairhaven?" a woman's voice says, warm and public. "This is Councilwoman Vera Lang. I just wanted to thank you for your *generous* donation to the literacy fund. Mr. Greeves spoke so highly of you—said you'd be too modest to accept recognition, but we're planning to feature you in next week's Driftwood Gazette."

My mouth goes dry. "That won't be necessary."

"Oh, don't be humble. It's a wonderful gesture. He even mentioned your late assistant's love of reading—that's such a touching tribute."

My vision tunnels. *"Excuse me?"*

"Mr. Greeves said it was in Kat's honor. I hope that was all right."

I hang up before I can hear the rest. For a long moment I just stand there, the dial tone humming against my palm, until the silence rushes back like a tide.

Kat's *name. My* shop. *My* cause. *My* donation. None of it truy *mine*.

He's using her fucking memory as currency. I want to strangle him. Or dice him up, and package him in a neat little bow.

The bell's linen wrapping sits like a bandage on the counter. I untie it, let the twine fall, and refasten the bell. The chime rings bright and clear again, as if reclaiming its place.

Then I reach for my phone.

Me: Need to meet. Now.

The response comes in under a minute.

Rakes: Where.

Me: Anywhere with witnesses.

I almost smile. It's the closest thing to a joke we've had since this began.

Outside, the wind shifts off the sea, bringing the faint scent of rain and diesel. The horizon darkens. I flip the sign to Closed and grab my coat.

If Thatcher wants to build me into his story, he's going to learn I've written a few of my own.

***

The café meet-up feels wrong before it even begins.

Rakes gets there first. I can see him through the window, back to the wall, jacket collar still damp from the drizzle that's returned to Driftwood like a recurring thought. He hasn't shaved. His posture says he's trying not to look like a cop, but everything else about him screams the opposite.

I push open the door. The bell chimes once, too bright. Heads turn—then turn away again. That's how gossip moves here... sideways, silent, polite.

He doesn't stand. Doesn't need to. Just tips his chin toward the seat across from him, a subtle gesture that still carries command. There's a newspaper on the table, folded to the local section. My name is there in bold, printed under a smiling mayor and Thatcher Greeves.

COMMUNITY FUND LAUDS FAIRHAVEN SPONSORSHIP. Below it: "In honor of her late assistant, Miss Kathleen Mathers."

My throat goes tight. I slide into the chair.

"He's rewriting the script," Rakes says, voice pitched low. "Line by line."

"He's writing me out of my own story." The words come sharper than I intend.

He studies me, that cop-stare dissecting expression from pulse. "He's not just playing charm games anymore. This—" He taps the headline with two fingers. "—this is stage-setting. He's establishing narrative control. Makes you look compliant. Makes him look clean."

"He used Kat." My voice splinters on her name. "He used her memory to—*what*—polish his reputation?"

"To bait you into reacting," Rakes says. "He's daring you to break character in public. One wrong move, one word too loud, and you look unstable. He keeps your composure, and you lose everything."

"He's already taken everything," I whisper. "My name, my story, my—"

Rakes leans forward, elbows on the table. "Not yet. That's why we're talking."

For a heartbeat I can't look at him. The noise of the café presses close—the hum of an espresso machine, a spoon clinking against porcelain, the muted chatter of people who think they're safe because they don't know what's hunting them. I catch my reflection in the window behind him.

Pale. Controlled. A ghost rehearsing how to haunt itself.

"How public is it?" I ask finally.

He opens a folder from his jacket, slides a few pages across the table—screenshots, timestamps, local reposts. The story's spread faster than gossip ever should.

"The council reposted. A couple of civic groups. One of the schools picked it up—something about scholarships. He's weaving you into the town's goodwill circuit, Jane. Makes it harder to question him without looking ungrateful."

I stare down at the paper. The printed photo is worse up close—his hand clasped around the mayor's, that faint smile of ownership. I can almost feel it at my throat.

"This isn't just manipulation," I say. "It's *branding*."

Rakes gives a humorless huff. "You'd be surprised how often those overlap."

He sits back, studies me again, slower this time. "You sleep?"

"Barely."

"Eat anything?" He asks, eyes blazing like he already knows the answer.

"Coffee counts."

He doesn't smile. "No, it doesn't."

"Are you going to lecture me on self-care now?"

"Maybe," he says. "You look like a live wire someone's been chewing on."

"I feel like one." I try for sarcasm, but it falls flat. "What's the play, Detective? Because I'm running out of patience."

His gaze holds steady. "The play is simple. You let him think it's working. You keep calm, keep showing up, keep letting him see you in public. But we start watching back. Not just cameras this time. People."

He's already written something on the back of one of the pages—a list of names. Merchants, clerks, a mail carrier. The small infrastructure of a town that talks without realizing it's talking.

"These are your neighbors," he says. "The ones he's touching through you. Watch for inconsistencies—who suddenly knows more about your business, who starts treating you differently. He's moving through social channels now, not just surveillance."

"So he's turning them into mirrors," I murmur. "Reflections I can't trust."

"Exactly."

A pause stretches. I can see his jaw working—something he's not saying. Finally, he adds, "And don't go home alone tonight."

I blink. "Excuse me?"

"It's not a suggestion." He lowers his voice further. "I checked your street before you got here. Two cars I didn't recognize were parked at the end of the block. Same model, same plates rotated between shifts. He's not watching you through lenses anymore. He's got boots on your block."

My stomach twists cold. "So what—he's escalating to intimidation?"

"No." His eyes meet mine. "To *ownership.*"

The word lands like a physical hit.

For a long time neither of us speaks. The air between us feels electric—unsteady, charged with something that's half fear, half something else neither of us wants to name. When he finally moves, it's to tear the article neatly in half and fold it into quarters.

"I'll trace the donations. I have a contact that owes me a favor," he says. "I'll follow the money. If he forged the paperwork, it'll lead somewhere."

"And if it doesn't?"

"Then we find another thread to pull."

He sounds so sure that I almost believe him.

Outside, the first drops of rain hit the glass, running down in fine, trembling lines. I realize my hand has drifted toward his across the table—not touching, not even close, just aligned. It feels like a mistake and a relief all at once.

"He's making it look like I'm a puppet," I say quietly.

Rakes' reply is a rasp. "Then we make it look like you don't."

CHAPTER 28

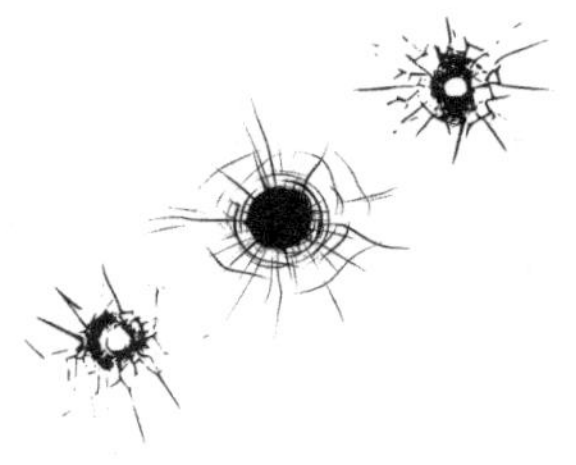

T he town looks different when you've been benched.

Same crooked lamps on Main, same salt-eaten benches, same gulls dive-bombing the trash bins by the docks—but when you're off the badge, the light hits everything wrong. The world stops moving for you. You stop being part of the machine that explains the noise. All that's left is the noise itself.

Driftwood hums low tonight, a bass note under the wind. Rain hasn't started yet, but it's coming. I can smell it—iron and brine and whatever chemicals Redhaven keeps dumping upriver. That food plant will be the death of Driftwood, but that's just another thing above my clearance. The streets gleam slick even without water, and the fog rolls in thin sheets, wrapping the lampposts like gauze.

Thatcher Greeves moves through it like he owns the weather.

Long coat, brimmed hat, hands easy in his pockets. The same patient gait he used when he trailed Jane outside Belladonna's, like he's rehearsed being seen just long enough to be remembered.

I park two blocks up, lights off, engine idling low. I shouldn't be here. Suspension isn't a suggestion—it's a leash. But I can't let it go. Kat's voice,

Jane's face, the bug under the lamp, all of it knots into a single truth I can't unsee.

Thatcher isn't just a stalker. He's the spark before the fire. And he's the missing connection that somehow ties it all together.

He turns left onto Harbor Row, heading toward the part of town where the seafood distributors share real estate with abandoned canneries. The place reeks of fish guts, diesel, and secrets. I kill the engine and slip out, keeping to the shadows, my shoes silent against the wet asphalt.

I tail him past the old cannery gate, through a gap in the fence where the chain hangs loose. He doesn't look back. He knows this ground too well—steps between puddles that would splash, skirts the metal scrap piles like he's mapped them.

A shape waits ahead, haloed by the glow of a single floodlight. A man in a pressed gray suit, too fine for this neighborhood. He's holding an umbrella he doesn't open. Even from this distance, I can see the flash of a cufflink.

That's no fisherman.

They meet in the open space between two containers. Their postures are all wrong for a casual chat—Thatcher loose but listening, the suit stiff as if someone's watching him too. I edge closer until the wind carries their voices.

"—timeline's accelerated," the suit says, every syllable clipped. "You'll need to secure her by week's end. Redhaven doesn't want this spilling into committee."

Secure her.

My chest goes tight.

Thatcher tilts his head, and I catch the faint glint of a smile. "You make it sound like she's a shipment, not a person."

"She's leverage," the man replies. "Don't get sentimental."

Leverage...*Jane*. The words fit together like lock and key.

I move another inch forward, shoulder brushing corrugated steel. The air vibrates with the low thrum of a generator, masking the sound. I can see Thatcher's profile now—clean, calm, like the idea of violence never touched him. The kind of man you'd trust to hold the knife because you'd never believe he'd use it.

"And the detective?" Thatcher asks.

"Handled," the suit says. "*Officially.*"

"Officially," Thatcher repeats, amused. "And unofficially?"

A beat passes between them, then the suit replies, "Unstable. Which is why this conversation never happened."

My fingers curl into a fist. I want to step out, shove my gun under the bastard's chin and ask what he means by secure her, or *unfuckingstable*. But the math doesn't add up. Two men. No badge. No backup. No idea who's waiting in the wings.

So I watch. That's what I've always been best at—watching the wolves before they turn their teeth.

The meeting lasts another three minutes. Thatcher receives a manila envelope. He doesn't open it. Just nods once and walks away, cutting through the fog toward the streetlights. The suited man stands there for a moment, breathing like he hates the air, then climbs into a black sedan and drives off without headlights.

When Thatcher reaches the end of the alley, he stops, and turns his head. Right toward *me*.

The angle's impossible. I'm buried in shadow. But the bastard still smiles—slow, measured, like he's been expecting me. Then he taps two fingers to the brim of his hat in mock salute, and disappears into the mist.

I stay frozen, heart hammering inside my chest, until the sound of his footsteps fades.

He *knows*.

He's always known.

***

I don't drive straight home. I circle the docks twice, checking mirrors, counting tail lights. By the time I park outside Jane's victorian, the clock on the dash reads 12:47 a.m. Her windows still glow soft amber. Looks like she hasn't slept either.

The rain finally arrives—fat, cold drops that hit the windshield like thrown stones. I step out, hood up, and climb the porch steps, the boards complaining under my boots. For a second, I just stand there, hand hovering near the doorframe. She told me to stop protecting her. But that was before I heard those words, before Redhaven's name entered the mix.

I knock once. Light shifts behind the frosted glass. The door opens halfway.

"Malcolm?" Her voice is small, sharp around the edges, like she's been swallowing fear all night and it's started to cut.

"Don't turn the lights up," I say. "We need to talk."

She lets me in without a word. The smell of coffee fills the parlor. She's been pacing, I can tell by the grooves in the rug. She's wearing one of those oversized sweaters that hides how tense she is, sleeves pushed up, hair caught messily at her neck.

"What happened?"

"Thatcher," I say. The name tastes metallic. "He's meeting people. Not locals. Government-adjacent. Redhaven."

Her expression shifts—disbelief, then something colder. "Redhaven Foods?"

"Not the kind that sells flour and soup," I answer. "The kind that launders budgets for Orion. But, I'm beginning to think you already knew that."

She goes still. Even her breath stops for a beat. "You're sure?"

"I heard it. *Secure her by week's end.*' Their words... Now, start talking."

Color drains from her face. She moves to the window, pulls the curtain just enough to look out, then lets it fall. "They're closing the circle."

"Which means what exactly?"

"It means whatever they wanted Kat for—they didn't get it. And now they think it's me." Her voice cracks on the last word, and I hate that I notice. I hate that my first instinct is to step closer instead of backing away like I should.

"Jane."

She looks at me then, and something shifts behind her eyes—steel flickering beneath glass, fear honed into precision. For a heartbeat, it's like seeing a stranger wearing Jane's face, someone older, harder, forged for this kind of danger.

"You were right," she says quietly. "It's not just Greeves. He's the hand. They're the reach."

I run a hand over my jaw. "Then we stop waiting for him to knock."

Her laugh is small, bitter. "You make it sound easy."

"It's not," I say. "But it's better than waiting for them to erase you."

That lands. Her eyes flicker, softening, then harden again. "You shouldn't be here, Rakes. If they're watching me, they're watching you."

"Then let them." I nod toward the window. "They'll see what they want to see—me doing what suspended cops do best. Breaking rules."

She doesn't answer, and the silence stretches taut. The rain drums against the eaves, thunder muttering far out over the bay. I can feel the electricity building between us—familiar, dangerous, the kind that makes you forget the storm isn't personal.

"You don't have to keep showing up," she says finally.

"I don't have to breathe either," I answer. "Doesn't mean I'm planning to stop."

Her mouth opens like she's going to argue, then closes. She turns back toward the table—the same one that used to hold the bugged lamp—and rests her fingers on its base. "What if we can't win this?"

"Then we make it expensive for them to try."

For the first time all night, she smiles. Barely. But it's there, ghostlike and exhausted and too alive for the ruin around us.

***

By two a.m., the rain has turned to mist. I sit in the car across the street again, notebook open, windshield fogging. I should sleep, but my pulse won't let me. Every time I blink, I see Thatcher's grin in the fog, and hear the words that were said between two men who didn't know they were being watched.

Jane's light goes out. The window stays open an inch for the sea air. I wait another hour, watching shadows move across her curtains that might be the ocean's reflection or might be something else.

When I finally start the engine, the rearview mirror catches movement at the corner of the block—a man standing under a streetlamp, collar high, face hidden by shadow. He isn't smoking. Isn't moving. Just standing there, turned toward her house.

I shift the car into drive. Headlights sweep over the pavement—and the spot is empty. No one there. No footprints, no retreating shape. Just the wet street shining like a mirror and the echo of my own breathing.

Thatcher's ghost, or the real thing? At this point, I can't tell the fucking difference.

I head for the cliffs, the old patrol route muscle-memory still etched into my legs. The sea crashes against the rocks below, angry and endless. Somewhere in that sound is the truth—Driftwood was never quiet. It only pretended to be.

And I'm not a detective anymore. I'm the bait that bit back.

Tomorrow, I'll tell Jane what I saw.

Tonight, I just watch the dark and wait for it to blink first.

CHAPTER 29

Quinn

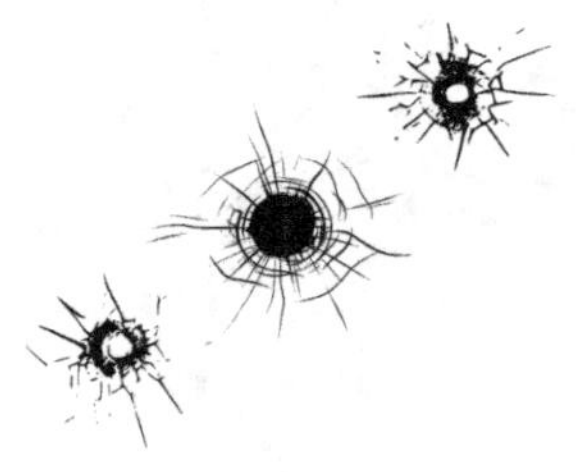

The rain has stopped, but Driftwood still smells like it's drowning.

The whole town feels swollen—gut-heavy clouds crouched low over the rooftops, streets slick enough to reflect the lamps in bruised amber streaks. When I unlock the door to the shop that morning, I half expect it to resist me, to catch like it has a reason to keep me out.

It doesn't. The key turns smooth. The bell sings its usual two-note chime.

And yet—something's wrong.

It isn't a sound. It's more of an absence. The heater's hum is too steady. The quiet between drips from the gutter is too thick. There's a stillness in the air that doesn't belong to ordinary mornings. It feels staged, like the silence on a film set before the director calls action.

My pulse stutters. I don't take a step yet.

Rakes' voice from last night drifts through my mind—his steady warning, that rough growl of restraint in it. But old habits die louder than they live. And this place, this shop, is supposed to be my *sanctuary*. My one piece of normal that keeps getting rewritten into a fucking nightmare.

I make myself move, the lock clicking behind me. My boots squeak once on the worn wood, a tiny sound that seems to echo in the shop.

The smell hits first. Not coffee, glue, or rain-soaked pages. Something chemical, sterile. Something wholly new to this space. And underneath it, faint but certain—*cash*. Old cash.

My gaze sweeps the counter, and at first, everything looks as it should. The register is closed, display case neat, the stack of flyers Belladonna designed for next week's poetry reading lying on top of the counter exactly where I left them.

Then I see it...

An envelope, *unmarked*, just sitting dead center on the countertop like it was placed there for me to find.

No note. No smudge of fingerprints. Just thick paper, folded once.

I stand motionless for a long beat, my heart fluttering in my chest like a frightened bird. My reflection in the front window looks like a woman frozen mid-thought, lips parted, shoulders tight. Jane Fairhaven could pick it up. She'd call the sheriff's office, make a record, pretend ignorance. But Jane Fairhaven isn't who they're after.

I reach for the envelope anyway.

It's heavier than it should be. The flap isn't sealed. Inside there's—*bills*. Neat stacks of twenties, maybe *thousands*. I thumb through enough of it to know it's real. The faint scent of latex gloves still clings to it, so minimal I would've missed it if not for my training.

And slipped between two folded notes is something else—thin, waxy paper, about the size of a page torn from a ledger.

My stomach turns, nausea roiling in my gut. It's Kat's handwriting, or what it *should* look like. The same looping script, the same red ink, but I can see the slight difference in the lean of the letters. It's small, but there. A single line runs across the top...

Payment received. Jane Fairhaven. Driftwood Bookshop.

And below that, a number that makes my heart stop.

Fifty thousand.

For a second, my vision narrows to a pinhole. My hands go slick. The room tilts.

I can feel Thatcher in it—the precision, the smug craftsmanship of the trap. He's done pretending to haunt me. Now he wants a stage.

The sound of tires crunching outside drags me back to the present, heart racing, palms slick with sweat. Through the fogged window, a shadow passes—the distinct shape of Rakes' truck pulling up at the curb. I shove the envelope beneath the counter before the door opens.

The bell rings, softer this time. He's careful like that. Always so fucking careful. He steps in, still wearing the leather jacket he never bothers to dry. His eyes catch on me, on my face, on whatever I'm failing to hide. "You didn't call last night." His voice is sanded down, half warning, half worry.

"I didn't sleep." I force the words out. "That count?"

He looks around, scanning the space. "Did you open up?"

"Trying to."

His gaze flicks to the counter, and I see the moment he notices the missing symmetry. "What happened?"

I don't answer. Not yet. I grab the envelope and lay it back on the counter like an accusation.

He hesitates for only a second. Then opens it, his brows pulling together when he sees the cash. "Tell me you didn't take this from anyone."

"I didn't. It was here when I walked in."

He finds the fake ledger slip, holds it up by the corner, the red ink catching in the light. "And this?"

"Not mine."

His eyes meet mine. "But it's supposed to be."

The words drop between us, heavy and exact. I nod once, only because I'm so tired of pretending

I'm not afraid. That I've got it all fucking figured out when I sure as hell don't.

He doesn't touch the bills again. He folds the paper, once, twice, slides it into an evidence sleeve from his pocket—muscle memory from a badge he no longer carries. "This is a frame," he says, low. "A clean one. Publicly done, too which suggests he's done waiting."

I grip the edge of the counter until my knuckles ache. He moves to the window, looks out through the warped glass. "He's shifting the hunt. You're not just prey anymore. You're the narrative."

Before I can answer, the bell over the door chimes again, and Belladonna enters the shop with more gusto than I feel. She's radiant as ever, curls pinned up, coat unbuttoned to show her painted scarf. The relief on her face when she sees me nearly undoes me. "Jane! Thank God you're open—I was just telling Thatcher how worried I was. He said he saw you heading home early last night."

Every muscle in my body locks. Rakes' head turns just slightly—enough for me to see his jaw tighten. I lick my lips, trying my best to keep my voice even. "It's not unusual for me to lock up early... Why were you worried?"

"You were supposed to come by for that lemon tart, and never did." Belladonna barrels on, oblivious to the tension rising in the room. "Anyway, I dropped off that box of new stock from the council drive. I told Thatcher to leave it in your back room since you weren't here."

My blood goes cold. "What box?"

She blinks. "The one for the literacy fund. He said you donated the bulk of the proceeds yourself. Honestly, Jane, you didn't have to—"

"I *didn't*," I say, sharper than I mean to. The words slice through the air. "I never—"

Belladonna's smile falters. Her eyes dart between me and Rakes, confusion shading to unease. "Oh. Well. Maybe I misunderstood."

"Maybe," Rakes says quietly. "Why don't you head home, Belladonna?"

Something in his tone—soft, protective—gets through to her. She squeezes my hand before leaving. "Call me later, okay?"

I nod, though I already know I won't. The door closes behind her. Silence stretches, brittle as glass.

Rakes moves first. He heads for the back room.

The second he opens the door, the smell hits us. Damp cardboard. Ink. Metal.

A shipping box sits square in the center of the floor. The tape's been sliced clean. Inside—books, yes, but not all mine.

Tucked between the spines is a silver case. Unmarked. Unmistakable.

He kneels, pops the latches, and tilts the lid open just enough for both of us to see the neat stack of bills, the glint of a small firearm, and a folded note with my name printed in red block letters: **Evidence. Intent. Jane Fairhaven, suspect.**

Rakes closes it fast, breath sharp. "He's building a case against you, Jane. Not just whispers this time. Physical evidence, traceable money. If the sheriff's office walks through that door tomorrow, this is what they'll find."

"He's fucking framing me," I whisper, repeating him like a broken record. Disbelief lodges in my chest making it hard to move past the static meant to distract me. "I'd *really* like to know why."

Rakes rises slowly, rubbing a hand over his mouth like he's trying to wipe away the thought. "Then we burn the script. I'll send out some pings to some trusted contacts. But you *have* to come clean, Jane."

"I can't." My voice cracks on it. "Not without proof that it's his hand on the pen."

He looks at me then, and the old softness—the part of him that still believes in rules—flickers behind his eyes. "You want proof? You'll *get* proof. But you're telling me everything first."

I should lie. It would be safer. Easier. But the part of me that's been stitched shut for a decade finally gives. "You won't believe me."

"Try me."

So I do.

I tell him about the years that don't exist. The ones erased from my record—the years in Boston under a different name, under orders I never fully understood. About the operation that went sideways, the handler who called himself a part of Orion, the woman who died to cover the exit. About the guilt that grew legs and followed me all the way to Driftwood. When I finish, I can't meet his eyes. "That's who I was. Quinn Blaire Maddox. The person Thatcher wants to resurrect just long enough to bury for real."

Silence. I hear the faint creak of the floorboard under his boot as he moves closer. Then, softly, like he's afraid to voice the thought out loud. "You think this LeClair you mentioned is the same one

Lawson and I tailed? *And* pulling the strings for Redhaven Foods in Driftwood?"

I nod. "And Thatcher's his face here, as much as his enforcer."

Rakes exhales, long, controlled. "Then we're already inside the fire."

He steps past me, shuts the back door, and pulls the blinds down in one clean motion. "We'll need to move the cash. Hide it, but not too well. Leave him something to think he's winning. And *you*—"

"What about me?"

"You stay visible, but unpredictable. And you *don't*, under *any* circumstances, go anywhere alone after dark."

"You can't be everywhere," I say, a smile twitching at the corner of my lips.

"No," he says, "but I can be enough."

The words hang between us like heat. He doesn't touch me. Doesn't have to. The space feels thinner already, like gravity's shifted around us. I swallow hard, trying to pretend I don't feel the electricity coursing between us. "And if they come for me anyway?"

"Then we stop reacting," he says. "We start attacking back."

***

That night, Driftwood feels different.

The air itself tastes like rumor—salt and metal and something electric waiting to spark. I lock the doors, kill the lights, and sit by the counter until the clock marks midnight. The silence has a pulse to it, slow and patient, like the town is holding its breath.

The box in the back room waits like an open wound. The envelope lies sealed again, a false confession folded neat inside, its paper already soft at the creases from how many times I've thought about burning it. It shouldn't exist. It shouldn't feel like it belongs to me. But that's Thatcher's game—rewrite the story, leave me the villain's script, then let the crowd fill in the rest.

Outside, the tide eats the shore in slow, patient bites. The wind drags through the gutters, carrying voices that aren't there. I tell myself it's nothing. I tell myself that twice. Then a third time for good measure even though I don't believe it.

When the phone vibrates—one short buzz, a coded text from Rakes—my pulse steadies before I even look.

Window clear. Eyes on the street.

I answer, *Copy.*

For a moment, I just stare at the glow of the screen until it fades. Then I breathe in slowly. The kind of slow inhale that tastes like exhaustion and resolve.

The mask I've been wearing doesn't feel so heavy anymore. I used to think of it as armor—something to shield what's left of me from the world. But tonight, it feels more like a weapon. Something precise... controlled. Built for cutting through lies as much as surviving them.

Thatcher's rewritten version of me might fool Driftwood. The murderer. The fraud. The woman who smiled too soon after a funeral. Let him feed the town that story. Let them eat their fill. Because I've spent years perfecting masks—and the next one I build won't be for hiding.

It'll be for *war*.

The thought steadies me. I stand, stretch the ache from my legs, and go to the window. The glass is cool beneath my fingers. Down the street, the lamplight sways in the wind, catching the wet gleam of pavement. No one there. No movement. Just the hum of a car idling somewhere too far to see.

He's out there. I can feel it in the way the air holds itself still. Watching, measuring, waiting to see if I'll flinch.

I turn off the phone and set it face-down.

There's no flinching left in me.

Tomorrow, Driftwood will wake to whatever story he's written overnight. The forged ledger page. The envelope. The whispers that will grow teeth. But tonight—just for tonight—I get to choose what version of me survives the telling.

I close my eyes and picture the tide rolling in, sweeping the footprints clean. When it recedes, the sand will look untouched. But I'll know better. The ocean always remembers.

And this time, I'll make damn sure it remembers *him* too.

CHAPTER 30

Rakes

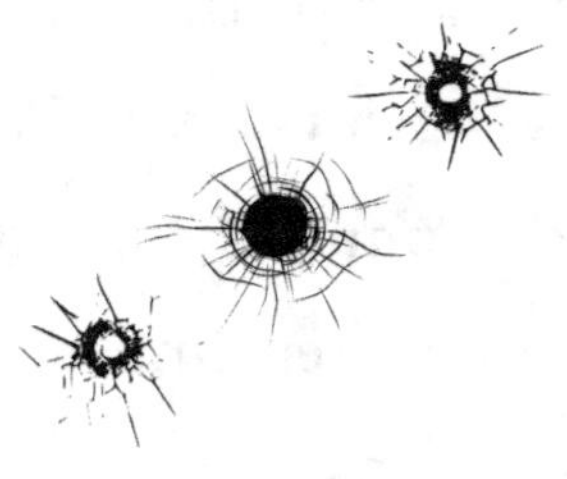

The house doesn't sleep. It ticks and breathes like something alive, old wood flexing in the tide-weathered frame. I make coffee thick enough to chew and stand at the window until the sky finds a color again. The ocean is a bruise at the edge of town, swollen and impatient. Somewhere out there, gulls carve daylight into the clouds.

Quinn's confession keeps looping in my head. Not the words exactly, but the weight behind them—the stillness she wore when she said her real name like it might bite if she wasn't careful. *Quinn Blaire Maddox.* A name that doesn't belong to the woman the town thinks it knows. A name I've seen whispered in the kind of files that don't survive redaction.

She didn't flinch when she said it. That's what stays with me. No apology. No plea for understanding. Just the truth laid bare between us like a blade on a table—sharp, steady, waiting to see what I'd do with it.

Now every silence feels loaded. Every sound outside this window, and every shadow that moves when the wind shifts. Whoever Thatcher really works for isn't just watching her, they seem to *know* her. They're rewriting her story, changing the narrative to fit whatever lie they're crafting.

One headline, one whisper, one careful setup at a time. And if I don't get ahead of it, they'll bury her alive in the lie.

The coffee burns going down. I keep drinking anyway.

Because somewhere between her truth and the one I thought I knew, the ground shifted—and I can't tell if I'm standing closer to saving her or falling straight into the same grave they've dug for us both.

Elias texts a single word at 5:11 a.m.—*Dock*.

He doesn't do pleasantries. He does coordinates.

I'm at Pier C by half past, the kind of cold that nails itself to the ribs crawling under my coat. The harbor's working—lines clacking, diesel engines turning over, a forklift coughing itself awake near the bait shack. Salt rides the air with the dull sweetness of old rope and fish scales gone to iron. If Driftwood has a pulse, it beats here before the shops open and the tourists decide we're quaint again.

Elias is a shape cut out of mist at the end of the slip, back to me, shoulders hunched in an army-green field jacket that's seen better winters. He wears a knit cap pulled low and a scar down his neck that always looks new in bad light. I never asked how he got it. He never asked what haunted mine.

"You look like hell," he says without turning.

"Good morning to you too." I stop at his side. The water shoulders the pylons and falls away again. "You asked for the view, or the exit?"

"Both." He flicks a cigarette into the Atlantic with a contempt that feels earned. "Phone?"

"Home," I lie. I don't need him to tell me how many ways a phone can be a throat to crawl down.

He snorts, eyes still on the heave and fall. "You're learning."

"I learned," I correct, and wait.

He opens his palm. A red USB drive sits there, cheap plastic trying to look like lacquer. He doesn't hand it to me. He holds it just out of reach, like a priest deciding if I deserve absolution or a bullet.

"You don't want this," he says.

"I do."

"You don't," he repeats, softer this time. "But you'll take it anyway."

"Tell me why I shouldn't," I say, because I need to hear him say it the way a condemned man needs to hear the door latch.

"Because once you plug it in, you're not just a cop with a bad month anymore." He finally looks at me. Elias has eyes that got hard a long time ago and never learned how to put themselves down. "You're a witness. And witnesses in this story don't get court dates."

"Redhaven?" I ask.

He doesn't blink. "And *friends.*"

The wind lifts, bringing the smell of diesel and kelp and something metallic, like rain waiting for permission. The harbor bell claps once and falls quiet.

"Say it straight," I tell him.

He rolls the drive once across his fingers, the motion crisp, a magician's habit he's never broken. "You were right about 'Greeves.' He isn't a person so much as a service. The records you pulled were scaffolding. A shell identity, modest income, clean taxes, and a couple of polite donations so it looks like civic engagement. The scrubbed edges? Paid for. The addresses that resolve to nowhere? Leased by a trust. I followed the money out through a set of Delaware LLCs into a logistics consultancy in Houston, and then into a procurement 'advisory collective' with a footprint that looks like charity and smells like bleach."

"Then it's Orion," I say.

"Indirectly through Redhaven Foods," Elias says. "They never hold the hot potato for long.

They push it to a subsidiary, which outsources a 'surge engagement,' which just happens to retain a boutique firm in Geneva to 'manage risk.' And you *know* what 'manage risk' means."

"I'm getting the impression it doesn't mean seat belts."

He smiles without softness. "It means you bury what bites."

I nod at the drive. "On there?"

"On here," he says. "Board minutes from an affiliate you can't FOIA, internal memos that talk about 'supply assurance' like it involves more than trucks, two procurement pipelines that never touch food but invoice like they feed a city. And—" He rolls the drive once more, then closes his hand around it. "—a list of handlers tied to that consultancy. One of the pseudonyms is 'Thatcher Greeves.' He doesn't exist. But the contract does. Six figures quarterly for three years."

"For *what*?" I ask, though I can taste the answer.

"'Community integration and narrative stabilization,'" Elias quotes, and he's so flat there can't be any humor left in him. "You know what a story costs? Whatever you'll pay not to read the real one."

The tide slaps the pier. A gull lands, decides we're not food, and launches again.

"I still don't understand why *her*," I say. "He's spreading whispers about her in public until the town forgets what they knew."

"Jane Fairhaven?" Elias's gaze slides back to the water. "He's done more than that."

Every part of me goes still. "Explain."

Elias works his jaw, like there's a splinter he can't dislodge. "He's building a file that would make your Captain sleep at night. Not just the odd receipt or a forged donation. A narrative. He feeds the town small bites—civic generosity with a forged signature, a rumor about an unpaid permit fee that turns out to be true because he redirected the notice to a dead mailbox, a 'concerned citizen' who claims he saw her leaving the shop at an hour she's never open. Independently, harmless. Together, cancer."

"What else," I ask.

"Bank accounts opened in her name, with just enough funds to interest the right auditor," Elias says. "A storage unit she didn't rent, under an address she doesn't use, paid in cash by a man in a hat you'll never find on camera."

"That's convenient," I say.

"That's the point," he says. "Clumsy enough to look local. Precise enough to hold up when the state boys decide they like an easy story. Add in one planted ledger page and one anonymous tip with the right nouns in the subject line, and congratulations, Detective—you're no longer chasing a murderer. You're processing a suspect."

The coffee in my gut turns to anchor chain. Hearing the words out loud is like stepping from shade into bright cold. I can feel my pupils slam narrow. "Stop there," I say, though we both know

I don't mean it. "Tell me the part where I can keep her out of a cage."

"By proving the real cage is *bigger*," Elias says. "By showing a judge that 'Greeves' is a corporate instrument and 'concerned citizens' don't come with false SSNs."

I look at his hand. He still hasn't passed me the drive.

"What else," I repeat.

Elias's breath ghost-smokes. He looks older all at once, like the air chose today to collect its debt from his lungs. "You asked me to pull the quiet years on Fairhaven. The gap you saw? She doesn't have a W-2 in that window because she didn't have a name you can *run* in that window. That kind of erasure doesn't come cheap. And it doesn't come local."

My chest tightens. I can hear the harbor bell again, distant, counting something down I can't see. "Who did it?"

"Someone with federal teeth and deniable hands," Elias says. "A black ledger. Not WITSEC, not officially. Off-books asset protection with a moral hangover. I found three references in places I shouldn't have seen. Two are burned. One flickers when you scratch it."

"Say the name," I tell him, and it's not a request anymore. It's the rail you grab when the boat rolls and you choose to stand.

He studies me long enough to decide if I've earned it. Then he opens his fist. The drive sits in the center like a wound dressed in plastic.

"Quinn Blaire Maddox," he says.

The name sits heavy, not a revelation but a weight I've been carrying. I knew all of this already. The gap in her file, the precision under her calm, the way she watches a room like she's mapped every ricochet before it happens—all of it pointed here. It's less a surprise than a reminder of how long I've been pretending not to know what she really is. I wasn't a coward with a badge. I was a man stalling for time, and now there's none left to stall.

I take the drive. It's warm from his palm. It shouldn't feel like a verdict. It does.

"Who else knows?" I ask. My voice has gone hoarse.

"People who don't write things down," Elias says. "And one or two who write it in pencil and keep the eraser close. You asked me to find her edges. The edges tell me she belonged to someone for a while. That someone decided she didn't anymore. And now someone else wants to collect whatever's left."

We stand with it. A fishing boat groans free of its berth and noses toward the mouth of the harbor, hull biting through a pewter sheen. A woman down the pier laughs, and the sound breaks apart in the wind.

"Why help me," I say finally. "This is the part where you should tell me to burn the town and start walking."

"I did," he says. "You didn't."

"Then tell me this is the last favor."

"It is," he says. "And Rakes?"

"What."

"If you plug that in at home, your house becomes a lighthouse. They'll see you from ten miles out. Don't do it."

"Where then."

He looks at the bait shack like it offends him. "Somewhere the silence is louder than you are."

He starts to turn away, then stops, nostrils flaring at something only he can smell. "One more thing."

I wait.

"Greeves," he says, "isn't even the tip of the spear. He's the hand that steadies it. The point is something with a better tailor and a family name that opens side doors. You won't see him until he wants his picture taken."

"Can I keep her breathing without seeing him?" I ask.

"For a while," Elias says. "But the men who write the quiet parts don't like loose ends."

He leaves like he arrived. Without ceremony, and without looking back. I watch him shrink to a shape and then to a shadow, and then the fog swallows him whole. My fingers tighten on the drive until the edges bite. The urge to throw it into the harbor is a wave that slams hard and recedes. I pocket it instead and head for the truck.

I don't go home. I drive out of town until the radio loses its grip on the station and the highway unwinds like a bandage. Twenty-two miles inland there's a chain motel with carpets that smell like lemon disinfectant and winter. I take a room at the end, second floor, no trees outside the window, only a lot choked with salt-stained sedans and a plow with a busted blade.

I pull the lamp's shade and unscrew the bulb to kill the hum. Old habit. My hands know how to make a room quiet in the ways that matter.

The motel TV gives me static when I ask for it. I drag the desk chair so I can feel the wall under my palm, a trick I picked up from a guy who never got surprised twice. Then I plug the drive into a machine I didn't buy with a salary I can explain.

It doesn't scream. It purrs. Folders open like mouths—nothing cute about the filenames, nothing on the nose. The doc titles mean nothing unless you know what ten other titles mean, which is how professionals hide wolves in filing cabinets.

I start with the way Elias told the story. Follow the invoices. There's a comfort to it, the discipline of a ledger. The numbers have no shame. Redhaven Foods Northeastern Procurement pays Remora Strategy Partners—no, rem0ra spelled like a hacker's joke—for "risk and crisis counseling." Remora pays Candela Logistics for "temperature-controlled emergency transport." Candela pays a boutique in Geneva with a website so tasteful it barely exists. The boutique pays a trust called Palmetto. Palmetto funds retainers for "community integration liaisons." One of those liaisons invoices under T. Greeves.

The amounts tell their own weather—regular, dependable storms. Nothing spiky enough to catch an analyst's eye. Enough to pay for a dozen careful lives.

The next folder is uglier. Signal. Captures. Clips. Maps of Driftwood with colored pins that line up too neatly with the places Jane breathes. Salt & Spines. The path to the café. The path home. The bluff where the wind talks louder than people do. Underneath each is a three-letter tag: MNR for "monitor," ASG for "assign," FLT for "float." The four-letter tag under Belladonna's is SEED.

I write the word down before I realize my hand has moved. *Seed.*

I slide into the Case folder. That's where the frame lives. I see it immediately because it's designed to be seen by the right eyes and missed by the rest. A scanned "donation receipt" thanking Jane Fairhaven for her "generous support of the Driftwood Harbor Improvement Fund." A copy of a "permit delinquency notice" mailed to a P .O. box that never belonged to her. A letter to the Friends of the Library congratulating her for underwriting "new archival materials"—which is funny, because the Friends haven't bought an archival box in five years. There are thumbnails: grainy stills from a camera across the street catching a person with her hair and her shape at an hour she wouldn't be there if she were asleep like a human being. There are two audio files. A woman who could be her saying "yes, that's fine" spliced from other phrases, stitched into a permission she never gave.

Then there's a PDF that makes my throat close. A ledger page I've never seen. Red ink. Clean hand. Kat's exact style. Two columns. A name that doesn't exist unless you know what to call it. *Jonas*

Kerr. Next to it—a sum and a date and the note *Alias?* And below that; *Q.B.M.—payment?*

If a detective who wants to sleep reads this, he solves the case in a paragraph. Motive, opportunity, identity collapse. Good night, Driftwood. Thatcher really did lay it all out neatly. *Fucker.*

I push the chair back and stand because I need my legs to remember how to hold me. The motel's air conditioner rattles inside the wall. Next door, someone sneezes and curses softly like they're trying not to wake a child. I put my palms on the desk and breathe until my head clears.

The last folder is called... *Quiet*. Elias didn't tell me about this one. Inside is a photograph scanned from paper that has creases in it like someone carried it a long time and then decided to stop. A younger woman looks out from the grain—the bones are the same as Jane's, but the eyes are sharper and the mouth hasn't learned its new rules yet. Her hair is different, freer, whipping past her face in long strands. The clothes are anonymous, and the stamp at the corner says, *Intake*. The name at the bottom says *Maddox, Quinn Blaire*.

There's a second image, buried just underneath the first. A copy of a form with half the fields blacked to nothing. Assignment has no words beside it. Release has a date. I do the math without meaning to. It lands right in the gap where Driftwood thinks generosity bought a bookstore.

I sit back down, hands trembling, looking at the drive like it might tell me what to do next.

What I feel isn't victory. It isn't even relief. It's a clean line snapping into focus—the kind of sight picture you get when your hands stop lying about what they're holding. I've spent weeks asking whether she's hiding guilt. I can see the clearly now. She's being erased. Not punished—*removed*. Tidied away by professionals who learned how to move whole lives a millimeter at a time until a person becomes a rumor becomes a warning becomes a gravestone.

I take the drive out and break it open with the motel's Gideon Bible because there's no rock handy. A splinter of board rips the plastic, cutting my palm and I let it. I pull the chip, bite down on it in a napkin, and pocket what's left. The laptop is clean enough to walk away from. I don't. I wipe it anyway. Old habits have a religion all their own.

By the time I'm back in the truck, the sun's found a way to make the frost look like glass. I'm halfway to Driftwood before I let the engine heat touch my hands.

I don't call Jane. I don't want a record of what I need to say. I drive the long way behind the cannery and park on the far side of her block where the map says there's nothing to see. There's always something to see. Thatcher's sedan isn't there. That makes my teeth hurt more than if it were.

I walk the last hundred yards and let the town wash over me—salt, wood smoke, the careful voices of people out early because they want to be, not because the job tells them to. A dog nails me with a bark and then decides I'm familiar enough to let go. Two teens in puffer jackets pass a vape and pretend the cloud is weather. Driftwood has a thousand eyes that aren't cameras. I keep my head down.

Her porch is the kind that knows how to store secrets under the boards. I don't step on the boards that announce your weight. She opens the door like she heard me thinking about the hinges.

"We shouldn't—" she starts.

"We should," I say, and I'm inside before her house decides to scream.

We don't go to the parlor with its lamp-shaped absence. We go to the kitchen because kitchens are where towns like this tell the truth when they must. She stands by the sink, palms braced, soaking in the morning like it owes her warmth. There's a coil of hair twisted at the nape of her neck that makes my hand move without permission. I do and then stop because I remember who we are.

"You were right," I say, and this time the words feel like a key. "It isn't just him. He's a hand. The arm is longer than the fucking harbor."

Something in her face closes and something else opens. She doesn't ask if I'm sure. She doesn't pretend surprise. She waits.

"He's seeding public story," I go on. "Forged receipts. Letters you didn't write. A storage unit you didn't rent. A ledger page that looks like Kat and says what they want it to say."

She looks at me like she's measuring the weight of every syllable. "And the part you haven't said yet."

"Your name," I say, and I can hear my pulse in it. "The one you wore before the town decided what to call you."

She could lie. She could laugh. She could turn the knife her direction and mine. She doesn't. She breathes in—under the breath is the click of an old machine turning over—and says nothing because nothing is smarter than everything right now.

"I don't care what you did for them," I tell her. "I care what they want to do to you."

The smallest muscle in her cheek moves. "And what do they want to do to me, Detective."

"Erase you," I say. "Make the town carry it for them."

She looks past me for a heartbeat, to the window, to the strip of yard where the damp climbs the fence like ivy, to the place where the ocean's voice carries if the wind slants right. When she looks back, the quiet in her isn't retreat. It's resolve. New. Ugly. Honest.

"What's the plan," she asks.

Finally... I've been waiting to be asked.

"We make their file useless," I say. "We take away any place a story can anchor. You don't go where you can be photographed doing what they want you to do. You don't carry anything you didn't touch in front of me."

"No one watches you?" She lifts an eyebrow—dry, almost fond, which is dangerous. "That's adorable."

"They watch me," I say. "But I'm already the man they talk about over lunch."

For the first time since the harbor, I feel it. The pivot the beats promised me. I stop wondering who she's hiding and start taking inventory of how to keep her from being killed. "They'll come at night," I say. "When the town lets them. When a hand on a shoulder looks like comfort and a car idling looks like weather."

"Let them," she says. "I know how to breathe in the dark."

I nod. "We do this together."

That makes her flinch—barely. It's there and gone, a fight between pride and survival, the kind of fight that leaves a scar you don't show anyone.

"They framed you," I say, because the word is a blade and I want it on the table where we can see it. "But they underestimated me without the badge."

"What are you now," she asks.

"Stubborn," I say. "And awake."

She huffs a sound that could be a laugh if the room had more oxygen. "That's a dangerous combination."

The kettle clicks. Neither of us remembers turning it on. She pours water over grounds with a steadiness that I don't deserve to watch. The steam curls up and carries the smell of earth and smoke and mornings before this one when the world pretended to be simpler.

She slides a mug toward me. Our fingers don't touch, but every nerve behaves as if they did.

Outside, a car idles and drifts on. The house registers it and lets it go. The ocean keeps working at the edge of the world like it intends to open it eventually.

I don't ask if I can stay. I take my coat and put it on the chair closest to the door because men like me don't get to be comfortable in houses like this. She doesn't tell me to leave. She doesn't tell me to keep my distance. She takes a sip and closes her eyes in a way that would undo me if I were a different kind of man.

On the table between us, the day folds itself into decisions...

Where to stand, who to call, which story to strangle before it learns to crawl.

I was asking the wrong question. The right one is simpler and sharper.

How do I keep her alive?

I take my phone out, turn it face-down, and slide it to the far corner where it can't hear what comes next even if it thinks it can. When I look up, she's watching me, one eyebrow lifted, the corner of her mouth considering an expression that would make men do unwise things.

"Lines crossed," I say.

"More like erased," she answers.

"Then we draw new ones," I tell her. "And we make sure they're cut deep."

Her eyes hold mine until the room forgets to breathe.

"Let's start," she says. "Before the town wakes up and puts us back where it wants us."

I nod, and the plan unspools—ugly, practical, fast. We will be smaller than the story that hunts us, until the story trips over us in the dark and breaks its teeth. We will make noise where the microphones are off and go quiet where cameras like to play.

And I will stop asking if I'm allowed to save her.

Because I finally understand the job. Not cop, or cousin. Not simply a man trying to be good.

No, it's... *Keeper of the page.*

CHAPTER 31

Quinn

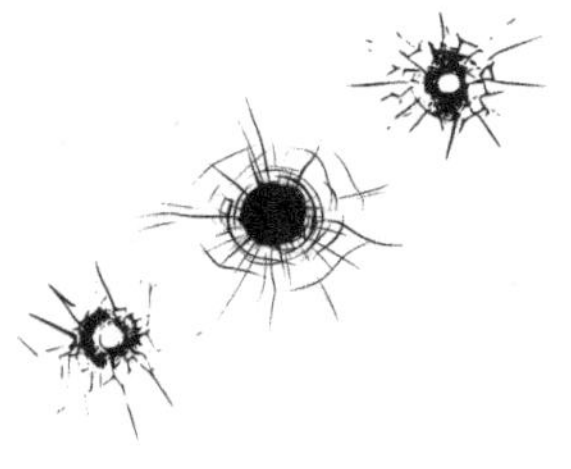

Morning light cuts across the floor in pale, brittle ribbons. It's the kind of light that makes the dust look like ash and every surface feel colder than it should. I stand in the doorway of the shop with my keys still in my hand, staring at the wreckage I didn't expect to find. It feels like groundhogs' day all over again.

The window is shattered inward. Not cracked or splintered, but obliterated. A scatter of glass spreads in a half-moon across the floorboards, glinting like ice under the muted gray light. A single rock sits in the middle of it, wrapped in torn paper that flutters in the draft from the sea.

It doesn't need to say anything. The message is already written in the violence of it.

For a long moment, I just stand there, listening. The shop has a different kind of silence now — thin, exposed. The kind that trembles with every gust of wind through the broken pane. I close the door behind me and twist the lock out of habit, even though it's pointless. The cold slides under my sleeves, runs up my spine, settles somewhere behind my ribs.

Whoever did this wasn't trying to sneak. They wanted me to see it in daylight, to find the mess when there was no one left to scream.

I crouch beside the glass. It's the old kind, from when Kat insisted we didn't need reinforced panels because "coastal charm" mattered more than paranoia. I almost laugh. The sound dies in my throat.

The note's paper is damp from sea air, edges curling. I pick it up with two fingers, careful not to disturb the rock, and unfold it just enough to read what's left.

LEAVE.

That's it. One word. Thick black ink bleeding down the grain of the page.

My pulse doesn't race anymore. It just *hurts*. Slow and deliberate, like my body's reminding me I'm still here.

I should call Rakes. I also shouldn't *want* to. That line between us blurred weeks ago, and pretending it hasn't only makes the fall harder. But I know the moment he sees this, he'll be here whether I ask him to or not.

I sweep the glass into a pile with a broom from behind the counter. The sound is sharp—a punctuation mark in a morning that hasn't decided how cruel it wants to be yet. The air smells like salt, dust, memory.

When I straighten, there's a shape in the window's reflection behind me.

"*Jesus*—"

"Easy," it says.

Rakes stands in the doorway, wind-tossed and already frowning. His jacket's still damp from the fog outside, a single drop hanging from the end of his hair. I hate how easily my relief finds him.

"You shouldn't be here," I say.

"You say that every time I show up," he answers, stepping over the threshold like the place belongs to him. "And *every time*, I turn out to be right about something."

I sigh. "You can't keep breaking the rules just because you're bored while you're on suspension."

"I'm not bored." His gaze lands on the glass. "Whoever did this wasn't either."

He moves closer, crouches by the window, and picks up the rock. His hands are bare — rough, steady, callused in a way that doesn't match his age. "They didn't throw from the street," he says. "Angle's too low. Someone got close."

"Close enough to what?"

"To make sure you'd hear it if you were here."

That stops me dead in my tracks. The idea of it — of footsteps outside while I closed up, of someone standing here long enough to aim — crawls under my skin like frost.

"I wasn't here," I manage. "I stayed home."

Rakes nods once. "Good."

He turns the rock in his palm, studies the wrapped paper, then looks up at me. "You recognize the handwriting?"

I don't have to. The thick strokes, the way the L cuts deep and the E barely finishes — I've seen it before. On notes tucked into packages, on lists written in too-perfect script. It's Thatcher's. I'm sure of it.

"I think so," I say quietly.

He doesn't push for more. Just stands, sets the rock on the counter, and rolls up his sleeves. "You got any plywood in the back?"

I stare at him in disbelief, mouth slightly ajar. "You're *not* patching my window."

"Then who is?" He asks.

"I can call someone," I argue.

"Who? The same someone who pretends not to see me when I pass them on Main?" His tone softens. "You don't have to like me to let me help."

I cross my arms. "That's a dangerous assumption."

"I make those for a living."

He's already moving before I can argue again, disappearing into the stockroom and returning with a spare board and an old hammer I keep under the register. It's ridiculous how natural he looks in the middle of my shop — like the chaos makes sense around him.

When he kneels to brace the wood, the morning light catches the side of his face, tracing the lines of exhaustion that weren't there weeks ago. He smells like rain and coffee and the kind of quiet I've never been able to find without a price.

"I didn't ask you to fix this," I say.

"No," he murmurs. "You didn't." He drives the first nail clean through, the sound splitting the air like a heartbeat.

I stand beside him, feeling completely useless. The rhythm of the hammer is steady, each hit loud and hard. The board fits too easily into the frame — temporary, fragile, but enough to hold the morning back for a while.

When he's done, he sits back on his heels. "That'll hold till we get proper glass."

"*We*?" I ask with a perfectly arched brow.

"You think I'm letting you sit here alone after this?" He asks, quirking a brow, shaking his head like he knows he didn't just hear what I said.

I open my mouth to argue, but the words don't come. Something in his expression stops me — not pity, not authority. Just care, unguarded and quiet. "I don't need—"

"Yeah, you *do*," he says softly.

The truth of it hangs between us, heavy as the salt air. I move to the counter, picking up a towel, pretending I have something to clean. "You can't keep showing up like this. People talk."

"Let them."

"I can't afford to let them, you know that. Not with how he's already changing the narrative."

He straightens, steps closer, his voice low. "You think I care what they say about me? About us?"

I gulp, "There is no '*us*,' Rakes."

He studies me, eyes narrowing just enough to make me feel seen in ways I didn't ask for. "Then why are you shaking?"

I glance down, clenching my jaw when I realize he's right. My fingers are trembling against the towel, barely visible, but not enough to hide. "Because this was my life *before* you," I whisper. "People leaving things—sending messages. Every time I think I've built something new, it finds me again."

He doesn't look away. "You're not alone in it anymore."

"I was supposed to be," I say, quieter. "That was the point."

He reaches out then — just one hand, rough palm, careful touch — and brushes a strand of hair from my face. His thumb grazes my jaw, calloused warmth against skin gone cold from fear. The contact feels both too much and not enough.

"Jane—"

"Quinn," I correct him without thinking.

The name hangs there, raw, like something newly born. His hand doesn't drop. His voice goes soft. "Quinn."

Hearing it from him does something I don't have language for. Like a lock turning somewhere I didn't know existed.

"Rakes," I start, but he shakes his head.

"Don't," he says. "Just... stop fighting for a minute."

And I do.

The air between us tightens, the sound of the ocean through the broken window replaced by something slower, quieter — the rhythm of breath meeting breath. When he leans in, it's not sudden. It's inevitable.

The kiss starts small, tentative—an apology neither of us knows how to phrase. Then something in it shifts, breaking open like a dam. His breath catches, and mine answers. The air between us collapses, and the kiss deepens, no longer searching but claiming—raw and real, pulling every lie we've told each other into something that almost feels like truth.

His hand slides from the back of my neck down to the curve of my spine, anchoring me even as the floor seems to tilt. My fingers catch his collar, then the buttons of his shirt, tugging him closer until there's no space left to hide behind. He tastes like rain and coffee and everything I've spent weeks denying myself.

The world outside fades to rhythm—the ocean's hush against the cliffs, the low hum of the boarded window, our breathing tangling in the half-light. His mouth moves with purpose now, deeper, hungrier. I can feel the restraint unraveling in him with every slow drag of his lips against mine.

I press closer. The counter digs into the backs of my thighs, but I don't care. His hands are everywhere—my waist, my jaw, the fabric at my hips that he fists as if to steady himself. I match him, pulling him in by his shirt, by the heat under it, feeling his heartbeat hammer through both of us until I can't tell whose pulse belongs to whom.

It shouldn't feel safe. It should feel like a mistake. But safety isn't what this is—it's surrender, and for one suspended breath, I let it happen.

He kisses me like he's trying to memorize me, like this is the only language left to tell the truth in. My hands find his hair, threading through it as his breath shudders against my skin. Everything in me that's been locked tight since Kat's death, since my past clawed back to life, comes loose all at once.

When we finally break apart, foreheads resting together, both of us unsteady, the world crashes back in—the sea roaring below the cliffs, the wind sneaking through the cracks in the boarded window. My pulse is thrumming so loud I can barely hear it.

"This doesn't change anything," I murmur.

"Sure," he grumbles, chuckling softly. "Keep telling yourself that."

A laugh slips out — small, fragile, but real. "You really *are* impossible."

"So are you."

He steps back, giving me space, but the room feels smaller now. Every breath between us charged with what we both refuse to name.

I glance toward the window. The board sits solid, pale wood catching the light, the world outside just a gray smear. For the first time, I think maybe Driftwood isn't big enough to hold all the versions of me I've been trying to keep apart.

Rakes walks the perimeter of the shop, scanning the corners, the shelves, every shadow that could hide a threat. When he stops, his voice is low again. "You're sure nothing else was touched?"

"Yes," I say automatically. Then... I see it.

In the far corner, on the lowest shelf where the light barely reaches, something pale catches my eye. I step closer, breath caught in my throat.

Nestled between two untouched books—Ghosts of the Coast and Salt and Silence—sits a single *yellow* lily.

For a heartbeat, my mind refuses to make sense of it. It's just a flower. Just another cruel reminder of Kat, maybe—like before. The kind of twisted joke people play when they think grief makes you too fragile to fight back.

But then the scent hits me. Sweet, cloying, *wrong*. The kind of sweetness that rots on the tongue.

And I suddenly remember a crucial detail. A lily means death in Orion's world. Their way of saying you're next.

My knees threaten to give. I brace against the shelf, fingertips pressing grooves into the wood. How could I have missed it before? How could I have looked at the lilies on Kat's grave and thought it was sentiment instead of a fucking signature? How could I have been so fucking *blind*?

The realization burns cold, crawling up my spine, hollowing out every excuse I'd built to stay calm. Whoever placed this didn't just want to scare me—they wanted me to understand exactly how close the blade already is.

Rakes sees my face and follows my gaze. His jaw tightens, the muscle ticking once. "That wasn't here before."

"No." My voice comes out hoarse. "It wasn't."

He moves first, crossing the floor in two strides. He picks up the flower carefully, examines the stem, the bloom. It's real — fresh, slick with morning dew that shouldn't be here.

The symbol is perfect. Too fucking perfect.

Rakes looks in my direction, "He's determined to prove a fucking point it would seem."

Rage slithers through me, cold and lethal. I'm tired of being fucked with. Tired of having my shop broken into, and my past dredged up. I wanted a quiet fucking life. *Retirement.* Was that really so much to ask for?

"Then we make some noise," I murmur, ignoring the pointed look Rakes throws in my direction. He moves toward the door, and I follow knowing damn good and well that things just got a *hell* of a lot more dangerous.

The light outside has shifted by the time we lock up, deeper gray rolling off the water, thick with rain that hasn't fallen yet. The air hums with something electric, like the world itself is holding its breath. I look back once at the boarded window, at the faint outline of the lily still burned into my vision.

Driftwood was supposed to be my refuge. Now it feels like the inside of a trap.

CHAPTER 32

Quinn

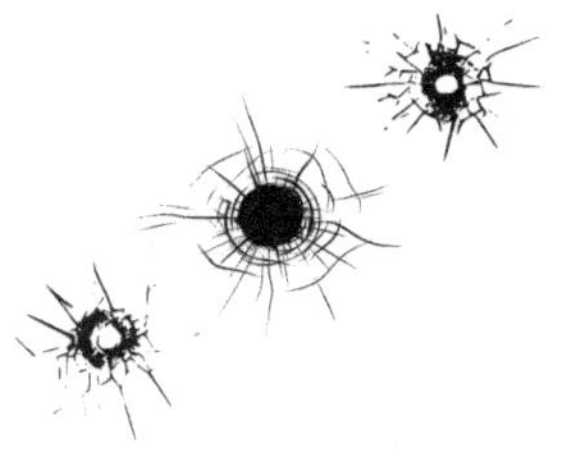

Driftwood looks almost kind in the early evening.

The fog hasn't rolled in yet. The harbor's visible from Main Street, water dark and flat, fishing boats rocking slow like they don't know a war's brewing beneath the surface. People move in pairs and threes—locals heading home, tourists lingering like they've got time to waste.

I walk because I need to feel the ground under my feet. Rakes walks because he doesn't trust stillness.

We don't touch, but he keeps pace just close enough that I can feel him there. It's infuriating. Comforting. Both.

"You're wound tight," he says eventually.

"I'm fine."

"That's not what I said."

I shoot him a look. "You planning to psychoanalyze me now?"

"No," he replies. "I'm planning to slow you down before you do something reckless."

I stop short. "Reckless would be pretending this goes away if I sit still."

He clenches his jaw, "I didn't say sit still."

"Then what did you mean?"

He nods ahead, toward the corner café glowing warm against the coming dusk. Belladonna's windows spill amber light onto the sidewalk. Safe. Familiar. Ordinary. "Coffee," he says. "Just five minutes, long enough for us to regroup."

"We don't need—"

"Quinn."

The way he says my name is quiet. Not commanding. Worse—it's steady. Certain even.

I hesitate, and that's the problem. He knows I will.

"Five minutes," I say finally. "Then we move out."

He doesn't smile. Just opens the door and ushers me inside, like this was part of his plan all along.

Belladonna's smells like espresso, old books and cinnamon—layers of comfort stacked intentionally to make people linger. I hate how easy it is to breathe in here.

We take a table near the window. A little out of the way, but not enough that I can't see anyone who would walk by. Visibility without exposure.

I shrug off my coat. He doesn't.

"You're not going after him half-cocked," Rakes says, low enough no one else can hear.

I blink, understanding flooding my veins. "I'm not half-cocked," I snap. "I've run recon my *entire* life."

"*Prepared* recon," he corrects. "With intel, exits, and fucking backup."

"And how exactly do you suggest I prepare when he's already five steps ahead?"

His gaze flicks—not to me. To the bar.

I feel it before I see it. That prickle at the base of my neck. The sense of a room subtly reorienting itself around a single presence. I already know who sits at the bar before I turn my gaze.

Thatcher Greeves sits at the counter like he belongs there. Casual jacket. No tie. Coffee cup cradled between his hands like he's just another man killing time before dinner. He laughs at something the barista says. Easily. Charming and ever the town's beloved do-gooder.

My pulse climbs in my throat. *There you are.*

I shift instinctively, angling for a better view. Rakes' hand comes down on the table—firm, grounding.

"Don't," he murmurs.

"He's *right* there," I argue.

"I know."

That's when it hits me. Rakes already knew. He fucking *knew.* "You already clocked him," I say quietly.

"Yes," he answers.

At least he's honest. I grit my teeth. "And you didn't tell me."

"No."

Anger flares, sharp and immediate. "You don't get to decide what I see."

"I do if what you see gets you *killed*," he replies without any real heat.

Thatcher turns slightly, enough that I catch his reflection in the window. His gaze skims the room, like he's searching for someone. He sweeps through once, then twice. Both times missing us completely. It has to be deliberate. "He's waiting for something," I whisper.

Rakes nods once. "Probably for you to make the first move."

My jaw tightens. "Then... I guess I don't."

"Good," he says. "Because right now, you're re-acting. Reacting will cause you to make mistakes. And he's counting on that."

Thatcher stands, tosses cash on the counter, and heads for the door. Doesn't look our way. Doesn't need to.

I'm already halfway out of my chair, but Rakes is faster. "Sit," he says, voice stern. "Let me."

"I'm not letting him—"

"You are," he cuts in softly. "Because chasing him without knowing his perimeter is exactly how you end up boxed in."

The kiss we shared earlier hums between us like an exposed wire. The tension isn't just tactical—it's personal now. He knows it. I know it. And I fucking hate that he knows it.

Thatcher exits, smug grin plastered on his face. The *bastard*.

Rakes drains his coffee in one swallow and stands. "Count to thirty."

"Rakes—"

"Thirty," he repeats. "If he circles back, I'll abort."

"And if he doesn't?"

His eyes meet mine. Dark gray storms filled with intent. "Then I follow him long enough to know what he wants you to do."

I don't like it, but I trust him anyway. He's gone before I can argue.

I sit there, fingers curled tight around my cup, counting heartbeats I don't need to measure. The street outside keeps moving. No alarms. No explosions.

Just Driftwood, pretending nothing's wrong. Turning on the same wheels it always does no matter the circumstance.

When Rakes returns, his expression has changed—not alarmed. Focused. "He's not hunting," he says, sliding back into the chair. "He's herding."

"Toward what?"

"Toward you losing every bit of your patience."

I exhale slowly. "Then what's the play?"

He studies me for a moment. Really studies me. "We don't take the bait," he says. "Not tonight."

"And tomorrow?" I ask.

"Tomorrow," he says carefully, "we make sure you're alive long enough to decide how this ends."

CHAPTER 33

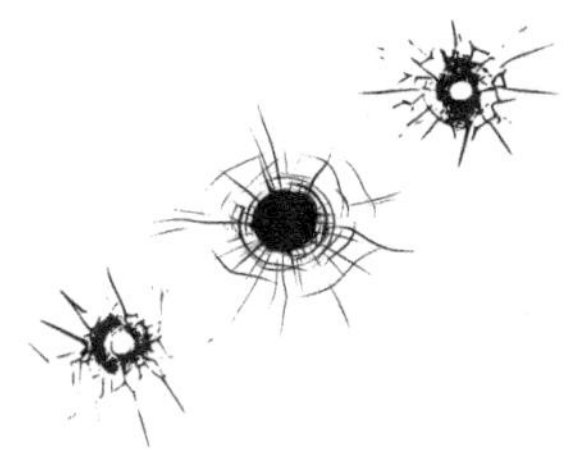

I don't stop driving until we're miles outside Driftwood—far enough that the ocean's hiss is only a rumor through the trees. The road narrows to gravel, then dirt, then the kind of forgotten track that makes you wonder who built it in the first place. The cabin that finally appears looks like it's been waiting decades for anyone to remember it's here.

Jane—no, Quinn—is fuming beside me, her silence louder than any shouting. I can't blame her. We left with nothing. No clothes. No food. No plan that extends past dawn. I even made her leave her phone behind, the same one that's practically an extension of her hand. A beacon, I told her. A liability we can't afford. What I didn't say was that the thought of anyone tracing her made my stomach twist hard enough to hurt.

The cabin sits tucked under the pines, their evergreen boughs hanging low, dripping gold in the dying light. In any other life it might've looked peaceful. Now it looks like a place where you go to wait for the world to forget you exist.

When I kill the engine, she's already out, boots crunching against the gravel as she stalks toward the door. Chin high, shoulders back. Defiant. The kind of posture that says she'll burn the place down before she lets it cage her.

I groan under my breath and shove a hand down my face before following, fishing the old key from my pocket. "Hold up—"

Too late. She's at the door, palm flat against it like she can will it open. I fit the key into the lock, the metal cold enough to sting, and twist. The bolt clicks back. She doesn't even look at me as she pushes past, stepping inside first and slamming the door with a force that rattles the frame.

I linger on the threshold, rubbing the back of my neck. Maybe I should've talked this through with her before I decided to play the hero. But at the time, it felt like the only move left—get her out, get distance, get quiet. Thatcher's making all these plays and she's starting to get reckless. All because she can't see the chess pieces moving on the board. She's too fucking close to it.

In the end, I push the door open. Because waiting outside feels like waiting for the other shoe to drop.

The air inside smells like dust and pine sap, the ghost of old fires still clinging to the stone hearth. A single window stares out at the woods. The light filtering through it turns her hair copper in places, but her expression's pure ice.

I let the silence hang a beat too long before I speak. "It's temporary. Just until I figure out how deep this runs."

Her laugh—short, prickly, disbelieving—cuts through the quiet. "Yeah, Malcolm, it feels a lot like hiding."

Her words from the car echo again, only now they sting harder, echoing in the ribs instead of the head. I clear my throat, trying to find something that isn't an excuse. "It's not hiding if we're still moving pieces."

She turns toward me, that look in her eyes—the one that reads like she's seconds from tearing her skin off just to get free.

And for the first time since this started, I'm not sure if I brought her here to protect her... or to keep her close enough that I don't lose her entirely.

She paces the cabin like a caged animal, boots scuffing against warped boards. Every movement is harsh, controlled—too controlled. The kind that only exists to keep something worse from breaking loose. I watch her for a long minute, my hands useless at my sides, until the silence presses too hard.

"You think I like this?" I ask. "Dragging you out here, in the middle of nowhere, like some paranoid—"

"Then *why* did you?" She cuts me off, spinning toward me. Her voice is low, but the tremor in it isn't fear—it's fury. "You don't get to make that call for me, Rakes. You don't get to decide what's safe."

"Someone has to," I fire back. "You saw the lily. You know what that means. *I* know what it means now."

Her jaw tightens. "I know exactly what it means."

"Then stop pretending this is some overreaction."

"I'm not pretending." She steps closer, the air between us charged and humming. "But you don't get to cage me because it makes you feel better. You don't get to drag me out here like a—" She cuts herself off, shakes her head. "Like I'm *yours* to keep."

That word hits harder than it should. *Yours.*

I move toward her before I've decided to. "You think this is about ownership?"

"Isn't it?" Her voice is shaking now, not from weakness, but from the effort of holding something in. "You don't trust me. You never have."

"Christ, Quinn, that's not—"

"Yes, it is." Her eyes are bright now, glassy in the half-light. "You're afraid of what happens if you stop holding every piece in your hands."

"And you're afraid of letting anyone help you," I retort.

The words hit their mark. Her shoulders pull back, expression sagging and it kills me to watch the light die in her eyes. "Because every time I do, someone dies."

The silence that follows isn't peace—it's the edge of a cliff. The kind you can only stand on for so long before something gives.

I take another step. "You think I don't know that feeling?"

Her breath catches. I can see the pulse hammering at her throat, the way her hands curl at her sides like she wants to push me away and pull me closer at the same time.

"I'm not your enemy," I say. "You don't have to fight me."

Her voice drops to a whisper. "Then stop treating me like I'm breakable."

That's what does it. The sound of her—small, angry, raw—snaps something I've been holding too long.

I close the last of the distance and kiss her.

It's not careful this time. It's not neat. It's all the things we've been choking back since Driftwood started to rot around us—fear, grief, hunger, guilt. My hands find her waist, the curve of her hip, the soft heat beneath her sweater. She gasps into my mouth and I swallow the sound, greedy. Her fingers twist in my shirt, dragging me closer until there's no air left to argue with.

The taste of her is a hint of bourbon and salt and something I can't name. I press her against the wall, the old wood creaking under us. She fists my collar, pulling until the kiss turns rougher, mouths open, teeth catching. Every breath is shared, every sound caught between us.

She breaks first, only to whisper against my mouth, "This is *insane*."

I kiss her again. "I know."

Her hands slip under my shirt, fingertips tracing the scars she's only ever seen in glimpses. I groan against her skin, the sound low, involuntary. She answers with a shudder that goes all the way through me.

When I drag my mouth from hers, it's only long enough to breathe her name—Quinn—before finding her again. The kiss deepens until it hurts, until the world narrows to the scrape of her nails, the rough stutter of my breath, the clean break of two people who stopped pretending they could stay apart.

I lose myself to it—to *her*. Letting time move differently, both of us learning the rhythm of each other.

***

<u>Quinn</u>

The kiss is everything I've been trying to deny—everything I've been running from since the moment he stepped into my sightline. I shouldn't want this. I shouldn't want him. But god, I do.

Maybe it's exhaustion. Maybe it's the sheer weight of pretending to be so many versions of myself that I've forgotten which one gets to want freely. Or maybe it's that with him, I don't have to hold any of them up at all.

I don't know, and I don't care. All I can think about is the heat of his palms under my sweater, the rough drag of his fingers over my skin, the way his thumb brushes the underside of my breast before his hand closes fully—possessive, reverent, hungry. His tongue tangles with mine, a slow, relentless rhythm that turns into a challenge, a claiming. Every nip, every catch of teeth pushes me closer to some invisible edge. It's too much—but not nearly enough.

He tightens his grip, body pressing me hard against the wall. The cabin shudders around us, dust raining from the rafters. I claw at his shirt, the buttons scattering like dropped coins, the sound small and shocking in the quiet. He growls low in his throat—a sound that vibrates through his chest and straight into mine.

My clothes follow, impatiently torn from me. The sweater. The shirt. Cool air licks at my skin, chased immediately by the heat of his mouth. He dips his head, tugging my bra down just far enough to bare me. His tongue circles my nipple once, slow enough to make me tremble, then again, harder, until my back arches against the wall.

I thread my fingers into his hair, gripping tight when he sucks harder, drawing a cry from somewhere deep in me. He shifts, one hand splayed against my ribs, the other tracing down,

down—mapping skin like he's been waiting for this, memorizing it. My breath breaks apart, uneven, and I realize I've stopped thinking entirely.

All that's left is sensation. Heat. Want. The low sound of his name against my throat.

His head dips lower, across my taut stomach, kisses trailing like fire in his wake. His fingers find the buttons on my jeans, and in seconds I'm standing bare before him. He looks up at me, eyes stormy with something dangerous.

"If you tell me to stop, it'll kill me," he says, voice rough. "But I'll stop—and walk away—before we do something you'll regret."

My head spins with sheer absurdity. "Shut the fuck up," I growl. "I want this—*you*—all of it. No more fucking pretending."

He doesn't wait. He spreads my thighs gently, hoisting a leg over his shoulder like he's been waiting for this exact moment. His breath is hot against my pussy, and I shiver. He looks up at me one last time before latching onto my clit, sucking and licking with a reverent sort of passion. He's merciless, tongue flicking faster with every second, each stroke featherlight.

I detonate faster than I ever have before. Legs quaking, body spasming, cries ringing into the air shamelessly. I buck and writhe, clinging to his shoulders so hard I know my nails have left marks. He takes it all, still flicking his tongue, forcing me to ride out every last wave of pleasure.

I come down, hazy, and he lifts me up like I weigh nothing, moving us down the hall and into a bedroom.

He lays me down on the bed like I'm the most precious thing he's ever seen, and something in me stirs at that. I don't want to put a name to it, so I let it linger in the air between us—an unspoken feeling neither of us seem willing to name.

Rakes covers me with his body, hands easily finding the same rhythm. Every kiss, every touch, is a prayer whispered into my skin. His fingers slip between my legs again, building me back up to that familiar high. "I need—" He pushes a finger inside, then two, curling them deliciously, spreading my inner walls in a slow, sinful massage that has my toes curling.

"More," I whisper, my voice raspy and coated with desire.

He growls, low and rough, sliding down again—his free hand cupping my breasts, gliding down across my stomach—until his lips find the sensitive bundle of nerves once more, latching on with careful precision.

I cry out, the sensation building to that familiar crescendo. Then, right before I come again, he pulls away.

"Damn it!" I snarl, only to gasp when he grabs me and yanks me toward him, shoving his pants down in one swift motion.

He's inside me with one easy, devastating stroke.

"God," he hisses, voice breaking against the rhythm. "You feel exactly like I thought you would."

"Shut up," I sigh, breath catching. "You're ruining it."

He laughs—a rough, low sound—and punishes me with deeper strokes, a faster pace, until we're nothing but ragged breaths and sweat-slick skin, moving like the world could end if we stop.

I'm burning up—heat building in my core, pleasure blinding behind my eyes. His fingers roam along my body, caressing, teasing, mapping my skin like he's memorizing every inch.

It's everything. Too much, and yet somehow not enough.

His fingers find my clit again, circling fast and feather-light, the rhythm so deep, so relentless, that I cry out—my release tearing through me with a scream so loud I'm sure the whole town of Driftwood could hear us even though we're miles away.

He isn't far behind. His body tenses, a shudder running through him, and his release follows with a groan that carries my name. Not Jane—*Quinn*.

That name hums in my veins long after the air stills, a reminder of who I am beneath every mask and lie. The sound of it—his voice tangled with mine, our breathing uneven—pulls something loose inside me that I didn't know was still capable of feeling.

He's still above me, body heavy and warm, heartbeat hammering in time with my own. The scent of sweat, salt, and pine clings to the air, a familiar yet heady aroma that only adds to the feelings swirling around inside me. His hand drifts to my face, thumb brushing my jaw, and it's so gentle it almost hurts.

For a moment, there's no running. No secrets. No ghosts waiting in the cracks between our words. Just this. Just him and me. Just the fragile illusion that we've outrun the world long enough to feel human again.

I could fall asleep like this—his chest rising beneath my cheek, the ocean faint beyond the walls, the sound of the wind combing through the trees. But the thought of rest feels dangerous. The thought of wanting more feels worse.

He murmurs my name again, softer this time, like a vow. "Quinn."

I swallow, the sound catching. "Don't say it like that."

"Like what?"

"Like it means something—*everything*."

His gaze meets mine, unreadable in the half-light. "It already does."

I don't have an answer for that. I never do when he stops sounding like the detective and starts sounding like the man underneath. So instead, I close my eyes, press a kiss to his shoulder, and let the silence between us be the only truth I can handle.

The world will find us again soon enough. For now, I let it stay quiet.

CHAPTER 34

Rakes

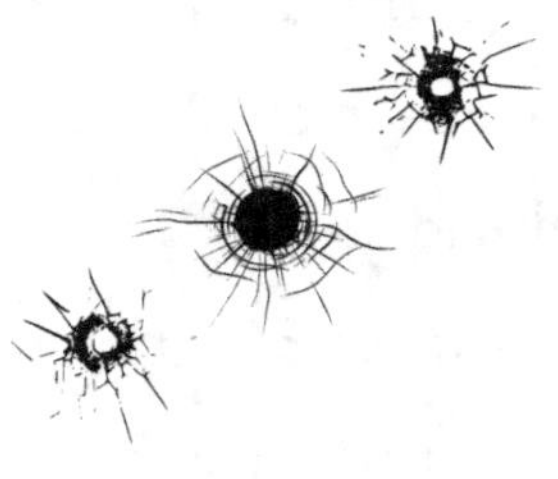

Morning comes slow through the trees. Pale gold light seeps between the blinds, sketching lines across the cabin's floorboards. The air smells like pine and ash — the faint trace of last night's fire still lingering, though we never really burned anything down except the distance between us.

I'm awake before she is. Have been for a while. My body forgot what real sleep feels like somewhere between Boston and Driftwood, and last night didn't help. There's an ache in my shoulders that isn't from the bed, and my thoughts run too loud to rest anyway.

Quinn's curled on her side, back to me, hair spilling across the pillow in dark waves. She looks nothing like the woman who tore into me hours ago — fierce, clawed, demanding. There's a peace here, fragile and fleeting, like something that knows it isn't meant to last. I trace the edge of it in silence, memorizing it for when things start to fall apart again.

When I finally move, it's slow. Carefully—like I'm afraid to disturb the silence. Coffee first. Reality second. I find the tin of grounds in a cabinet that's been empty for years and an old enamel percolator that might've belonged to whoever abandoned this place. It sputters and hisses like it resents being woken.

By the time she stirs, the smell has filled the cabin.

"You're... *loud*," she mutters into the pillow, voice thick with sleep.

"You're welcome," I answer, pouring two cups into mismatched mugs.

She sits up, hair a mess, sweater slipping off one shoulder. "What's this? A domestic fantasy?"

"Something like that." I hand her a mug and take the seat opposite her at the edge of the bed. "Only difference is, I didn't burn the toast."

A small smile ghosts her lips, gone before I can fully catch it. She blows on the coffee, watching the steam rise like she's trying to read something in it. "I didn't expect you to make coffee."

"I didn't expect you to sleep so soundly," I retort, snorting into my cup.

Her gaze lifts, sharp and questioning. "And did I?"

"Enough to make me jealous."

That earns me a snort. "You really don't stop, do you?"

"Not when I've got something worth watching."

That does it — the blush, faint but there, a small flare of color breaking through the exhaustion. She takes a sip to hide it, and the sight of it hits me harder than it should. I didn't plan for softness. I didn't plan for this to feel anything like peace.

But peace doesn't last long with us. It never does.

When she finally sets the mug down, she glances toward the door. "We can't stay here."

"I know."

"They'll come looking."

"Which is why we move quietly," I tell her, pulling my jacket from the chair. "There's a place a few miles out — diner with decent breakfast and a back road that won't show up on the grid. We'll stop there. Figure out what comes next."

She watches me for a long moment, like she's deciding whether to trust me again or call me a fool. "You really think *pancakes* are going to fix this?"

"No," I say, buttoning my shirt. "But it's a start."

***

The road out is narrow, lined with cedar and moss. The world looks cleaner here — no cameras, no whispers, no Driftwood gossip curdled into poison. Just trees, light, and the hum of the engine beneath us.

Quinn rides silent beside me, staring out the window. The morning sun cuts through the glass, painting her profile in gold. She doesn't look like a woman running for her life. She looks like someone remembering what it was like to live.

I want to tell her that, but I don't. I keep my eyes on the road and pretend that's enough.

We don't talk until the diner comes into view — a small roadside place with a rusted sign that reads *Millie's Breakfast & Lunch,* half the bulbs burned out. The parking lot's gravel, the kind that crunches loud enough to announce you. There are only two cars here, maybe three if you count the rusted pickup out back.

Inside, it's all linoleum and sun-faded booths. A waitress with silver hair and a name tag that says *June* greets us with a smile that feels like it's been practiced for forty years.

"Anywhere you like," she says.

We take a booth near the back, far from the windows. The smell of bacon and coffee clings to everything. Quinn slides into her seat with quiet grace, but I can see the tension still coiled under her skin. Every movement in the room pulls her eyes. Every door creak makes her flinch, just enough for me to notice.

June brings menus we won't read and pours coffee we don't really need. When she leaves, I finally say what's been chewing at me since the sun came up.

"I've been thinking about last night," I say.

Her gaze lifts, wary but steady. "About what?"

"About how fast it went sideways." I pause. "About how I didn't give you enough room to decide if you were ready for that."

She studies my face, searching for the angle. "That's not like you."

"No," I admit. "And I don't like that it wasn't."

The silence stretches—not uncomfortable, just charged.

"You didn't hesitate," I add more quietly. "You read the room. You listened to my concerns. You moved when it mattered. That tells me something."

"About me?" she asks.

"About *us*," I say, before I can stop myself. Then I correct it. "About how this works when we're not pretending it's just procedure. How this works when it's two of us calling the shots. I should've taken what you wanted into consideration."

"Maybe that's why we work so well together," she says, shrugging like she's feigning indifference but I know better. "You're making better choices than me under the pressure. You watch out for all the variables, even the ones I'm too blind to see. I'm... *too* close to it. I knew it the minute you stopped me from making a reckless decision at Belladonna's... I just didn't want to admit it."

I suck in a sharp breath. Her words stick in my head like a splinter. I want to tell her this isn't supposed to work — not like this, not when every move puts us closer to the edge. I want to tell her that I've made so many reckless decisions already when it comes to her. I'm no saint. Definitely not perfect. But the way she's looking at me — like she already knows, like she's choosing to stay *anyway* — kills the argument before it starts.

Breakfast comes—French toast for her, eggs and bacon for me. The plates steam between us, syrup glinting in the light. She cuts the toast into small, deliberate bites, dragging each through the syrup like she's testing whether she still remembers how to enjoy something simple.

Normal food for people who live normal lives.

For a few minutes, we pretend that's what we are. Two strangers sharing breakfast in a nowhere town, not a detective and a woman with too many names. Not fugitives waiting for the world to catch up. Just a man watching a woman lick sugar from her thumb, trying not to think about how long it's been since anything tasted this human.

"Tell me something true," she says suddenly.

I blink. "What?"

"You've been staring at your coffee for ten minutes. So tell me something true. Anything."

I think about it. There's too much truth and not enough of it that doesn't hurt. "When I was a kid, I used to think if you looked at the ocean long enough, it'd start to talk back."

"Did it?"

"Not in words."

She smiles, faintly. "That's almost poetic, Detective."

"Don't tell anyone, I have a reputation to uphold."

The silence that follows isn't sharp this time. It's warm. Comfortable. Then I catch the reflection of something in the window — a flash of light where there shouldn't be one. Chrome, or metal. Moving fast past the lot.

My gut tightens.

"Stay here," I say, already sliding out of the booth.

"Rakes—"

But I'm already moving.

Outside, the cold hits hard and clean, too bright for what waits in the gravel. My car sits wrong—nose dipped, stance uneven. I don't need to get close to know.

I do anyway.

Two front tires, sliced clean through. Not punctured. *Opened*. Cleanly cut, the rubber curling back like skin.

Message received, loud and clear.

Behind me, the door creaks. Quinn steps onto the stoop, eyes already moving, already cataloging. "That bad?"

"Worse," I say. "Stay there."

She doesn't argue. She shifts instead—subtle, controlled—using the glass and reflections to sweep the lot. I crouch, fingers tracing the edge of one cut. The blade was sharp. The hand steady. Whoever did this wanted us delayed, stranded, exposed.

I straighten and meet her gaze. She already knows.

Inside, we regroup without ceremony. Quinn claims our booth near the wall again, back protected, sightlines clean. I pull my phone, already scrolling.

"We're not driving anywhere," I say. "I'll call it in, and get us towed to a private shop. Cash only."

She nods once. "And a ride?"

"I know a guy who owes me a favor and doesn't ask questions."

"Good." She glances toward the lot. "Because we're not going to be sitting ducks out there."

The waitress refills our cups without comment. Normalcy as camouflage.

I make the call. Keep it short. When I hang up, Quinn's watching the reflection in the window again.

"Black sedan," she says quietly. "Same position. Engine on."

"They want to see how we react," I wager.

"They want to see if we *panic*," she argues.

I meet her eyes. "Then we don't."

"No," she agrees. "We finish our coffee. We let them think this slowed us down."

"And when the tow shows?" I ask.

"We leave separately." Her mouth curves, sharp and knowing. "You with your guy. Me on foot. I loop back."

"Not alone," I say, shaking my head.

She doesn't bristle—just considers. "Parallel routes, then? Same destination."

I nod. It's as close to compromise as either of us gets.

The truck arrives fifteen minutes later, loud and inconvenient. Heads turn. The sedan stays put.

Quinn rises first, pulling on her jacket, calm as a woman heading back to work instead of walking into a surveillance net. As she passes me, her fingers brush my wrist—brief, deliberate. The sensation sends a shiver of anticipation crawling down my spine.

"Don't be obvious," she murmurs.

"Never am."

Outside, the tow hooks up my car while I watch the sedan watch us. Quinn disappears down the sidewalk without a glance back.

They wanted us stuck. Instead, we've just changed the board.

And whoever's sitting in that sedan?

They're about to realize we don't wait very well.

CHAPTER 35

Quinn

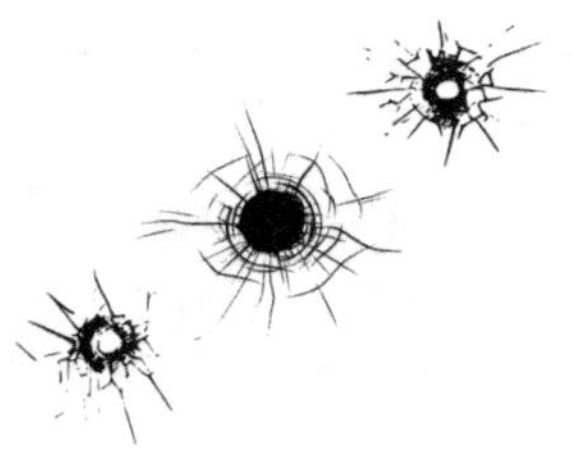

We don't stay separated long.

It isn't fear that pulls us back together—it's timing. The kind you learn to trust when plans are liabilities and instinct is the only thing that hasn't failed you yet. I cut through the back end of the neighboring town, keep to streets that smell like salt and diesel instead of tourists, and wait where the highway bends toward the cliffs. No landmarks. No witnesses. Just a stretch of road that doesn't care who passes through it.

Rakes rolls in five minutes later, different car, same posture. He doesn't ask where I've been. I don't ask what he saw. I slide into the passenger seat, and he pulls out without a word.

Whatever we agreed to back there—space, distance, separate angles—lasts exactly as long as it takes for the road to narrow and the ocean to reappear.

By the time we reach the coast road, the sky has collapsed into storm light. Thick clouds roll over the water, turning everything silver and bruised. The cliffs rise sharp on one side, waves gnash below on the other. I keep my eyes on the horizon, even though every instinct in me screams to look back.

Rakes drives in silence, fingers drumming the steering wheel, jaw locked tight. He hasn't said it, but I know the thought clawing through him: we can't stay gone forever. Driftwood doesn't let go that easily.

"Back to Driftwood," he says finally, voice rough from too much quiet.

I nod. "Time to stop running."

He glances at me. "You sure?"

"No," I admit. "But hidings' a language I'm tired of speaking."

That earns me a small, crooked smile—the kind that flashes and fades before it can mean too much.

It's gone by the time we reach the edge of town. He's already taking the left toward his contact, and I take the right toward the lie I still call home.

The sea air thickens the closer I get to my house. Salt clings to the railings, the stone steps slick from mist. My Victorian sits hunched on the cliff like a sentinel — white trim weathered to gray, a widow's walk curling above the second story. The waves pound somewhere below, an endless argument between tide and rock.

Inside, the air smells of lavender polish and damp wood. I lock the door behind me out of habit. My bag lands on the hall table with a soft thud. The whole house exhales.

It's strange, coming back after a few days away. The walls hold sound differently. The floorboards seem to remember footsteps that aren't mine. I stand for a long time, listening. Only the ocean answers.

Upstairs, I peel off my jacket and wash the road from my hands. My reflection in the mirror looks hollow-eyed, hair wind-tossed. Not Jane. Not even Quinn. Something in between.

I light a candle on the vanity — the one with wax already hardened around its base — and the scent of salt and smoke curls upward. The sound of the waves slides in through the cracked window, a lullaby older than the town itself.

Normal, I tell myself. You're home.

But normal doesn't hold. Not anymore.

***

By ten, the house has gone still. I leave the downstairs lamp on, the way I always do when Rakes is somewhere in town chasing ghosts. I pour tea instead of bourbon, though my hands ache for the burn. The cup warms my fingers, and for a brief second, I let myself believe the lie that this is safety.

The first sound is soft — a click from the back porch.

The sound of a handle being turned. I freeze, cup halfway to my mouth. Another sound follows shortly after. The metallic rasp of something sliding against the lock, careful, patient.

My pulse hammers in my chest. I move to the kitchen, barefoot, the tile biting cold against my soles. The porch light outside glows dim through the curtains, just enough to paint the silhouette of the door.

Then—the sharp pop of splitting wood, and the door swings open with a groan.

I grab the Glock from the drawer under the sink. The cup shatters on the floor, hot tea searing across my foot, but I barely feel it. I kill the lamp, plunging the house into shadow.

Bootsteps cross the threshold. Not rushed. Measured. Confident in the chase. And from the sounds of it... *One* man.

He pauses in the dark, head turning like he can smell me. I can hear his breath, calm and even, the kind you only learn in training. This isn't a drifter. This is a fucking *professional*.

The floorboards creak again — closer now. I back into the parlor, breath tight, gun raised. The only light comes from the candle flickering up-stairs, throwing a thin line down the stairwell.

It catches his mask — black, smooth, featureless — for half a heartbeat before he moves.

I fire on instinct. The shot tears through the air, splinters the banister. He drops, rolls, comes up low. A knife flashes in his hand.

He lunges toward me, and I dive sideways, shoulder crashing into the edge of the sofa. His blade carves the air where I was standing. The sound of steel cutting fabric. I fire again—missing a second time. He's fast, controlled as hell.

He slams into me, and we hit the floor hard. The Glock skids out of reach, clattering beneath the table. I twist, knee driving toward his stomach. He blocks, catches my arm, and tries to pin me. His strength is in the stillness—every move efficient, brutal.

"Why me?" I rasp, breath scraping my throat.

He doesn't answer. He doesn't need to. The knife lifts, the gleam of the blade catching the candlelight.

Then—headlights flare through the front windows. Tires screech. Doors slam.

He hesitates for just a second, and it's all I need.

I drive my palm into his chin, shove him backward, scramble for the poker by the fireplace. He recovers fast, slashing the air between us. I swing wide, and he ducks under, the poker slamming into the doorframe instead. Wood splinters from the hit, sparks leaping from the fire.

The front door bursts open, and my heart drops to my stomach. "Quinn!" Malcolm's voice cuts through the chaos, deep and sharp.

The intruder twists toward it. I swing again—connecting this time with a hard thunk. The poker cracks across his shoulder with a sound like breaking bone. He roars, stumbles, and Rakes is already there, moving fast, a gun up, stance steady.

"Down!" Rakes shouts.

I drop, heart thumping, adrenaline coursing through my body.

The gunshot is deafening in the small room. The masked man jerks sideways, glass exploding as the bullet punches through the window behind him. He crashes through it, a blur swallowed by the rain and darkness outside.

For a moment, all I can hear is the wind screaming through the shattered glass and Malcolm's rough breathing beside me.

He lowers the gun slowly, eyes sweeping the room. "You hurt?"

I shake my head, even though my shoulder screams and my palms are bleeding from the glass. "He didn't get that far."

He moves closer, eyes flicking over me, the mess, the splintered furniture, the scorch mark near the hearth. *"Son of a bitch,"* he swears. "He was armed?"

"Knife. Tactical blade from the look. Military training. He knew exactly what he was doing."

Rakes steps past me, crouching near the broken window. He looks out into the dark—nothing but rain and surf. Then he turns back, jaw tight. "He'll come back, Quinn. You can't stay here."

"Then I'll be ready for him next time," I argue. I refuse to comment on the second part.

He exhales, dragging a hand down his face in exasperation, then holsters his weapon and looks at me like he's trying to memorize every inch that isn't bleeding. "Let me see your hands."

"I'm fine."

He takes them anyway, his grip firm but careful. His thumb brushes a cut along my palm. His voice softens. "You could've been dead before I hit the porch."

"Could've," I admit. "But I wasn't."

He looks up at me, something fierce and desperate flaring behind the calm. "You're not staying here tonight."

"This is *my* house."

"It's a target, Quinn," he argues, narrowing his eyes at me.

"Then so am I."

"Not while I'm breathing," he growls.

The air between us is still humming with gunpowder and adrenaline. I meet his gaze, steady. "Then I guess you'd better keep breathing, Detective."

He exhales, a rough sound that could be a laugh if it didn't sound so frayed. "You don't make anything easy, do you?"

"Wasn't aware I was supposed to." I set the poker back against the mantle, shaking glass dust from my fingers. My pulse is still hammering, but I keep my movements steady. He doesn't need to see the tremor.

"Quinn—"

"I handled it."

"Barely."

"Still breathing, aren't I?" I turn, arms crossed. "You planning on lecturing me or helping me check the perimeter?"

He stares for a moment, something flickering behind his eyes — frustration, worry, the same thing that's been simmering between us for weeks. Then he swears under his breath and nods. "Grab a light. I'll take the west side."

"Together," I say. "We do it together."

***

The rain starts again as we step outside, fine and cold, slicking my hair to my temples. The flashlight beam cuts through the dark, catching the edges of fresh footprints in the mud. Rakes crouches, hand braced on the porch rail.

"Same tread as the print from the shop," he murmurs. "Deep stride. Taller than me."

"Strong," I add. "But favoring the right side. You clipped him good."

His head tilts up. "You saw that?"

"I see everything."

That earns me a brief look — equal parts respect and warning. He straightens, scanning the shadows. "Tracks head toward the cliffs. Tide will wash them out by morning."

"So he knew the ground," I say.

"Or he's been here before," he counters, shooting me a look that screams *yes*.

The wind picks up, carrying salt and rain and the faint copper tang of gunfire. We finish the sweep in silence, moving like two people who've already accepted they're being backed into a corner. Every creak, every shift of the trees feels amplified.

Back inside, I start to reach for a broom. Rakes takes it from my hand before I can protest.

"Sit," he says.

"I'm not fragile."

"Didn't say you were." He nods toward the couch. "But you're bleeding."

I glance down — tiny glass cuts stippled along my forearm, the thin edge of red gleaming under the light. "I'll live."

"Humor me."

I glare but sink onto the couch anyway, letting him sweep the glass and wedge a chair beneath the door handle. It's a poor lock, but it'll do. For now.

When he finally looks up, the storm light hits his face just right — the hard lines softened by exhaustion, a streak of rain still tracing his jaw. His shirt clings to his shoulders. He looks wrecked. Alive. Human.

"You should get some rest," he says quietly. "I'll take first watch."

I shake my head. "You need sleep more than I do."

"Not happening."

"Then don't pretend I'm the only one who needs a bed."

His mouth twitches. "My house?"

"Too far." The words are out before I can stop them. "Stay here."

We stand there in the half-light, the sound of the sea filling the silence between us. Then he grunts, like it pained him to agree, and nods once. Then flicks off the lamp, and follows me upstairs.

The candle on the vanity has burned down to its last inch, its flame trembling across the walls like a pulse that refuses to quit. I sit on the edge of the bed, stripped down to a camisole, the smell of rain, smoke, and gunpowder still clinging to my skin. Rakes stands in the doorway, shirt plastered to him, hair dripping, holster still strapped across his chest.

"You don't have to—" I start, but my voice is thin.

"I know," he says quietly.

He crosses the room, the floorboards sighing under his weight. Without a word, he takes the first-aid kit from the dresser, kneels in front of me, and uncaps the antiseptic. The sting hits sharp when the cloth meets my arm. I hiss through my teeth.

"Easy," he murmurs. "I'm just getting started."

His hands are steady, work-worn and gentle, tracing the small cuts along my wrist and forearm. He wipes each one clean, tapes gauze where the blood still seeps, his touch careful in a way that feels almost reverent. I don't look at him while he works. I can't. The nearness feels too raw, too *human*.

When he finishes, he leans back on his heels, studying his work with a frown that's half worry, half pride. "You'll bruise," he says.

"I've had worse."

"I know," he answers, soft again. His eyes lift, meeting mine. "Doesn't mean I have to like it."

Something tightens in my chest. Before I can reply, he reaches up and brushes a damp strand of hair away from my face. The movement is small. Thoughtless. It undoes me anyway.

He hesitates, a breath hanging between us — then kisses me. Soft. Barely there. The kind of kiss that asks permission while pretending it doesn't need to. I could stop it. I don't.

When it ends, neither of us speaks. He presses one last kiss to my bandaged wrist, stands, and strips off his holster, laying it beside the bed. The mattress dips as he slides in next to me, warmth radiating through the thin space that separates us.

For a long while, we just listen — to the wind, to the rain, to the ocean's slow breathing beneath the cliffs.

I tell myself it's nothing. Just exhaustion. A human response to fear and adrenaline. His arm brushing mine means comfort, not confession. The kiss was gratitude, not promise.

I repeat those lies until they almost sound true.

But when his hand finds mine beneath the sheets, fingers lacing instinctively, the truth hums louder than the storm outside.

It *means* something.

And I fall asleep still trying to pretend it doesn't.

Chapter 36

Rakes

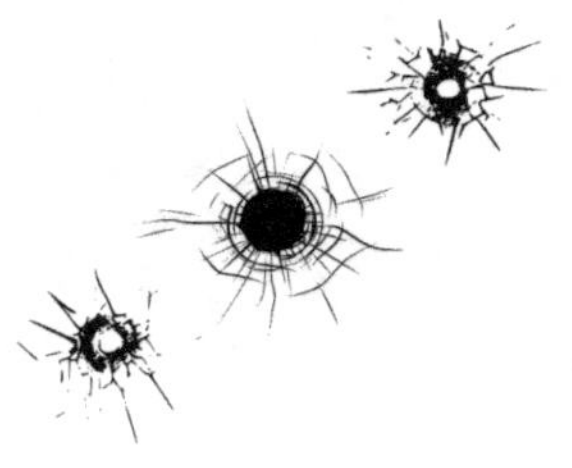

The house creaks as if it's waking too, timber shifting under the push of wind off the water. Light leaks in through the curtains — the color of old bone, not warmth. Driftwood looks harmless again from up here, all fog and salt air and gulls crying over the cliffs, but the illusion doesn't hold long. It never does anymore.

Quinn's still asleep beside me. Her hair's a dark sprawl across the pillow, her arm bent toward where I'd been lying before I got up. Her skin glows faint in the gray light, soft against the bruises that map her shoulder. I watch her breathe — steady, measured, alive — and tell myself that's enough for now.

When she stirs, she doesn't startle. She just blinks once, then groans. "You're *watching* me... Why the fuck are you watching me? That's creepy."

"Making sure you're still breathing," I say.

"Morbid habit, Detective."

"Occupational hazard," I argue, even though a smile tugs at the corners of my mouth.

Her mouth curves, tired but genuine. "Coffee?"

"I'll make it," I say, rising out of bed before she can object. I listen to Quinn's soft chuckling, grinning all the way downstairs.

In the kitchen, the morning light feels too clean for the night we had. The coffee maker hisses, old and temperamental, the smell of grounds cutting through the ghosts that still hang in the air. Quinn appears a few minutes later, bare feet silent on the tile, sweater hanging off one shoulder. She takes a mug from my hand without looking at me.

For a moment, we just stand there, sipping in silence. The kind of quiet that only happens after adrenaline drains and you realize what's left underneath.

"Did you sleep well?" I ask.

She nods once. "Enough to remember what it feels like."

"That's something."

She leans against the counter, studying the chipped mug in her hand. "This shouldn't feel normal. This *thing*... building between us."

"It's not," I say, knowing damn good and well it does.

"Then stop looking at me like it is."

I don't answer. I can't. There's a small bruise under her jaw, a shadow of the night before, and my fingers twitch with the urge to trace it.

Instead, I set my cup down and cross to the front window. The view over the street is pale and quiet. No traffic. No pedestrians. But the air feels wrong — like someone's been standing out there too long, breathing the same patch of wind.

Quinn comes up beside me, mug cradled in both hands. "What is it?"

"Not sure," I say finally, scanning the street again.

"You always say that right before you decide you are."

"Stay here," I tell her, already moving for the door. Though, I know she won't.

"Not a chance," she says, confirming my suspicions. I have to fight to hold in the laughter that begs to escape.

Outside, Driftwood looks like a painting left out in the rain. The air tastes like rust and salt, and the wind cuts colder than it should for morning. The street is too quiet—no gulls, no foot traffic, no engine hum—just the distant crash of the tide below the cliffs.

The car sits where I left it under the maple, but there's a sheen on the windshield that isn't dew. I move closer. Fingerprints. A perfect half-moon smudge where someone leaned in to look. Not kids, not curiosity—too perfect to be a coincidence.

"Rakes?" Quinn's voice behind me.

I don't turn, eyes still glued to the handprint. "Someone's been here."

She joins me, squinting through the glass. "Inside the vehicle?"

"No sign of a break." I step back, scanning the street. "But they wanted us to know they were close enough to try."

Her eyes sweep the neighborhood—the quiet porches, the half-drawn curtains, the way a single black sedan idles two houses down. Not moving. Not hiding. Watching. "He's getting way too comfortable," she says.

"Yeah."

"Then we move first."

I nod once. "Offense is cleaner than defense."

A muscle jumps in her jaw, not fear, but calculation. "You still have a contact?"

"Marrow," I confirm. "Ex-Bureau. He's seen Orion's ledgers from the inside out."

"Then let's find him." There's no hesitation in her voice, just decision—sharp, final. She's past the point of running, and so am I.

"Alright," I say, already scanning the horizon. "But we keep it quiet. No predictable routes. If they're watching, we make it a blur."

Her mouth tilts, faint and defiant. "Then let's give them something worth losing sight of."

***

The drive inland feels longer than it should. The roads between Driftwood and the next town twist through fog and forest, cliffs rising and falling on either side. Every turn of the tires sounds too loud, every crow overhead too knowing.

Quinn sits beside me, hair pulled back, gaze steady on the road ahead. The silence between us isn't uneasy—it's focus, wired tight enough to snap.

Finally, I glance at her. "Who do you think's *really* running this?"

She doesn't answer right away. The highway opens into a stretch of wet asphalt and static hums low through the radio, filling the space where trust is supposed to live.

"Red Haven's the mask," she says at last. "It's too polished, too public. A front built to make Orion look like a rumor instead of a system. They handle the shipments, the manifests, the paper trail—but the money, the muscle, the orders? That's probably Orion."

"Red Haven moves the product," I say, thinking aloud. "Orion moves the people."

"Exactly. And when one gets burned, the other sheds the skin and starts again under a new name."

I glance over. "You sound certain."

"I've seen it before," she says quietly. "You don't build something that clean without dirty hands guiding it."

There's no tremor in her voice, just precision—a kind of deadly calm honed by too many close calls. I don't push, she'll talk when she's ready. The road dips, the fog thinning enough to reveal the faint shape of Port Cormac ahead—a dock town long past its prime. It still smells like fish, oil, and lies.

Marrow lives in the kind of building you'd only find if you already knew where it was—back alley, no number, door marked by a single red chalk line.

He's waiting for us when we knock — thick set, gray at the temples, a pistol lying casual beside his coffee mug like it's part of the crockery. The place smells of solder and old tobacco, monitors stacked like windows into other people's mistakes.

Marrow squints at me as he wipes his hands on a rag. "Jesus. They said you'd been hung out to dry."

"Nope." I step inside, peel off my wet jacket. "They suspended me. Same difference, in their book."

He grins, not quite reaching his eyes. "And who's the woman?"

Quinn's reply is a blade. "The one who keeps him from getting himself killed."

Marrow laughs once, low and genuine. "Alright then. Come in." He clears a space on the workbench with a sweep of his arm and brings the main rig to life. Wires hum. Drives spin like tiny constellations.

"So what's the problem this time, Rakes?" he says, sliding a mug toward me.

"Orion," I say. "Red Haven Foods. I need a link. Something that ties the front to the patron."

Marrow whistles, the sound half admiration, half warning. "That's... *ambitious*."

He starts pulling up shells and corporate scaffolding, ghost accounts and distributor names that exist on paper and nowhere else. Quinn leans over his shoulder, pointing, directing — every motion exact She's not pretending, she's fully in her element.

"Watch the timestamps," she says. "Those transfers — way too neat. Two domestic legs, one offshore. Triangular routing. That's their signature."

Marrow's fingers fly. "You know your ghosts," he says, looking at her in a way that asks whether she means it.

"I built parts of that rail once," she says flatly. "Before I walked."

He goes still for a beat, then explodes. "And you're still fucking *breathing*?!"

"Mostly," she replies.

He swears, turning his attention back to the monitor. Lines of code and spreadsheets rearrange until Marrow freezes, taps the screen and spins it to face us. The ledger bloom on the monitor shows charity routing, donor IDs, then — the approving signature? None other than Thatcher fucking Greeves.

"Found your smoking gun," he says. "Red Haven's parent has been channeling Orion cash through a nonprofit in the harbor district. Someone signed off on the transfers."

I feel the room narrow. "Thatcher Greeves," I say. "He's managing their cover."

Marrow rubs his chin, eyes tired. "So he's the accountant in the suit. Either greedy, ambitious — or he knows where his bread is buttered." He looks at both of us. "You want advice? Don't try to outmaneuver Orion. Those folks don't play by the rules of the rest of us. They built the board."

Quinn folds her arms, steady and small. "We're *not* playing."

He studies her a long beat and then, with a slow nod, smiles that crooked smile of a man who's seen too much to be surprised. "Then you'd better come prepared. Weapons you can't trace, wheels that don't talk, a location you can lay low, and more patience than either of you probably own."

"Know anyone who can supply that?" I ask.

Marrow's smirk turns private. "Always do. But you didn't get it from me."

We leave an hour later with a duffel bag in the trunk and a folder thick with names, dates, and coordinates. The sun's dipping low, turning the water copper and the air colder. Quinn sits with the folder open on her lap, scanning the top page while I drive.

"Shipment leaves the harbor tomorrow night," she says. "Red Haven manifest. Offload scheduled for midnight. Thatcher supervising personally."

I grip the wheel tighter. "That's our opening."

She nods, jaw tight. "Orion's not sending him to manage logistics. He's there to clean up."

"Meaning?"

"Meaning they're done hiding the bodies."

The words hit harder than I want them to. I glance at her, but she's staring straight ahead, profile carved sharp against the window. The kind of calm that only exists right before something explodes.

"You still sure you want in on this?" I ask.

She looks at me then — really looks — and I know the answer before she says it.

"I'm *already* in it. Let's go before shit hits the fan."

***

Back at the Victorian, the house feels different. Charged. Like every sound is louder, every shadow heavier. The lamp light flickers against the walls, catching on the edges of the photos arranged with intention.

I spread the papers across the kitchen table. Quinn pours two glasses of bourbon, slides one toward me, and leans against the counter.

"We can't trust the precinct," I say.

She nods. "They're already compromised. Callahan's in deeper than he lets on. He has to be for you to be suspended."

"We always knew we would have to move alone."

She raises her glass. "To ghosts."

"To ghosts," I echo, and we drink.

The bourbon burns all the way down — clean, hard, grounding.

Outside, the sea's restless again. Somewhere down the hill, I swear I hear a car door close, soft and deliberate. When I look at Quinn, she's already glancing toward the window, eyes narrowing.

"They're watching again," she says.

"Good."

"Good?"

"If they're watching, it means they're worried."

She smiles then — not sweet, not safe, but something sharp and hungry. "Then let's give them a reason."

For a heartbeat, the air between us hums — that electric quiet before a storm decides where to land. No hesitation. No retreat left to run to.

The silence doesn't break; it hardens into purpose. She turns first, wordless, already moving through the room, pulling open drawers, checking locks, taking stock. I follow.

We pack methodically. Ammunition. Knives. Gloves. Cash. She moves like she's done it a hundred times before — and I realize it's because she *has*. I watch her, and for the first time, I understand that this isn't me protecting her. It's *us* hunting *them*.

When everything's ready, she turns to me, hair falling loose over one shoulder, eyes steady. "We hit the harbor tomorrow night. No more second guessing."

"Agreed."

"Then we get some rest."

For a moment, neither of us moves. The room smells like oil and salt and gunmetal, the air heavy with everything we're not saying. The adrenaline's fading, leaving something rawer behind. Something dangerously close to peace.

She closes the duffel, smooths the strap, and glances at me through the lamplight — that unreadable look she gets when she's halfway between armor and surrender. "You really think we'll find what we're looking for?"

"I think we'll find something," I say. "And whatever it is, we finish it."

A faint smile ghosts across her lips — not hope, not quite — and then she moves. She crosses the room, fingertips grazing my arm as she passes, the lightest touch and somehow enough to set my pulse racing. It feels like both a promise and a warning.

Upstairs, the wind picks up, rattling the window panes. The house creaks in rhythm with the tide, the sound of a place remembering how to breathe. I watch her climb the stairs until the last of her shadow slips out of sight.

The quiet that follows isn't empty. It's charged, waiting for what's to come.

I pour what's left of the bourbon and stare out at the dark sea. The waves break against the cliffs in long, slow heartbeats. Somewhere out there, a ship horn sounds — distant, hollow, like a signal meant for the dead.

Tomorrow, the ghosts will stop hiding.

And this time... *we* will be the ones waiting in the dark.

CHAPTER 37

Quinn

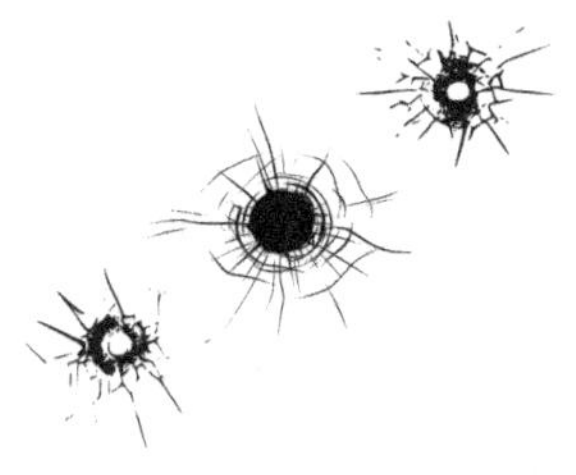

The docks look different at night. Quieter. Meaner, somehow. The tide's out, the harbor breathing in long, shallow gasps that smell of salt and metal. The warehouses crouch along the water like sleeping giants, each one ribbed with rust and shadow.

We park three blocks away. No headlights. No conversation. Just the ticking of the engine and the sound of Rakes loading the unmarked Glock with the same quiet concentration he uses to breathe.

"Marrow's intel said west end," he murmurs. "Unit forty-two."

"Marrow also said he hadn't been on Orion's radar in five years," I remind him, chambering a round. "He could've been fed false coordinates and never realized it."

"Yeah," he says, glancing at me with that half-smile that isn't humor. "We'll find out the hard way, I guess."

The wind comes in off the sea, cold enough to bite. We move along the service road, boots silent on wet asphalt, ducking between freight containers that gleam like whale backs under the distant floodlights.

Every sound feels amplified—the clang of a rope, the low moan of a ship against its moorings. My pulse keeps time with the tide.

The warehouse door stands cracked open. Not wide. Just enough.

Rakes raises two fingers. I nod, covering him as he pushes it open. The hinges groan, swallowed fast by the cavernous dark inside.

The smell hits first. Oil, damp wood, and something metallic underneath—something old and harsh. *Blood*.

He sweeps the flashlight across the floor. Dust motes drift through the beam, catching on chains bolted to the concrete, coils of wire, overturned chairs.

"This isn't storage," I whisper.

"No," he says. "It's something else."

A shape glints in the far corner—metal crates, stacked in uneven rows. He moves toward them, light steady, steps measured. I keep to his flank, gun drawn, every muscle wired tight.

He stops suddenly, flashlight cutting across a monitor setup—two screens still glowing faint blue in the dark. A looping feed plays. Not live, but recent enough.

Women.

Dirty. Shackled to walls, faces obscured by their hair. The camera pans, deliberate, lingering on their wrists, the bruises, the fear. My stomach turns.

"Oh, *God*," I breathe. "They're running a trafficking ring through here."

He doesn't answer. His jaw is locked, eyes fixed on the screen like it's holding him there.

A faint click echoes from behind us.

"Down!" He shoves me aside just as the first shot cracks. Metal screams. Sparks bloom off the crate beside me. I drop low, returning fire toward the shadows near the catwalk. More movement—boots on steel, voices shouting.

"Two on the mezzanine!" I yell.

"I've got 'em!"

He fires twice, controlled bursts, one target dropping with a shout, the other scattering into dark. I roll behind a pallet, bullets chewing into the concrete where my leg had been.

"They knew we were coming!"

"Yeah," he snarls, ducking beside me. "Marrow's intel was garbage. Or a trap."

I look up toward the flickering light, disbelief and exasperation flooding me. "You think he sold us out?"

He doesn't answer. Doesn't need to. The look on his face says everything.

The shooting pauses—just long enough for me to hear the low, rhythmic scrape of boots closing in. Three, maybe four left.

Rakes gestures, quick and sharp. I nod, sprinting to the opposite side, drawing fire. The noise explodes again, deafening in the enclosed space. I pop up, shoot, duck, move again.

One figure drops from the catwalk, landing hard. I catch him mid-motion, one clean shot center-mass. He folds, gun clattering.

The others hesitate—just a heartbeat—but it's all Rakes needs. He moves like a storm breaking, crossing open ground in three strides, tackling the next shooter into a stack of crates. They crash down together, the impact echoing through the warehouse.

The lights die, and we're plunged into total darkness.

I blink hard, useless. Sound becomes *everything*—grunts, shuffling, the sharp whine of a knife scraping the floor.

"Rakes!" I scream.

A shadow barrels toward me. I pivot, then fire. The muzzle flash lights up his mask for half a second before he drops. The smell of cordite mixes with blood and dust.

Silence, except for the sound of the ocean just beyond the walls.

"Malcolm?" I whisper, my nerves crackling like live wires.

"I'm here." His voice—hoarse, but close. I find him by the crates, his arm bleeding from a shallow cut, shirt ripped from the tussle.

"Let's move," he says. "They'll circle back with more."

We start toward the side exit, but the flicker of the monitors catches my eye again—the feed still looping, the women still staring at nothing. Something in me hardens.

"No," I say.

He turns. "Quinn—"

"They'll *wipe* it. Every file, every fucking trace. It will be like it *never* happened."

He drags a hand through his hair, scanning the room. "We don't have the time."

"We *make* time," I argue.

For a moment, we just look at each other through the dark, the glow of the screens painting his face in blue and shadow. Then he nods, resigned. "Make it count."

He rips the drives from the towers, wires snapping like tendons. I grab a rusted can of solvent from the nearby shelf, tipping it until the chemical reek fills the air. The floor glistens in the light. Rakes finds a road flare in his pack and lights it, the red flame guttering to life.

"Ready?" he says.

I meet his gaze. "Do it."

He tosses the flare.

The solvent catches instantly, racing in a bright, feral crawl along the concrete. Flames lick the chains, the crates, the walls—the ghosts of what was done here. The heat builds, fast and furious. Smoke rises, curling around us like the warehouse itself is trying to breathe.

We run.

Out the side door, down the dock. The wind off the harbor hits like knives. Behind us, the fire roars, spreading fast through the oil-soaked air. The explosion that follows is small but violent—enough to blow out the windows, enough to wake the sea birds.

Shattered glass rains down. My pulse pounds, threatening to break through my damn chest. Rakes shoves me forward, coughing through the smoke. "Go, go!"

We sprint for the car. By the time we reach it, flames are devouring the roofline, thick black smoke curling toward the stars.

He throws the gun into the back seat, bracing his hands on the roof, breath ragged. The orange glow paints him in broken light, blood and soot streaking together across his jaw.

"You think it'll be enough?" I ask.

He shakes his head, still staring at the inferno. "It's never enough. But it's a start."

The fire's reflection dances across his eyes—rage and something like grief intertwined. I swallow hard, chest tight.

"Then drive," he says.

I floor it, tires spinning on the slick asphalt as we tear down the service road. In the mirror, the warehouse collapses inward, a beast folding back into its own ashes.

Neither of us speaks. The only sound is the distant thunder of the waves and the low growl of the engine. The air inside the car smells like smoke and adrenaline and everything we can't say.

We don't stop until Driftwood's skyline appears—ghostly through the fog, familiar and foreign all at once.

The adrenaline keeps us upright until we're halfway into town. Then the shakes start. Mine first, then his. By the time we hit Driftwood's edge, neither of us says a word.

We clean up in silence at my house.

The water in the basin runs pink, then clear. His hands are steady even when mine aren't. He tapes my shoulder, I patch his arm. Small rituals in the aftermath of chaos.

When it's done, I pour two mugs of black coffee. He takes his with a nod, lowering himself into the chair across from me.

For a moment, it almost looks normal—two people shaking off a bad day. But the blood on the cuffs of his shirt, the bruise spreading along my ribs, the faint hum of my gun on the table—they're reminders of what we really are.

He finally breaks the silence. "You saw those feeds."

I nod. "Cells. Women." My voice feels scraped raw. "I can't believe Orion's running human cargo now, not just money."

He looks at me, eyes dark and distant. "They've been doing it for years. We just never had proof."

I swallow thickly, knowing he's probably right. "Now we do."

"Now we're on their radar," he says, turning his gaze to the window.

The words hang between us, heavier than the steam curling from our mugs. Outside, morning

edges into gray. Driftwood's waking up—fishermen heading to the pier, gulls screaming overhead. Life goes on like the night didn't just crack
open.

He leans back, rubbing his temple. "We can't
disappear again. People need to see us—alive,
calm, unbroken."

"So we go out."

He arches a brow. "Coffee date?"

"Breakfast," I correct, though the word feels
strange on my tongue.

He smirks faintly. "Sure. Breakfast."

***

We walk into town twenty minutes later,
cleaned up but still frayed around the edges. My
sweater hides the bruises; his jacket conceals the
bandage. The café on Main smells like cinnamon

and burnt espresso, the kind of scent that tries too hard to be comforting. People glance up when we enter—habit, not suspicion—but their stares feel longer than usual, like they can sense something just under the surface.

He orders two coffees, one black, one with cream, the way he always does, as if repetition itself might make the world normal again. I claim the corner booth facing the street, where I can see the reflection in the glass if anyone follows us.

When he slides into the seat across from me, there's a heartbeat where it almost feels like the kind of morning I had before everything went to hell.

"How's your arm?" I ask.

"Hurts less than it should." His voice is steady but frayed at the edges. "Yours?"

"Stings," I say. "Bruises are blooming."

He smirks faintly. "Purple suits you."

"Don't start," I mutter, but the corner of my mouth betrays me anyway.

The silence that follows isn't awkward. It's intentional—a mutual decision to pretend, just for a few minutes, that we're two normal people sharing caffeine instead of blood and secrets.

Then the TV behind the counter shifts from weather to breaking news.

A local anchor fills the screen, her smile a brittle mask. Behind her are flashing lights, smoke-streaked air, and the skeletal frame of a burning warehouse. Port authorities investigating possible arson at the Red Haven shipping site. No fatalities reported. The reporter's voice drones on about vandalism and "unconfirmed activity." No mention of cages. No mention of the women. Just another incident in a town that pretends it doesn't see what rots beneath its own boardwalk.

My pulse skitters, nerves swirling around in my stomach like scattered butterflies. "They're cleaning it already."

Rakes doesn't turn to look. "They'll make it vanish before dinner. Files, evidence, the bodies—gone. It's a good thing we took what we could."

The words settle like ash. I stir my coffee just to have something to do with my hands. The spoon clinks, rhythmic, fragile.

We finish the coffee without another word between us. What's left of the morning sun filters through the café's windows like a lie — too clean, too bright for what's waiting outside.

Rakes drops a few bills on the counter and gestures for the door. "Come on. We'll plan next steps at your house."

I don't argue. The adrenaline has faded, leaving only exhaustion and the dull ache of bruises beginning to bloom. The walk back to the house is quiet, each step heavy but measured, both of us tuned to the same invisible pulse.

Inside, the air feels close. Safe isn't a word that applies anymore, but the walls at least remember how to pretend. He tosses his jacket over the chair, holster still attached, and leans against the counter while I set the kettle on the stove. The smells of chamomile and lavender assault my senses. The perfect tea to help calm us down.

"We should get some rest. We've been going for hours," he says, voice low.

"Sleep," I correct softly. "Rest sounds optional."

He almost smiles, but it doesn't make it all the way there. "You first."

"Not a chance."

I pour two mugs anyway, handing him one. He takes it, eyes on mine instead of the rising steam. "We'll move again after dark. Figure out where the trail leads now that Red Haven's blown open."

"Fine," I say, curling into the couch. "But only after you get some sleep."

He nods once, sinks into the armchair across from me. For a few quiet minutes, it's almost peaceful. Then the silence breaks — a vibration, faint at first, then insistent.

His phone.

Rakes fishes it from his pocket, glances at the screen. "Connor," he mutters.

"From the precinct?"

"Yeah." His brows draw together. "He wouldn't call without reason."

He answers, putting the phone on speaker. "Connor, what's wrong?"

Static hums for a moment before a voice slips through, tight with adrenaline. "Rakes, I don't have long. You didn't hear this from me, you understand?"

Rakes straightens, every trace of fatigue gone. "Understood. What's happened?"

"It's *Elias*."

The air leaves the room. I watch his knuckles go white around the phone. "What about him?" He asks, jaw clenched.

"They just found him," Connor says, the words coming fast and low. "Construction lot off Route 6. Two bullet wounds. They're already trying to spin it, but you need to get down here now."

Rakes doesn't move, doesn't breathe. "How long ago?"

"Twenty minutes, maybe. Scene's not locked down yet. You didn't hear that from me."

"Copy," he says automatically.

"Rakes—" Connor hesitates, the kind of pause that means the truth is worse than the report. "Whoever did this wanted a message sent. Be *careful*."

The line clicks dead. For a heartbeat, the house seems to stop breathing with us. Then Rakes lowers the phone slowly, staring at nothing. "Elias," he says quietly. "He's *gone*."

Something cold drags its fingers down my spine. "Jesus."

Rakes runs a hand over his mouth, the motion sharp and restless. "They're still on scene."

I stand, already moving toward the door. "Then what are we waiting for?"

He catches my arm, not rough, but enough to make me look back. "You don't have to—"

"I do," I cut in. "They're attacking from every direction. You think I'm sitting this out?"

His jaw works, but he doesn't argue. "Alright," he says finally. "Grab your jacket. We move now."

The house is already quiet when we step outside. The kettle's been abandoned on the counter, cooling into silence, like it knows better than to follow us. Gray light presses in from every direction—low clouds, wet air, the smell of salt and rain clinging to the path as if the coast itself is watching us go.

We don't talk. There's nothing left to negotiate, nothing left to soften.

We get into the car. The doors shut. The engine turns over.

And that's it. No ceremony. No promises.

Just the road ahead—and the reckoning waiting at the end of it.

CHAPTER 38

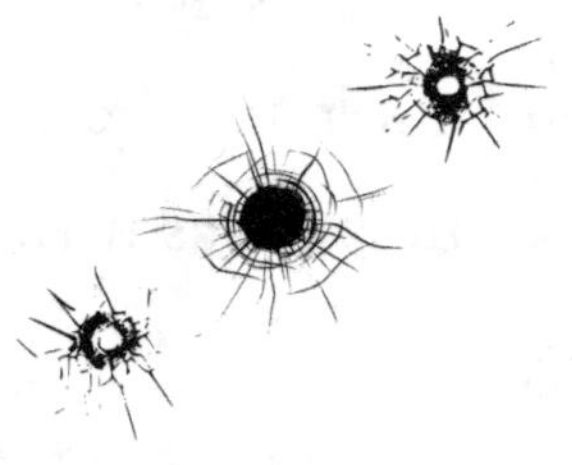

I get to the shoreline before my shoes realize the ground's moving beneath them. Flood-lights stomach the dark, carving the pier into hard planes of white. The wind off the ocean bites through my jacket like a hand with knives. Yellow tape hisses against the rail, and a dozen faces blur into a smear of coats and cameras and the blue flash of uniforms trying to hold order while the tide keeps forgetting it's supposed to be polite.

Quinn's hand is tight on my arm—iron instead of apology—and I take comfort from the pressure. We move up the gangway like men walking into a wound. Someone parts for us, someone else points. I don't want spectacle, but I smell diesel and antiseptic and the sudden, wrong scent I know too well. Copper and clean paper. *Blood.*

They push us back before I can make sense of the shapes. A rookie with trembling hands leans too close and then stumbles away when I look at him. "You can't—" Callahan starts, but I don't hear him. My eyes find Elias before anything else—the way bodies tell a story even when mouths are taped shut.

Elias is a heap at the waterline, half on the planks and half in the surf, like driftwood finally decided to stay. He's been laid out in a way that reads like a message. Arms splayed, coat flared, shoes still laced. The light catches on the shadows under his cheek, the back of his neck. I taste salt and cold and the sudden bright knife of grief that always hits me first now—hard enough I can't breathe for a second.

On his chest, pinned through the fabric with something crude and personal, is the calling card. Not really a card, but a fisherman's knife. Its blade sunk into the canvas of his jacket, the hilt turned so the handle faces up. Someone knew enough to plant it so only we would read it. The symbol carved into the wooden grip—small, precise, obscene with intent—makes my stomach drop. Elias knew it as a sigil, an emblem of a thing we never spoke about in reports. He knew what the mark meant because he'd walked too close to the furnace and learned how hot it burned.

"Jesus," one of the rookies murmurs behind the barrier. A whisper climbs the small crowd and blooms—what we do in public to make the dead small. "That's brutal."

It is. It's a declaration. It's the kind of calibrated cruelty that wants us to see it and tremble. Whoever did this wanted to make us all look at it and understand we'd been warned.

The cops are professional in the way people teach themselves to keep breathing: method, distance, gloves. But Callahan sees me again, and the air snaps tight with everything he's been holding back. He crosses the deck at a stiff angle, whole body a badge of authority about to be used as a cudgel.

"*Rakes*," he says, the name a hammer. "You're still suspended. Get the hell out before I haul you in myself."

For a second I think I can answer him with a list—a litany of injustices, of the way the world lets men hide under licenses and linen—but the words lodge like splinters. The sight of Elias on the pier takes out the rest of me. I step forward because something in me—stubborn, stupid, faithful—wants to touch the shoulder of a dead man and tell him I'm sorry. Callahan's hand snaps up, a block that's half legal threat and half hurt.

"Get back, Malcolm," he snaps. "You've been told once. Now go."

I taste something sour—anger, fear, the memory of all the times I've let the uniform do the talking. My hands open and close. For a second the world narrows to the space between Callahan and Elias and the knife and every stupid promise I made to myself.

If I had a badge in my pocket, I'd fling it. If I had reason, I'd argue. Instead I feel Quinn there—*solid and real*—and the instinct to punch the man who stood between me and the truth is almost strong enough to make me move.

Quinn steps into my path like a breaker between two storms and the town's history of easy violence. She presses her hand against my chest—hard, public—and it's not just to stop me. It's to say... *Not here. Not like this.*

Callahan's face is a map of compromise he refuses. "I'm telling you as your captain and your superior... *leave.* You're compromising the scene."

"You're compromising *Elias,*" I say cooly. The sound comes out dry and small. "He didn't get a chance to—"

"Enough." Callahan's voice is iron. He leans in, too close. "You heard me. Get out. Before I write a report that makes you disappear for good."

There's a look in his eyes I've seen before—fear dressed as edict—and for a moment something that might have been compassion flickers and dies. He says something about protocol and community trust and the way investigations proceed, but the words are machinery. He wants me gone, and he is making sure I understand the cost of not obeying.

We're forced off the gangway like a pair of trespassers. I stand at the edge of the crowd with

Quinn at my side and watch the men in suits and blue paint circle Elias like they're carving a story from him. The ocean hammers at the pilings beneath our feet, the salt air stings the back of my throat. We can't cross the tape. The tape is a cordoning of lives. All I can do is watch.

Elias's face doesn't look like anything that belongs entirely to death. It looks like a man who held too many keys and finally found out the doors they unlocked were all on the same chain. Blood beads in the grain of the pier; a tangle of tideweed curls into it. The fisherman's knife glints with malicious ceremony.

"Why him?" Quinn asks, voice low enough that the crowd dims out like a radio at the edge of town. Her hand tightens on mine. She sounds small and huge at the same time—a snarl folded into softness.

"Because he helped me," I say, and it's more than a sentence. It's a confession. Elias dug. He rifled through files and lies and shadow accounting. He unpicked a seam and found a nest of teeth. He taught me moving parts I didn't want to know. He paid with his life for his honesty.

A rookie nearby mutters something about brutality again, and a woman with a camera snaps another photograph—one more evidence that the system knows how to forget. A detective in a suit consoles a crying relative with practiced cruelty; a forensics tech bags a section of clothing with gentle, severe hands.

I kneel on the damp planks because staying upright is an affectation I don't need to maintain in front of Elias. The rope the first responders use to mark the body's perimeter is still frayed, still sensual with smell and meaning. I stare at the knife hilt where the symbol lives, and my chest tightens until I'm sure my ribs will grind.

"Elias," I murmur, his name like a useless prayer on my lips. "I'll make them pay for this. I don't care what it costs."

The words are small when they leave me, but the promise makes the air taste different. Quinn's fingers squeeze mine until I think she might break bone to make it real. The crowd hums with questions that won't be asked in the right order. Callahan, distant now, barks orders into a radio like he's trying to drown out his own conscience.

We're moved down the pier by hands whose gloves smell like bleach and who know nothing about loss. When I finally stand, the cold of the boards has sunk through my soles. The ocean keeps pulling, as if nothing at all has changed.

I keep the vow in my mouth like a coin. I will make them spend for this. Not for revenge's sake but because men who make messages out of bodies deserve to be unreadable next time. I will find who built this sigil into a threat and burn the ledger that names them.

Quinn leaves a hand on my shoulder before we go—brief, anchoring. We tuck the moment, private and hot, under the tape and the yellow lights and the questions. Someone in the crowd calls my name, but I don't answer. Callahan watches until we reach the lot, then turns away like the sight is something he'd rather forget.

The tide takes and takes. The pier smells of salt and iron and the small, arrogant cruelty of men who think a public killing will buy them quiet. It won't. Not if I have anything to say about it.

I stand there a long time, looking at where Elias is laid out like a lesson across the lot, and whisper to him again, softer this time, "I'll *burn* them for this." Then I add the only thing I can make honest: "*I swear it.*"

CHAPTER 39

Quinn

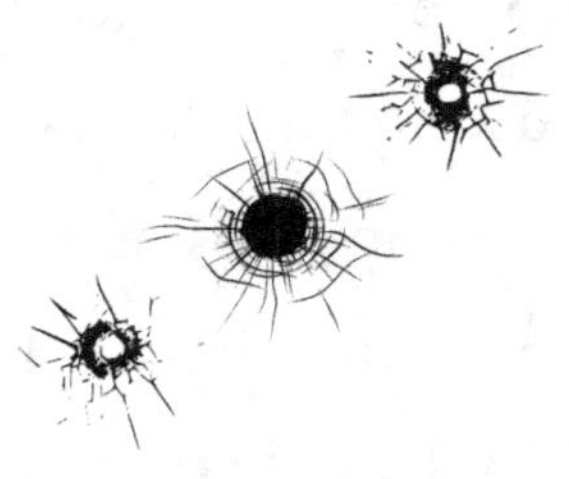

The house hasn't known silence like this since the night the storm rolled through. For two days, Rakes hasn't left. His jacket hangs by the door, his gun lives on the table beside the kettle, and the ghosts of Elias and Orion follows us from room to room. I make coffee. He fixes the loose hinge on the window. We pretend that counts as living.

Grief sits between us like a third presence—polite, watchful, refusing to leave first.

Every night he falls asleep in the armchair, and every morning I wake to find a blanket draped over me that I don't remember pulling close.

By the third morning, the quiet feels staged. Like manufactured peace. The air hums with something that wants to break.

I'm sorting through inbox trash—vendor invoices, newsletters, the endless debris of a life that once felt normal—when the new message lands. No sender name. No subject. Just a string of characters that look like static. I suck in a sharp breath, and Rakes notices, glancing in my direction.

"Spam?" Rakes asks from the couch, half-distracted by the paper he isn't reading.

"Maybe." But my gut says otherwise. The address line isn't random. It's one of Kat's old handles. A literal fucking ghost from Driftwood's underbelly.

I open it, mentally preparing myself for whatever is about to flood my screen.

The screen floods white, then black. Lines of code ripple like water, a lock breaking itself. Rakes is beside me in two steps, one hand braced on the desk, the other hovering near his weapon.

"Quinn—"

"I've got it."

The static clears. A video feed loads—grainy, handheld. The lighting's sickly, fluorescent. A concrete room. Pipes dripping somewhere off-screen.

Then movement from the corner, a woman being dragged into frame. Hair matted. Lip split. Eyes wide enough to swallow the light.

Kat.

I stop breathing. The world folds in. She's thinner, bruised and beaten, but it's her—she's alive. A guard yanks her upright, but she fights. Weakly, but she still fights. Then the camera dips as if the person filming wants us to see.

Rakes swears under his breath, the word venomous.

Kat's voice cuts through the distortion—hoarse, terrified. "*Please*... tell him... I didn't talk—"

A hand shoves her back. The feed jerks. The sound of a slap cracks the air. Then nothing. Just the echo of her breathing before the video cuts to black.

For a moment, I think I've imagined it. That grief and hope have built another hallucination for me to fall into. But the file keeps looping, stuttering at the last frame—Kat's eyes, staring straight at the lens.

Rakes is already moving, jaw tight, body wound for violence. "*Where* did it come from?"

"An encrypted relay. Origin is scrubbed. But the code signature—" I swallow hard. "It's Orion's. One of their internal tags."

He slams his fist against the wall, the sound sharp enough to make the glass rattle. "*Thatcher*. It fucking has to be!"

"Rakes—"

"He's got her, Quinn!" His voice cracks open, half fury, half disbelief. "All this time... she's been *alive*."

The room feels too small for what's happening inside it. The air's full of static, grief transmuting into rage.

I replay the footage once more, needing to be sure. Kat flinches at something offscreen—someone calling orders. There's a symbol spray-painted on the wall behind her, and my eyes narrow in on it making out the small details. It's a red haven emblem crossed through with white chalk. A clear mark of ownership.

Rakes leans in, fists braced on either side of the laptop. "That's a message."

"It's bait," I whisper. "They want us to come."

He looks at me then, eyes raw. "They got what they wanted the second they showed me this."

I should tell him to think. To wait. To plan. But the same wildfire that's eating him is crawling under my ribs too. Kat's alive. Hurt. Probably fucking terrified. And he made sure we'd see it.

He paces once, twice, then stops, voice steady but lethal. "We find the source. Tonight."

"Rakes—"

"No, no more waiting. No bureaucracy. Thatcher's holding her, and I swear to God I'll put him in the ground before he touches her again."

The promise hangs between us like thunder about to break.

Outside, the sea hammers the rocks relentlessly. The wind howls through the shutters, and somewhere in the distance a gull cries—a sound like grief and warning all at once.

I close the laptop, heart splitting between terror and relief. The thought barrels through my mind again like lightning.

Kat's *alive*.

***

It's late. The house hums with restless quiet, and Rakes has been pacing for the past hour—packing, re-packing, burning holes in the floor with his temper. He's finally sitting in the armchair by the windows, watching the sea as it crests against the cliffs. I've been trying to talk him down, but words aren't cutting through the fury. Something in my gut keeps whispering wait, but I can't explain it—*not yet*.

So I try something else.

I start with a touch—a slow drag of my hand over his shoulder, the faint scrape of my nails against fabric. He stiffens, not from surprise, but from the effort it takes not to break apart. I lean in, my lips brushing the shell of his ear.

He turns, and for a heartbeat the fire in him falters. His eyes roam—shock, then awe, then something darker—as he takes in the black lace I slipped into when he wasn't looking.

"What's all this?" he asks, voice rough.

I don't bother lying. "A distraction." His throat works around a swallow, gaze tracing every inch of exposed skin like a man starved. "Is it working?"

Rakes doesn't wait for an answer. His hands find my waist, and suddenly I'm in his lap, the world narrowing to heat and breath and the rough sound he makes when our mouths meet. The kiss starts slow—careful, deliberate—but it doesn't stay that way. It builds, wild and consuming, every pull of his lips demanding something deeper, truer.

I'm not hiding this time. Not using him to forget the world outside. I'm choosing him—here, now, despite the storm waiting for us.

And he feels it. I can tell by the way his touch changes, how his hands move over me like a confession he's too afraid to speak aloud. Every kiss becomes a language neither of us can unlearn.

He rises from the chair with me still in his arms, moving toward the bed with a purpose that steals my breath. When he lays me down, it's with a reverence that undoes me—like I'm something *sacred* instead of scarred. The look in his eyes turns my skin fever-warm, blush blooming across my cheeks before his hands even find me.

They roam slowly at first, exploring, claiming. His palms trace my sides, his thumbs drag lazy circles over my hips, then up to cup my breasts. He teases the hardened peaks with deft, quick fingers, and the sound that leaves my throat is half moan, half plea. I arch into him, the ache sharpening into an intense feeling of need.

He strips the lace away in one fluid motion, the cool air meeting the heat he's left behind. His gaze darkens—molten, hungry—before he lowers his mouth to me.

The first stroke of his tongue sends a shock through my body. I gasp, fingers fisting in the sheets as he works me with patient precision, each flick and swirl a new kind of undoing. The quiet of the room fills with the sound of my breathing, his low groan vibrating against my skin as he tastes me deeper, slower, harder.

"Rakes," I whisper—then louder, a cry that fractures the stillness.

He doesn't stop. He hums against me, the vibration coaxing another shiver from my core.

"I need more," I gasp, voice breaking between moans.

He pauses only long enough to lift his head, mouth glistening, eyes wild and tender all at once. "Tell me what you want, Quinn. I need to hear you say it."

"I need *you*, Malcolm. I need you inside me."

The words come out shameless, breathless—my modesty long gone when it comes to the Detective worshipping my body.

His shirt comes off first, pants undone second. In a heartbeat he's bare before me—muscle and sinew cut in shadow and light, power wrapped in control. His cock stands hard and ready, proof of everything he's been holding back.

He joins me in the next breath, sliding inside with a deep, shuddering groan that rips through the quiet. I move to meet him, hips finding his rhythm as heat blooms through every nerve. Each thrust sends sparks skittering beneath my skin, our breath tangling, the sound of us filling the space where silence used to live.

I've never wanted anyone the way I want Malcolm Rakes—completely, recklessly, as if wanting him could burn the rest of the world away.

He moves against me, every breath a clash of heat and restraint, every touch a silent vow. The world outside the walls falls away until there's only this rhythm between us—urgent, breaking, remade again. His name trembles from my lips, a thread that binds the dark to the light.

The air thickens. The sheets twist. His hands find mine, fingers locking, grounding me as everything else slips. The sound that leaves me is half cry, half release—something too fierce to name.

When the storm finally breaks, it isn't gentle. It's the shattering kind—wild and consuming, leaving us both gasping in its wake. For a long moment we stay there, suspended in the aftermath, the pulse of the sea outside echoing the one still racing between us.

He presses his forehead to mine, his breath rough, uneven. I don't say anything. Neither does he. There's nothing left to say.

Only the quiet. Only the heat still clinging to our skin. Only the unspoken truth that something has changed, and there's no turning it back.

He starts to move, slow and restless, reaching for his clothes. The fight is still in him—I can feel it in the set of his shoulders, the need to do something, to make someone pay.

"Don't," I whisper, catching his wrist. "Not tonight."

He hesitates, jaw tight. "If we wait, they'll move again."

"They already have." I sit up, the sheet slipping from my skin, and meet his eyes. "You're running on fumes, Malcolm. You go out there like this, and you'll get yourself killed. I'm done watching people I care about die."

The words hang between us, raw and heavy. He stares at me as if I've stepped off a cliff and he can't tell whether to follow. For a long beat there's nothing but the sound of our breathing and the distant hush of the ocean. He doesn't argue. He doesn't launch into a plan or a protest. He just says, quietly, like it surprises him to hear it. "You... you *care*."

"I do." My voice is small and sudden and true. "I want us to survive."

Those two lines land, hitting him flat in the chest. The hard line of his shoulders eases—just a fraction—and for a moment I see the man under the fury. Raw, worn, stunned by the idea that someone might refuse to walk away. I shift closer, press my palm to his chest so I can feel the steady thrum beneath his ribs. "We stay. We think. Then, in the morning, we'll go. *Together*. No one else dies because of us."

He searches my face, something unspoken flickering in his eyes before he finally nods. "Alright. Morning."

I nod once, then tug him back toward the bed. He doesn't resist. When he lies beside me, the tension slowly drains from him, leaving only the quiet weight of grief and the faint rhythm of his heartbeat under my cheek.

"I promise," I murmur into the darkness. "We'll finish it. But we're going to do it right."

His hand finds mine beneath the covers, a wordless agreement.

Outside, the tide pulls back from the shore, carrying the night with it. For the first time in what feels like forever, I let myself breathe. Letting the sounds of the tide lull me into a fitful sleep.

CHAPTER 40

Quinn

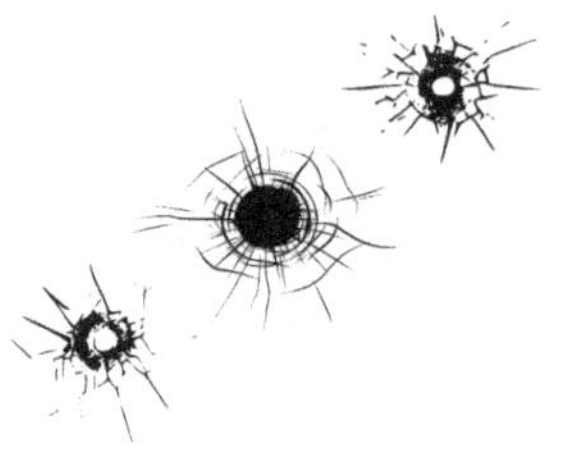

Morning creeps in gray and slow, sunlight barely cutting through the fog that's settled over Driftwood like a second skin. The air smells of salt and wet cedar, a storm waiting just offshore. I move through the kitchen with the kind of precision that only exhaustion can sharpen—coffee brewing, laptop open, the hum of the old generator filling the silence that's stretched between us since dawn.

Rakes leans against the counter, half-dressed, hair still damp from the shower. He looks better in the daylight—less like a man unraveling and more like one waiting for the right thread to pull.

"You're sure you want to go through with this?" he asks, eyes flicking to the screen.

"Sure? No," I say, typing in another set of coordinates. "Ready? Always."

He exhales, rubbing a hand over his jaw. "You've run Thatcher's list three times."

"Four," I correct him. "But one address keeps pulsing red. Closer to town, near the cliffs. If I were hiding something—or someone—I'd pick a place with an escape route."

Rakes steps closer, scanning the data over my shoulder. "It's old property—abandoned, looks like. Used to belong to a fishing outfit before Red Haven bought it out."

"Perfect place for a ghost to hide," I murmur.

His hand brushes my shoulder briefly. "We go in light and fast. You hang back until I clear the inside."

I give him a look. "You know I won't."

He smirks, just slightly. "Didn't think you would, but I had to try."

I grin, shoving him a little as we grab our gear and rush out the door.

***

By the time we reach the cliffs, the fog has thickened to a living thing, curling between the pines and spilling over the dirt road. The building waits at the end of the track—a weather-beaten structure that might've been a lodge once, windows shuttered, siding grayed by sea spray.

It's too quiet.

I feel it before I hear it—the stillness that isn't still at all, the kind that hums beneath the skin. "Something's *wrong*," I whisper.

Rakes cuts the engine, scanning the tree line. "Stay sharp."

We move in tandem. His gun clears its holster, and my blade slides free from my boot. The front door hangs crooked, open just enough to suggest invitation.

Inside smells like dust and brine, but underneath—faint oil, metal, something too clean. The floorboards creak beneath our weight. Sunlight knife's through the gaps in the boards overhead, slicing the dark into strips.

A sound—soft, intentionally hidden, stirs from behind us. Rakes spins, gun raised. "Show yourself."

The answer comes in the click of a safety sliding off.

"Detective," a voice drawls from the shadows. Smooth. Mocking. "You're a hard man to get off the leash."

Thatcher Greeves steps into the light. Impeccable as always. Slate-gray suit, gloves, the faintest smirk that never reaches his eyes. Behind him, two men flank the door—one with a rifle, the other with a knife that gleams like fresh bone.

"Quinn," he says, voice a purr. "Or should I say *Agent Maddox?*"

My stomach knots. The blade in my hand feels heavier, but my arm doesn't tremble. "You don't get to use that name."

"Oh, but I do," he murmurs. "It's the reason we're all here, isn't it?"

Rakes shifts beside me, gun steady. "You've got five seconds to start explaining before I redecorate the walls with your teeth."

Greeves only laughs, low and quiet. "Still the brute. I can see why she keeps you around."

He snaps his fingers. A door behind him slams open—two more men appear, weapons drawn. The sound of boots echoes through the building, upstairs and down. We're surrounded.

Rakes swears under his breath. "Trap."

"*Obviously*," I hiss. "Move!"

We duck as gunfire explodes, wood splintering, glass shattering. I dive behind an overturned table, returning fire with quick, measured bursts. Rakes hits one target square in the chest before a second shot drives him backward, grazing his shoulder.

"Malcolm!"

"I'm fine," he growls, blood darkening the fabric of his jacket. "Back door!"

We push toward the hall, but two figures block the way. I throw my knife—hits the first in the thigh. He goes down screaming. Rakes takes the second with a punch that sounds like breaking stone.

We crash through another room, only to find it already occupied. Four men this time. We spin, trapped between two exits, both closing fast.

"Drop it," Greeves calls, stepping through the wreckage. His pistol gleams silver in the fractured light. "Let's not make this messier than it needs to be."

Rakes doesn't lower his gun. Neither do I.

"So this is about Driftwood, then?" I ask. "Or Orion?"

"Oh, Quinn," he says softly. "You really don't remember what this is about, do you?"

His tone makes my blood run cold. He steps closer, boots crunching over the broken glass, eyes locked on mine. "Think back, *sweetheart*. Paris. 2016. Operation codename... *LeClair*."

The name hits like a bullet, I suck in a breath, and Malcolm visibly tenses. My hand falters. The air vanishing from the room.

He smiles, slow and poisonous. "You should remember Alexandre LeClair. You put two in his chest before the fire took the rest. Or did the agency neglect to tell you what you *really* burned that night?"

Rakes turns toward me, confusion and shock cutting through the tension. "Quinn?"

I can't breathe. My vision tunnels. "No," I whisper. "He's *lying*."

But I'm not so sure anymore.

Greeves tilts his head, watching me like a man who's just found the crack in the glass. "You and I both know the truth, Agent Maddox. This—" he gestures to the chaos around us, the men, the guns, the blood on the floor "—this is just the reckoning."

He raises his weapon, but Rakes moves first.

Gunfire detonates, deafening in the close quarters—glass bursts, splinters rain from the ceiling. I dive for cover, return fire, but there are too many. Muzzle flashes strobe the room, every burst a symphony of chaos—Rakes grappling one man to the ground, another grabbing my arm hard enough to bruise.

I twist, slam an elbow into his throat, but something sharp bites into my shoulder. A sting, then pure unbridled fire that courses my veins. My limbs go slack before I can process it. He fucking hit me with a tranquilizer.

"Malcolm—" I manage, the word breaking apart on my tongue.

He's still fighting, blood streaking down his temple, wild and furious until the butt of a rifle catches him across the jaw. He drops to one knee, snarling, trying to rise again.

"*Easy*, Detective," Greeves says smoothly, stepping through the haze. "You're far more useful alive."

My vision flickers, edges dimming. The floor tilts beneath me, everything narrowing to shapes and shadows. I feel rough hands catch my wrists, zip-tie them tight.

Through the blur, I see Rakes go down beside me—half-conscious, still reaching for me even as they drag him back.

"Get them in the truck," Greeves orders. "We've wasted enough time."

The men haul us toward the door, boots scuffing against broken glass. The last thing I see before the darkness takes me is the glint of the ocean through the shattered window—cold, gray, endless.

And the sound of Greeves's voice, low and satisfied, following me into unconsciousness.

"Welcome back to the game, Agent Maddox."

CHAPTER 41

Quinn

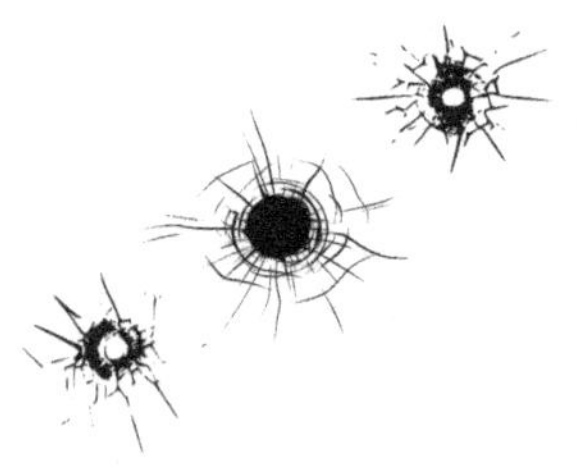

The world comes back in fragments—sound first. The low hum of machinery. The rhythmic drip of water somewhere close. The echo of footsteps pacing above us, methodical and unhurried.

Then... *pain*. My wrists ache where the zip-ties bite in. My knuckles throb, split and swollen, every throb a painful reminder of what we went through. One eye burns, heavy and tight, the skin around it already swelling shut. My throat feels raw, like I've been screaming in my sleep.

Light seeps through the edges of a corrugated metal ceiling—cold, artificial, sterile. A warehouse, maybe? The air tastes like rust and old oil.

When I shift, something solid brushes my arm. *Rakes.*

He's slumped against a support beam beside me, one eye swelling shut, blood crusted at his temple. Still breathing. Still fighting, even unconscious—his hand curls instinctively when I whisper his name. "Malcolm."

He stirs, groans, the sound low and guttural. "Quinn...?"

"Yeah," I rasp. "Still here."

He blinks against the light, looks around, and his jaw tightens. "Where the *hell*—"

"Somewhere we're not supposed to be." I test the ties, feel the plastic bite deeper, and grit my teeth. "They moved us. Probably while we were under."

The door creaks. Rakes straightens as best he can, muscles coiled even bound. The sound of expensive shoes echoes off the concrete, slow and careful. Like he has all the time in the world.

"Don't bother," the voice says, smooth as velvet over a blade. "You won't get out of those."

Thatcher steps into view—or at least, that's who I think it is. But the man who walks toward us isn't the polished suit we've known. His jacket's gone, sleeves rolled to the elbows. The precision's still there, but it's colder now. *Emptier.*

And then I see it—the small, deliberate smile. The one I saw years ago, right before a building in Marseilles went up in flames.

"*Alexandre,*" I whisper, horrified disbelief crawling through my gut.

Rakes stiffens. "*What*?!"

Thatcher—no, *LeClair*—grins wider. "So you *do* remember. I was beginning to think they'd erased me completely."

"LeClair's *dead*." My voice is steady, but the world is tilting under the weight of it. "I killed him."

He laughs. It's a soft sound, almost pitying. "You killed someone. Just not me."

Rakes turns to me, confused. "Quinn, what is he talking about?"

I can't answer. The images come too fast—the mission brief, the intel drop, the explosion. My hands shaking afterward, blood on my boots.

Alexandre keeps walking until he's close enough that I can see the faint scar at his temple—the kind you only get from shrapnel. "I knew they were sending you. That's why I sent my double in first. Poor bastard didn't even know he was actually playing me until the end."

"You *staged* your own death," I scoff, spewing venom. "To *what*? Crawl back to your father's empire?"

"To build it bigger," he says, tone almost gentle. "Victor needed a foothold. Orion provided it. Redhaven made it look legitimate through multiple corporations across the country. We needed somewhere quiet, safe. Just like Driftwood. But you, Agent Maddox—you gave me the excuse. The perfect tragedy to vanish behind."

Rakes growls low in his throat. "You son of a bitch. You've been running Driftwood like a damn puppet show."

Alexandre's eyes flick toward him. "Oh, Detective. You really think this is about you? You're just the leverage. The means to keep her in line."

He turns back to me. "You were *always* the prize, Quinn. The agency's *golden* girl. I watched you dismantle syndicates, burn networks to the ground. And all the while, I wondered—what would you do if you realized you'd been fighting shadows of your own making?"

The words hit harder than the tranquilizer ever did. "You *used* us," I manage.

"No," he says softly. "I *learned* from you. And now you'll help me finish what your handlers started."

Rakes strains against the bindings, face red with fury. "Over my dead fucking body."

"That," Alexandre says, voice turning silky again, "can be arranged."

He crouches beside me, fingers brushing my chin. I jerk away, but his grip snaps tighter, forcing my gaze up to meet his. His eyes are sharp, endless—no longer hiding the madness humming beneath the surface.

"You remember Paris," he murmurs. "The hotel balcony. That deal that never went through. You looked me in the eye then, too, right before you pulled the trigger. Well, you thought you did."

I can still smell the smoke. The way the world had tilted as I walked away, believing it was over.

"I told myself I'd never make that mistake again," he continues. "This time, I'll make sure you know exactly who you're killing. I'd make you face... me."

He stands, straightens his sleeves, all composure again. "Welcome to Orion's heart, Agent Maddox. Redhaven was only the door."

He gestures toward the far wall. A faint hum rises—hidden panels sliding open to reveal monitors, a row of them, each displaying faces. Some I know. Others I wish I didn't. Agents. Targets. Contacts long thought dead.

Every one of them tagged ACTIVE.

Rakes stares, jaw clenched. "Jesus Christ."

LeClair's smile deepens. "You see now? Orion doesn't just own this town. It *is* this town. And by the time we're done, Driftwood will be a memory too."

He steps back, nods to one of his men. "Move them. We've got a long night ahead."

The guard yanks me to my feet, plastic biting into my wrists, limbs screaming in pain. I fight it, digging my heels into the concrete, but it's useless.

As they drag us toward the corridor, Rakes twists to catch my eyes. There's blood on his cheek, fury in his stare. "Quinn—whatever this is, we end it. You hear me?"

I nod once. "Together."

LeClair's laughter follows us down the hall—low, satisfied, and terrible.

"Of course together," he says behind us. "After all... I went to all this trouble just to keep you two together."

And somewhere deep inside, under the fear and rage, I finally understand—this was never about Kat.

It's about finishing the story I thought I ended six years ago.

CHAPTER 42

Rakes

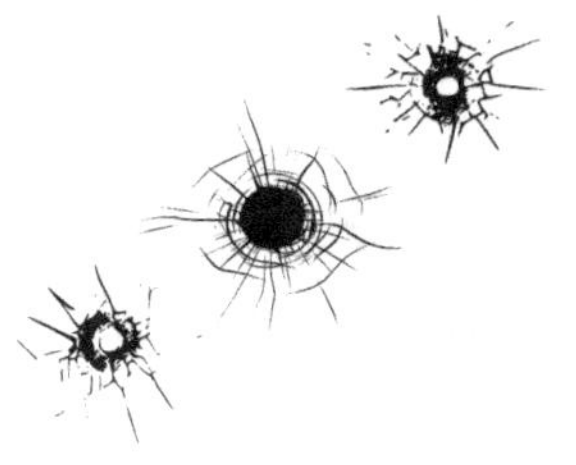

T he drive is long, silent, and disorienting. I can't see much from the back of the van—just glimpses through rusted slats. Pine trees bending with the wind, a strip of coastline in retreat. The ocean's gone gray, the kind of color that promises bad storms.

They don't speak. Not the driver, or the guards in the back. Their silence is practiced. Military in tone.

My wrists burn against the zip ties, my shoulder still slick with dried blood. Quinn's beside me, half-slumped, her eyes open but distant. There's a shadow in her I've never seen before—one that looks too much like resignation.

"Hey," I murmur, leaning close. "You still with me?"

She blinks, breath catching. "Yeah." Her voice is low, cracked. "Thinking."

"About what?"

"How to make them regret letting us live this long."

I smirk. That's the Quinn I've come to know. The one who doesn't break—she *burns*.

The van jolts off the road and slows. Gravel under the tires. The air changes—wet, earthy, heavy with the scent of pine and smoke. Then the door slams open. "Out," a voice orders.

They drag us into the daylight. We're in the middle of nowhere. The property's old, sprawling—what used to be an estate, maybe, long before the salt air ate it. The main house leans against the wind, its windows black holes. Outbuildings crumble in the distance.

Greeves—no, LeClair—waits by the porch, coat off, sleeves rolled. He looks like the devil about to offer a deal.

"Welcome home," he says. "I thought you'd appreciate a bit of nostalgia before the end."

He gestures for them to move us inside. The guards shove us toward the door, but the second one hesitates, fumbling with his radio. Static bursts, shrill and sharp. LeClair turns, irritated.

That's all the time I need.

I throw my weight sideways, shoulder-check the first guard hard enough to break his grip. The plastic at my wrists snaps against the blade of his own knife as I twist it out of his hand. Pain flares, hot and clean.

"Quinn, move!"

She doesn't hesitate. She slams her heel into the second guard's knee, grabs his gun, and fires. The shot cracks through the open air. Chaos follows.

LeClair's men scramble, shouting, diving for cover. I grab Quinn's arm and pull her toward the house. It's the only shelter we've got.

Inside, it smells of rot and memory. Dust, oil, the ghost of old smoke. We race through the hall, boards groaning beneath us. I kick a table over for cover just as bullets chew into the plaster.

"They'll flank from the east side!" she shouts.

"Then we don't give them the chance!" I drag open a cabinet near the fireplace—old bottles, kerosene, maybe meant for lamps. I toss one to her. "If we're going down, we take the place with us."

She gives me a look—half terror, half defiance. "You're *insane*."

"Yeah," I say, striking the lighter. "But it works."

The flame catches. The bottle shatters against the far wall, fire blooming up the wood like it's been waiting years for this. The house becomes a furnace in minutes.

"Out the back!" I yell.

We crash through the rear door just as the heat hits our backs. Outside, gunfire cuts through the haze. A bullet grazes my ribs. I don't feel it until Quinn's hand is on my arm, pulling me toward the trees.

"Malcolm!" she cries. "You're hit—"

"Keep moving!"

We dive into the underbrush, the world behind us turning into an inferno. The explosion comes a second later—a deep, rolling thunder that shakes the ground beneath our feet. The house collapses in on itself, sparks scattering into the fog.

I fall to my knees, breath tearing at my chest. Blood pools warm against my side. Quinn drops beside me, eyes wide, wild, streaked with soot.

"Stay awake," she orders, pressing her hands against the wound. "Don't you *dare* close your eyes. Don't you dare leave me, Malcolm Rakes."

"Not... planning to," I choke out.

She tears a strip from her shirt, ties it tight around me, hands trembling but steady. The firelight flickers across her face—ash on her skin, sweat on her temples. She looks like something risen from the wreckage.

*****

Quinn

He's losing too much blood. I can feel his pulse weaken beneath my hands, each beat slower than the last. The smoke carries downwind, dragging our trail through the trees, and I know LeClair's men will be back once the fire dies.

We can't stay here. "Come on," I whisper. "We have to move."

Rakes groans but forces himself upright. I slip under his arm, half-carrying him through the tree-line. Every step feels like it should be our last, but adrenaline keeps us moving. The air is heavy with ash. The fire behind us roars, licking the horizon, turning the estate into a funeral pyre.

Branches snap behind us. Not the fire—footsteps.

"Quinn," Rakes rasps, breath ragged. "They're on us."

"Keep moving," I fuss, pushing us forward a little faster.

We stumble downhill, the slope slick with pine needles. A bullet cracks through the air, close enough to shear bark from a tree inches from my head. I shove Rakes down behind a fallen log, drawing my gun. Another shot follows—then two more.

"They're sweeping!" I hiss.

"Three of them," he says, grimacing as he reloads with shaking hands. "Maybe four."

"We don't have ammo for four."

He gives a tight, humorless grin. "Guess we make the first three count."

The world narrows to sound and shadow. I can see their shapes moving between the trees—black-clad, methodical, weapons raised. The light from the burning house flickers through the smoke, throwing everything into disorienting color.

One steps closer, and I take the shot. He goes down, not dead but loud. The others shout. That's all the opening we need.

Rakes fires twice, then hisses, "Move!"

We break from cover, half-running, half-dragging each other toward the service road. Rakes is limping badly, every step a jolt that pulls against my grip, but I won't let him fall. My lungs burn, vision narrowing to the shimmer of smoke and fire ahead. Behind us, boots hammer the earth, shouts cutting through the haze. Bullets slice the air close enough that I can feel their heat as they pass. I tighten my hold on him, forcing his arm over my shoulder. "Almost there," I hiss, breathless, even though neither of us believes it.

"There!" one yells.

We hit the asphalt, the skeletal line of the road winding toward the coast. Headlights flare up ahead—an old sedan parked sideways near a rusted gate, engine still idling.

"Someone's waiting," Rakes warns.

"Then we take it from them."

I break into a run. The driver turns, startled, and goes for his gun. I reach him first. My elbow cracks across his jaw, sending him sprawling. I wrench the weapon from his hand and swing it hard enough to make sure he stays down.

Rakes limps to the passenger side, face pale, blood soaking his shirt. "You drive," he says. "You're the one who still has full use of both lungs."

I don't argue. I shove him in, slide behind the wheel, and slam my foot on the gas. Tires squeal, gravel sprays. The car fishtails onto the road just as another burst of gunfire follows us. A bullet punches through the rear window, glass exploding inward.

Rakes ducks, cursing. "They're not letting up!"

"They will when we hit the coast!" I shout, knuckles white on the wheel.

He reaches down, fumbling with his jacket, and pulls out a small, metal canister—military grade. My stomach drops. "Tell me that's *not* what I think it is."

He grins through the blood on his lip. "Picked it up off one of LeClair's boys. A... Souvenir if you will."

"Malcolm," I hiss. "You are not—"

But he's already pulling the pin. The world explodes behind us in a flash of orange and thunder. The shockwave punches the car forward, metal groaning as shrapnel pelts the trunk. I scream, wrenching the wheel to keep us on the narrow coastal road. The rearview mirror shows a wall of fire blooming through the trees, devouring the road we came from.

"You absolute *lunatic*!" I snap, breath ragged. "You could've killed us!"

"Could've," he manages, voice faint but amused. "Didn't."

Another volley of gunfire echoes in the distance, but it's fading. The explosion bought us time. I push the car harder, engine roaring, tires screeching against the bends. Every corner feels like a coin toss between freedom and the cliff's edge.

"Stay with me, Rakes," I mutter, eyes flicking between the road and his face. His skin's gone gray, his jaw slackening. "Don't you dare close your eyes."

"I'm fine," he mumbles. "Just... tired."

"No, you don't get to be tired. You threw a damn grenade."

A faint smile twitches at the corner of his mouth. "It worked, didn't it?"

We tear down the final stretch of road, the sea opening wide beside us—a violent black mirror catching the first light of dawn. The fire's reflection turns the cliffs red, a wound against the horizon. I spot an old maintenance turnout and wrench the wheel, sliding the car behind a stone wall half-swallowed by vines.

The engine ticks as it cools. Smoke still curls from the shattered rear window. Rakes slumps against the seat, eyes half-lidded.

"Hey," I whisper, grabbing his hand. It's cold, slick with blood. Panic rises in my throat, but I shove it down. "You stay awake, do you hear me? You promised."

He exhales, a sound between a groan and a laugh. "I'm here. Still annoying you."

"Barely." I tear open the med kit, pressing gauze to his side. "You're reckless, you know that?"

"I'm effective."

I glare at him, but the fight drains out of me fast. "You're bleeding through your bandage, effective man."

"Just a scratch," he argues.

"Liar."

He doesn't answer this time. His head lolls back, eyes slipping shut, breath shallow but even. The horizon glows faintly orange, the sea murmuring below like it's catching secrets. I sit there with him, pulse hammering, the smell of smoke and salt thick in the air. For a long time, there's nothing but silence and the sound of waves against the rocks.

Finally, I speak, voice low. "We didn't find her."

Rakes stirs, barely conscious. "No."

"But she's alive," I say, more to myself than him.

His hand tightens weakly around mine. "We'll finish this—find *her*. We have to."

I look out over the coast, at the faint trail of black smoke twisting up into the dawn. "We end it."

He smiles faintly, lips barely moving. "Together."

We've burned the bridge behind us. There's no going back to Driftwood.

LeClair wanted to bury us. Instead, he lit the match. And when we go after him next, it won't be for answers.

It'll be for *blood*.

CHAPTER 43

Quinn

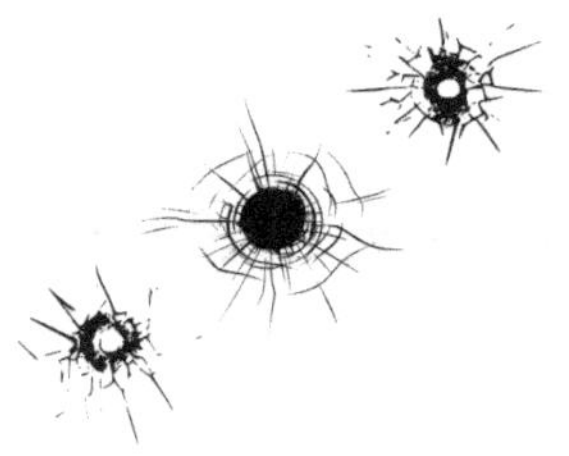

The safehouse smells like dust, bleach, and the faint ghost of cigarettes.

Rakes is still half-unconscious when I drag him through the door. He's heavy in the way only the wounded are — all muscle and dead weight, every breath a gamble.

The woman who answers doesn't speak. Just looks me up and down, reads the blood on my hands, and gestures toward the narrow hallway. Her name is Lorna, though that isn't the one on her passport. She used to run cleanup jobs for the Agency before she started selling silence to people like me.

"Upstairs," she says. "And if anyone followed you, you're already dead."

"No one followed."

She gives a single nod and moves ahead of us. I shoulder Rakes' arm across my back, half-dragging him up the narrow staircase. Each step knocks loose more of the dust that coats everything here — picture frames, the stair rail, the air itself. The only light comes from the hall lamp, jaundiced and weak.

When we reach the spare room, Lorna already has her kit laid out. Strips of gauze, sutures, saline, morphine, and whiskey. No questions, no sympathy. She just goes to work.

I stand against the wall, one arm wrapped around my ribs, watching as she cuts away Malcolm's shirt and peels back the soaked bandages. The wound at his side looks worse in proper light — a deep graze that tracked too close to bone, angry and red at the edges.

"Bullet missed anything vital," she mutters. "Lucky bastard."

"Not luck," I say quietly. "Stubbornness."

Her eyes flick toward me once, sharp. "Same thing."

He stirs as she injects the anesthetic, his hand twitching until I take it. He doesn't open his eyes, but his fingers close around mine, weak but certain.

"Don't die," I whisper, more to the universe than to him. "You don't get to do that, not after all this."

Lorna finishes stitching and tapes the wound with the neat precision of someone who's patched too many people who didn't deserve saving. She stands, wipes her hands on a rag, and faces me. "He'll need rest. Pain meds, antibiotics. You've got maybe six hours before he's able to move without passing out."

"I can't give him six."

"You'll give him what you can, then you'll move fast."

I press a wad of bills into her palm. She doesn't count it — just slides it into her pocket. "You were never here," I say.

"You know my rules, Quinn. I was never *born*."

When she leaves, the room feels smaller. The wind rattles the shutters, and a distant freight train cuts across the night.

I kneel beside him, press a damp cloth to his forehead. The fever's climbing already. His lips part, the whisper escaping like smoke. "Kat..."

My throat tightens. "We'll find her," I tell him, though I don't know if I still believe it. "We're not done."

He fades again, drifting into whatever place pain can't follow. I stay there until dawn bleeds through the cracks in the blinds, painting the room in tired gold.

***

By the time he wakes, I've scrubbed most of the blood off the floor and cleaned myself up enough to pass for alive. The bruises along my jaw are hidden beneath makeup, the split on my lip softened by a trace of red. My reflection in the cracked mirror looks almost human again—almost.

He stirs, a low groan escaping him as he tries to move. His eyes blink open, unfocused at first, before finding me. "Where the hell—"

"Safe house," I cut in gently. "Friend of mine. You needed stitches, and rest."

He blinks again, trying to orient himself, and his voice comes out rough. "Still do."

"Don't," I say, moving closer, pressing a hand lightly to his shoulder before he can test the stitches. "Don't push it."

"How long?" he asks.

"Four hours."

He exhales through his teeth, head falling back against the pillow. "You should've left me."

"That's not how this works."

His gaze drags up to me then, slow but steady. The corner of his mouth lifts, the faintest ghost of a smile. "You look worse than I do."

I scoff, "Flattery won't get you morphine."

He chuckles softly, and it's the first real sound of life I've heard from him since the warehouse. "Worth a shot."

I pour a glass of water from the bottle beside the bed, hold it to his lips. "Drink. You're dehydrated."

He obeys, eyes on me the whole time, something unspoken flickering in the quiet between us. When he finishes, I set the glass aside, and for a moment, neither of us moves. Then his hand finds mine, fingers brushing over the faint scrape on my knuckles. "I can't believe you stayed."

"I always do," I say, softer than I mean to.

He studies me, jaw tightening as if he wants to argue, then lets it go. "Where now?"

I stand, grabbing my go-bag from the corner, checking the clip on the pistol inside. "Driftwood's too hot. It's obvious LeClair's reach is longer than I thought, deeper than I ever dreamed."

"So... *where*?" he presses, voice strained but lucid now.

I glance toward the window, where sunlight glints off the distant highway. "Texas."

That gets his full attention. "*Texas?*"

"There's someone there I trust."

He gives a humorless laugh. "That list can't be long."

"It isn't." I meet his eyes. "Beau Maddox."

Recognition flickers across his face — the name means something, even to him. "Your brother," he says quietly.

"My brother," I confirm, voice rough but certain. "He's the only one left I'd trust with either of our lives."

Rakes leans back against the pillow, wincing. "You think he'll take us in?"

"If I ask," I say, tightening the strap on the bag. "He will."

"You sound sure."

"I am." I hesitate, then move closer, brushing the hair from his forehead, my thumb grazing the edge of a bruise on his temple. "Beau and I—he's not like me. He stayed clean, followed orders. But he owes me one."

Rakes looks at me then, really looks, his eyes darker than before but gentler somehow. "You really do care."

"I care about a handful of people in this world," I whisper. "You're both on the list."

The admission surprises him—I can see it in the way his breath catches, the faint, startled blink. "Quinn—"

"Don't," I say, cutting him off with a small shake of my head. "We'll deal with the rest later. Right now, you need to heal, and I need to make sure we're still alive tomorrow."

He smiles faintly, but there's no humor in it. "You're bossy when you're scared."

"I'm always scared." The truth lands heavier than either of us expects.

He reaches up then, fingers brushing my wrist. "Thank you," he says quietly.

"For what?" I ask.

"For dragging me out. For not giving up on me," he whispers.

I force a small, tired smile. "Don't make me regret it."

His hand tightens briefly, warm despite the fever still clinging to him. "You won't."

"Rest while I finish packing," I tell him. "We'll move in thirty minutes."

He nods, eyes already fluttering closed, and I stay there for a long while, listening to the rhythm of his breathing, the faint pulse of life under bruised skin. When I finally rise, it's to pack what little we have left—guns, cash, a fake passport, the last of the antibiotics.

In an hour, he'll be on his feet. By tomorrow night, we'll be on a plane.

And by the time LeClair realizes where we've gone, we'll be halfway to Texas.

To Beau.

The only person in this world who might still be able to save us.

***

We leave just before the sun crests over the horizon.

Lorna doesn't say a word, just watches from the porch with a cigarette burning low between her fingers. The Buick she lends me rattles like it's one bad turn from collapsing, but it'll get us where we need to go.

Rakes limps down the steps behind me, stitched and stubborn, the afternoon light cutting across his bruised jaw.

"You're pushing too hard," I warn.

He grunts. "You're not pushing hard enough."

"Keep that up and I'll start calling you *dead-weight*."

That earns me half a grin. "Nah, it's... Bullets over bourbon," he mutters. "That's what we are."

"Terrible brand name," I say, sliding behind the wheel.

"Catchy slogan," he counters, grinning like an idiot.

"Sure. Guaranteed to self-destruct," I snort.

He laughs under his breath, and for a second it feels like the world hasn't caught fire.

The drive out of the county is long and quiet. The static from the dead radio fills the space between us, a white noise that feels almost peaceful after the chaos. He dozes on and off, head turned toward the window, every now and then mumbling something I can't quite hear.

At a truck stop, I grab supplies—coffee, antiseptic, a couple of clean shirts. When I come back, he's sitting up straighter, color back in his face, pretending he's not hurting.

"Nice of you to fully rejoin the land of the living," I say, tossing him a bottle of water.

He catches it clumsily, shooting me a look that tells me he knows exactly what I'm doing. "Didn't plan on leaving it anytime soon." He studies me for a moment, quiet, that same look carving through the silence—part worry, part something softer.

"You sure you're up for the flight?" he asks instead.

"I should be asking *you* that question. I've done worse on less sleep," I say, taking a sip of lukewarm coffee.

"Yeah," he murmurs, a faint smirk ghosting across his bruised face. "That's what worries me."

I glance at him, lips twitching. "Do try to keep up, Detective. We've got a plane to catch."

He leans back, wincing but smiling all the same. "Wouldn't miss it."

The airfield looks half-abandoned by the time we get there—just a rusted hangar, one bored attendant, and a runway fading into heat haze. It's perfect. I hand the attendant an envelope thick enough to shut him up. "Fuel it and forget you saw us."

He glances at Rakes, at the limp, the stitched shirt, then back at me. "Whatever you say, lady."

Inside the hangar, the little prop plane hums to life. I help Rakes up the steps, ignoring the grunt that escapes him. Once inside, he sinks into the seat, exhaustion dragging at his features.

As the engines roar and the ground falls away, he looks over at me. "You really trust where we're going?"

"With my life," I say simply, and reach for his hand as the plane banks through the clouds.

Driftwood shrinks to a bruise on the horizon, swallowed by mist and distance. The world below burns gold and endless.

Rakes closes his eyes, his thumb brushing against my knuckles — a small, human tether amid the hum of the engines. "Falling asleep on me?" I ask, relishing in how safe he feels with me.

His lips curve, faint and tired. "Wasn't planning to."

"Good."

For a moment, that's all there is — the sound of wind against the fuselage, the steady rhythm of his breathing, the slow retreat of the world we burned behind us. Texas waits somewhere beneath that bright, indifferent sky — dust, heat, and the promise of one more reckoning.

We don't run from the fire anymore... we already learned how to walk through it.

CHAPTER 44

Quinn

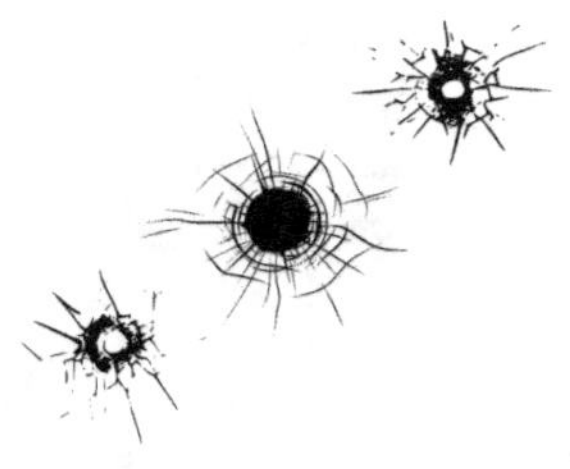

The road to Beau's ranch winds through the kind of country that remembers every storm. Red dust clings to the fenders, tall grass brushing against the car like whispering hands. By the time we reach the gate, the engine's rattling itself to death.

The headlights sweep over iron bars strung with barbed wire. Fixed to one post, a weathered sign leans crooked, its paint sun-bleached and half gone — Copper Creek Ranch. The name looks older than the metal it hangs on — worn soft by time and storms, but still standing.

Beyond it, the land opens in wide, shadowed waves. Pastures stretch out under the moon, fence posts marching into the dark. A barn crouches against the horizon, its tin roof catching faint light like an old scar. Somewhere out there, a dog barks once—sharp, lonely—and silence folds over the fields again.

The gate groans shut behind us, swallowed by the dark. The gravel road narrows to a single lane that winds through open pasture, grass swaying like slow-moving tides beneath the headlights. The air is thick with the scent of hay, damp earth, and the faint metallic whisper of the creek that gives the ranch its name. It smells like history—stubborn, grounding, unshakable.

Rakes leans against me as we climb the last rise toward the house. He's lighter than he should be, blood loss and pride carving him hollow. The porch light burns ahead, a small, steady flame in the dark.

Copper Creek's house stands two stories high—brick and timber weathered by years of storms. Rocking chairs guard the porch like sentries, their shadows stretching long across the steps. It doesn't look like a place that tolerates lies. It looks like a place that demands the truth.

I ease the door open without knocking.

Inside, the air smells of cedar, gun oil, and old coffee. A ceiling fan hums lazily overhead, stirring the heavy heat. Somewhere deeper in the house, floorboards creak—the unmistakable rhythm of my brother's gait.

Beau steps into the kitchen doorway, taller than I remember, his expression sharp with disbelief that softens into concern. "*Jesus, Quinn!* You look like shit." His voice is rough from sleep—or maybe from worry. "What the *hell* did you get yourself into this time?"

For a moment, I can't answer. The words dry up in my throat, though I desperately want to tell him why I look like I crawled out of the gutter. I just can't bring myself to. Not yet. The crickets outside keep singing, and the world feels suspended—like the night itself is waiting to see what we'll do next.

"Hey, brother," I whisper, my voice breaking on the last word.

Beau doesn't hesitate—he pulls me into his arms before I can say another word. The hug is rough, grounding, full of dust and unspoken worry. When he finally lets go, his gaze cuts past me to Rakes. "You brought company."

"Long story."

Before I can say more, a voice slips out from the shadows of the hallway—low, steady, and edged with that familiar precision I'd hoped I'd never hear again. "You're bleeding all over the porch."

I'd know that tone anywhere.

Victoria stands behind Beau, sleeves rolled, hair shorter, the same sharp eyes that once saw every move I made before I made it. My old partner. My near downfall.

"Well, *I'll be damned*," I say, forcing a smile that doesn't quite reach my eyes. "Didn't expect to find you shacked up with my brother."

Her mouth curves, amusement flashing in those eyes. "World's small, Quinn. You should've figured that out by now. Doesn't change the fact you look like hell. You *need* to let me take a look at your eye."

"Looks worse than it feels," I argue, refusing to meet her gaze head on. The air tightens, memory threading between us—too many nights, too many secrets, the weight of things neither of us said when it all fell apart.

Beau clears his throat, breaking the tension like he's cutting a wire. "Alright," he mutters, rubbing the back of his neck. "Save the reunion for *after*. Preferably, when no one's bleeding."

I exhale through my nose, the ghost of a grin tugging at my mouth. "You always did have great timing."

"Comes with big brother territory," Beau says. He jerks his chin toward the door. "Get inside, both of you. Before you pass out or start shooting."

***

Inside, the house smells like home — the same as every safehouse Beaux ever built for himself. The scent feels like muscle memory. Late nights, loaded weapons, secrets that don't stay buried.

Victoria moves through it like she's lived here a long time. She doesn't speak, just grabs the first-aid kit from the counter, sets out towels, water, and a bottle of antiseptic that looks like it's seen a few wars of its own. The lamplight cuts across her face—sharper now than I remember, but the precision in her hands hasn't dulled.

Rakes sits at the kitchen table, shirt off, a line of half-healed stitches running down his side. Lorna's work—rough, fast, meant to buy time. It's unraveling now, bit by bit. Blood seeps through the gauze, and I clench my teeth to keep from hissing.

"Hold still," Victoria murmurs, her tone all business, but her eyes flick to me once—just once—as if to ask how far gone he is.

"He doesn't do '*still*,'" I say, leaning against the counter.

Rakes tries for humor, teeth bared in something that might be a grin. "Still is for dead men."

Victoria doesn't blink. "Then stop trying so hard to join them."

The needle flashes in her hand, steady as ever. She rethreads the line, gloved fingers pressing the torn skin together with practiced grace. The faint scent of alcohol stings the air. Rakes grunts once but doesn't move, muscles tightening under her touch.

Beau stands behind her, arms crossed, jaw working. "You want to tell me why you look like you crawled out of a war zone?"

"Because we did," I say simply.

He doesn't smile. "You bring it with you?"

"Didn't have to. It followed."

Rakes exhales through his nose, voice low. "And it's not done."

That earns him a long look from Victoria—part curiosity, part calculation, maybe even something like pity. "You're Malcolm Rakes," she says after a moment, recognition threading through her voice. "Boston Division. You and Quinn made quite the mess."

Rakes tilts his head, watching her closely. "You talk like someone who read the report."

"I wrote half of it," she replies, tying off the last stitch. Her tone is calm, but I can feel the ripple in the air between them—two professionals, two ghosts comparing scars.

Beau arches a brow. "Care to elaborate?"

Victoria doesn't glance at him. "It was a sting gone sideways. Too many players, not enough intel. Quinn's op went dark for six weeks. When she resurfaced, half the Bureau wanted her blacklisted."

Rakes glances at me, that old question flickering behind his eyes. "And you?"

"I survived," I say, voice flat. "That's all that mattered."

Victoria snips the thread, wipes away the excess blood, and presses new gauze into place. "You always did have a talent for survival," she says softly, not quite looking at me.

"Better than *disappearing*," I shoot back.

That earns the faintest smirk from her. "Touché."

Beau clears his throat, the sound sharp in the silence. "Alright, ladies. As much fun as this reunion is, maybe we talk strategy before someone else shows up bleeding on my floor."

Rakes reaches for his shirt, grimacing. "Your sister's got that covered already."

"Don't remind me," Beau mutters, rubbing a hand over his face.

Victoria stands, peeling off her gloves, the sound sharp in the quiet. "Save your breath," she says, her voice low but steady. "We already have a sense of who's making your life hell."

I narrow my eyes. "You do?"

Beau exchanges a glance with her before answering. "Just a trail. Crates moving through old freight lines, false manifests, money changing hands through ghost accounts. Same patterns I saw before everything went sideways in Harrington."

Victoria wipes her hands with a rag, gaze flicking between us. "Whatever you're tangled up in—it's been circling here too. We figured it was corporate muscle shaking down suppliers, but if you're involved..." Her eyes land on me, cool and certain. "It's never just business when you're in the middle."

"Still like old times," I mutter.

"Worse," she says flatly. "This time the ghosts have uniforms."

Rakes shifts, wincing as the stitches pull. "You've seen them?"

Beau nods once. "Enough to know they're not local."

I glance at Victoria, reading between the lines. "So you've been running your own op."

She shrugs. "More like surviving someone else's."

The air tightens, thick with what none of us are saying. Beau pushes off the counter, jaw set. "We'll talk details after he's back on his feet. You both look like hell."

"Always the charmer," I say, shooting my brother a smirk. He ignores it.

Victoria steps toward the hall, her tone calm but deliberate. "Get some rest while you can. You're not the only ones they're watching."

As she walks past, her shoulder brushes mine—intentional, measured. The scent of smoke and mint antiseptic follows her, ghosting the air between us.

I hold her gaze a moment too long. "Still chasing phantoms, *Vic*?"

"Still catching them," she says, and disappears down the hall.

Beau exhales, rubbing the back of his neck. "Hell of a homecoming, sis."

"Could've been worse," I say, sinking into the chair across from Rakes.

He manages a grin that doesn't quite make it. "You people have a funny definition of '*safe house*.'"

"You haven't even seen Texas yet." I pour a shot of bourbon, slide it across to him, then pour my own.

He takes it, our glasses clinking soft as the thunder outside rolls over the horizon. The air smells like rain and something else—something coming. "The quiet doesn't last long in places like this," I say softly.

Rakes glances at the window, then back at me. "Good thing we're not built for quiet."

Outside, lightning flashes over the ridge—brief, bright, and far too close. And I know with a deep certainty.

The storm's not coming.

It's already *here*.

About The Author

B is a devoted wife and dog mom who has always had a passion for writing. When the opportunity arose, she channeled all her energy into creating an immersive world that captivated readers from the very first page. B loves traveling, reading, photography, and video gaming with her husband. B actively shares her journey on social media, connecting with readers who love paranormal, dark, and fantasy romance.

ACKNOWLEDGEMENTS

This book exists because a whole lot of people refused to let me quit when it would have been easier to disappear.

First, to my husband — my steady, my anchor, my safe place. Thank you for loving a woman who lives in her head, in her stories, in her chaos. Thank you for the late nights, the cold coffee, the patience when I'm lost in worlds you can't see, and the quiet ways you show up every single day. I could not do this without you. I would not want to.

To my Golden Light people — my authors, my publishing team, my creative chaos crew — thank you for building something with me instead of just working for me. Thank you for trusting my vision, matching my energy, and standing in the fire with me when things get hard. This imprint is what it is because of you. You are not just colleagues. You are chosen family.

To my alpha and beta readers, MA Worrell, Jenn & Vickie B — the brave souls who read the messy drafts, the unhinged scenes, the emotional wreckage and still came back for more. Thank you for catching what I missed, pushing me harder, and believing in these characters as fiercely as I do. Your feedback shapes these stories more than you know.

To my family and friends — thank you for loving me even when I'm distracted, tired, or emotionally unavailable because I'm knee-deep in fictional trauma. Thank you for understanding that this isn't "just a hobby." It's who I am. Your support means more than I ever say out loud.

And finally... to my readers...

You are the reason I do this.

You are the ones who hold these stories with care, who feel them, who see yourselves in the broken pieces and the sharp edges. If you found comfort, strength, rage, or even recognition in these pages — then this book did what it was meant to do.

Thank you for trusting me with your hearts.

This one was written with teeth.

And it's for *you*.

— B. Wills

ALSO BY B WILLS

The Eternal Darkness Chronicles

Book 1 – Shadows & Starlight

Book 2 – Flames & Ash – Coming soon...

Sacred Flames of Ruin

Book 1 – Chasing The Flame

Book 2 – Embracing The Fire – Coming soon...

Bloodwritten Flames of Ruin

Book 1 – Written In Blood

Book 2 – TBA

The Breakfast Murder Club Series

Book 1 by Yvonne Hamilton – Blades Over Break-

fast

Book 2 by B Wills – Bullets Over Bourbon

Book 3 by B Wills & Yvonne Hamilton – TBA

Hexed Christmas Romance

Book 1 – Hex The Halls

Masked Riders Dark Romance

Book 1 – Long Live the Queen

9 781970 692075